THE RETURN OF ABSENT SOULS

SOULS

AFTER THE RIFT, BOOK 6

C.J. ARCHER

WWW.CJARCHER.COM

CHAPTER 1

*T*he shock of Dane's arrest at the hands of the Freedland authorities didn't hit me until Balthazar, Quentin, Erik and I returned to the lair of Max's former gang where we were temporarily hiding. I managed to keep my hands from shaking long enough to stitch the wound in Erik's side, but once he fell asleep from the effects of the Mother's Milk, I finally sat down on the bed beside him and burst into tears. Dane was in a holding cell, awaiting trial for murder; the only way to free him was to use a magic wish.

A wish we did not have.

"What happened?" Kitty asked as she stroked Erik's forehead.

Meg sat beside me and placed her arm around my shoulders. "Where's Dane?"

I shook my head, too overwhelmed to explain. Besides, Jenny was there. She and Max's other friends didn't know about magic, and we wanted to keep it that way. Explaining what happened to Dane would mean revealing his memory loss and his past.

"We were set upon by bandits in the street," Balthazar lied. "There was a fight, and Dane was arrested."

Jenny arched her brows. "Bandits? What'd they look like?

Were they real big? Did the leader have a scar down his right cheek? I bet it was the Bruiser gang."

"I didn't notice," Balthazar said heavily.

Jenny waited, but Quentin and I didn't offer answers either. He was crying into Theodore's shoulder. With a click of her tongue, Jenny left to make us something to eat.

"Where are Vance and the others?" Balthazar asked.

"Out thieving," Max said, staring down at Erik. "So what really happened?"

"And where *is* Dane?" Theodore added ominously. "Is he..." He gazed at Erik. "Is he dead?"

"Not yet," Quentin wailed. He pulled away and wiped his nose on the back of his hand. "He really did get arrested."

Theodore, Max and Meg turned to Balthazar, the only one who'd been present and was still capable of speaking sensibly. But even Balthazar seemed overwhelmed by what had happened as he searched for a place to begin.

"You went to the house of Tabitha's parents," Theodore prompted.

Tabitha was a servant from the palace with a missing memory. Quentin had found a poster of her asking for information of her whereabouts. That led us to visit her parents who explained that she was the maid to a wealthy young woman.

"Her mistress's name was Laylana," Balthazar told the others.

Theodore and Max gasped. Laylana was another palace servant who lost her memory; not once, as the others had, but repeatedly. It was wiped every few days and she had to start again, knowing nothing. She had some sketches and notes to help her, but her situation made her fearful.

"So you visited Laylana's family next?" Meg asked.

Balathazar nodded. "Her brother is one of the wealthiest men in Freedland. But the most shocking thing we learned tonight wasn't that Laylana and Dane were betrothed—"

Meg let out a small squeal of surprise, only to quickly cover it with her hand. Her gaze fell on me, as did the gazes of the others.

"How is that not the most shocking thing you learned?" Kitty asked carefully.

"Laylana's brother and sister-in-law took us to the house of Dane's mother, and it was there that we learned Dane is the grandson of the former king."

Meg sat heavily on the bed near Erik's feet. "He's Freedland royalty?"

"He would be the heir," Balthazar said. "If there were a throne to inherit."

"Which there isn't," Max added. When no one responded, he tilted his head to the side. "Bal?"

"Dane's mother and some noble families want to overthrow the Freedland republic and restore the monarchy with Dane as king. As a woman, she could not become queen, but ever since Dane was born, she has been grooming him to take up his birthright. His arrest over a year ago and apparent death ended her dreams, but tonight, they reignited upon seeing him."

"Merdu," Theodore breathed. "That's why he was arrested, wasn't it? Because the authorities don't want the heir to the throne alive. His reappearance could mean the end of the government."

"Another war, at least," Balthazar said, nodding. "I don't know if the royalists have the numbers, though."

"They don't," I said, speaking for the first time since Erik had fallen asleep. "When Dane was first arrested, they gave up all hope and disbanded their mercenary forces, so the maid told me. It will take time to gather them again."

Martha had remained behind at the house to await the return of Yelena, Dane's mother. She had been devastated by Dane's arrest, whereas his mother had been angry. Yelena had immediately stepped into action to gather support to get him out of the prison, whereas Martha had been a forlorn and lonely figure as we left her at the cottage.

"Is that why Dane was arrested the first time and sent to the prison mine to rot?" Meg asked. "Because they learned about his existence?"

Balthazar nodded. "Laylana tried to free him, but her attempt failed and she too was sent to prison."

"Poor Laylana," Theodore muttered.

We fell into silence as weighty as the sadness pressing down on me. The horror and hopelessness of Dane's predicament had begun to sink in. With his very existence jeopardizing the republic, it made sense that the ministers would want to get rid of him. A conviction for murder would take care of that without raising an eyebrow. He was, after all, supposedly guilty of murdering all those guards in the prison escape months ago.

But what worried me now was the speed at which he might be tried, convicted and hanged. The longer they waited, the more time it gave the royalists to gather their forces. If the high minister was wise, he would eliminate Dane quickly. He could be hanged within days, perhaps even tomorrow.

"But how did the authorities learn Dane was the heir?" Meg asked. "Last year, I mean. If he'd been hiding since birth, who told them?"

"Perhaps it was a noble family who turned against them," I said. "Perhaps they thought they were better off under this regime after all." I shrugged. It didn't matter. Not now. Getting Dane out was the only thing that we should be worried about.

"Josie," Kitty said in a small voice. "Will Erik...?" Her eyes filled with tears as she blinked down at her lover's pale face. He'd lost a lot of blood, but the bleeding had stopped now, thank Hailia.

"He'll survive," I told her. "He needs to rest and keep the wound clean."

Dane was also injured, having been struck by a sword in his lower back. I'd stitched and bandaged the wound, but keeping it clean in a prison cell would be impossible.

"Why didn't they arrest Dane's mother?" Quentin asked from where he stood by the bed, sniffling. "Why did they just let her go?"

"She's not a threat," Balthazar said.

"I reckon she's more of a threat than Dane. He doesn't want the throne; she does."

"She can't inherit it, and she's too old to give birth to more sons. The threat of her gathering forces will be nullified once Dane is executed."

4

Quentin's face crumpled. "Don't say that! Don't say he's going to die, because he's not! We'll think of something to get him out. We always do." He looked to me. "Josie? You've got an idea, haven't you?"

I rose and strode towards the door. I opened it without answering him and headed for the room Balthazar shared with some of the other men. I rummaged through his pack until I found the whalebone tube that contained not only our maps, but also the magic gem.

A hand clamped over mine before I had a chance to reach into the tube and remove the false base. "No," Max said quietly.

"Using a wish is the only way!" I cried.

Quentin and Meg rushed in, followed by Theodore and finally Balthazar. I couldn't meet his gaze. I didn't want to see the censure in his eyes, the disappointment.

"I don't care what you think," I told them. "Only magic can free him and you all know it."

Theodore and Quentin looked to Balthazar, but Meg was watching Max with a curious frown. She mouthed "why" at him, but he didn't seem to notice. He was too busy prying the tube from my hands.

Balthazar settled his hands over the head of his walking stick. "We may have the gem, but we don't have the wishes. Brant does, and we'll never find him in time."

"We might!" I snapped.

"And if we do, will you murder him to get them?"

"Yes."

He shook his head. "I can't allow you to do that."

"*You* were going to murder him to get the wishes."

"I still might, *when* we catch him. But not you. We won't catch him in time, anyway. He fled the city after being recognized. He could be half way to Glancia by now. We have to find another way."

"There is no other way! The royalists have good intentions but without their mercenaries, they have no army. So what do you propose we do, Bal?"

"Get him out ourselves, through the proper legal channels."

I scoffed.

"We tell them he's not the man they think he is, that they've made a mistake and he's merely the captain of the Glancian palace guards."

I shook my head at the ceiling. "He was arrested in Yelena's house. How do we explain his presence there if he's not her son?"

"We say we were attempting to dupe her for money. We discovered he looked like Dane March and decided to take advantage. That explanation saves them admitting they lied about his recapture and execution along with the other prisoners, and it negates the royalist cause."

I made another scoffing sound. "Don't be naïve, Bal. That leaves it open for Dane to say that was a lie after his release. They won't let him live. They *can't* let him live. It's too much of a risk."

"Then what do you propose?" Balthazar spat back. "Storm the holding cells? Poison the guards?" It was the most vehement I'd seen him. He rarely snapped at others. He preferred sarcasm, not wrath.

"Yes," I said. "Why not?"

He sighed heavily. "It didn't work in Merrin."

"I learned from that failure. This attempt to free Dane *will* work." I crossed my arms over my chest against a wave of despair. "It has to," I added, voice trembling.

Meg put her arm around me. "We'll find another way. Let's put our heads together and come up with something."

Max slapped the map tube into the palm of his hand. "I already have an idea."

"Go on," Theodore said on a hushed breath.

"Dane's in prison, and prison cells are locked."

Quentin snorted. "Stating the obvious ain't going to help."

"All we need is someone who can open locks without a key." He headed for the door. "And I know where to find such folk."

We followed him into the kitchen where Jenny was stirring a stew in a pot over the fire. She looked up as we entered and bade us sit at the table.

"You can each have a bowl," she said. "But no more. There ain't more to give. It ain't cheap feeding all of you."

"We can pay you back," Theodore said. "Balthazar?"

Balthazar sat at the table with a groan. "I suspect we're about to give them every last ell we have."

"I expect Vance'll tell you to keep what little you have to help you get away from here. Max can't stay. There's a noose with his name on it." She clutched Max's arm and gave him a grim smile. "We don't want to see him swing for murdering them guards."

I slid onto a chair, feeling sick to my stomach.

Max accepted a bowl of stew from Jenny. "When's Vance getting home? We've got a business proposition for him."

We had to wait some time before Vance, Drew and Gillon returned with their evening's takings. Among the coins they dumped on the table were a silver shoe buckle, a shell hair comb, two brass buttons and a silver candlestick.

Jenny handed Vance a bowl of stew and inspected the stolen goods. "Not bad but I don't see no jewelry. Weren't you going to break into the Wellerby house tonight?"

"Later," Gillon said as he accepted the bowl from his sister.

Jenny flicked her long dark braid over her shoulder. "Don't leave it too late. We need more than this. Max's friends are costing us a fortune."

Vance grabbed her wrist. "That's enough, Jenny. Max's friends are our friends too. Got it?"

She pulled away, her eyes flashing. "Sure, as long as they don't cause trouble, but I ain't putting no wager on that. The leader got arrested."

Vance's gaze connected with Max's. "And the Marginer?"

"Erik is injured," Max told him. "He's recovering with Kitty watching over him. But Jenny's right. Dane got arrested tonight."

"What for?"

Max told him the same story we'd told Jenny, that we were set upon in the street and Dane was arrested for beating up the other man.

"That's self-defense," Gillon said. "Ain't no magistrate will convict him for that."

Drew agreed. "He'll be free soon, but if I were you, I'd leave Noxford as soon as he's released."

Vance said nothing. He stroked his chin and watched Max intently. The flickering light from the candles glinted in the gold rings on his fingers and the silver objects on the table.

Max studied his empty bowl, unable to meet Vance's gaze. Vance knew we weren't telling the truth, and Max hated lying.

I decided to make it easier for him. If we were going to ask for their help, they needed to know more anyway. "Dane was arrested for the same reason Max would be if the authorities knew he was here. He escaped from the prison mine."

"What?" Jenny exploded.

"Why didn't you tell us from the start?" Drew asked.

"Aye," Gillon said darkly. "Why lie?"

Vance continued to stroke his chin and glare at Max.

Max pushed his bowl away. "We're not sure how to explain it to you."

"Try," Drew growled.

Jenny pointed her wooden spoon at Max. "You're better than this. You been with them too long. Before, you'd never lie to us. Never."

Vance suddenly leaned forward. "So he's going to hang for murdering the guards. That's why you all look like miserable dogs."

"He's not going to hang," I said. "We're going to get him out."

The four gang members stared at me as if I'd gone mad before turning to Max. He nodded.

Jenny snorted and returned to the pot over the fire. "You're all barking. Ain't no one gets free of the hangman's noose."

"That's why we're going to break him out of the jailhouse before he heads to the scaffold," Max said.

"Tonight," I added. "But we can't do it without your help."

Drew, Gillon and Jenny either shook their heads or returned to their bowls of stew, dismissing us.

All except Vance. "What you're proposing is dangerous. He'll be heavily guarded. It's not just getting him out of the prison, but you have to get him out of the city too."

"We know," Max said. "So will you help us? We can pay you."

"How much?" Jenny asked.

"We've got twenty-eight ells left," Theodore said with a glance at Balthazar. "You can have it all."

"Twenty-eight?" Jenny screwed her nose up. "That ain't much."

Vance nodded at the objects and coins on the table. "We get that much in two nights."

"It's all we have," Balthazar said.

"It's not enough. I can't risk—"

"Please," Meg said. "We're begging you, help us. Help us get Dane out."

"Do it for me," Max said. "Am I not your friend?"

Drew crossed his arms and stretched out his legs. "A friend wouldn't ask us to risk our lives for someone we don't know for so little in return."

"Vance?"

Vance shook his head.

Max thumped his fist on the table and swore.

Meg placed her hand over his and rubbed her thumb over his knuckles. Max opened his fist and turned his hand over to hold hers. Vance watched their silent exchange of affection from beneath half-closed lids.

"Perhaps you can teach us to pick locks so we can break in without you," Meg said.

Gillon nodded at Max. "He already knows how. The rest of you, sure. But it ain't just picking locks you'll have to do, it's sneaking in, knowing your way around the jailhouse in the dark."

"It's knowing the guards' routines," Drew went on. "You ain't got time to learn all that. Besides, without the Marginer, it's just Max, some women, an old man and them two. They don't look too strong."

Quentin puffed out his chest. "I can wield a sword and throw a punch as good as the next man."

Drew pointed at Theodore. "That's because the next man is him."

Vance had fallen quiet again. He seemed to be concentrating on his stew, but when he looked up at Max, I saw a spark in his eyes that hadn't been there before. Our plan appealed to him. Perhaps he liked the idea of beating the authorities at their own game, or perhaps he simply liked thrilling adventures. Whatever put that spark in his eyes, I knew how to exploit it.

"Do you know the guards' routines and your way around the prison in the dark?" I asked him.

"Of course."

"Vance," Jenny warned. "It might have changed since then."

Vance dug his spoon into the stew. "About a year ago, we thought of breaking in and going through their records to find out what really happened to you, Max. We set to watching them, memorized when they changed shift, how many they had on at the front door and inside."

"Why didn't you go through with it?" Max asked.

"We couldn't find a way to make it work. There were just too many guards."

"It was too much of a risk," Jenny said., hand on hip "Still is. Ain't no way we're doing it for someone we don't know."

Drew, Gillon and even Vance nodded in agreement.

I picked up the silver buckle and flipped it over. It was thin, not a quality piece. "What if we promised you solid silver buckles? And candlesticks and plate. More ells than you have here, too. Much more. Will that persuade you?"

"You don't have it," Jenny said with a sneer.

"We can get it. Money, jewels, you ask for it, and we can provide it. Dane's mother's friends will pay whatever you need."

"He's got family here?" Gillon asked.

"Then why aren't you staying with them?" Jenny asked.

My gaze locked on to Vance. "She's friends with the Rotherhydes."

Vance's eyes flared. For a man who showed little surprise or emotion, it was telling. He was very interested now.

"Merdu and Hailia," Gillon murmured.

"They'll agree to pay you whatever you want to get Dane out," Max said to Vance.

Jenny stormed back to the fire, her annoyance clear in her stomping footsteps and indistinct mutterings.

Vance sat back and regarded Max. "You want to tell us what's really going on?"

"What do you mean?" Max asked.

"Why's Dane so important to the merchants?"

"He's one of them."

Vance looked to me and I knew we had to give him more if we wanted to win him over. "He's supposed to marry the sister of Ewen Rotherhyde."

"Merdu!" Gillon blurted out.

Drew chuckled. "Guess he didn't want to marry her then. I guess he thought he needed to get as far from Freedland as possible to escape the Rotherhydes."

"Who wouldn't want to marry that much money?" Jenny said from the fire. "Especially if he's poor."

Vance's eyes darkened. "From what I recall, the Rotherhyde girl went to the prison mine and was also later executed."

The other gang members frowned and became very interested in Max's response. But Max said nothing.

Vance fidgeted with the gold skull ring on his middle finger. "Tell me the truth or we won't help."

Max looked to Balthazar. Balthazar hesitated.

So I told them instead. I told them all about the magic and what we'd learned about the palace servants so far, and even about Dane's relationship to the last king of Averlea, the former name for Freedland.

They listened in shocked silence until the end. And then the questions came. I answered them as best as I could until their curiosity seemed satisfied. Drew, Gillon and Jenny looked like they believed me, but Vance's expression was unreadable.

"Well?" Max asked. "Will you help us get him out? The Rotherhydes and other royalists will pay you a fortune."

Vance rubbed his jaw. "I don't think it will work. The reason we abandoned the idea of breaking in the first time was because there are too many guards."

Gillon clicked his fingers. "There needs to be a distraction. Something that will get them out, or most of them."

"We can provide that," I said. "I have medicines that will make them purge." It hadn't worked in Merrin, but I meant it when I said I'd learned from the mistakes I made there. This time there would be no mistakes.

Vance pushed his chair out and stood. "Sorry, Max, my answer is no."

Max shot to his feet. "Why?"

Vance went to walk off, but Max intercepted him. He grabbed Vance by the front of his jerkin and pulled him closer until they were nose to nose. Neither blinked an eye.

Vance threw a quick jab, low in Max's gut. Max released him with a grunt and threw a punch of his own. Vance dodged it and caught Max's fist. Being the stronger of the two, Max pulled free. He stepped back and settled into a fighting stance, but Vance didn't attack.

"You used to be quicker," Drew said.

Jenny snorted. "Palace living has made him slow."

Max ignored their taunts. "Why won't you help?" he growled at Vance.

"It's too dangerous," I said. "He can't risk their lives."

"That's not why," Vance said.

"Danger don't scare us," Gillon agreed. "It's the Rotherhydes and their money we don't want. Not for this."

"Not just the Rotherhydes," Vance added. "We don't want money from any of the royalists to release the heir to the throne. We don't want another king in Freedland. The last one almost ruined this country."

"Dane's not like that," I said. "He's a good man."

"And he doesn't want the throne," Balthazar added.

Vance shook his head. "He won't have a choice. If he's the heir, he has to take it. It's his birthright."

"There is always a choice," I said. "Dane won't take it even if it's offered to him on a platter. He's a different person now than he was before his first arrest last year. Just like Max is different."

Vance looked to Max and sighed. "He has changed," he conceded.

"So you'll do it?" I asked. "You'll help us free him?"

Vance twisted his skull ring and regarded me then Max. After a moment, he said, "You've got to promise you'll get him away from Freedland immediately."

"We will," I said, even though my head told me it wasn't my decision to make. For now, I would promise Vance the moon if it bought his assistance.

"And never let him come back," Vance added.

"We'll make sure of it," Theodore said. "So you'll do it?"

"There's one problem." Vance sat again. "We won't ask for money—for Max's sake, you understand. But I have a friend with a boat who'll agree to take you all the way to Glancia if you pay him. It'll cost more than twenty-eight ells though. A lot more."

We all studied the loot on the table. We couldn't ask them to donate it to us. They needed it. It wasn't much anyway.

I started thinking of items we could sell, but we didn't carry anything of value. We'd sold some of the horses to the last innkeeper to pay for our rooms, but we still had three. They should fetch a good sum, but would it be enough for all of us to secure passage to Glancia? If not, who should be left behind?

"I'll sell this." Kitty stood in the doorway and reached behind her neck. She unclipped the necklace she wore beneath her clothes and dropped it on the table. The gold and gems dazzled in the candlelight.

Drew gawped at it. "Who'd you steal that from?"

"My husband."

Jenny picked it up and held it to the light. "Are they real?"

"Of course," Kitty snipped. "If you can't tell real jewels from fake, perhaps you're in the wrong business."

Jenny put the necklace on herself and admired her reflection in the silver candlestick.

"Is it enough?" I asked Vance.

He nodded.

I closed my eyes and exhaled. I felt light-headed all of a sudden and hardly heard them as they made plans. The only thing I did hear was the timeframe—they would free Dane tomorrow night.

I opened my eyes. "Why not tonight? We must get him out without delay."

"I need to speak to my friend with the boat," Vance said. "And we need to go over what we know about the courthouse routine and learn if it has changed. I won't send anyone in until I'm sure it's safe."

He was right. It couldn't be rushed. I prayed tomorrow night wouldn't be too late.

CHAPTER 2

*T*he following day dragged. We had to remain in the lair as Vance refused to allow our men to go with him to the docks to speak to his friend the boat captain. They couldn't afford to be recognized as escaped prisoners. Even with a patient to occupy my time, and herbal emetics to prepare, it felt like an age before night fell.

"Do you think it will work?" Meg asked as she peered over my shoulder at the pot of steeping herbs.

"It has to."

Balthazar, seated at the kitchen table, cleared his throat. "The guards in Merrin fetched others as soon as they felt ill. That might happen again."

"Someone will be watching all exits. If a guard attempts to leave, he'll be dispatched." I eyed Balthazar first, then Meg. "In Merrin, I was reluctant to do what needed to be done to free Dane. This time, I won't hesitate."

"Josie," Meg began.

"Don't." I turned away. "Don't lecture me until it's Max's neck in a noose."

She sighed but thankfully said no more. My conscience couldn't cope with the guilt. She finally left to join the others in the bedroom where Erik was recovering. He wasn't well enough to help free Dane but he insisted on being involved in the planning with Vance, Max and the other men.

Drew had already gone out that morning and reported back that Dane's trial had been the first of the day. He'd been sentenced to hang tomorrow. There was no gossip about him at the market, not a whiff of a suggestion that he was anyone other than a man from Glancia being hanged for murder. His true identity had been suppressed.

Vance insisted that was a good thing. If the public knew who Dane was, the crowd would swell overnight in the hopes of getting the best view of his hanging. It would make his getaway more difficult, not just with the extra people, but the extra people determined that he should not be allowed to escape. The notion of the royal family returning was not a popular one, so Vance assured us.

I went to follow Meg out of the kitchen to see how the plans were going, but Balthazar asked me to stay. He patted the chair beside him and I sat. Going by the ominous look on his face, I was about to receive a lecture.

"I don't want you to join the rescue attempt." He put up his hands for silence when I began to protest and asked me to hear him out. "You can wait on the boat with me, Erik and the others."

"I'm needed at the jailhouse. In Merrin, I didn't watch the guards drink the ale myself. This time, I want to see them."

"You're going to put more into the ale, aren't you?"

"I didn't add enough in Merrin. I didn't factor in the larger size of the guards. But that also means the smaller ones could become quite ill."

"That's not the real reason you want to be there, is it?"

I rose, but he caught my wrist.

"Don't go tonight," he said. "Come to the docks and wait."

"I'm tired of waiting." I tried to pull away but he held my wrist firmly. "Don't, Bal. I don't want to hear your lecture."

"You need to hear it, because no one else will say this to you. It's too dangerous. I'm forbidding you to be there. Let Vance and his men—"

"Save your breath, Bal. Nothing you say will convince me not to be there."

"You'll be sentenced to hang too if the plan fails."

"Then it better not fail."

He clicked his tongue in frustration.

I jerked my wrist free and walked off. "My mind is made up."

"Josie, think about the consequences."

"I have," I said from the doorway.

"I'm begging you not to do it."

I stopped and lowered my head. Tears burned the backs of my eyes. "I can't sit by while Dane is hanged for a crime he didn't commit and let others who are not his friends take all the risk. What if it becomes too dangerous and they abandon the rescue before the job is finished?"

"*You* should leave if it becomes too dangerous." His voice sounded thin and far away.

I closed my eyes. "I have to be there."

He didn't speak and I thought I'd got through to him, but as I went to walk off, he said, "Losing Dane will be terrible. But losing you too... I can't even comprehend it."

My throat constricted. I dared to look at him, but he was staring down at the floor, his knotty fingers holding tightly to the head of his walking stick. I crossed back to him and kissed the top of his head.

"I promise I'll be careful." As an assurance, it was weak, but I couldn't offer more. I certainly wouldn't do as he wanted and wait for Dane to come to me at the docks. Waiting and blindly hoping wasn't in my nature these days.

* * *

In Merrin, we'd waited for the day of Dane's hanging to rescue him. It left us with no time to form an alternative plan if we failed. We would not make the same mistake.

By the time Kitty and Jenny returned from visiting the gang's goldsmith acquaintance in the late afternoon, my emetic was ready, and so were we. They had come via the courthouse where the prisoners were being held in the holding cells before their execution in the morning.

"There are no extra guards on duty," Jenny reported. "The shift changed as the temple bells rang at midday."

"We counted eight guards arriving and eight leaving," Kitty added.

"There'll be another change at dusk," Vance said, nodding.

"Was the scaffold erected?" Gillon asked.

I swallowed the lump rising up my throat.

Kitty hooked my arm with hers. "Let's not talk about that."

"Did you get enough for the necklace?" Vance asked.

The boat captain had demanded an exorbitant sum to take all of us back to Glancia. He hadn't been made aware that Dane was the heir to the throne, but he must have sensed our desperation. Asking to depart in the middle of the night and avoid docking until we were out of Freedland were very big clues.

Kitty removed two full purses from the pack she carried beneath her cloak and set them on the table with a dull clank. "It leaves us a little left over after we pay him."

Vance checked inside the purses. "We make our way to the Sandpiper Tavern at dusk. Jenny, take the money. You'll be in charge of getting the women and the infirm men to the boat."

Quentin stamped his hands on his hips. "Who're you calling infirm?"

"The Marginer and the old man."

Quentin lowered his hands with a sniff. "Right. Me and Theo will come with you."

"You'll stay with the horses."

I didn't remind him that I would be joining them. We'd already had this argument. Vance had given in when I explained how accurate the quantity of emetic needed to be. Too much and the guards would die. Too little and they would not be sick enough.

A shrill whistle from the doorman filled the cottage. Vance, Max and the other men stood and reached for weapons.

A bow-legged man with a cluster of gray hair clinging to the back of his otherwise bald head wandered in. Vance and his friends let go of their sword hilts.

"This here is Captain Obsidian," Vance said. "He's the one taking you tonight on his boat."

The captain scratched his dark red whiskers. His lips, almost entirely hidden beneath all the hair, twisted to the side. "That's the thing. We can't go tonight."

"It has to be tonight!" I cried. "We can't stay in Noxford a moment longer than necessary."

"Sorry, miss, but a barge hit us and the hull needs repairs."

"How long will that take?" Vance asked.

"Two days, maybe three." Captain Obsidian shrugged, as if it were not important, just a small delay without consequence.

But it had a very big consequence. It meant hiding in Noxford at a time when every constable and soldier would be looking for Dane after we broke him free from the courthouse jail.

"We can stay here," Max said.

Vance scrubbed a hand over his face. When it came away, he looked worried. "*You* can stay, Max. But not them, and especially not Dane."

"But you have to hide us!" Quentin whined.

"It's too dangerous."

Quentin was about to protest until Theodore rested a hand on his shoulder. "He's right. This is his place, and he decides who can stay. We'll find somewhere else until the boat's ready to sail."

"Where?" Quentin whined.

"I know a place," I said, rising. "Meg, Kitty, will you come with me?"

"Do you need our help persuading people?" Kitty asked, following me out of the kitchen.

"I simply need your moral support. Dane's mother is not someone I want to face alone."

* * *

YELENA WAS NOT at her cottage, but Martha said she could be found at the Rotherhydes' residence. "They're trying to think of a way to get Dane out of prison tonight," she said. "But I don't see how. They haven't got the support." Her face crumpled as her tears welled.

I hugged her, suddenly overwhelmed with love for the woman who had known Dane all his life; she had tended to his childhood scrapes, cooked his favorite meals, and probably been more of a mother to him than Yelena. "It'll be all right, Martha." I drew away and clasped her hands in mine. "Go and pack for yourself and your mistress. If a rescue attempt is successful, it may not be safe here for you after tonight."

"How can it be successful? It's hopeless."

"Just do as I say and be prepared to flee."

I left her looking small and miserable in the doorway and headed off with Kitty and Meg. We followed the river until we came across the area where the Rotherhydes lived in a mansion set amid extensive grounds.

"Civilization at last," Kitty said when she spied the grand residences at the end of tree-lined drives. "It reminds me of our townhouse in Tilting. The house on Gladstow's country estate is much larger, of course, but our townhouse is rather like these."

"You can't even see them," Meg said with a roll of her eyes. "Just the gatehouses."

"With gatehouses as grand as these, the houses themselves must be lovely."

Although the guards at the gatehouse recognized me from the night Dane and I first visited, I reintroduced myself as a friend of Laylana's. Still, they hesitated.

"Tell your master and mistress that I have a plan," I added.

One of the guards ran off to check at the house. He returned moments later, out of breath, and immediately opened the gate. The driveway was illuminated by torches, reminding me of the avenue leading to the palace at Mull in the evenings. My heart pinched with longing for my village, the palace, and my friends.

If tonight went horribly wrong, I would never see them again.

The door opened and we were ushered into the same drawing room as last time. Yelena was there with Ewen and Eeliss Rotherhyde. Yelena grasped my elbows before I had a chance to set two feet in the room.

"What is your plan?" she pressed.

I tried to extricate myself from her grip but it was too tight. "Before we get to that—"

"Tell me!"

"Yelena, perhaps you should calm yourself." Ewen indicated she should sit. When she did not let me go, Eeliss pried her fingers off and steered her away.

I introduced Kitty and Meg to the Rotherhydes and Dane's mother. Meg did not make any attempt to hide her birthmark, despite Eeliss's stares. Yelena didn't seem to notice her at all. She sat regally, her chin high, her shoulders back. But the hands in her lap twisted together in a white-knuckled clasp.

Kitty performed a perfect curtsy to Yelena. Yelena blinked hard, taken aback. Then she put out her hand, and Kitty kissed it.

"It's a pleasure to meet you," Yelena said formally. "What did you say your name is?"

"Kitty, the duchess of Gladstow."

"Kitty!" both Meg and I cried.

She shushed us. "These people won't tell my husband that I'm still alive. They have a greater secret of their own to keep."

"Not for much longer," Yelena said.

Eeliss eyed Kitty up and down, her nose wrinkled. "You don't look like a duchess."

Kitty touched the hair at the nape of her neck. Without a maid to fix it every day, it had become unruly. "It's been a long few weeks traveling in less than favorable conditions."

Yelena cut her off with a hand signal that had Kitty's nostrils flaring in indignation. "Miss Cully, please elaborate on this plan you mentioned to the guard. You are referring to releasing my son, are you not?"

"I am," I said.

She drew in a deep breath, as if it were the first proper one she'd taken in some time.

Ewen angled a chair towards Kitty, encouraging her to sit with a smile. She cast a pointed look at Meg and me and he hastily arranged chairs for us too.

"How do you propose to have Dane released?" Yelena asked.

"We're going to break him out of the prison," I said.

Ewen crossed his legs and shook his head. "It can't be done. Not without an armed force, and I doubt you have that. You haven't been here long enough to gather the right sort of support."

Yelena sat forward. "Do not endanger my son's life by employing Freedland mercenaries. They might go to the government, demand more, and then tell them your plans. You can't trust them."

Ewen agreed. "You need mercenaries from Dreen or Vytill, ones with no interest in Freedland affairs. I can't even call on my own guards for this. My captain informed me his men won't be involved in any attempts to free someone from prison. I threatened to relieve them of their positions, but he was still doubtful. So much for loyalty."

"What if you explained the man they were freeing was the rightful heir to the throne?" Kitty asked. "Did you suggest your captain tell his men that?"

Ewen pressed his lips together. "That would be unwise at this juncture."

Kitty frowned, somewhat confused, but Meg and I knew why. There wasn't enough support for a monarchy in the lower and middle orders of Noxford. If the wealthy could gather their forces quickly enough then it might be a different story, but the royalists knew they didn't have the numbers. Guards, and men like them, would not risk their necks for a man they didn't want to see free. The Rotherhydes couldn't even use their money to bribe the prison warden and guards. Sometimes, money wasn't enough.

Ewen and Yelena's warnings drove home the precariousness of Dane's position. We could not rely on assistance from anyone. If ordinary folk knew who we were breaking out of prison, they would inform the authorities immediately. We were extremely fortunate that Vance and his gang had agreed to help. I suspected that was because we promised to take Dane back to Glancia, and they loved Max too much to allow him to do it alone.

No wonder Yelena was keen to hear our plan; they evidently

had none. I briefly outlined how we would remove the threat of the jailhouse guards and get Dane out, without mentioning Vance's name. I went on to tell them how the boat we planned to use to leave Noxford needed repairs and Dane needed a place to hide until it was ready to set sail.

"Leave?" Yelena shook her head over and over. "No! He cannot leave. He's needed here. He must show his face to our supporters. None will believe he's really alive if they don't see him in person."

I stared at her. She would risk the life of her own son for a cause that only a few wealthy families believed in? "The longer Dane stays in Freedland, the more likely his discovery," I said. "He has to leave. Staying is too dangerous."

"You do not have a say in this. He is *my* son and the heir to Averlea."

"I agree that it's not my decision. It's Dane's."

Yelena looked as if she would argue the point further, but she resumed her regal pose with stiff back and superior air. It was Ewen who protested.

"Now listen here. Dane must lead the foreign mercenaries and any other forces we can muster. He isn't merely a figurehead to rally behind, he is a very capable leader. When the people see how capable, they will change their minds and want him as their king."

"Quite right," Eeliss said. "Dane is a magnificent man and will be a popular leader. He shines with a sword in his hand and on horseback. I've seen him practicing myself. You can't deny him the opportunity to prove himself to the people, Miss Cully."

"I am not denying him anything. I am advising caution."

"He's been preparing for this his whole life," Ewen added. "We believe the time has finally come to reveal the royal heir to the people and let them see what he's capable of, and imagine how powerful Averlea could be with him on the throne. He *deserves* this opportunity."

"He'll be in danger if he stays!" I appealed to Yelena in the hope she would consider her son's life too important to risk.

But she simply regarded me levelly. "If he had his memory, he would never agree to leave with you."

I doubted Dane would be so foolish.

"How long will it take you to gather enough support to take back the throne?" Meg asked.

Kitty and I stared wide-eyed at her. What was she up to?

"Two months," Ewen said. "Three at the most."

"Then I have a proposition that may suit everyone. Your friends will believe your word, surely," she said to Ewen and Eeliss. "If you tell them you saw Dane in person, and he is safely in Glancia with Laylana, won't that be enough for them to offer their support?"

Yelena clicked her tongue and muttered under her breath.

Eeliss looked to her husband. "They would believe us," she said.

"Then why not let Dane leave while you continue to work here," Meg went on. "When you are satisfied that you're sufficiently ready, you can send word to him in Mull and he can return."

Three months would give Dane enough time to decide if he wanted to pursue his birthright. It would also give us time to find Brant. With his memory back, Dane could make a calculated decision on what he believed was best. Not what his mother thought, or the Rotherhydes, or even me. It would truly be his decision.

I couldn't believe I was even thinking about him becoming king here. Mere days ago, he was just the captain of the guards and my lover. I tried not to allow myself to wonder what him claiming his birthright meant for us.

One step at a time. Firstly, he had to avoid execution in the morning.

"Very well," Yelena said. "We will travel to Glancia and await word there. Ewen, can Dane hide here until it's time for him to leave?"

"He can hide in the tunnels under the house," Ewen said. "They're dark, and the air is stale, but he'll be safe. Not even the captain of my guards knows about them."

It was agreed, and we left them with a suggestion they be alert. We also agreed that Yelena and Martha should hide in the tunnels too. Their cottage would be the first to be searched after

Dane's escape was discovered. When they didn't find Dane, the ministers might take their frustrations out on his mother, the former princess.

* * *

THE SHRILL WHISTLE SIGNALED that all was safe for me to approach the inn's rear courtyard. I clutched my pack tightly to my chest and crept along the alley. Moonlight lit the way, but I still got a fright when Max suddenly appeared in a doorway.

"Down there," he whispered. "Hurry. They could come out at any moment."

Drew waited at the top of a steep staircase that led to an underground storeroom in the inn's yard. According to Vance, this small inn supplied ale to the courthouse's guards. A barrel was delivered every evening by two inn staff who were due to collect it soon.

I descended the stairs in the dark with Drew as my guide. A small flicker of torchlight at the bottom didn't reach the steps, but we navigated them safely. I could just make out several barrels stored in the corner. The smell of ale must be wafting from those.

Vance waved me over with the torch and indicated an unsealed barrel with an X marked in white chalk. I silently tipped the emetic tonic in and he helped Drew reseal it. The taps on the wooden lid seemed far too loud.

Thankfully no one came and we ascended the stairs and ran out of the empty yard undetected.

A short while later, a man pushing a barrow took no notice of us as he passed. He chatted to another man as they headed towards the courthouse where Dane was imprisoned in one of the six holding cells. We followed at a discreet distance and watched as they looked up at the gallows. The structure loomed with grim authority over the courtyard, blocking out the stars.

I swallowed and concentrated on the inn's staff as they hailed the guards on the door. Instead of letting them in, one of the guards stopped them.

"What's happening?" Max hissed.

We strained to hear, but I caught nothing of their conversation. The inn staff appeared to be arguing with the guards and one of the guards shooed them away while another knocked on the door.

It opened, revealing many guards inside. Far more than the eight that were supposed to be on duty. One emerged and spoke to the inn staff who finally turned to go.

My heart lurched into my throat as they passed us, shaking their heads and muttering their disappointment that their ale had been refused tonight when it never had been in all the years they'd been supplying it to the courthouse.

"I don't understand," Drew said when they were out of sight.

"You said the ale would be accepted without question," Max growled at Vance. "You said they took the ale every night at this time."

Vance studied the guards at the courthouse entrance, his brow furrowed. "Something's amiss."

A breeze whipped up, chilling me to the bone. I folded my arms against the cold. "There are more than eight guards," I pointed out.

"They're taking extra precautions with their special prisoner," Drew said.

"Or they've been alerted to an attempted escape," Vance said as he strode off.

I thought about the Rotherhydes and their own guards. Ewen had spoken to his captain about freeing Dane. Had he assumed an attempt would go ahead and betrayed his employer because he didn't believe in the royalist cause?

"Are you giving up already?" Max snapped at Vance.

"I'm going back to the inn to get that barrel and deliver it myself," Vance said. "I can be very persuasive when I want to be."

Max snorted as he fell into step alongside Vance.

I remained at the courthouse with Drew and we were soon joined by Gillon who'd been setting Quentin and Theodore up with horses around the corner. He swore after we told him what happened.

"I've got a bad feeling about this," he said.

"Go home if you want," I told him. "We can do this without your help."

"I only abandon an operation when there's no chance of it succeeding. If Vance thinks we can still get him out, then I'll stay." Gillon clasped my arm and gave me a grim smile. "Have faith, Josie."

Faith was a finite commodity, and my stores were severely depleted.

It felt like an interminable amount of time before Vance and Max returned, pushing the small barrow with the barrel of ale on it. The white chalk X was clearly visible in the moonlight, as were their determined faces.

"How did you get it?" I asked.

"Stole it," Max said.

"Now what?"

Gillon flashed me a grin. "Now we watch Vance in action."

Vance removed the rings from his fingers and handed them to Drew. He then picked up an apron from the barrow that I hadn't noticed and tied it around his waist. He pulled down his hat brim, hunched his shoulders, and thrust out his jaw. It changed the character of his entire face.

He pushed the barrow up to the guards on the courthouse door. We couldn't hear what he was saying, but his manner looked friendly.

"What's his plan?" I asked.

"He's giving it to them for free," Max said, sounding skeptical.

"They won't believe that."

"He's pretending to be the innkeeper. None have probably met him since all deliveries are done by staff, so he reckons they'll believe his story about trying a new brew and wanting their opinion."

Like before, one of the guards opened the door and spoke to someone inside. The same man as earlier emerged and spoke to Vance. He must be their captain. He didn't immediately dismiss Vance, but seemed interested in what he had to say. Other guards joined him at the door and finally they stepped aside, allowing Vance in.

He emerged with an empty barrow moments later and rejoined us. He grinned as he accepted his rings from Drew. "They fell for it. They're very enthusiastic about a new brew. Enthusiastic enough to disregard orders forbidding them to drink tonight."

Gillon clapped him on the shoulder. "Your idea is even better than the original plan. This way they'll try it immediately."

Even as he said it, a guard emerged and handed a cup to each of the guards on the door. They sipped and stared into the cups then discussed it. One drank the lot but the other hesitated.

"Drink it," I muttered. "Drink it, damn you."

The first guard banged on the door at his back and it reopened. The guard took his cup and waited for the other. With a shrug, the second guard drank and handed his cup back too.

We waited. It seemed like an age before the emetic began to have an effect. The smaller of the guards touched his stomach and spoke to his companion; he banged on the door at his back. It opened and he swapped with another guard. Soon, he too was clutching his stomach and banging on the door. When it opened, the torchlight inside revealed a skeleton staff.

"It has taken effect on almost all," Max said.

"They'll be in the latrines, throwing up their last meal," Vance said with delight.

One of the guards at the door doubled over suddenly. The new one who'd come out as a replacement addressed him only to find himself in the firing line as his colleague threw up all over his boots.

The sick one disappeared inside, leaving only one guard on duty. He did not look ill.

"He didn't drink it," I said.

"Wait a bit longer," Vance said.

"He's smaller than the other two. If he'd drunk the ale, he would be sick by now, but he looks fine."

Vance watched a moment longer then swore.

"What do we do?" Gillon asked.

"We resort to the backup plan. Josie, you should go to the Rotherhydes' house with the others. You'll be safer there."

"I'm not going anywhere until Dane is free," I said.

Vance grunted. "Are all Glancian women as stubborn as her?"

I could swear Max's lips curved into a small smile before they flattened again. "Just the brave ones."

"At least wait here while we talk to the guard," Vance said. "Someone needs to be lookout for this part."

Vance set off before I had a chance to respond. Max, Drew and Gillon followed in his wake while I waited in the shadows. I wrapped my hand around the surgical knife I kept in my skirt pocket and kept a close eye on proceedings as well as looking out for anyone approaching from the street.

The guard halted the men. Even from where I stood I could see his nervousness. One man against four were not good odds, and if they'd been warned to expect trouble, he would be wary of strangers. If he was smart, he'd alert any companions left inside of potential danger.

My fears were realized when he let out a shout. Max punched him in the gut before he had a chance to shout a second time. Vance and Drew disarmed him while Gillon removed the rope he carried around his neck. He tied a cloth around the guard's mouth then tied the guard's hands and feet together. Drew and Gillon carried him between them around the side of the courthouse where he wouldn't be discovered for some time.

I didn't wait for a signal to join them but ran up to the door and followed the men inside. To my surprise, there were no more guards. Not in the small outer chamber or the inner one. They'd all drunk the emetic.

Using the moonlight to see, we silently searched the office for keys but found none. Remembering how the keys had been hanging just outside the cell doors in the Merrin prison, I set off in the direction I assumed the holding cells to be.

"Not that way," Vance hissed. "That's the courtroom." He pointed at another door. "Through there."

"The latrines?" Max asked.

"Behind the cell block."

We headed into a dimly lit corridor but stopped as the sounds of a man vomiting reached our ears. Max put up his hand for us to wait but Vance pushed past Max and forged ahead.

"Oi!" came the voice of a guard. "Who're you?"

There was a grunt and a thud. I followed Max and we passed the guard who'd fallen into his own vomit. Vance stood over him, shaking out his hand. I made sure the unconscious guard lay in such a way that he couldn't choke on his vomit before following the men further into the corridor.

Max grabbed a torch from the wall and led the way. He held it close to the bars of each cell we passed. Prisoners squinted at the light from where they sat on the floor at the back. Only one prisoner stood near the bars, arms crossed, looking as though he'd been waiting for us.

"Dane!" I ran to the bars and thrust my arms through. He grinned and clasped my hands.

"I knew you'd come," he said. His jaw was covered in stubble and he looked filthy and tired, but I'd never seen a more beautiful sight.

I wiped my tears on my shoulder. "You have more faith in us than we have in ourselves."

"Save the loving reunion for when he's out," Vance said, inspecting the lock.

Max held the torch high and checked the wall beside Dane's cell. It was bare. "Where are the keys?"

"The warden keeps them on his belt." Dane touched my chin. "Emetic?"

I nodded.

"That's my girl."

"We need to get the fucking key!" Max snapped.

"Panic is making you forgetful," Vance said. "I suggest you calm down and stand guard while the professionals get to work." He removed some slender metal strips from his pocket.

I clutched Dane's hand and willed Vance to work faster. Judging by his grunts, and the worried look exchanged between Drew and Gillon, the lock was proving more complicated than they expected.

"Hurry up," Max growled.

"He's working as fast as he can," Drew snapped back. "Merdu, Max, you never used to be this annoying."

"Maybe that's because I never cared about anything this much before."

Dane's fingers tightened around mine.

"You going to free us next?" came a voice from the next cell.

"Sure," Vance said. I didn't know if he meant it or was simply appeasing the prisoner to keep him quiet.

"None of you are going anywhere," said another voice from the corridor's entrance. "You're under arrest for helping a prisoner to escape."

The man speaking wore a black uniform with gold braid at the shoulder. A set of keys hung from the belt at his waist. He was not alone. Six guards stood behind him. All carried swords. None looked ill.

Had I misjudged the amount of emetic? If they'd been warned of an escape attempt tonight by the Rotherhydes' guard, then they could have tricked us into thinking they'd all taken it. That seemed more likely; I doubted I'd made a mistake.

"Step aside!" the captain bellowed.

"Keep working," Max said to Vance. "You get that lock open, and we'll keep them back." He drew his sword and settled into a fighting stance.

My stomach plunged, along with all hope. Max, Gillon and Drew could not keep seven trained guards at bay.

CHAPTER 3

"*P*ut your weapons down!" the warden commanded.

Max adjusted his grip on his sword hilt. Drew swallowed heavily but kept his gaze on the seven guards.

"Hurry," Gillon whispered to Vance.

Vance's tongue wedged in the corner of his mouth, the tip poking out as he concentrated on the lock. I picked up the torch Max had set down but Vance didn't need it. He was working by instinct alone.

"Josie, get back," Dane said.

I moved to the end of the corridor and held the torch like the men held their swords. The warden gave one more warning. When Max didn't drop his weapon, he charged forward.

Max met him half way. Gillon and Drew engaged two guards each but that left two more unimpeded. They strode past the fight and shoved Vance aside.

Vance drew his sword as he fell and thrust it into the stomach of a surprised guard. The second one engaged Vance. With his back to me, he didn't see me coming.

I smashed the torch into his head, sending him reeling. Vance finished him off.

"Now I see why Max lets women come along," he said, swiftly returning to work on the lock again.

Gillon cried out as he was struck. Max managed to push

the warden back and help Gillon before a plunging blade sliced through him, but the warden quickly recovered. Instead of wasting time on Max, he went straight for Vance, ignoring me.

That was a mistake. He tripped over my outstretched foot. His momentum took him past Vance and into the bars of Dane's cell. Dane stabbed him in the shoulder with the surgical knife I'd passed to him moments earlier.

Before the cry of pain had even left the warden's lips, I'd removed the keys from his belt and pushed Vance out of the way. With a grunt, he joined in the fight.

But he wasn't needed. One of the guards suddenly bent over and threw up, and the warden vomited onto the floor. The remaining three guards ran away, clutching their stomachs.

My emetic had worked after all. They must have been experiencing a lull between bouts of purging. Others might too, and they may be well enough to come for us. The sooner we got away the better.

"It's the last key on the ring," Dane told me after my first attempt failed.

I thrust the last key into the lock and it clicked open. Dane rushed out, grabbed my hand, and snatched up a sword from one of the fallen guards. We left the torch behind and Dane led the way through the chambers then outside.

No one followed us.

We sprinted around the corner and almost smacked into Quentin and Theodore with the horses.

Theodore clasped Dane's shoulder. "You did it!"

Quentin gave Dane a brief but fierce hug. "Two people per horse," he said, wiping away tears. "You ride with Josie, unless you prefer to be with me."

Dane laughed. "I'll take Josie." He helped me onto the saddle and climbed up behind me. Theodore and Quentin mounted another horse, while Max held the reins of a third.

"Gillon, your shoulder?" he asked.

"It'll be fine," Gillon said, gripping Max's arm in a friendly shake.

"Thank you. We owe you so much."

"You pay us back by showing us around that palace one day," Drew said.

"Maybe even give us a key," Gillon added with a wink.

Max gave them a weak smile then his gaze settled on Vance as he mounted one of the horses. "Goodbye, Vance."

Vance grunted. "There's no time for goodbyes. The guards are probably fetching soldiers now. You've got to go or all our hard work will be for nothing."

"*Your* hard work?" Max teased. "Josie made the guards sick and opened the lock."

Vance's grunt was full of humor this time. "You better go and not come back to Freedland. Not unless you bring Josie with you to get you out of prison."

Max clasped Vance's arm. He nodded.

Vance nodded back, and I could swear his eyes shone. But he quickly looked away and urged his horse forward.

Max mounted and we headed in the opposite direction.

Dane's arms tightened around my waist as his hands held the reins. "Where are we going?"

"Rotherhydes," I said. "They have tunnels under the house." I explained about the boat, Kitty's necklace, and the delay in leaving.

He was silent the whole way, only speaking when he greeted the others inside the tunnels. We approached the property from a side garden gate that Ewen had made sure would not be guarded. We were met by Ewen himself, who took the horses and directed us to a clutch of trees abutting the high garden wall.

"The entrance is in there," he said. "Eeliss is waiting for you."

We crept close to the wall then followed an overgrown path to the trees, using only the moonlight to show the way. It was fortunate that Eeliss met us or we would not have found the trapdoor in the dark.

"I'll replace the leaves and soil over the top once you're safely inside," she said as I climbed down the ladder. "Your friends are waiting for you in the main tunnel."

I looked up to see Dane following me. Below, candlelight flickered. I couldn't see who held it.

It grew cooler the closer I got to the bottom of the shaft but I was still warm from our flight. The air smelled of earth and felt damp, but if the tunnel kept us safe, I didn't care. I would live like a rat down here for weeks if necessary.

"Josie! Thank Hailia." It was Kitty's voice but Meg's arms that embraced me.

"Dane?" said Yelena. "Where's Dane?"

"Here," he said as he jumped to the ground, skipping the last few rungs. His mother embraced him as fiercely as the girls hugged me.

I squinted into the dim light to see Balthazar holding the candlestick and Martha alongside him. She shed silent tears, but he simply looked relieved. He smiled weakly at me, and I smiled back.

Then he turned and walked off, taking the only light with him. "Come with me and mind your heads."

Our rather large party made its way, single file, through the narrow tunnel. Dane kept one hand linked with mine and the other on the tunnel roof to warn him when to duck. He alerted Meg, Kitty and I to also duck at certain points, but the others did not have to worry.

We didn't speak until the tunnel gave way to a small chamber where Erik sat on a straw pallet, a single candle beside him. His teeth showed white in the darkness.

"You are free! This is good news. Very good news." He tried to rise, but Dane ordered him to remain seated. They clasped arms warmly. "I am glad you didn't die yet."

"So am I," Dane said.

Martha made a choking sound, and Meg wrapped a comforting arm around her. "We have enough food and water to sustain us for three days," she said. "It's stored in another small chamber along the corridor. We can't cook anything down here, and the perishable food must be eaten first."

Quentin snorted. "We won't be dining like royalty then."

"Quentin," Theodore hissed, jerking his head at Yelena.

Quentin winced. "Sorry, Princess. I meant no offence."

Yelena ignored him. She took Dane's hands in both of hers. "Did they torture you?"

"They treated me well enough." He scrubbed his jaw. "I

wouldn't mind a shave, though. Funnily enough, barbers aren't allowed to visit condemned prisoners."

Quentin chuckled then threw his arms around Dane again. "It's so good to have you back in one piece. We missed you."

Dane clapped him on the back. "I missed you too. I see you took care of Josie for me."

"Of course."

"I think *she* took care of *him*," Theodore said, slapping Dane on the shoulder. "Come with me. I'll shave you."

Dane's eyes shone in the darkness as he smiled at me. He winked and I winked back before he followed Theodore out of the chamber.

I checked Erik's wound and was pleased to see it was healing nicely. Hopefully the stitches in Dane's back had not come out in the struggles during his arrest. There was no telling what state it would be in if it became infected from the prison filth.

I went to follow him, but Yelena caught my arm. "Leave him be."

"I need to check his wound," I said.

"He needs to rest."

"I know."

Her grip tightened around my arm before she released me. "Thank you for what you did tonight. Your loyalty won't be forgotten."

"It had nothing to do with loyalty, but I appreciate you acknowledging my efforts."

I followed Dane and Theodore's voices in the dark to the next chamber and found Dane holding up the candle to his jaw while Theodore carefully shaved him.

"This could have waited for the morning," I said.

"Until you have unwanted whiskers, you can't comment," Dane said.

I smiled. "You're in a good mood."

"I may have exchanged one small dark place for another, but at least I'm free."

"Not necessarily. You can't go anywhere until the boat is ready and it's time to leave. None of us can. It's too much of a risk. Even Kitty, Meg and I must stay in here. If anyone sees

Glancian women walking down the street, they'll follow us back."

Balthazar entered, taking us by surprise. The packed earth floor dulled the tops of his walking stick.

"Is nowhere private anymore?" Dane asked without moving his jaw.

Balthazar leaned his walking stick against the wall and searched for somewhere to sit among the barrels of water, pails, and basins. He ended up perching on the edge of the small table where brushes and other grooming implements had been laid.

"It's just like old times at the palace," Theodore said. "The four of us discussing palace politics and plotting intrigues. It's not exactly Bal's office, but it's not too bad down here."

"I never plotted," Balthazar said.

We looked at him.

"I merely reacted to the machinations of others." He glanced at the entrance. "Speaking of which, I've had the good fortune to speak to your mother while we waited for your return, Dane. She's an interesting woman."

"I hardly know her," Dane said.

"She's very forthright, which is not unexpected in a member of the royal household."

No one mentioned that she wasn't a member of any royal household anymore.

"Did you know she's coming to Glancia with us?" Balthazar went on.

"Josie explained as much on the way here. If Yelena stays in Freedland, her life is in danger."

"Only while you live."

"Don't kill me off too soon, Bal."

"I won't. Quentin would be inconsolable, and I can't stand excessive weeping." Balthazar inspected a hair comb made of bone as if it intrigued him, but I knew it was a technique he employed to disguise his emotions.

"Go on," Dane said, not fooled either. "Out with it."

Balthazar set the comb aside. "Now that the Freedland ministers know you're alive, they'll pursue you, even if that means chasing you all the way back to Glancia. They can't afford for you to live."

Theodore lowered the blade. "Not back to Glancia, surely?"

Balthazar nodded.

Theodore indicated he'd finished and set about washing the blade in a basin of water. "We'll just have to fight them in Glancia, then. At least we'll be on home soil."

No one reminded him that his real home was more likely to be in Dreen than Glancia.

"Yes," Balthazar said heavily. "We'll just have to fight them when they come for him. Or he must hide out his days somewhere, perhaps change his name. Leave Mull and go somewhere no one will find him."

Dane leaned forward and rested his elbows on his knees. He dragged his hand through his ragged hair and sighed heavily.

Balthazar pushed off from the table and collected his walking stick. "Or he embraces his birthright and leads a royalist force to take back the Averlea throne. The Rotherhydes will send word to me at the palace when they have gathered enough support."

"*If* they get enough support," I said. "It doesn't seem like many in Freedland will risk their lives for the royal family."

"They will get the soldiers they need," Balthazar said with confidence. "The Rotherhydes have a vast fortune, so Vance told me, and international mercenaries go where the money takes them."

"How long before they'll be ready?" Dane asked.

"It's a matter of months," I said, recalling what Ewen had told Meg. "You don't need to make a decision about your future yet."

"Come on, Bal," Theodore said cheerfully. He passed a basin of fresh water to me with a clean cloth. "I'll leave him in your hands, Josie. Try to remember he's tired."

"And that sound travels in these tunnels," Balthazar added as he limped off.

I hugged the basin until they were gone then set it down near Dane's feet. I sat on his lap and stroked his hair off his forehead. "You look worried."

"There's a lot to think about."

"One thing at a time. Escaping first; taking over Freedland later."

He shook his head. "Loving you first. Everything else can wait."

* * *

THE FIRST THING Dane did after waking from a long sleep was to ask his mother about his father. Yelena told him he was Glancian, as we'd suspected. He'd come to Noxford to forge new trading alliances but died shortly before Dane's birth.

"He was a good man," Yelena said, her voice softening. "I liked his company. We had lengthy discussions about all sorts of things." She smiled and touched Dane's cheek. "You have his eyes."

"He was a merchant?" Dane asked.

"He had extensive interests all over The Fist."

"Did he know you were the princess of Averlea?"

"He did. When I fell pregnant, he understood what it meant if I had a boy."

Quentin snorted softly. "All this could have been avoided if Dane was born a girl."

Meg kicked him, and he gave her a questioning look.

We sat on the pallets in the larger of the two rooms since there was nowhere else to go except the tunnels where the men slept at night. There was no opportunity for private conversation so my interaction with Dane had been limited. We exchanged whispered words but nothing more. I had expected him to wait until he could be alone with his mother before pressing her about his past, but it seemed he couldn't wait.

"Does he still have family in Glancia?" Dane asked.

Yelena shook her head.

Dane crossed his legs at the ankles. His booted foot touched mine. It was as intimate as we could get in these cramped quarters. "That explains why he was happy to live here and not there."

I glanced at Martha, who sat as far from us as possible, her back against the wall. She caught me looking and lowered her gaze to her lap.

Yelena took Dane's hand in her own. "Your father understood you would have a destiny to fulfill if you were a boy. He told me it pleased him to know his unborn child could be the heir to the Averlea throne. He prayed to the goddess for a boy."

Out of the corner of my eye I caught sight of Meg crossing her arms and shaking her head. Max nudged her with his elbow and winked when she looked at him. She smirked and nudged him back.

"He would be immensely proud of you, Son," Yelena said softly.

Dane suddenly took her hand. I couldn't see his eyes from where I sat, but I suspected they were bright and his throat too tight to respond. My own was.

"You have turned out better than either of us could have hoped," Yelena went on. "I know your father would have been pleased to see you re-take what is rightfully yours."

Dane let go of her hand. "I haven't decided if I want it."

"Pardon?"

"The throne. I'm yet to decide if the upheaval is worth it. I doubt it is, but I want to wait until I have my memory back before I make that decision."

She swayed as if he'd pushed her and stared at him. "You're yet to decide?" she echoed. "What decision is there to make?"

He frowned. "A very big one. Surely you can't expect me to lead an army of mercenaries into Noxford and slaughter all the ministers and soldiers who are against me without careful consideration."

"Why not?" she growled. "That's what they did to my family. To *your* family."

Dane rubbed his forehead. "We'll discuss this later."

"What do you think you'll do instead?" she went on. It was as if none of us were there, as invisible as the palace servants had been when they served the nobles.

Dane glanced around the room, at the faces watching them and at those discreetly turned away so as not to embarrass him. "Can we talk about this when we're on the boat?"

"No, we cannot. It'll be too late then."

"Too late?" He turned to face her fully. "You don't want me to leave, do you? You expect me to stay here even though the entire country is looking for me."

"We will remain in hiding until the time is right."

"It could be months!"

"You're strong and healthy, and I'll endure it with you." He went to protest again, but she cut him off. "Don't run off to Glancia. You were never a coward, Dane."

"He's not a coward now," I snapped.

Yelena's nostrils flared. "She can stay too, if you wish. Her presence will make the wait more pleasurable for you. Ewen and Eeliss won't mind, as long as the betrothal with Laylana stands."

Dane set his jaw. "I'm leaving on that boat, and I don't want to hear another word about staying."

She set her jaw just as firmly. "You are the heir. The Averlea throne is your birthright, your destiny. You can't ignore it."

"If you believe in destiny then you have to accept that my destiny was to lose my memory and be a guard in the Glancian palace. *That* is what happened, and maybe it happened for a reason." He stood and peered down at her. "I won't be making any decisions until my memory returns and I understand myself."

He went to walk off but she grabbed his hand and rose onto her knees. "You *do* understand yourself. Search your heart and you'll find your true nature." She tapped her chest. "You don't need a memory for that."

He pulled free and walked off, out of the chamber.

"What would you do if you don't accept your birthright?" she called after him. "Hide for the rest of your life? They know you're alive now, and they won't rest until your head is on a spike. Is that the life you want for Josie, for your children? You will be looking over your shoulder for the rest of your days if you take that boat to Glancia and abandon everything I've worked so hard to achieve for you."

"That's enough," I hissed at her. "He knows the consequences." I picked up a candle and strode after Dane, Yelena's glare burning into my back.

I found him leaning against the wall at the base of the ladder, his arms crossed over his chest. He looked up upon my arrival and opened his arms to me. I set the candle down on the ground and went to him. His sigh ruffled my hair.

We embraced for some time, neither speaking, until I pulled away and indicated the ladder. "You're not thinking of leaving, are you?"

"No. This was the furthest point from the room."

"You could have followed the tunnel in the other direction. I believe it's longer."

"There are more tunnels that way, so Martha says. I'm worried I'd get lost."

I smiled. "The amazing Dane March has no sense of direction? I don't believe it."

He laughed softly. "March. I'm not yet used to it."

I took his hands in mine. "I'm glad you know who you are now, even if it means you're far above me in station."

"Don't joke about it. I'm still an ordinary man."

"Your mother doesn't think so," I said, keeping my voice low.

His chest deflated with another deep sigh. "Perhaps if I could remember, I would want to please her, but I feel no sentimentality towards her. I'm a terrible person for thinking that."

"You're not. Everyone in your position would feel the same. Look at Max and Vance. They were as close as brothers, yet Max can easily walk away. When your memory returns, you'll feel a connection to her again."

It was what I dreaded most now, that his memories would return and his desires and wishes would change to what they had been before. If he thought reinstating the royal family in Freedland was a good idea then, why wouldn't he still think that way now?

It was impossible to know how any of them would react when their memories returned. All I did know was that Dane was a good man then and he was still a good man now.

"You'll make the right decision," I said. "Have faith in yourself."

He tugged me closer and put his arms around me again. He kissed my forehead and worked his way down to my lips. The kiss was sweet at first but quickly escalated to one of yearning and desire. He broke the kiss before it went too far, but he did not push me away. He closed his eyes and tipped his head back against the wall.

"Are you thinking about Laylana?" I asked.

He frowned. "No."

"Oh. Right. Of course you wouldn't think of her at a time like this."

He touched my chin. "I think we need to address this before your imagination starts running off in the wrong direction."

I thrust my hand on my hip. "I'm very practically minded."

His lips stretched into a smile. "So you weren't thinking that I'll get back to Glancia and decide Laylana needs rescuing, and since we're already betrothed I might as well just marry her?"

"No."

He arched his brows.

"Very well, it crossed my mind."

"Then let me assure you, I won't marry her, with or without my memory. It seems as though it was an arranged marriage for political reasons and we weren't in love."

"She tried to free you from prison. That sounds to me like love."

"Or a royalist supporter with her own interests at heart. Her future depended on me regaining the throne." He kissed me lightly on the lips. "When we get back to the palace, I'm going to tell her about the betrothal but I'll also tell her I'm calling it off."

I checked the vicinity before whispering, "You're going to break your promise to her?"

"Yes."

"Before or after we get Brant to wish for your memories back?"

"Regaining my memory won't affect my decision. I don't want to marry Laylana." He pressed his forehead to mine. "I want to marry you."

My heart flipped in my chest, and a wave of warm tingles washed over me. I couldn't help my smile, even though I fought hard to suppress it.

It was only wiped from my face when Dane kissed me again,

fiercely this time. I buried my fingers in his hair and kissed him back. I pressed my body against his, wanting to feel more of him, all of him. But we could not lie together. Not here, and not when my mind still whirled with questions and uncertainties.

I broke the kiss and our combined sighs of frustration filled the tunnel.

"You shouldn't make hasty decisions," I said. "Not until your memory returns. I agree with Yelena on that score."

He settled his hands on my shoulders and dipped his head to meet my gaze. "I've been in that prison cell for two days with nothing but time to think. I know what I'm doing, and I am comfortable with my decision to break the betrothal to Laylana. Just as I'm comfortable with not taking back the Averlea throne."

My breath hitched, and I looked along the tunnel to make sure Yelena hadn't heard.

"Don't tell her yet," he said, reading my thoughts. "It's not the right time."

"That's a big decision to make, Dane, especially not knowing your past."

His lips twitched with his smile. "Do you want to be queen? Is that why you're questioning my decision?"

"You are not taking this seriously enough. In this instance, what I want is irrelevant."

"If you're going to be my wife, you have to be involved in important decisions."

His wife. It was a thrilling notion but somewhat humbling too. "I suppose so."

"Before you start imagining how big your crown should be, I should tell you what I learned from the other prisoners," he said.

"Again, you don't seem to be taking this seriously enough."

"I am, I promise."

"So what did you learn from the prisoners in the holding cell?" I asked.

"Not just the prisoners, but the guards too. I asked them about the current system of government in Freedland. They said it was corrupt, taxes were too high, and there wasn't enough work."

"That sounds terrible."

"But they all agreed it was better than what they had forty years ago. One prisoner even remembered King Diamedes. He said he was a vain, small-minded man without compassion. The lower orders were little better than slaves, working for poor wages in horrendous conditions for noble families, and my grandfather encouraged that system. Anyone who spoke against him was tortured and killed, and not just the dissenter but their family too."

I gasped. "How horrific."

"The corruption under the royal family was far worse than the corruption of the current regime. All the prisoners and guards agreed that they never wanted to see the country in the hands of a king again. They preferred their leader to be elected by the people."

I stood beside him and leaned back against the wall for support too. Trust Dane to find out what the ordinary folk thought instead of listening to people like the Rotherhydes. He'd never had much respect for that sort.

"I don't want to be king in a country that doesn't want one." He huffed out a humorless laugh. "I don't want to be king even if they *did* want to reinstate the monarchy."

"You'd make a good king," I pointed out.

"I don't want to sit on a throne and issue commands."

"You already issue commands, every day. But I understand what you're saying. Being a good monarch means being diplomatic, and you don't like politics."

He nodded thoughtfully. "I'm returning to Glancia with you, and I will never come back here." After a long moment in which neither of us spoke, he said, "Say something."

I clasped his face in my hands and kissed him. "I am very happy with your decision. Very happy."

It meant hiding in Glancia somewhere, but so be it. We would do what needed to be done to keep him safe from the Freedland authorities. Part of me still worried that he had made the decision without having his memories, but I doubted that would make a difference. Like he said, he had new memories now, and those ones had shaped him just as much as the ones he'd lost.

* * *

I HAD no idea how long we were down in the hidden chambers and tunnels. Time slipped by unnoticed with no daylight to mark its passing. We ate when we were hungry and slept when we were tired. We played cards and dice that Jenny had given to Erik, and we talked. Yelena did not pressure Dane about the throne again, but they didn't talk much, either. She often set herself apart from the rest of us.

I was pleased to see he chatted easily with Martha. His attention lifted her spirits, and she delighted in telling him all about his childhood, his friends, and what he liked and didn't like, most of which were the same as now. She told him anecdotes of the various scrapes he'd got into as a boy, and she grew a little misty-eyed when she spoke about a stray dog that had followed him home one day and he'd adopted as a pet. I listened but tried not to intrude, although in the cramped chamber, it was impossible not to feel a part of their discussion.

Dane didn't hide his love for me from anyone, choosing to kiss me in front of his mother whenever he felt like it. She kept her face impassive and pretended not to notice. Martha always looked away, but not before I saw the worry in her eyes.

When he wasn't chatting to Martha, Dane seemed distracted. He often walked the length of the tunnels and did not get lost once. He sparred with Max and Quentin, and he walked with Erik as the Marginer began to feel better. The lack of exercise and light seemed to frustrate Dane, however, and his restlessness only grew worse as we headed into what I guessed to be our third day underground.

Dane was on one of his tunnel walks when Eeliss arrived with Jenny. As a Freedland woman, her arrival at the Rotherhydes' house would not raise any suspicions if the house was being watched. With a basket of laundry in her arms, her disguise wouldn't be questioned.

We all rose to greet them and peppered Jenny with questions about the boat.

"If you let me speak, I'll tell you," she said with a grunt. "The boat's been fixed and the captain's ready. You leave tonight."

We all breathed sighs of relief. Then came more questions about our departure. Jenny passed on the instructions from the captain before she left with Eeliss, but not before she embraced Max one last time.

He watched her go, his expression thoughtful, until Meg took his hand in hers. Then he smiled at her and kissed her gently on the mouth.

"Captain'll be pleased to get out of these tunnels," Quentin said. "He can't stand being cooped up down here."

"He's been gone a while," Theodore said, looking along the tunnel. "I hope he didn't get lost."

"He knows his way around," Max said.

Max and Quentin went in search of him, only to both return with confused frowns. My heart plunged and my gut tightened.

"We looked everywhere," Max said. "He's gone."

CHAPTER 4

"*M*erdu, no!" Yelena cried. "They've taken him!" She picked up her skirts and ran off in the direction of the ladder.

"No one has come down here except Eeliss and Jenny," I called after her.

She disappeared around the corner. I followed her to bring her back before she exposed our location.

"Listen to me," I said when I caught up to her. When she still didn't stop, I grabbed her arm.

She tried to shake me off, but I held firmly. She hissed at me. "Let go."

"If someone entered from the trapdoor in the garden, they would have had to pass us. We would have seen them. If they'd come the other way, from the house, it's unlikely they would have gone unnoticed. If they did, then we would have heard Dane defending himself. Sounds travel in these tunnels."

The others crowded behind us. Someone held up a candle and I could make out the wildness in Yelena's eyes as she glared at me. That and her fear. I sympathized. I felt it too. Despite what I'd said, I wasn't entirely sure Dane had left of his own accord.

"Why would he just walk out there into danger?" she snapped. "It's madness."

Madness or a calculated risk—time would reveal which. He

must have gone to speak to the authorities to either clear his name or pretend he was merely a lookalike for the deceased Dane March. Whatever his plan, it was not only flawed, it was foolish.

I felt utter despair at the thought of him once again returning to a prison cell to await his execution. This time they might not wait to execute him. They might dispatch him the moment he showed his face.

I clutched my throat as bile rose.

Yelena took my hand, a sudden and unexpected sympathizer.

"It was the only way," Balthazar said, his voice clear.

We all turned to him. "You knew," Theodore said, accusing. "Why didn't you say?"

"He asked me not to."

Yelena stiffened. "You should have informed me."

"No, I should not. It was Dane's request that no one be told until his absence was discovered. He didn't want anyone trying to stop him before he had time to speak to the ministers."

Yelena snapped her skirts out of the way then put a hand to the ladder. "You just signed his death warrant."

"Max, stop her," Balthazar said. "I'm going back to the room and taking the light with me. I suggest you bring anyone with you who is likely to go after Dane. Until we have word that he is successful or not, we must remain here. There's a chance he'll need to escape to somewhere safe, and this is the safest place in the city."

"You fool!" Yelena cried.

Balthazar walked away, passing Martha as she silently cried at the back of the gathering. I put my arm around her shoulders, but it was difficult to comfort her when I needed comforting too. I was so very tempted to go after Dane, just as his mother tried to, but I knew it would achieve nothing.

Max marched Yelena back along the corridor, his hand on her arm. "Sorry, ma'am, but Bal's right. Dane knows what he's doing."

I wish I could be as confident. Dane might know what he was doing most of the time, but he was not in the Glancian palace and the ministers were not selfish and malleable like Leon. And he was not simply the captain of the guards here.

We returned to the main chamber and waited. If time had dragged before, it crawled now. Max stood guard at the door, not allowing anyone out. Yelena brooded in the corner while Martha's misery infected everyone. I lost all hope that Dane would succeed in his mad plan as time stretched on and on.

Sounds might easily travel in the tunnels, but footfalls were deadened by the earthen floor. So Dane's sudden appearance behind Max took us all by surprise. Max was the first to embrace him and tell him he was a fool for leaving, but we all got our turn.

"Thank the god and goddess," I murmured in his ear as I hugged him with all the ferocity of someone who thought she'd never see him again. "You scared me."

"I know, and I'm sorry." He apologized to his mother and Martha next, then to everyone. "But I had to keep it a secret. I knew you'd all try to stop me. Everyone except Bal. He understood what I had to do."

"I understood it," Balthazar said. "But I didn't like it. I'm relieved you're back. Does this mean it was a success?"

Dane grinned. "We can leave Freedland without fear of anyone trying to stop us."

"Is this true?" Erik asked.

"How?" said Theodore.

"You lied, didn't you?"

"They believed you when you said you're not Dane March?" Quentin asked, wide-eyed.

Dane put up his hands for calm. "I didn't lie. I told them I am indeed Dane March, heir of Averlea."

Quentin's eyes grew even bigger. "And they're just letting you go?"

Yelena's sudden intake of breath had us all turning to her. "What did you do?" she whispered, lips trembling. "Dane, *what did you do?*"

Dane pulled out a folded document from inside his doublet. "I signed this. They have copies. One will be kept in the high minister's archives, another sent to the high temple, here in

Noxford, for their archives, and another to the supreme temple in Fahl."

"No." Yelena's voice sounded strangled. She clutched her throat. "No!"

Dane unfolded the document and signaled for Theodore to bring the candle close. "I have given up all rights to the Averlea throne in exchange for a pardon for myself and all my friends."

"We're free?" Max asked. "We can show our faces in Freedland now?"

"Freedland, Vytill, Glancia, Dreen." Dane nodded at Theodore, who looked as though he was about to cry. "Everyone's sentences have been considered completed."

Balthazar put on his spectacles and peered at the document. "You do mean everyone," he muttered in wonder. "This says they admitted they didn't capture every escaped prisoner, and that those who did manage to get away have had their sentences commuted to the time already served. Every prisoner is now free."

"Except for those in the palace cells," Dane pointed out. "Those men are evil. We don't want them released."

Quentin threw himself at Dane. Dane hugged him, laughing. Max turned to Meg, his eyes bright with tears. She put her arms around him and smiled at me over his shoulder.

Erik let out a whoop of delight and picked Kitty up to spin her around until I snapped at him to put her down again. "Do you want to pull out your stitches?"

"We are free!" he said, wrapping his arms around me. "Free to go home."

I smiled even though tears began to fall. "Yes. Free to go home with no one chasing Dane." He would not have to flee in the night. He wouldn't have to hide for the rest of his life. He wouldn't have to marry someone he didn't want to. I hadn't realized how heavy the weight on my shoulders had been until it had lifted upon his announcement.

"It says here you gave up the right on behalf of any future children you may have," Yelena said, studying the document by the candlelight.

"On behalf of my heirs until the end of time, I believe it

says." Dane took the document from her and folded it up. "The high minister wanted to be very thorough. This document also states that I must leave Noxford tonight, and never let it be known that I am the grandson of King Diamedes. He doesn't want people rallying in my name. Since only a few people knew he had a grandson, that won't be difficult."

"He thought of everything," Balthazar said with a nod of approval.

"I found him to be clever," Dane said. "One of his advisors, however, was even more astute. I think the government will do well if it learns from some of their mistakes."

Yelena let out a high-pitched wail and flung herself at him. She pounded her fists into his chest and shoulders. "How *could* you? After everything I've done for you!"

Dane caught her wrists and held her at arm's length. She struggled and bared her teeth but quietened when she realized her anger was futile. Dane loosened his grip but didn't let go.

"I'm sorry," he said gently. "But this is my life, and I am the only one who decides what I do with it."

Her face twisted with rage, and I thought she might spit at him or try to strike him, but she simply turned her face away, as if she could no longer bear to look at him.

"Yelena, I know this isn't what you wanted, and I hope you will find it in your heart to forgive me, one day. But from the moment I learned I was heir to the throne, I've been trying to think of a way to be free of the obligation you forced on me."

She turned back to face him. Her cheeks were wet and her eyes brimmed with tears. It was the first time I'd seen her cry. "I didn't force it on you. You wanted it. You will again when you get your memory back."

He shook his head. "I will never regret signing that document. You can be assured of that."

Her face momentarily crumpled before she regained her composure. She tossed her head and peered up at him. "You used to take advice from me. Right up until the day you were arrested, you shared my hopes and dreams. You wanted what I wanted, Dane."

"Did I? Or did I not want to disappoint you?"

She didn't appear to hear him. She gazed into his eyes, as if looking into the past and seeing the man he used to be, not the one he had become. "Everything I did, I did for you."

"No. You did it for you."

My arm was still around Martha, and I felt her body shake. She was no longer crying but staring at her mistress and the man she'd raised with wonder. I wasn't sure if she was terrified by Dane's declaration or pleased.

Yelena pulled free of Dane's grip. The fire had returned to her eyes, the tears all gone. "You should not have signed that document without knowing your past. You would think differently if you had your memories."

Dane shook his head. "You said yourself that I understand myself without them. You told me I don't need a memory to know my true nature and to search my heart to find it. So I did. And this is what my heart wants. To live a peaceful life with Josie, with no crown weighing me down. The Freedland people don't want a king, and the country is better off the way it is."

"Shedding our people's blood to regain the throne didn't sit well with me either. I will concede that point." She sounded oddly pleased that they had found something to agree on. "But taking back the throne was the *right* thing to do. The people would want *you*, once they got to know how just and good you are, how honorable and strong. You are what they need—"

"Enough! It's over."

Yelena's nostrils flared, and her lips twisted. Was she smiling? It looked so odd, so out of place considering the situation. She was up to something, I was sure of it.

Martha rushed towards her. "Mistress, are we still going with the master to Glancia?"

"Of course. He's my son. Where he goes, I go."

"Then please come and show me how you would like me to pack. Please, mistress." Martha bobbed a curtsy and indicated the door. Their things had been stored in the other chamber. "Please, mistress, come with me."

"In a moment. There's something I have to tell him."

"Don't do this, mistress. Not now. He's not ready. Please, I'm begging you to wait."

We all turned frowns towards the maid.

"Martha?" Dane asked carefully. "What's wrong?"

Distress was etched into every line on her face. She was torn between obeying her mistress and answering her master.

"She's referring to me telling you about your father," Yelena said.

Dane tilted his head to the side. "You told me he was a Glancian merchant."

"I never said merchant. I said he had trading interests all over The Fist. But he wasn't a merchant. Nor was his name March."

"My name is not Dane March?"

"That was the name he used when he came to Averlea, in secret, to visit me. I wrote to him and requested he come, as it was too difficult for me to go to him in Glancia."

"You were friends?"

"We'd never met before I wrote to him."

"I don't understand. You invited a man you'd never met to your home? Why?"

"To marry me and beget an heir."

"He simply agreed, without question?"

"I had to prove I was the princess, of course. That was easy enough to do with the Rotherhydes and other families vouching for me."

"I don't understand," Dane said again, his voice thin. "What are you saying?"

Balthazar's hand found mine, and I suddenly understood. We all understood. All except Dane. He simply stood there, his face blank except for the dark swirl in his eyes as he stared at his mother.

Yelena clutched his elbows and gazed up at him, her eyes clear and bright. "My son, you are not only the heir to Averlea. You are the rightful king of Glancia. Your father was Prince Hugo, King Alain's son. Your name is not Dane March, it's Dane Lockhart."

CHAPTER 5

"Say something," Yelena prompted when Dane continued to stare at her, his mouth agape.

He shook his head, over and over. "I can't comprehend it."

She touched his cheek. "It's overwhelming, I understand. Ask me anything. I will answer your questions freely."

Balthazar shuffled forward. "You should have answered them from the beginning."

"I never lied to him," Yelena said.

"You withheld the truth."

She turned back to Dane, presenting her shoulder to Balthazar. "I continued to use the name March to keep your true identity a secret. It was too much of a risk to use Lockhart, even here. It's known all over The Fist to be the family name of the kings of Glancia."

Dane glanced at me, but I could give him no advice. My mind was still reeling. "You chose to marry Prince Hugo because you wanted your child to be the heir of both kingdoms," he said to his mother. "Why? Insurance, for situations like this, when one didn't work out?" His biting tone did not deter her. She continued to smile in that hopeful way.

"It was the sensible thing to do," she said.

"Sensible," Dane scoffed.

"It's what royal families do. They form alliances with other kingdoms through marriage and trade. I didn't invent the practice, Dane."

"You should have told me the night we met."

Martha made a small sobbing sound and clutched at her throat.

"Go and pack," Yelena ordered her maid.

Martha hurried out, and Meg followed, indicating the others should leave us alone. I remained behind, as did Balthazar. The lines scoring his brow had only grown deeper.

Yelena clutched Dane's hands. "I know this is a shock, but you will grow used to it. You have the journey home to the palace to think."

Dane removed his hands from hers and dragged them through his hair and down his face. When he removed them, his gaze flicked to me. I didn't see a man who was thrilled with the idea of becoming king. I saw a man who looked trapped.

Being king of a monarchy like Glancia wasn't the same as taking back the throne in a bloody coup in Freedland. The Glancian people would welcome him if it meant the dukes would stop fighting and King Phillip of Vytill was kept at bay. Indeed, Dane's inheritance meant a bloodless succession.

I should be pleased for my country and its people. I should feel glad that a war could be averted. I shouldn't feel as though this was the worst possible outcome.

"You inherited the title upon King Alain's death," Yelena went on. "Since I thought you dead too, I did not care that the pretender Leon assumed the throne. But now that he is dead, and you are alive, your path is clear and unencumbered."

"It's not as simple as arriving at the palace and announcing he is the rightful king," Balthazar said. "Evidence will be required."

"Dane," she said gently, "I chose Hugo because he would have made a good king, if he'd lived. He was keen to have a son to rule both kingdoms too—"

"So he was ruthless," Dane said.

"Ambitious."

"You never told King Alain about the union?" Balthazar asked. "It's my understanding that upon his death, the only paperwork regarding an heir was that conjured up by the magician for Leon. We know that document to be false. Why was King Alain not informed by Prince Hugo himself before his death?"

Yelena's lips tightened. "The king would not have liked tying his son and heir to the defunct Freedland royal family. He wouldn't have understood the need for his grandchild to fight for a foreign throne."

"Because he knew it meant plunging the republic back into turmoil and he didn't want the expense or loss of Glancian life fighting for a lost foreign cause. Yes?"

Yelena's jaw hardened. "He would have taken Dane from me and insisted he reside in Glancia and forget the Averlea throne."

"And the Averlea throne was always your primary objective," Balthazar went on. "So you decided to wait for his death and present Dane to the people of Glancia."

"If I had known the sorcerer would change everything, I would have played it differently."

"Played," Dane growled. "This is not a game." He went to walk away.

"You cannot dismiss this as you did your claim to the Averlea crown," his mother called after him.

He stopped and rounded on her. "I can if there's no evidence. The dukes and lords won't simply accept your word. Didn't you say you sent the marriage and my birth documents to the master of Merdu's Guards in Tilting?"

"I did."

"Then there is a problem, because if those documents still existed, Balthazar would have found them. He searched high and low for a reason to explain why he left the city in secret to come here, and he found nothing. I think a child born to a princess who is supposed to be dead would have been something he noticed."

My breath caught in my throat, just as Dane seemed to realize the implications of what he'd said too. Neither Balthazar nor Yelena looked surprised. She had already known and he had come to the conclusion before us.

"He brought the documents to Freedland," I said, thinking

out loud. "Over a year ago, he had with him the evidence of Dane's birthright, which he showed to Dane when they met. The papers were probably confiscated when Balthazar was arrested soon afterwards."

"Arrested because he possessed knowledge that could endanger the republic," Dane added.

Yelena closed her eyes. Her nod was slight, as if it gave her pain. "Dane informed me after the priest's visit that he had the documents on him as proof." She opened her eyes and glared at Balthazar. Her jaw clenched so hard it didn't move as she spoke. "His visit not only triggered your arrest, Dane, but it also lost us those priceless documents. Stupid, stupid man. I should scratch his eyes out for what he has done."

Dane shifted towards her, as if worried she might actually attack.

Balthazar, however, merely lifted his chin. "I still fail to see how my visit triggered his arrest. Nobody knew I was here, let alone why. I told no one."

"You priests are all the same," Yelena spat. "You think you are above the law, above the king. You think you are owed explanations in matters of state that don't concern you, and you think you are the arbiters of justice. You are *not*."

I hooked my arm through Balthazar's, but he didn't need my support. He was frail in body, not in mind or spirit. He wasn't the sort to let the venom of a former princess trouble him.

He merely shook his head and walked out of the room.

Dane went to follow him, but Yelena caught his hand. "I was going to tell you the night you returned, but you were arrested before I could. And these last few days have been unsettling, to say the least. The timing wasn't right. I thought you should stay here and fight for this throne before leaving for Glancia and claiming your birthright there. But since you gave up on Averlea and decided to return anyway…"

"I know why you kept it from me," Dane said levelly. "But it seems I can't claim the Glancian throne anyway. There is no evidence I am Prince Hugo's son. When Leon's claim came out of the blue, the skeptics circled until he presented definitive proof. They won't believe the claim of a second unknown son, particularly one with no evidence. Let's leave it at that and forget about it."

She clutched him harder as he went to walk off. "I have copies of the marriage and birth certificate in my possession."

"They'll say you forged them. Unless they are in the possession of the priests, it won't be enough."

"Then use one of the wishes to conjure the correct paperwork into existence. If you word it just so, perhaps a single wish could get your memory back *and* put right this wrong."

Dane extricated himself from her grip. "No, Yelena. You are welcome to come with us to Glancia. I will do my best to take care of you and Martha. But I won't be attempting to claim the Glancian throne. There'll be no more discussion of the matter."

She released him. "Very well. It's your decision. I'll take you up on your offer of coming with you, if that's all right with Josie. I don't want to intrude on your lives any more than I already have."

"It's no intrusion," I said and meant it. "You're his mother. You'll always be welcome wherever Dane is."

She smiled and thanked me. Dane nodded stiffly and walked away, his back straight. She watched him go, blinking back her tears.

"Give him time," I said gently. "He's feeling overwhelmed, but he'll forgive you and accept you."

She smiled wistfully, and I was glad to see that she did seem to have maternal instincts. She had simply set them aside for her ambition. Hopefully now she could be a proper mother to a grown son. "He doesn't like things being out of his control," she said wryly. "Something I'm sure you've discovered."

"I certainly have."

We walked out together and met the others in the second chamber. With our meager belongings packed, we departed our cramped quarters and headed along the tunnel and up the ladder. We emerged from the trapdoor in the copse of trees then followed the lights towards the house.

The guards looked surprised to see us, wondering how we'd got past them at the gate, but the footman let us in without question. Eeliss and Ewen met us in the sitting room and immediately voiced their concerns about the guards noticing us.

"I'm afraid I cannot trust them," Ewen said apologetically.

Eeliss tried to shoo us out the door. "Make haste! You must get to the boat before someone alerts the authorities."

"There's been a change of plans." Dane quickly explained the bargain he'd made with the ministers and told them he could leave Noxford without risking recapture.

When he finished, utter silence filled the room. Then Eeliss muttered a small sound as she fainted onto the daybed. Meg and Kitty went to her, but her husband merely stood there, staring at Dane as if he hadn't heard a word.

Yelena took Dane's arm. "I think we should go. They need time to consider—"

"You!" Ewen suddenly growled at her. "You assured us he would accept his birthright. You told us he was eager to become king!"

"He was, before his memory loss. Come, Dane. We must go. The boat is waiting."

"Everything has changed," Dane added. "I'm sorry, but—"

"You're sorry?" Ewen scoffed. "You're *sorry*! Do you know how much gold I've spent on you? All your tutors were paid by me. Your mother's cottage and allowance, every loaf of bread on your table, every grain, all paid out of my pocket. The mercenaries, the bribes, the spies; they have all cost me a fortune." He jabbed Dane in the chest with his finger. "And now, because you've *changed your mind*, I am to receive nothing in return?"

"We are grateful," Yelena began.

"Spare me your pitiful gratitude," he snapped.

She straightened. "That is enough. Do not speak to me or my son that way."

"I will speak to you how I treat all my servants, because that's all you are to me now. Servants I pay to perform duties. Except you did not perform your duty." He poked Dane again. "Do you know what I do to servants who fail to do their job? I whip them."

Martha gasped then clamped her hand over her mouth.

Yelena swallowed heavily. She looked afraid, and if Yelena was afraid of the Rotherhydes, then we should be too.

"Let's go," I said to Dane.

He pushed Ewen's finger aside with a deliberate sweep of his arm. He showed no urgency and no fear. "Thank you for taking care of my mother and me all these years. It's appreciated."

"Appreciated!" Ewen blocked Dane's exit and once again stabbed him in the chest. "We didn't do it out of kindness!"

"So I understand. Move aside, Ewen. We have a boat to catch."

Ewen planted both hands on his hips and settled his feet apart.

Max drew his sword. "Get out of the way."

Eeliss whimpered from the daybed.

"Guards!" Ewen shouted. "Take this man to the authorities. He's wanted for...crimes." Ewen grinned in triumph as two guards filed in, looking at their master with confusion. "Change your mind, Dane, or I will have them take you to the sheriff where you will no doubt be arrested on whatever charge I see fit."

Merdu, he might do it, too. He had enough money to bribe the sheriff into arresting Dane on a false charge of burglary.

Dane merely smiled. "The high minister wants me out of the country and my identity kept secret. A public arrest and trial is against his interests."

The color drained from Ewen's face, yet he didn't order his men to let us pass.

Dane removed the signed document from inside his doublet and addressed the guards. "This proves my pardon. Either you believe it and step aside, or I will have my men kill you. It's your choice."

The guards glanced at one another and stepped out of the way. Clearly the Rotherhydes weren't paying them enough to risk their lives.

We hurried away. Ewen's frenzied shouts roused the sleeping birds from their nests, creating a chorus for our departure. We headed for the docks, glancing over our shoulders at every turn, jumping at unexpected sounds. I breathed a sigh of relief when we reached the water's edge without being stopped by constables or Rotherhyde guards, but I didn't fully relax until the pier was behind us.

"Ewen was always greedier than his father," Yelena said as she stood on the deck and looked back at the moored boats. "He always wanted something in return for his loyalty, whereas his father gave it unconditionally."

"Is that why you promised Dane would marry Laylana?" Theodore asked.

"It was Ewen's price from the moment he took over the family empire." She settled both hands on the deck rail and watched the dark hulking forms of the city's warehouses slip past in the eerie quiet. "He's going to regret the way he spoke to me."

She left to join Martha below deck. The others remained, listening to the light splash of the oars in the water as Captain Obsidian navigated out of Noxford's congested river port. It was the sound of freedom.

"I hope Yelena doesn't mind swapping one cramped quarters for another," Meg said, breaking the silence. "It's not exactly accommodation fit for a princess."

"She's not a princess anymore," Quentin piped up.

"Quentin," Kitty scolded.

"He's right," Dane said. "It's time she grew used to being an ordinary person. No one will treat her like royalty in Mull."

"Don't say that to her," I told him. "It hurts to be reminded of what is lost."

"I won't, but I'm not sure she deserves our consideration."

"She's your mother!"

"She was about to force me to accept something I didn't want, as well as plunge Freedland into another war, for her own selfish reasons."

"To be fair," Balthazar pointed out, "it was what you wanted too, once."

We stood on the deck for some time, watching the city pass by and filling our lungs with the cool, fresh autumn air. It was cathartic after spending so much time underground. We talked quietly of our enthusiasm for seeing our friends again, of telling them about their pasts, even the dark parts.

"They'll be pleased just to have some of the missing pieces," Max said.

Erik agreed. "And to know they do not have to go to prison again even if they go home to Freedland."

"Or wherever they came from," Theodore added.

Quentin looked at him. "Will you go to Dreen to search for your family after you get your memory back?"

"I haven't yet decided."

"What about you, Bal? Will you return to Tilting?"

Balthazar took a moment to answer then shook his head. "The temple didn't feel like home. Mull and the palace do. I hope to regain my position there…if the new king will have me."

Quentin glanced at Dane, but everyone else kept their gazes studiously on the river bank.

"Me too," Max said. "Mull and the palace are my home, not Freedland."

Meg placed her hand over his on the rail. "You might think differently when your memory returns."

He turned his hand over, palm up, and clasped hers. "I won't."

She smiled, but it lacked confidence. It warmed my heart to see them getting along so well, but Meg was right. A small measure of doubt would remain for me too until Dane got his memory back.

Erik put his arm around Kitty's waist and she leaned into him. "What about you, Duchess? You must be careful when we arrive in Mull. You are supposed to be dead."

Kitty couldn't stay in Mull or Tilting. She couldn't go anywhere near her husband's estate, either. She must travel to somewhere remote where her peers would never go. Hiding in uncivilized villages was not in Kitty's nature, but she had done a serviceable job of it so far.

"There's a place called Brawle, in the north," Meg said. "I have cousins there. They could find work for you until the duke dies and it's safe for you to reveal yourself."

"Brawle," Kitty said, drawing the word out. "It sounds rough."

The fishing village was smaller than Mull, and it was indeed rough. Smugglers and pirates made it their home, and I doubted there was work for an educated, privileged woman. Not unless she was willing to spread her legs.

"Or you could travel to Dreen," I said, trying to sound cheerful. "I hear Logios is beautiful and interesting, and it will be large enough for you to get lost in. You could find work as a governess or nurse to the children of students and teachers."

"You can travel with me," Quentin said, puffing out his chest. "I'll be your protection on the road."

"You're going to try to get into the medical college?" I asked him.

His teeth flashed white in the darkness. "I am. Do you think I can get a recommendation?"

"I'll write to my father's friends and see what can be done."

"What do you think, Kitty?" he asked.

Kitty merely shrugged. "I don't know."

"You could go back to Merrin Fahl," Theodore said.

When Kitty sighed, Quentin added, "Or you can travel with Erik to the Margin."

"I am not going there," Erik said. "Not yet. Maybe when I know why I left, but I could ride into danger if I return."

"You think you're a wanted man in your homeland?"

"It is possible, since I was imprisoned for theft in Freedland."

"You wouldn't have been sent to a prison mine just for theft," Quentin said.

"Multiple thefts, maybe."

"Or for the simple fact you are from the Margin," Theodore said with grim certainty.

"Or I made love to a woman with a powerful husband and she was so satisfied that he became jealous." He nodded, liking the idea. "Many, many jealous husbands."

Theodore patted Erik's back. "It's a good idea for you to stay in Glancia, but try to stay away from the wives of powerful men."

My gaze slid to Kitty, but she was too occupied with yawning to notice. She bade us goodnight and departed for the women's sleeping quarters. Her sad smile worried me, but the decision of what to do next was hers alone. She knew the dangers she faced if she stayed in Glancia. I hoped she would take up Quentin's offer of accompanying him to Dreen. At least that way they would both have a friend in a strange city.

The others soon left too, leaving Dane and I alone. He wrapped his arms around me from behind, resting his chin on my head. I gazed up at the sky, my heart full, my nerves tingling. The last time we'd studied the stars, we had made love on the riverbank and Dane declared he would marry me.

So much had changed since then, yet nothing had at the same time. We both still loved one another, and we wanted to be together, now and always. If I asked him, Dane would still declare his intention to marry me. But I wouldn't ask. I didn't want him to break that promise, something he may yet be forced to do, not by anyone else but by his own conscience.

The more I thought about it, the more I realized Dane could save my country from destroying itself. And a king could not marry a commoner.

* * *

THE JOURNEY down Blood River to Lake Torment took a day and a half with the sails full most of the way. The remainder of our journey would take us up the Upway River along the Vytill-Dreen border and a short distance along the Vytill-Glancia border to Tilting, where we would continue by road to Mull.

Yelena kept to her bed, below deck, from the beginning. The river voyage was calm, so I didn't think it was seasickness, yet she complained of tiredness and stomach cramps. I nursed her with Martha's help. Together we made sure Yelena drank the tisane I gave her to settle her stomach, and when that ran out, we simply tried to make her feel comfortable.

Thankfully, she rallied when we docked in Upway, the capital of Dreen, which sprawled along the western bank of the Upway River. Like Tilting, it was a city of contrasts, with the flat-faced Dreenian folk making up the majority of the population, but a number of Vytillians and Glancians worked alongside them at the dock. It was a relief to see Yelena up and about again, and even well enough to go to market with us while the boat unloaded its cargo.

We looked around the city first, taking in its interesting architecture of pointed roofs and ochre colored buildings before heading to the market to stock up on necessities for the rest of the journey. We split up into smaller groups and came together at the market entrance to return to the boat. Yelena took me aside and pressed a book into my hand.

"What's this?" I asked, reading the title. "A medical book?"

"Dane told me you lost many of your belongings after your house was confiscated, including your father's precious books. I don't know if that's one you can use, but it was the only medical text the bookseller had."

"Oh. Yes, it is. Thank you, that's very kind of you, but you didn't have to give me anything."

"It's just a small gift in appreciation for your doctoring skills on the boat."

"It was nothing. I'm not sure the tisane helped you much anyway."

She fell into step beside me and nodded at Martha, walking up ahead with Meg and Kitty. "She's good to me, but she fusses. Your no-nonsense manner calmed her, and that calmed me."

I cradled the book to my chest. "I'll treasure it."

She smiled, and I could almost feel Dane's gaze on my back as he walked behind us. He was far enough away, and our voices low enough, that I doubted he could hear us.

"Dane told me all about how the two of you met," she went on. "He is full of praise for you. Anyone with eyes can see that he loves you."

"And I love him," I assured her. "I'm glad you two have talked some more, and not just about the succession."

"We've talked about that too, naturally. He knows what I think."

"He doesn't want to be king, even of a peaceful country."

Her gaze turned distant. "Sometimes we must set aside our heart's desire and do what is right for the greater good." Her gaze suddenly snapped to mine. "You know Dane's becoming king is the right thing. For your country, your people." She nodded at Meg. "Your friends. A war will destroy lives and livelihoods. It will tear Glancia apart. I saw it happen forty years ago in Averlea."

"And yet you wanted him to start another war there."

"I let my anger for the regime that destroyed my life rule me. I acknowledge that anger now, and I have set aside those ambitions. But this is different. Dane has it in his power to stop a war before it begins." She clasped my hand. "I know you think so too. I see it in your eyes when you look at him. They're sad because you think it means you'll lose him. But he doesn't have to give you up altogether. Kings are—"

"What are you two talking about?" Dane's attempt at casual conversation fell flat. He was worried about what his mother was saying to me and we all knew it.

She released me and smiled up at him. "We're discussing the future and how bright it can be."

"Mother," he said on a sigh.

Her smile widened. "That's the first time you've called me that without me prompting you."

She lengthened her strides and joined the others ahead, while Theodore joined us.

"I've been thinking about your dilemma," Theodore began, breaking through my thoughts.

"What dilemma?" I asked, all innocence.

"You know." He jerked his head at Dane. "Him being king of Glancia and what that means for you."

Dane let go of my hand. "I'll leave you two to your gossip."

"I don't gossip," Theodore said crisply. Once Dane was out of earshot, he said, "Diplomacy is not his strength."

I laughed. "True."

"Even so, I think he'll make a good king."

"So do I," I said quietly.

"He does have a difficult streak, though. Once he has made up his mind, he rarely changes it."

I eyed him sideways. "Are you stating a general fact or are you working up to something?"

He huffed out a breath. "It won't be easy, him being king, but if you have your heart set on him, then I think you'll make an excellent queen. I like the idea of you ruling over the nobles who once lorded it over you."

"Only the Deerhorns did that."

"Is that not enough?" He patted my arm. "It'll be satisfying seeing them squirm when you take away their wealth and influence. As king, it would be within Dane's power to strip them of their titles. Now that would be something I'd like to see."

He snickered, and I nudged him with my elbow. "You're getting ahead of yourself. Dane says he's not going to declare himself."

"He must. We all know it, including you. It's nothing to be saddened by, Josie. He *can* marry you, no matter what his mother says. The dukes and other nobles will express their displeasure about it, and present all sorts of reasons why a political alliance would be better, but at the end of the day, the king can do what he wants." He patted my arm again. "You'll make a wonderful queen, Josie, and he will make an excellent king. He's honorable, clever, commanding yet fair, not to mention handsome."

"I'm quite sure that's not a requirement for being king."

"He is also stubborn enough that if he decides on something, he won't let people like the Deerhorns talk him out of it. He's the perfect king, in my opinion. With a lovely Glancian wife by his side—you—he cannot fail to win the hearts of the people, especially when they realize he is the answer to avoiding war."

The end of Balthazar's walking stick tapped my hip. I didn't realize he'd been so close. Dane walked a little behind him, talking quietly with Quentin. As if he knew I were watching him, his gaze lifted and connected with mine.

"Theodore and I are of like mind," Balthazar said. "There's no reason you can't be queen."

"Not you too," I said on a sigh. "It would be very unpopular, and not just with the nobles. The people will want a princess, someone born to the role." And I knew precisely who would make an excellent queen. Princess Illiriyia was regal to her core.

"They'll grow to love you," Theodore said.

Balthazar nodded. "Having a Glancian woman as queen will please the people, and you will become used to the role and responsibility in time."

I snorted. "I doubt it."

"You are the most adaptable and clever woman I know," he said.

"Balthazar, you know five women in total." I indicated Kitty, Meg, Yelena and Martha, up ahead. "Besides, we all know Princess Illiriya should marry the next king of Glancia. A marriage alliance will stop her father from invading and trying to take the crown for himself. It'll shore up peace between the two nations."

Their silence was all the proof I needed that they agreed.

"Not you too," I heard Dane growl at Quentin.

I turned to see him striding towards me, a thunderous scowl darkening his brow. "Dane?"

He grabbed my hand. "Listen to me," he said to Quentin, Theodore and Balthazar. "I will not be taking the Glancian throne. Not only do I not want it, there is also no evidence that I am Prince Hugo's son. That is the end of it. Talk about me being king ends here and now. Understand?"

Theodore nodded, but Balthazar merely forged ahead at his slow pace, one hand on his walking stick, the other tucked behind his back.

Dane frowned after him. "Pigheaded old man."

"I heard that," Balthazar said over his shoulder.

"You were meant to."

Balthazar stopped up ahead with the others. I initially thought they were waiting for us but noticed they all stared at one particular ship, moored amongst the others at the dock. The figurehead of Merdu clutching sword and shield on the brigantine's bow glinted gold in the sunlight, but it was the flapping flags that drew my attention. There were two. One sported the Vytill flag of a white diamond on a blue background, while the other depicted the royal family's emblem of a hawk with outstretched wings clutching an eye in its beak. This ship was reserved for the Vytill king's personal use.

Quentin swore. "We have to get aboard and hide. If he finds out we're here, he'll come for what we promised him."

"We'll tell him we don't have the gem and wishes," Theodore said, but not even he seemed convinced that King Phillip would believe us and simply let us go.

We had betrayed him by promising what we didn't have and killing the guards he sent to bring us back as we fled his country. If he learned we were nearby, he would enact his revenge, no matter that we were on Dreen soil.

Quentin was right. We had to hide on our boat and hope the captain was ready to set sail sooner rather than later.

CHAPTER 6

Our boat was anchored far enough from the Vytill royal ship that we could not easily be seen from it, but we remained cautious and went immediately below deck. Dane asked the captain to join us and inquired after our departure.

"We leave tomorrow, as planned," Captain Obsidian said. "The Dreen customs officers are methodical. Too bloody methodical to make an earlier departure."

"The king of Vytill's ship is docked here," Dane went on. "We ran afoul of his laws when we passed through Merrin and don't want to attract his attention. Please inform your sailors not to discuss who you have on board."

"My men are used to keeping quiet."

I'd suspected he might be a smuggler, and his answer had confirmed it. I felt relieved to have a fellow fugitive on our side.

"Besides, it ain't the king on that ship," the captain went on, one hand on the ladder. "It's the princess."

We released a collective sigh of relief.

"Thank Hailia it's her," Kitty said as she leaned against a wall.

"Why?" Yelena asked. "Is she not out for revenge too?"

"She understood why I promised the gem and wishes when I didn't have them," I told her. "It was the only way to save

71

Dane's life, and she was kind enough to let us leave the city, as long as we didn't return."

Yelena nodded, thoughtful. "She is a fair ruler. If women could rule, she would make a better monarch than her fool of a brother, the heir."

I returned to the quarters I shared with the other women and lay on the narrow bed with my eyes closed. Princess Illiriya was fair and kind, strong and capable. She would be an excellent queen. And Dane would make an excellent king. Together, they would make Glancia a vibrant, progressive and just country. They were what Glancia needed as its wealth increased from more trade. The entire Fist would become more peaceful with an alliance forged between Glancia and Vytill through their marriage.

All these things swirled in my head as I lay there, feeling as though my heart was sinking through my chest into the mattress. It was impossible to shake the melancholy that had settled over me since learning of Dane's birthright. His choice in Freedland had been relatively easy. His choice in Glancia less so. Much less.

I must have drifted off to sleep because I awoke to Meg leaning over me, shaking me awake. I sat up in a hurry, almost butting her head with my own.

"What is it, Meg? What's wrong?"

"Princess Illiriya is on board. Dane wanted me to fetch you."

I gasped. "Has she brought guards to arrest us?"

Her eyes twinkled like stars. "It seems she merely came to wish us well on our journey."

"Oh. That's odd," I said as we headed down the corridor to the captain's cabin. "How did she know we were docked here? Did one of the sailors let it slip?"

Her lips flattened. "Yelena fetched her. Apparently she thinks the princess will be a worthy ally if Dane takes the Glancian throne. But I don't see how. She has no power over her father. That was proved when she couldn't free Dane in Merrin."

I knew why Yelena really wanted Princess Illiriya on board, and it wasn't for her influence with King Phillip. She hoped that the more Dane got to know her, the more accepting he'd be when she was presented to him as his future wife and queen.

I shook the notion off. I was being ridiculous and jealous. Dane would never set me aside, not even if it meant he could rule the Fist in its entirety.

I pushed open the door and forced a smile to my lips as I curtseyed for the princess.

"Josie," she said, putting out a hand as I rose. "I'm so happy and relieved to see you safe and well."

I kissed her hand and kept my smile in place. "You look well too, your highness."

"Travel agrees with me. I adore seeing new places. I rarely get away from home, but I insisted on this journey. I'm visiting the far flung corners of Vytill on behalf of my father. It's been so long since he has visited the outlying villages and there are many responsibilities keeping him in Merrin, so I offered to go in his stead. We're traveling the length of the river to visit the villages on the Vytill side, but Upway is the only city large enough for us to make repairs to our ship, so we'll anchor here for a few days. How fortunate that our paths have crossed."

I glanced towards Dane, standing at Balthazar's shoulder by the table in the center of the room. Theodore was with them and Yelena sat on one of the dining chairs. She was the only one smiling.

I turned to Meg to ask her to stay, but she was already bowing out of the room. "How fortunate indeed," I said to the princess.

"Please, be seated," she said as if it were her ship. "All of you. Come, Dane, you too. There is no need for ceremony. We are all friends, especially now."

"Why now?" I asked carefully.

But I knew. *I knew.* It was the reason Yelena was the only one of our party who looked pleased.

"My mother met with Princess Illiriya," Dane explained. "She invited her here for refreshments."

He indicated the wine cups on the table as Theodore poured another for me. The cups were plain tin, the room also plain with little adornment. It smelled of fish and faintly of sweat. The princess wouldn't be used to such conditions, but she made no sign that her surroundings disgusted her.

"On the way, Yelena told her highness that my father was Prince Hugo." Dane raised his glass in salute of his mother.

Her smile withered beneath his scowl. "The princess could be a valuable ally, when the time comes," she said.

Dane grunted. "It seems Bal agrees."

I arched my brows at Balthazar and he nodded, although the cool glare he slid in Dane's direction left me in no doubt he disliked Dane's sarcastic tone.

"I've been thinking about the situation," Balthazar said, "and that of Glancia, and I agree with Yelena. Dane should become king. It's the best course of action for the country and its people. It will avoid war."

"You don't have to sell the idea to me, Bal," I said gently.

He released a breath.

Dane sat forward. "Josie?"

"I know what you becoming king means. It's a good thing for Glancia." I looked down at my hands folded in my lap. "I might not personally like it, but Glancia needs you."

He sat back slowly, his brow furrowed in question.

"Let's not make hasty decisions," Yelena said. "This requires consideration and planning. Knowing we have the princess's support is one step up the ladder but there are more rungs to climb."

"Agreed," Balthazar said.

I wondered if Yelena had already promised the princess that Dane would marry her if he became king. She was good at betrothing him to make alliances.

"Have you had recent news of Glancia?" I asked the princess. "How close is a war between the dukes?"

"Very."

"Thanks to your father's interference," Dane said.

"If it's true that he sent false reports to the dukes to mislead them about the amount of support they had, I am truly sorry." She did not flinch from his hard glare but met it with fortitude. "The situation in Glancia is dire. War could be announced within days."

"Days!" Theodore cried.

"I'll write to the dukes again, advising restraint." Dane shook his head. "But I doubt they'll listen to me."

Yelena set her palms flat on the table. "They will if you inform them that you are the true son of Prince Hugo."

"We've been through this. They won't accept me without evidence."

"It'll give them a reason to pause. Send letters to both dukes, the advisors and ministers, and the high priest and declare yourself. It might be enough to delay a war while they investigate your claim. It's the only way, Dane. You know it is."

She was right. A delay would give us time to reach Glancia, where Balthazar and Dane could speak to the dukes face to face and try to convince them that the only person to benefit from a war now would be King Phillip. It was the wisest course of action.

But Dane didn't agree. "I will send letters, but not to announce myself as the heir. The letters will mention our suspicions of interference and request the dukes meet us upon our return to the palace. Your highness, when we last met, you said you didn't want your father taking the Glancian throne. Has your opinion changed?"

She hesitated.

"You are among friends here," Yelena assured her.

Princess Illiriya swallowed heavily but otherwise kept her composure. "I am against war, whether in my country or a neighboring one. I wish to spend my entire life on the Fist, not on distant shores I know nothing about, and that means keeping Glancia and the other Fist nations independent to ensure all potential marital prospects remain available to me. I will do what I can to help you, but I am in no position to act against my father's interests."

"I understand," Dane said.

"And yet I sense you have a request for me?"

"Vytill ships come and go from this port all the time, and some of them are very fast vessels. If Balthazar and I write those letters now and we give them to you, sealed, will you see that they're delivered as quickly as possible by one of the ships heading to Tilting?"

The princess hesitated before nodding. "If they are sealed, I can't possibly know what's in them. I'll wait while you write."

Dane and Balthazar rose and moved to the captain's desk in the corner of the room where the inkstand had been nailed to the desk surface to stop it sliding off in rough weather. They set to work immediately.

Yelena indicated to Theodore to refill the princess's wine cup. "You are very brave, highness. Your courage is appreciated and, dare I say it, admired." Her gaze drifted to Dane, leaning over Balthazar at the desk.

If the princess understood Yelena's meaning, she didn't show it. "I wish I could do more. Glancia has been a good neighbor to Vytill, particularly now as displaced residents from The Thumb flee to Mull."

Theodore set the cup down before her, thumping it a little too hard on the table. Wine almost sloshed over the rim. It was uncharacteristic behavior by the usually smooth valet. "It's surprising not more has been done to help those people resettle on the Vytill mainland," he said.

Yelena went quite still, but Princess Illiriya fixed a concerned frown on him. "I see it troubles you as much as it troubles me. Our people are free to move where they wish, of course, even if it means they leave Vytill. That is the freedom we all enjoy with peace on the peninsula. However, I think it's only right that we do more for those who can no longer find work in Port Haven. I've spoken with one of my father's advisors, who thinks as I do, and he is in the early stages of planning the resettlement of skilled labor to Skene, a small port in the south that will become Vytill's main trading center. I only wish we could have managed to do something earlier. I'll always regret that we did not."

"We women can only do so much," Yelena assured her. "Your people are fortunate to have such a kind yet determined princess. Perhaps one day, you will have more influence. A good king should listen to his queen, particularly a queen skilled in the art of diplomacy as you are."

Every word felt like the nick of a blade tip on my skin. I was not skilled in anything except doctoring. Diplomacy was an art I lacked, as was ruling. Yelena knew the power of words and had designed her speech to point out my deficiencies while conveying her wish to the princess that she would make the perfect queen for Dane.

Princess Illiriya could not have failed to understand Yelena's meaning, however she continued to talk about the plans for enlarging Skene's port as well as build a new one on the Vytill banks of Lake Torment. She must have been involved in the planning because she knew quite a lot of detail, including the value of trade lost by the Rift and an estimate of what could be regained in twelve months. Clearly she wasn't just kind and diplomatic. She knew about economics and trade, too.

She would be an asset to Glancia, and to a man who would need a steadying hand to guide him.

I looked to Dane, still dictating to Balthazar. Broad shoulders and a strong back would be required to be king, not just physically but metaphorically too. He would make a better king than either of the dukes. He was precisely what Glancia needed and wanted, and I could see him sitting on the throne, the crown on his head, reigning over people who adored him.

And when I saw Dane on the king's throne, I saw Illiriya beside him as his queen.

* * *

WE DECIDED NOT to stop in Tilting any longer than necessary for fear of being recognized. We didn't want word reaching the Deerhorns and Brant of our return to Glancia before we arrived in Mull. If they learned we were back, they'd stop at nothing to force us to give up the gem. We needed to catch Brant by surprise, not the other way around, and that meant we must continue on as quickly as possible. Even so, we could not leave Tilting until the afternoon of the day we docked. There were horses and carriages to hire, and provisions to purchase.

Talk at the market was all about one thing: war. I tried to listen to as many conversations as I could to gauge which duke had the most support, but few outwardly stated who they wanted to be king. Everyone was unanimous that they didn't want to be swallowed up by King Phillip of Vytill, and most wished the dukes could come to an arrangement to avoid war altogether.

"It won't end well for anyone," said the elderly fishwife.

"We'll lose our best young men," said her customer with a shake of her head.

"Who'll fund it?" asked another. "That's what I want to know."

The fishwife handed over the fish with one hand and took the coins with the other. "I heard a declaration is imminent, but they said that over a week ago too. What are they waiting for?"

"Who cares, as long as it's delayed? Maybe they're having another think and it won't happen after all."

A delay! Dane's letters must have worked, thank the goddess.

But clearly the plan for war had not been abandoned altogether. The blacksmiths were all busy. Forges blazed fiercely and all seemed to have several apprentices buzzing about. Activity had also increased at the saddler and bootmakers' workshops, but there was no excitement in the extra energy, only somber faces. These men were the lucky ones. Their work was necessary to the war effort, and they would not be pressed to join one army or another if they didn't want to. Many others wouldn't have that choice. Tenant farmers had to follow their feudal lord's allegiance and his orders. If Lord So-and-so chose to support one duke over another, his able-bodied tenants would have to take up arms and join the paid mercenaries. With very little training in weaponry and fighting, many wouldn't stand a chance.

Dane's mood had been grim too, ever since leaving Upway. We'd hardly spoken to one another since the meeting with Princess Illiriya. The blame for that lay entirely with me. I avoided being alone with him. The shared cabins on the boat made it easy, but once we settled into the Tilting inn for the night, I couldn't avoid bumping into him.

Especially when he hooked me around the waist as we passed on the landing and pulled me against his chest.

"What do I have to do to get your attention these days?" he asked.

"I don't know what you're talking about."

"Do I need to dance naked around a fire?"

I smiled, despite myself. "It would certainly get my attention when the fire set the boat alight."

He frowned in mock seriousness. "You're right. It would also earn the attention of Captain Obsidian and his men. Very well, no fires, just dancing naked."

"Apparently you're quite a good dancer."

The reminder of his tutored upbringing in all the courtly arts wiped the smile off his face. I winced, wishing I could take back the quip.

Erik and Kitty squeezed past us on their way upstairs so Dane took my hand and led me down and outside.

"Where are we going?" I asked.

"To the river to be alone."

"But the sun won't set for some time yet."

He smirked. "I meant for us to talk, but it's nice to know your mind wandered elsewhere."

I swatted him lightly and his expression sobered.

We kept our faces averted as we headed through the streets towards the river. We weren't close to the docks, but the river-bank was muddy and smelly, not at all like the grassy bank where we'd made love in Noxford.

We continued on and found an area of parkland where women were gathering in washing after laying it out on the grass to dry. Dane steered me towards a large tree and pressed me back against the trunk. He did not kiss me, however. He looked serious.

"I need to know if you still care for me," he said with earnest. "Or do you just desire me?"

My quip of earlier still bothered him. That, and perhaps what I'd said about Glancia needing a good king like him. It would seem we were both in need of reassurance. Sometimes I forgot how vulnerable he could be.

I stroked his cheek. "Can I not love you and desire you at the same time?"

His gaze searched mine, that small furrow still connecting his brows. Then it cleared and he suddenly and very thoroughly kissed me. It was a passionate kiss, full of contrasts. It was desperate yet loving, giving as well as taking, both needing and wanting.

In that moment, our troubles faded to nothing. I could believe that we would always be together, that Glancia would stay peaceful, and that he would always love me. His kiss made me feel alive, invincible, and very, very fortunate.

But as soon as the kiss ended, the doubts returned. I could see they did for him too.

"You want me to take it," he said darkly. There was no need to explain what he meant. His Glancian birthright had weighed on both our minds to the exclusion of almost everything else since learning about it.

"It's the right thing to do," I said. "Your claim will end the war before it begins. How can that not be a good thing?"

"That didn't answer my question. I want to know if *you* want me to take it, not what everyone else wants."

"Yes." I closed my eyes. "No. I don't know, Dane."

He stepped back and looked around then settled his hands on my hips. "Forget what's best for the country, just tell me if it's what *you* want."

"I can't answer that."

"Do you want to be queen?"

I blinked. "No. I'd make a terrible queen."

"You'd make an excellent queen, but that's not what I'm asking. I'm asking if you want to rule over Glancia."

"No."

He released a breath. "Good."

"Good?"

"I don't want to be king, but I'd consider it if you had your heart set on being queen."

A bubble of laughter escaped my lips. "You've got it back to front. Your decision shouldn't depend on me. And before you say anything," I said, cutting off his protest with a finger to his lips. "Just because you don't want to be king now doesn't mean you'll always think that way."

He removed my finger and clasped my hand between both of his. His earnest gaze drilled into me, the one that made me feel like I had no secrets from him. "So it is as I thought. You want me to marry Illiriya."

"See, you already call her by her first name."

"This is not a joke!"

One of the washerwomen glanced our way with a scowl then settled her basket on her ample hip and walked away.

"If I take the throne," Dane said, quieter but with no less earnestness, "I am not marrying her. Kitty and Balthazar both confirmed that a king can marry whomever he wants. There are no laws to say he has to wed a princess."

I tipped my head back against the tree trunk and sighed. My heart felt too sore to argue with him. I didn't want to argue with him. I wanted to cherish every moment we had together because the future was uncertain.

I put my arms around his neck and kissed him lightly on the lips. This kiss was much less fierce, but the passion was still there in abundance, only it was a quieter, deeper passion that went beyond surface desire. It was all the more wonderful because of it.

We walked back to the inn in silence. I suspected he was thinking about the future just as much as I was, and he confirmed it when he stopped me outside near the door.

"I'll consider declaring myself to the dukes," he said, "but only after I get my memory back and only if you are my queen."

My heart lodged in my throat. "The duke of Buxton will guide you."

"Not about marriage. I'll be ruled by my heart in that matter and my heart wants you." His fingers skimmed mine. "I am never giving you up, Josie, so if you want me to become king, you'd better be prepared to be queen."

He kissed me lightly on the lips, an exclamation point at the end of his declaration. In so many ways, he's said precisely what I hoped he would say. My heart was full with his love for me and the love I felt for him in return.

But my head protested all the way back to my room where I lay on the bed and stared up at the ceiling until dinnertime.

CHAPTER 7

*W*e traveled swiftly and reached the palace as dusk fell three days after leaving Tilting, just as we'd planned. Instead of going straight to the palace itself, the women stayed in the cottage on the estate. Hidden in the forest, the cottage had been my refuge from the clutches of the Deerhorns on more than one occasion. We needed that refuge again. With Kitty supposedly dead, she could not show her face, and Meg and I were vulnerable. If Brant caught either of us, he could use us to blackmail Dane and Max into handing over the gem. As much as I hated hiding, and as much as Meg and I both wanted to return to Mull, we stayed in the cottage while the men traveled on to the garrison.

Meg took the delay well, although her frustration boiled over when Yelena began pacing back and forth around the sitting room. It was such a small room that she was in danger of wearing out the floor and had refused all reasonable requests to sit down. Martha even offered to bring her food and a glass of wine, but Yelena merely waved her away, as if she hadn't heard a word.

"Do stop," Meg snapped. "The wait is excruciating enough."

Yelena bristled. "What can *you* possibly have to worry about? You're young, healthy, have a man who loves you and not a care in the world."

"My brother may have to go away to fight soon, I haven't seen my family in months, and the last time we were in Mull, there'd been rioting. Perhaps those worries pale when compared to yours, but they are worries nevertheless."

Yelena's nostrils flared. "I'm going for a walk in the garden until Dane returns."

"But it's dark," Kitty protested.

"Mind the rabbit traps," I called after her.

The front door slammed, making Kitty jump. "Honestly, you'd think she'd be more patient after waiting so long for Dane to grow up and fulfill his destiny."

"There's no such thing as destiny," Meg chided.

"You sound like Miranda. I believe in destiny, fate, or whatever you want to call it."

"So you believe I was born to be a village girl and you were born to be a duchess?"

"Well, yes, I suppose so."

"What about Josie? Is her destiny to be a village girl or queen?"

Kitty flounced onto a chair. "I don't know. I'm not a fortune teller. Whatever happens is meant to be, that's all I know."

I put a hand on Meg's arm and shook my head. There was no point arguing with Kitty. She'd never change her mind.

"If it helps," Kitty went on, "I understand your frustration. It's bad enough for me being so close to the palace and all its luxuries, but it must be awful for you being near your family and not able to hug them. Come and sit with me and we'll commiserate together."

Meg smiled, her temper cooled. It was impossible to stay mad at Kitty for long, even when the spoiled duchess came to the fore. She was a thousand times better company than Yelena.

I looked at the door. I should speak to her.

The door suddenly opened, however, and Yelena rushed in, followed by Dane. "There now," she told him. "We are all here. Tell us how your meeting with the dukes went."

"How did the other servants react?" I asked.

Kitty indicated that Dane should sit with a lazy wave of her hand. "Did they take the news of their imprisonment well?"

He smiled. "One question at a time. The dukes haven't arrived at the palace yet but are due tomorrow. We went straight to the garrison and the guards there were pleased to see us—and relieved. They reported that some of the servants who'd traveled with us to Tilting had returned, deciding to wait for news rather than go on alone. I called a meeting with the heads of each department, as well as the maid named Tabitha who'd been Laylana's maid in Noxford before their arrest. When they arrived, we told them everything."

"Everything?" Yelena and I asked in unison.

"Not about myself," he clarified. "Everything about the prison mine, the likely reasons for their arrests, and how the sorcerer whisked all of us here when the palace was ready upon Leon's wish. We told them how the Freedland authorities put out the story that we all escaped but were subsequently recaptured and executed. Then I told them they are all pardoned and can return home, if they wish. Theo told Tabitha about her parents and what we knew of her life in Noxford." He smiled. "She was overwhelmed but excited to learn of her loved ones."

"I'd wager they were all overwhelmed with the news," I said.

"There were a few moments of stunned silence then quite a bit of rejoicing. They couldn't wait to pass on the information to the staff in their departments."

"And Laylana?" I asked in a small voice.

His smiled faded. "I spoke to her separately, alone. I told her what we knew of her life and that she and I are betrothed."

My heart skipped a beat. "And?"

"And she read the notes she'd written on the back of the paper with a drawing of my face. Then she released me from the obligation before I asked her to."

My fingers ached, and I realized I'd been digging my nails into the cushioned chair arm. I released it, leaving half-moon dents in the fabric.

Kitty reached over and patted my hand. "There, see. All that worry for nothing."

Meg smiled at me. "That is a relief. Did Laylana say why she quickly made up her mind?"

"Apparently the notes on my portrait told her that I had feelings for Josie and she for me. Laylana also has her own love interest now. She shares a room with the footman who sketched our profiles. She was relieved to release me because now she knows that she is free to wed him, as long as he is free to wed her."

Kitty clapped her hands. "Wonderful news. I do love a wedding."

Yelena made a harsh sound in her throat. "I should see her."

Dane shook his head. "She doesn't remember you."

"I should still see her and tell her what her life was like before she lost her memory."

I glanced at Dane, but he was looking at his mother and didn't notice. "It doesn't matter what you tell her," he said. "She won't retain the information for longer than a few days, maybe some weeks at the most. She loses her memory over and over again."

Yelena frowned. "How odd. Is she the only one?"

He nodded. "We don't know why."

"Perhaps wait until after the wish is granted," Meg said. "Once they all get their memories back, you can see her, but I agree with Dane that it's pointless now."

Yelena's gaze narrowed but Meg merely smiled sweetly. I suspected she was worried that Yelena might talk Laylana into taking back her word and not releasing Dane from the betrothal. I didn't think Laylana would do so, but Meg always had my interests at heart.

"Was Brant there?" I asked.

Dane shook his head. "He had been back to the palace, but he has since vanished. I asked the heads of the departments to check if any of their staff knew where to find him."

Max entered and greeted us, smiling. It would seem the servants were in good spirits after learning about their pasts and that lifted the spirits of our men.

"It can't be soon enough," Meg said, welcoming him inside.

Martha brought out wine in cups then returned to the kitchen after curtseying to Yelena. Yelena only had eyes for Dane, however.

"So you plan to wait for your memory to return before you tell the dukes who your father is?" she said.

He hesitated. "Our meeting tomorrow will be about King Phillip's manipulation only." It neither confirmed nor denied whether he would tell them he was the rightful king.

"Don't wait or it might be too late," she urged. "They will leave immediately after tomorrow's meeting to visit the lords whose support they've not yet secured and you might not have a chance to speak to them again."

"Mother," he said levelly.

"It will solve all of Glancia's problems without bloodshed. Glancia is not full of revolutionaries like Freedland. It's crying out for a good, strong king, and everyone who knows you believes you will be precisely what the country needs. I don't understand why you're hesitating. You taking the throne is the best outcome for the country."

"But is it the best outcome for me?"

"Of course it is," she bit off.

He studied the wine in his cup as he swirled it. "It doesn't matter, anyway. The dukes won't believe me without evidence. No one will."

Yelena stared at him, her gaze fixed only on Dane. He must have felt the ferocity in it because he looked up.

"I have evidence," she said with a defiant lift of her chin. "I have irrefutable proof that you are Prince Hugo's son. All they need are some documents with his handwriting on them and the letters I carry with me can be compared to those. It will be obvious to anyone who looks that they were written in the same hand."

Dane went very still. "Do the letters talk about your marriage and my birth? Because if they don't—"

"They do. They are not love letters, if that's what you're thinking. We were never in love, which is why I never wanted them revealed to you. They will show that we entered into marriage for purely political reasons. When you were younger, I worried that might upset you. You were not an overly sensitive child, but you had an idealized picture of your father. You believed we'd been in love, that us being together was destiny and your birth was fated by the god and goddess, as was your inheritance of the two kingdoms of Averlea and Glancia."

"And you didn't want to shake that belief," Dane said, his voice guttural.

"It can still be considered fate," Kitty cut in. "If one believes in destiny then all this was supposed to happen, even the memory loss."

"Not now," Meg whispered.

"Where are these letters?" Dane asked.

"I'll produce them when the time comes," Yelena said.

"I'll take them."

"They stay with me."

"You don't trust me?" he asked.

"Not at this juncture. You are just as likely to burn them before you even read them. I will keep them safe until it's time to present them to the dukes."

He pushed to his feet. "Do I at least get to choose when that time is?"

"It must be tomorrow. If you wait—"

"It will not be tomorrow," he growled. "After I get my memory back—"

"Why wait?" she spat.

"Because I am not ready yet!"

She stood too, her eyes flashing, her lips pinched. "Very well. Get your memories back first. Then you will realize that you've been ready for this for years. You've had more than enough time to get used to the idea of being king." She picked up her skirts and stormed off up the stairs.

Dane opened the door and left too, out into the night. I hesitated but followed him. Now might not be a good time to tell him my plan for finding Brant, but there would never be a good time for that. He wasn't going to like it.

I found him stroking Lightning's nose. The horse nuzzled closer, enjoying being with his master again.

"He missed you," I said.

"And I missed him."

"Are you returning to the garrison tonight?"

He nodded. "The cottage isn't large enough for the five of

you, let alone me. I'll wait for Max and we'll return together. Do you have everything you need?"

I put my arms around his waist from behind and rested my cheek against his back. "Not quite."

I felt rather than heard his deep sigh. "Sorry for my outburst in there."

"Actually I thought you were rather restrained. She shouldn't have kept those letters from you."

"Their existence has come as a shock. I'd made up my mind not to mention my father's identity to the dukes because there was no evidence. But now..." He turned in my arms and cupped my face in his hands. "What do I do now, Josie?"

"I can't answer that for you."

"Advise me," he said hotly. He closed his eyes and rested his forehead against mine. "Sorry. I hate this. I hate what it's doing to us, and what it might continue to do if my mother has her way."

I kissed him lightly on the lips. "You did the right thing. You told her you're going to wait until you get your memory back."

"That doesn't change who I am or the fact the letters exist."

"No, but it will buy you time to think about what you want."

He gave me a little shake. "I know what I want. That has never been in question. I want you."

I leaned into him and closed my eyes. I did not tell him he could be king and have me too. It wasn't my decision to make. Nor was it the best decision for Glancia.

"Dane," I said pulling away. "I've thought of a way to find Brant."

"Go on," he said in that dark tone that could mean he was still mad at his mother or that he'd realized what I planned.

"I don't think appealing to his better nature will work."

"Agreed. He doesn't have a better nature."

"So we must bargain with him. We have to offer him something in exchange for a wish to return the memories. It has to be something better than what the Deerhorns have offered, if they have in fact made him an offer."

"They will have, I'm sure of it. Whether that's money or a position in exchange for a wish, I don't know."

"Perhaps both. He wouldn't give up a single wish for just a single thing, he'll be demanding two or more. So that's what we must do. We promise him money, of course. He could sell jewels or ornaments from the king's private collection."

"And the second thing?" he asked.

"Make him captain of the palace guards with a good salary."

He arched his brows. "You want him to have my job?"

"It's something he wants. If he thinks he can lord it over you by taking it from you, then it's a very big carrot to dangle in front of him."

He nodded, thoughtful. "I doubt the men will accept him."

"That's for him to worry about."

"What if he does what Leon did and ask to be a rich king with the third wish? It's just the sort of thing he'd do, despite seeing what a disaster Leon made of it."

"Then we point out how it ended in Leon's death. Brant is selfish but not a fool. He knows Leon's fate could be his own if he was greedy and asked for too much."

Dane nodded slowly. "Very well, we've decided how to bargain with him for one of the wishes. How do you propose we find him?"

"We'll draw him out of his hiding place. We'll make him come to us."

His hands tightened at my waist and even in the darkness, I could feel the ferocity of his glare. "No."

"It's the only way, Dane."

"You are not going to be the bait. Is that understood? We'll look for him before we resort to that tactic."

"Listen to me." When he turned his head away, I clasped it and made him look at me. "You think Meg and I are the only vulnerable ones to kidnap? What about Balthazar and Theodore? What if Brant gets his hands on Quentin? He hates Quentin, and it wouldn't surprise me if he hurt him just to get back at you. The palace servants know Bal, Theo and Quentin are back. If a servant knows where Brant is, it won't be long before he tries to kidnap one of them and blackmails you into giving up the gem. You can't watch them and us, and we can't all hide away here. If

Brant succeeds in capturing one of us, we have no bargaining power. We lose all advantage."

"I don't want you to be the bait," he said, his voice strained.

"I am the most obvious choice. He'll go after me, just because he knows what I mean to you. This is the only way, Dane. We have to strike first."

He tipped his head back and blinked up at the stars, but I doubted he saw them. I took his silence as ascent that he agreed to my plan.

I stroked his cheek again and he turned to me. I pointed to the sky. "Don't look at me."

"But I like looking at you."

"Look up there."

He tipped his head back and searched the sky. "Why?"

"Because you're not noticing the stars."

He smiled. "You remembered our conversation from the riverbank in Noxford."

"I remember everything about that night. But yes, I remember what you said about not truly seeing the stars until then. I don't want you to return to the days when the stars were invisible to you. I want you to see them, always."

"It's this place," he muttered. "It distracts me from the stars. And from you."

"The stars are always here, Dane, ready for when you have the time to look. And so am I."

* * *

THE SERVANTS KNEW EVERY NOOK, cranny and room in the palace, including the hidden ones that the nobles never saw. By hiding in a small space behind a wall panel in the council chamber, I was able to listen in to the meeting with the dukes.

They had arrived separately, at around midday, accompanied by their armed guards and closest supporters. Those supporters and the dukes now crammed into the council chamber along with Dane, Balthazar, Theodore and the high priest of Glancia, who had arrived that morning. I watched proceedings through the spy hole in the wall along with Max. It was just us. No one else could fit.

Lord Deerhorn and his daughter, Lady Violette Morgrave, flanked the duke of Gladstow, with Lord Xavier and Lady Deerhorn walking in behind. Dane and Balthazar didn't bow, but Theodore gave a small one.

They ignored him.

"What is the meaning of your letters?" the duke of Gladstow bellowed.

Theodore pulled out a chair and Balthazar bade the duke to sit. "Let's make this as civilized as possible."

Theodore set goblets of wine in front of each nobleman, but Lady Deerhorn pushed hers away. Her family followed suit.

"It's not poisoned," Dane said.

Lady Deerhorn glared at him. "How has King Phillip been manipulating the situation?"

Dane told them about the letters supposedly sent from Glancian lords pledging their allegiance that had since been proved false. "The high priest can confirm it," Dane said.

The high priest nodded. "It's true. I didn't want to interfere in this matter—"

"Then don't," Lady Deerhorn snapped.

The high priest pressed his lips together.

He had greeted us warmly upon his arrival, and he paid particular care to Balthazar, noting his frail appearance, his bent back and squint, even when he wore his spectacles. The high priest looked worried, and that worried me. Our travels had taken a toll on Balthazar. We should have taken better care of him and ridden at a slower pace. He'd not once complained and so we hadn't seen what his friend now saw—an aging man who didn't have long left in this world.

"It's quite an accusation you make," the duke of Buxton said. "Particularly without proof."

"The proof should be easy enough to gather," Dane said. "There are two ways you can do it. Sit down with your counterpart," he nodded at the duke of Gladstow, "and compare a list of nobles that have pledged their support. If the same name appears on both lists, something is amiss."

Lord Deerhorn snorted. "You are naïve if you think they should reveal that information to their enemy."

Lord Xavier snorted too.

"Or," Dane went on, unruffled, "you can visit the nobles who have pledged their support only by letter and find out from them in person if they sent it or not."

"That will take time," Lord Deerhorn said even as the duke of Gladstow nodded his head.

Balthazar lifted his goblet in salute. "You are correct, my lord."

Lord Deerhorn frowned, as if he wasn't sure if Balthazar was being condescending or not.

"He's right," the duke of Buxton said, turning to Gladstow. "We must delay. It's in both our interests."

"Why?" Lord Deerhorn sneered. "Because you know you don't have the numbers?"

"Neither do you. Come, Gladstow, agree to a delay."

The duke of Gladstow contemplated his wine.

"If you start a war too soon," Balthazar pressed, "both armies will be decimated. Your soldiers aren't ready. Is that what you want? To kill your young men by the hundreds?"

"Of course not," the duke of Gladstow snapped.

"Don't listen to them," Lord Deerhorn said. "They're manipulating us because they know we'll win and they're on Buxton's side."

"For Merdu's sake," the high priest muttered. "All you will be doing is playing into Vytill's hands. The only person to win from this situation is King Phillip. Do you want to be ruled by Vytill?"

"Aren't you supposed to be neutral?" Lady Deerhorn hissed at him.

The high priest sat back and blinked at her, stunned by her open hostility. He didn't know her like we did. This display was nothing.

"He's right." The duke of Buxton reached across the table, hand outstretched towards his counterpart. "We call a temporary truce while both sides confirm numbers."

The duke of Gladstow sat forward, preparing to shake his

enemy's hand, when Lady Deerhorn suddenly rose. The legs of her chair scraped against the tiled floor.

"We only have their word about the interference," she said. "Come. It was a mistake to agree to this meeting."

The duke of Buxton pulled back his hand, shaking his head at Gladstow, as if he couldn't believe he could let Lady Deerhorn make the decisions for him. Indeed, Gladstow used to be more forthright than this. He wouldn't have allowed anyone to speak for him, let alone a woman.

"Can the duke of Gladstow not speak for himself?" Balthazar asked.

"Of course I can," Gladstow growled.

"I have his best interests at heart." Lady Deerhorn indicated her daughter, Lady Morgrave, sitting meekly at the back of the room. She smiled dutifully at her mother. "You wouldn't know since you've been away, but my daughter is now the duchess of Gladstow."

I clamped my hand over my mouth to make sure I emitted no sound. We had expected them to wed, but not so soon after Kitty's supposed death.

"How quickly you two fell in love," Balthazar said flatly.

The duke bristled. "Hold your tongue. Priest or no, I will gladly flay you for your insolent tone."

"No," the high priest said, his voice grating. "You will not."

Balthazar smiled benignly. When he bestowed such a smile on me, I always found it a little irritating because it usually preceded a sarcastic comment. "I doubt their marriage cut out the duke's tongue. I'm sure he would prefer to speak for himself about such an important matter as whether to start a war or not."

The duke of Gladstow stood and his supporters followed suit. "Lady Deerhorn is one of my most trusted advisors. I value her opinion."

The duke of Buxton made a scoffing sound. "So you'll listen to her mad advice over your own conscience? You're willing to see the lives and livelihoods of your best tenants ruined and your own coffers emptied just to appease your mother-in-law's thirst for blood?"

"I am not appeasing anyone!" The duke of Gladstow tugged on his doublet hem as he fought to regain his composure. "While I value the opinion of my advisors, my decisions are my own. I'll agree to the delay."

Lady Deerhorn looked as though she wanted to throttle him. Her husband watched her carefully, as if he expected her to fly at the duke of Gladstow at any moment. But she kept her mouth shut. The flare of her nostrils indicated the effort it took to remain calm, however.

"One more thing before you go," Balthazar said as the duke of Gladstow headed for the door. "I would like to have my position back as master of the palace."

The high priest turned in his chair to look properly at him. "But your place is at the temple of Merdu's Guards in Tilting."

"Your Graces? I need the agreement of you both."

"Of course you can," the duke of Buxton said. "I don't know how much there is for you to do here, but you've proven yourself to be competent at running this place and your sage advice is welcome too. You'll be a valuable asset, no matter who wins."

The high priest shook his head sadly.

Balthazar turned to the duke of Gladstow.

"No," Lady Deerhorn snapped. "We don't agree to it. We don't trust you."

Balthazar's unnerving gaze remained on the duke.

He hesitated then nodded. "The palace servants need to be brought into line. Let some of them go. There are too many when there's no king in residence."

Everyone in that room knew why he'd gone against Lady Deerhorn. He'd wanted to prove that he was not ruled by her, that she had no power over him. Even in something as small as this. I wanted to laugh.

"And Dane should be reinstated as captain of the guards," Balthazar went on. "The men are loyal to him and he has always been loyal to the crown."

"There is no one wearing the crown at the moment," the duke of Gladstow pointed out. "I vote no."

Lady Deerhorn smiled that tight, cruel smile of hers that always sent a shiver down my spine.

The duke of Buxton sighed. "Sorry, Captain. I was going to say yes, but there's no point if he doesn't."

Dane shrugged. "I was going to refuse it anyway. I have other plans. Sorry, Bal."

The duke of Buxton rose and shook Dane's hand. "Thank you for everything you've done. The realm is a little more secure tonight because of your efforts in unearthing King Phillip's interference. Yours too, Your Eminence," he said to the high priest.

The duke of Gladstow left without a word. His wife and brother-in-law went with him, and his father-in-law followed close behind. Lady Deerhorn, however, lingered. Her gaze scanned the room. She knew I was hiding behind a wall. It was as if she'd sniffed me out.

"Tell the midwife that she'll find the village much changed since she left," she said idly. "It's amazing what doors are re-opened when you're related to a duke. Everything she tried to destroy is once more ours, and if she tries to take it away again, the consequences will be drastic for her and those who assist her. The villagers know that now. They won't dare take her side. Every single one of them knows who employs them. The magistrate, the jailor...all Deerhorn men. Even the new sheriff."

Dane's head snapped up. "What did you do to Neerim?"

"Made an example of him."

Hailia, no. The sheriff had been a good man. He hated injustice and had always done his best to defend the weak against the might of the Deerhorns. I prayed for him but feared the worst.

Dane closed his eyes and lowered his head.

Lady Deerhorn's lips stretched into a smile. "That precious item you have in your possession...it's useless without Brant. What a shame you don't know where he is."

"I suppose you do," Balthazar said stiffly.

She walked off in the middle of his sentence. "Not at all," she tossed over her shoulder.

I didn't believe her for a moment.

"What was that about?" the high priest asked after she'd gone. "What item? Who is Brant?"

"Just a man," Balthazar said, slumping in the chair. He

looked and sounded exhausted from the confrontation. "Theo, more wine, please."

Dane opened the hidden door and assisted me out of the secret room, much to the high priest's surprise. "Pour some for Josie, too. She looks like she needs it."

"Poor Sheriff Neerim," I murmured. "He fought for me. He got the people to support me when he could not openly do it. Do you think the Deerhorns killed him?"

Dane's answer was to fold me into his arms and tuck my head under his chin. "We'll set it right, Josie. We won't let the Deerhorns win."

I wished I could be as confident. But all I felt was overwhelming sorrow and a sense of hopelessness. If the duke of Gladstow had enough support, the entire country could soon be under his rule. And Lady Deerhorn would take full advantage of her new position as the queen's mother.

CHAPTER 8

"The turd! The prick! The vile piece of—"

"Kitty!" Meg cried. "Mind your language. You are still a duchess."

Kitty spread her fingers and attempted to throttle the air in the vicinity of the duke of Gladstow's neck as if he'd been standing before her. "I hate him."

"He is not worth another moment's thought," I said.

"Clearly he never loved me. He hardly even mourned me."

"And you never loved him, so what does it matter? Besides, you expected him to marry Violette quickly. The Deerhorns would have been pushing for the union."

Kitty flopped onto one of the chairs at the cottage's kitchen table, her bottom lip thrust forward in a pout. Then she suddenly grabbed Dane's hand as he passed, taking him by surprise. "You must listen to your mother and claim what's rightfully yours."

He extricated his hand and folded his arms over his chest. "So you can reveal that you're alive and scuttle their plans?"

"I was thinking more of stripping him of his title, confiscating his estate, and watching them have to work to survive. He could be a tenant farmer for the new landlord and she could be a whore. She's as good as one anyway."

Meg and I burst out laughing, and Dane looked as though he was struggling to contain his smile.

"If it were in my power, I would do it myself," Kitty declared.

Meg pulled a face behind Kitty's back. "Will you be all right here alone if we go to the village?"

"Yes, go, see your family. I'll be fine here." Her morose tone implied otherwise. Martha and Yelena had already gone to the village. Of all of us, they were deemed safe to walk out alone. Brant knew nothing about their connection to us.

"I'll send Erik to keep you company," Dane said.

"Only if he wants to come."

"He will."

Meg and I returned to the palace with Dane, where we stopped by the servants' commons. I exchanged greetings with the maids I knew, and we traveled to Mull in one of the carriages that wasn't currently in use. With only the two dukes and their small retinues at the palace, the royal carriages were sitting idle. We didn't travel in one of the luxurious conveyances reserved for the king, of course, but used one of the lesser, unmarked ones.

Dane followed on horseback.

We went straight to Meg's house. I tried to avoid looking at the Ashmoles' cottage, but I couldn't resist taking a peek. Then I forced myself to look away. Even that small glance tore a small strip off my heart. I had so many fond memories of the cottage that had once belonged to me, but those memories were in danger of being tarnished by the venomous new doctor and his wife. If I wanted to retain my wonderful memories, I could not think about them living there.

Meg's sisters squealed with delight when she walked in and smothered her with hugs and kisses. Mistress Diver burst into tears.

We stayed for some time, drinking tea and talking about the places we'd seen. We had to repeat ourselves when Meg's father and brother returned home from work, and Dane joined us too after keeping watch outside.

"We thought you'd come home after the duchess's death," Lyle said with a pointed glare for his sister.

"Ignore him," their mother said to Meg. "He's jealous that you've had more interesting adventures than him."

"I am not!"

Meg gave him a smug smile. "You should get out of Mull once in a while, Lyle, and broaden your horizons."

"I will when the war starts."

That smothered our good mood like a wet blanket. Mr. and Mistress Diver exchanged worried glances and even Lyle looked as though he regretted mentioning it.

"Maybe there won't be a war," Meg said, trying to sound cheerful. "I hear there has been a delay."

"But for how long?" Mr. Diver said with a shrug. "Nobody knows. The dukes tell us nothing. We're always the last to find out anything and the first they call on to fight."

Lyle folded his arms high up his chest, tucking his hands beneath his armpits. "Bloody nobles," he muttered. "I don't want to die for either duke."

"Then don't fight," Meg said.

"I might have to pick a side if it looks like Gladstow's going to win. None of us in Mull want him as king. He's well on the way to ruining this village now he's in bed with the Deerhorns."

His parents nodded solemnly before Mistress Diver shooed the younger girls away. Once they'd gone, Mr. Diver said, "Ever since Gladstow married Lady Violette, things started to change for the worse here."

"We heard about Sheriff Neerim," Dane said.

Mistress Diver pressed a hand to her chest. "They say it was an accidental drowning, but no one believes that."

"The new sheriff is the Deerhorns' man." Mr. Diver wagged a finger at me. "You'd better be careful, Josie. Don't go fixing people's wounds. If anyone asks you to, you send them to Dr. Ashmole."

Mistress Diver wrinkled her nose. "Loathsome man. His wife's no better."

Lyle chuckled. "I hear the women of the village are turning their husbands away from their beds because they're too worried about getting pregnant and having her deliver their babies."

His mother smacked his arm. "It's not a joke. Anyway, now that Josie's back, she can be the midwife again."

I shook my head. "Mistress Ashmole won't be willing to give up the role, not to me, and I don't want to stir up trouble with them."

"Then what will you do?"

I kept my gaze strictly averted from Dane. "I'm considering my options."

Lyle and his parents all looked to Dane.

"I'll take care of Josie," he said. "We're getting married."

Mistress Diver clamped her hands to her cheeks. "Oh, how marvelous. Why didn't you say sooner?"

"Yes, Josie," Meg bit off. "Why didn't you?"

"We haven't thought much about it yet," I said. "We don't even know where we're going to live."

"At the palace," Mistress Diver said, as if it were an easy decision to make.

I gave her a tight smile. Dane simply said, "We'll see."

Mistress Diver reached across the table and patted my hand. "I am so relieved that you'll have him to take care of you. Your parents would have been pleased with your choice."

"If I were you," Lyle said, "I'd start a new life together away from Mull."

"Why?" Meg snapped. "Mull is her home. All of her friends are here."

"You'll find Mull has changed even more since you left. It's not just the change in sheriffs, but everything is back under the Deerhorns' control and just when we thought we were rid of them, too."

His father agreed. "It's worse than ever 'round here. It's like they're punishing the villagers for the riots, and for destroying their castle to save you, Josie."

"How are they punishing everyone?" I asked weakly.

"Supplies are slow to be processed in the customs' house, unless the cargo came on Deerhorn ships or is destined for the Deerhorn estate. No new buildings are being built to house the poor, food is in short supply and costs are still high."

"But when we left, there was plenty of grain," Meg said. "We released it from the Deerhorns' own stores."

"All gone and supplies are once again low, thanks to the slow processing of cargo."

"And the dukes are just allowing this to go on?"

"Buxton is too busy elsewhere in the country," Mr. Diver said, "and Gladstow wants his wife's family to prosper because he'll reap the rewards too. He needs money for mercenaries and weapons."

"He needs the support of the people," Meg shot back. "Why aren't the villagers rioting again?"

Lyle snorted. "Maybe they're waiting for you to lead them, Sis."

His mother smacked his arm again. "Don't encourage her."

Dane and I left Meg with her family and walked to the green at the village's heart where I hoped to see old friends. Dane kept his distance, his gaze darting around, watching for Brant or Deerhorns, anyone who might want to kidnap me and use me to bargain for the gem.

While I didn't recognize many of the people conducting business or meeting up in the village green and on the forecourts and steps of the public buildings, I did see quite a number of familiar faces.

Except those faces were not as friendly as they used to be. Few would look me in the eye and most hurried away after a brief greeting.

When I spotted Sara Cotter with the baby I'd delivered some months ago, I hailed her. She scanned the vicinity before smiling at me. It was a little forced, but there was genuine warmth there too.

"He's adorable," I said, putting my arms out to hold her baby.

She hesitated before handing him over. "He's always hungry," she said. "But healthy, thank Hailia." She looked around again then asked for him back. "How long are you in Mull?"

"Permanently. This is my home, after all." The edge to my

tone made her bite her lip. "I'm sorry, Sara, but why is everyone being so rude to me? I feel as though I'm not welcome here."

"It's not that." She shifted the baby from her right hip to her left. "We're all very grateful for the hard work you did as a midwife over the years, and when you assisted Dr. Cully too."

"But?"

She sighed. "But you seem to get yourself into a lot of trouble with the Deerhorns, and when that happens, the village suffers."

"Oh."

"The fire in The Row was most likely set by the governor, under instruction from the Deerhorns, because you accused them of trying to buy the land cheaply and throw out the slum dwellers. You encouraged us to oppose the sale and look what happened. They just burnt the place to the ground and the governor sold the land to them anyway."

"That's hardly my fault."

"And that led to the riots, which could have ended badly if the warrior priests from Merdu's Guards hadn't come. Then when the Deerhorns had you arrested and took you to their castle, the entire village stormed it and destroyed it in order to free you."

"I didn't ask them to destroy the castle."

"Now the Deerhorns are back and they've increased rents, withheld grain, and are employing outsiders rather than local villagers because we supported you."

My heart sank a little further with every word. "I'm sorry," I whispered pathetically.

She jiggled the baby on her hip as he began to grizzle. "Not only do the Deerhorns own most of the land and buildings in this village, they also own us. They own the shops and lease them out to shopkeepers. They own warehouses they lease to businesses. Their ships, warehouses and docks employ many of our men. Our livelihoods depend on them."

As much as it hurt to hear, she was right. The Deerhorns' influence in Mull was vast, and as Mull grew in size and prosperity, the Deerhorns' wealth and influence grew too. If they wanted to punish the villagers, they could. With the governor and sheriff in their pocket, no one could stop them.

"It was bad before," Sara went on, "but it became worse after Lady Violette married the duke of Gladstow. Now that you're back, some of us are afraid trouble will follow." She winced, as if it pained her to say these things. "I'm sorry, Josie. I hate to be the one to bring bad news, but we've known each other a long time and, well, someone's got to say it. We're all truly grateful for everything you and your parents have done over the years, but we have young ones to protect."

"I know," I muttered.

She winced. "If I were you, I'd leave the village and not come back. And don't go near the Ashmoles. She'll accuse you of doctoring if she catches even a whiff of you helping someone." She gave me a flat-lipped smile of sympathy then hurried off, head ducked as if she didn't want anyone to recognize her.

I joined Dane, now frowning at me. "Let's go back to the palace."

"Are you all right?" he asked.

"The Deerhorns have infected this place."

I looked around the green, edged by shops that were closing up for the day. The market had long since ended, the shutters on the permanent carts now locked. Men hurried home from the docks, their heads lowered, their steps determined. The sinking sun had taken the warmth with it, but even so, the air was merely crisp, not wintry. Yet hats were pulled down and hoods flipped up to avoid making eye contact with others.

"They seem miserable," Dane muttered.

"The Deerhorns are making them afraid. Sara told me I should leave Mull. The villagers won't show me support because they fear the Deerhorns will punish them. I have no friends here anymore."

He took my hand in his. "You *do* have friends here. And you have me."

I tried to give him a reassuring smile. "Thank you, Dane."

"You don't have to thank me for loving you."

I looked around at the streets radiating off the green, the shadowy recesses between buildings, and the people lurking in doorways. There seemed to be quite a number just sitting about, idle. Mostly men, but some women and children too. They were the homeless, I realized, the dispossessed from The Row's fire. They still had nowhere to go, even after all this time. No temporary accommodation had been built for them, not even tents erected on vacant land. With winter coming, the need to house them would become desperate, but the governor wouldn't build them anything unless the Deerhorns allowed it, and they wouldn't allow it unless the tenants paid a high price. These people couldn't afford their next meal, let alone a new roof over their heads.

I wasn't much better off, I realized with shock. With no work, I had no way of paying for food. Nor did Dane. At least we had the cottage on the palace estate, but it might only be a matter of time before it was discovered and we were evicted. We had no right to be there.

Dane tugged on my hand. "Let's ride back to the cottage. We could go via the pond in the forest if you like."

"It's too cool for a dip."

"Who says we're going in the water?"

I nudged him and smiled, despite my misery.

We headed back to the Divers' house. As I was about to knock, someone hailed me from the other side of the street. I turned to see Mistress Ashmole striding over, a look of determination on her pinched face.

I sighed. She was the last person I wanted to see. "I am not here to take back your business," I said heavily. "You are the midwife now and that is the end of it."

She bristled and glared at me through the slits of her eyes made narrower by the severe pulling back of her hair. "If I catch you giving so much as advice to an expectant mother, I will see that the sheriff hears of it." Her lips stretched in what I suspected was her attempt at a grin. "It's a new man, one who understands the way of the world, not that fool, Neerim. Thank the goddess for taking him from us and giving us this—"

I lifted my hand to strike her, but she stumbled back with a gasp, and Dane quickly stepped between us.

"Josie can be a midwife if she wants," he said. "There's no law against there being two in the village."

Mistress Ashmole bared her teeth as she pointed a boney

finger at me. "You are fortunate your guard dog is here to stop you doing something stupid, Miss Cully."

Dane folded his arms. I turned away and knocked on the Divers' door so did not see her walk off, although I heard her stomping all the way back across the street.

We dined with the Divers and Dane left to pay a visit to Jon and Marnie. I'd first met the Vytill-born couple and their children in The Row after they moved to Mull. Marnie had given birth to her third child in the slum, but they'd managed to get out before the fire, after Jon was given a job as constable by Sheriff Neerim. Dane wanted his opinion of the new sheriff. I hoped Dane's presence didn't bring trouble to their door.

Lyle and Mr. Diver also left after dinner to meet with friends at The Anchor. I urged Mistress Diver to spend some time with her younger daughters while Meg and I cleaned up. We were in the middle of a hushed debate about whether she should stay with her family that night or return to the safety of the forest cottage with us when her mother poked her head into the kitchen.

"Visitor for you, Josie, by the name of Brant. He says he's one of the captain's men."

Brant! Our plan had worked. He'd heard of my return and now he wanted to talk. Indeed, our plan had worked better than we'd hoped. We'd thought he would try to kidnap me and use me as a bargaining tool, but he'd announced himself. This way we could have a civilized conversation in the open.

"Wait for Dane to return," Meg warned.

"No harm will come from talking to him," I said. "Besides, this is what we want—a chance to reason with him."

Meg followed me to the front door but remained hidden to the side as I opened it.

The man standing there was not Brant. I didn't recognize him.

I looked left then right. Someone lurked in the dark not far away. "Who are you?" I demanded.

The stranger on the doorstep clamped his hand over my mouth and hooked me around the waist, trapping my arms to my sides. I struggled against him and kicked out, but my feet missed him altogether. I tried to shout a warning to Meg not to attempt a rescue. With the second figure nearby, we couldn't fight both by ourselves. She must have understood my muffled pleas because she remained hidden.

The man dragged me away from the house. I managed to get in one good kick to his shin, but it didn't slow him down. He was broad, strong, and his big hand restricted my breathing. I tried to gasp in air but gagged on the smell of onions and sweat.

The figure in the darkness led the way to the alley where the brute half-carried, half-pushed me. I couldn't make out who the other man was, but his silhouette wasn't big enough for it to be Brant.

It must be Lord Xavier.

Fear gripped my insides. Last time he'd got his hands on me, I'd been taken to the dungeon in his family's castle where he'd threatened to rape and torture me. I'd escaped thanks to the help from the villagers and palace guards. But Sara had made it clear there would be no rescue attempt from the villagers again, and the guards were too far away to rally in time. Lord Xavier wouldn't wait to perform his cruelty on me. He'd been thwarted before and learned from that mistake.

The figure ahead stopped and turned, hands on hips. Lord Xavier's eyes were two black pits gleaming with the promise of cruelty. "Welcome home, my pet. I've been waiting for you."

The brute shoved me back against the wall and let me go. My head smacked into the bricks and stars burst in my vision. But my hands were free. There was no time to pull the knife from my skirt pocket, however. There wasn't even time to blink away the stars.

Instinct took over and I lashed out at Lord Xavier, wanting to wipe that smile off his lips. My fingernails raked across his jaw, scraping skin.

"You bitch!" He smacked me across the mouth, slamming my head against the wall again.

Pain spiked. Everything went black. I felt myself falling, my knees too weak to hold me up. I struggled to remain alert. I needed to be strong if I wanted to talk my way to freedom.

But I couldn't even think what to say, let alone sound

convincing. Nor was I capable of fighting off both men, not even if I caught them by surprise with my knife.

The footsteps were so light that I didn't hear the approach of my rescuer. Nor did Lord Xavier and his thug. It wasn't until the fingers digging into my shoulders released me that I knew something had happened.

Someone cried out in pain then swore. "This ain't worth it." The growled voice belonged to the brute.

My vision cleared in time to see him run off, clutching his arm. A woman with her back to me, sword in hand, watched him go. Meg, also clutching a sword, held Lord Xavier at bay with the point aimed at his throat.

He swallowed hard. "You'll pay for this."

Mistress Diver turned to him. "You touch my family and I will kill you myself."

His lip curled in a sneer. "I know where you live."

"And I have the gem," I said. "If you want it, you won't harm anyone. That is my price. Do you agree to it?"

"You don't have it," he snarled. "Your lover does."

"I don't have it with me now, but I can get it. Dane will agree to give it to you, if you promise to leave us all alone."

A beat passed. Two. He was considering my proposal, at least. "Lord Barborough wrote to us," he said. "He told us that you spoke to him in Noxford. He told us everything you learned from the Zemayan."

"You lie. He would inform the king of Vytill, not you."

"He claimed he can't return there. He bargained for a position on the Glancian council, after Gladstow wins the war. Lord Barborough will be a senior advisor. In exchange, he informed us that Brant was telling the truth all along. He did inherit the remaining wishes when he killed Leon. So it seems you can't offer me what I want, only half of it."

"I never promised you the wishes, only the gem," I said with as much defiance as I could muster. "It shouldn't be too hard for your family to find Brant. You have the resources to look."

The sneer became a genuine smile. A knowing smile.

My heart pounded in warning. "Do you know where he is?"

The smile turned slick.

"Do you know where he is?" I demanded.

He pushed away Meg's blade.

She stepped back in line with her mother. They clutched one another, their terrified gazes on Lord Xavier. But he only had eyes for me.

"Give me the gem, or you will never be safe," he said. "Not you, not your lover, your friend, her family. None of you. You have no warrior priests to protect you now. You have few friends in the village. We made sure of that while you were away. Get me the gem, my pet, and I will do my best to keep you alive while I have my way with you. Perhaps you'll even enjoy it...but I doubt it."

Mistress Diver made a choking sound in her throat. She grabbed Meg and tried to usher her back along the alley, but Meg resisted. "Josie," she pleaded. "Come."

"Am I clear, pet?" Lord Xavier taunted. "The gem in exchange for their lives."

"And their freedom," I said.

He nodded.

"Bring it to me this time tomorrow or your ugly friend here will be the first to feel my wrath."

I picked up my skirts and raced with Meg and Mistress Diver back along the alley. We slammed the door shut and bolted it. We didn't reopen it until Dane knocked.

It was only then that I apologized to Mistress Diver and begged her forgiveness for placing her family in danger. She gave a curt nod and walked away, taking Meg with her.

"What is it?" Dane pressed. "What's happened?"

He wanted to march to Deerhorn Castle as soon as I told him, but common sense prevailed, thankfully. He pressed his palms to the door and lowered his head.

"I should have been here," he muttered.

I touched his shoulder. "It's my fault. I shouldn't have opened the door. I thought it was Brant..."

He suddenly turned and grasped my shoulders. The candle-light danced a wild dance in his eyes. In that moment, I worried that common sense had fled. "He admitted he has Brant?"

"Not in words, but I suspect Brant is in hiding at their castle."

"Perhaps, or perhaps not. Brant wouldn't go willingly."

"You think he's being held captive?"

"It's likely. We can mount a rescue mission and storm it again."

"They'll be expecting that," I said. "He might not even be at the castle. If I were them, I'd hide him somewhere we wouldn't think of looking."

He swore under his breath.

"Dane, we have to proceed with caution. And we have to make sure Meg and her family are safe. If we don't deliver the gem by tomorrow night, Lord Xavier won't waste a moment in punishing them." I choked on the last words. The horror of our predicament was only now sinking in. We had no choice but to give the Deerhorns the gem or the Divers would suffer. That only gave us one day to find Brant. If we couldn't retrieve him from their clutches before we handed over the gem, they'd have all the power they could want at their fingertips.

We waited for Lyle and his father to return before leaving for the palace. Meg decided to stay behind with her family, and Dane promised to send guards, just in case Lord Xavier broke the agreement.

I rode with Dane back to the cottage. The close proximity would usually lend itself to intimacy between us, but not tonight. We both had too much on our minds. His solid, familiar presence was a comfort, nevertheless.

Yelena and Martha were relieved to see us, but Erik and Kitty didn't look at all worried by our long absence.

"We tell them you will be with Meg's family," Erik whispered as he passed me to join Dane by the horses.

Yelena was ahead of him, trying to convince Dane to stay and eat something. "Martha cooked for you."

"I ate at the Divers' house," he told her. "I must get back to the palace. My absence might be noticed, and if the dukes catch wind of you all living here..." He eyed me over his mother's head and gave a firm nod.

We had agreed that I would tell Kitty about my meeting with Lord Xavier and he would tell the others in the garrison. I wasn't looking forward to the discussion but it was necessary.

I watched as he and Erik rode off through the dark forest and returned inside with Yelena to where Martha and Kitty sat in the small parlor. I locked all the doors then told them why.

"Lord Xavier is despicable," Kitty spat. "I've always loathed him."

"He's even worse now that the Deerhorns have more power, thanks to Violette's marriage to your husband," I said.

She stared at the flames licking the logs in the fireplace. "I should reveal myself."

"Not yet."

"It's the only way to take away their power."

"They will still have some power." I reached across the gap and clutched her hand. "If you reveal yourself, Gladstow or the Deerhorns could kill you. It's far too dangerous."

"But I need to do something," she whined.

"There is only one thing to do." Yelena's voice cut through the air with sharp clarity. "If you want your friends to be safe, Josie, then Dane must come forward and declare himself to be the rightful king."

My insides recoiled. I shook my head.

"It's the only way," she went on. "As king, he can protect them. The Deerhorns and dukes won't dare harm your friends."

I squeezed the bridge of my nose. "He doesn't want to be king."

"I was in the village today and I heard about the lack of grain, the dire need for work and housing. The Deerhorns' corruption is strangling Mull. Dane can stop that. Not just here but all over Glancia. He has it in his power, Josie. And you have it in your power to convince him that he must become king."

"I can't!"

"You can," she bit off. "But you won't. You want him all to yourself." She pushed to her feet and marched towards the stairs. She paused, one hand on the railing, and turned a cool glare on me. "Stop being selfish. Think of your friends, your village, your country. It's time to accept what he is. The king of Glancia."

* * *

I SLEPT on the floor in the parlor. I didn't want to be in the same room as Yelena. I tossed and turned as a thousand things raced through my mind, all jumbling together in a tangled mess. I must have dozed off, however, because I awoke with a start to the pounding of a fist on the front door.

"Josie!" It was Quentin. "Josie, come quick!"

I wrenched the door open. Quentin stood there, breathing heavily, his doublet unfastened, and terror in his eyes. My heart dove. "Quentin, what is it?"

"Get your medical bag. It's Dane. He's been poisoned."

CHAPTER 9

*D*ane lay in his old bed in the room next to the king's bedchamber. Despite no longer being the captain of the guards, no one had been appointed to replace him. According to Quentin, Dane had returned there as if it were the normal thing to do.

I took the information in as I assessed Dane's condition. He was pale, warm to touch, and had thrown up in the basin. It had been at that point that he'd shouted for Theodore. The valet had also continued to sleep in his usual place, on a roll out bed in the king's bedchamber. Theodore had immediately woken the guards and Quentin had ridden to the cottage to fetch me.

I had never seen Dane look so weak. His physical strength had always reassured me but now he probably couldn't even wield a sword. Seeing him like that made the world seem wrong. The notion that he might succumb to the poison in his body rocked me to my core. If that happened, my life would be forever cast in shadow. There would always be a piece of me missing.

"Well?" Balthazar asked. He hovered nearby, as did Theodore, Quentin, Yelena, and Martha. "Will he live?"

"Of course I will," Dane snapped.

His vehement response was like a hammer tapping on the glass of our fear, shattering it. A collective sigh was heaved, relieved smiles were exchanged. I breathed again and silently thanked the goddess for answering my prayers.

Balthazar suddenly sat on the chair, nodding to himself. He looked as pale as Dane, now struggling to sit up.

Yelena helped him and plumped the pillow at his back. "Thank the merciful goddess. She saved you. She has blessed you."

"My lack of appetite saved me." Dane indicated a plate on the small table by the window with half of a pie slice on it. "That was waiting for me when I returned but I dined at the Divers' tonight and wasn't hungry."

I sniffed the pie. It smelled of direweed's earthiness. The poisoner hadn't used the rarer and more lethal traitor's ease, thank Hailia. "If you'd eaten all of this pie, you would have thrown up more than once," I said. "Your condition would also be more perilous than it is now."

"Thank Mistress Diver and her delicious cooking." He smiled at me.

I did not smile back. I was still shaken. Now that the immediate danger had passed, I couldn't help picturing how badly this might have ended. If he'd ingested more of the poison, I could not have made up an antidote without my father's equipment and all the ingredients. Dane was strong, but not even he could have survived a large dose. Going by the smell of that pie, the dose had been large indeed.

Someone wanted to kill him.

"From now on, you eat only what Martha cooks for you," I said. "You are not to touch a single thing from the palace kitchen."

Martha pressed a hand to her stomach, but the look of determination on her face helped my own frayed nerves. "I'll only use ingredients purchased directly from the village market," she said emphatically. "You're not to touch a thing from the palace, Dane. Do you hear? Not a drop of water, not a single crumb or lettuce leaf."

His smile gentled. "Yes, ma'am."

"Who could have done it?" Yelena snapped.

"Not the Deerhorns or anyone connected to them," Balthazar

said, frowning. "They need Dane alive or they know we'll never give them the gem."

Dane closed his eyes and leaned back against the pillows with a heavy sigh. The dark circles under his eyes worried me. He might not be entirely out of danger. My father had ordered Miranda to sleep after she'd been poisoned, and I suspected Dane needed it to.

"Everybody out," I said. "He needs a thorough rest." I shooed them towards the door, but Yelena didn't get up.

"He's my son. He should be watched in case he takes a turn for the worse."

"I'll be fine," he said. "Get some rest. Josie will stay."

"But I am your mother."

"If I do take a turn for the worse, she'll know what to do. Will you?"

Her nostrils flared. Then with a tilt of her chin, she followed the others out.

Dane patted the bed beside him and I sat on top of the covers. Then I threw my arms around him and fell against his chest. I didn't speak. I didn't tell him of all the horrible scenarios going through my head. I just held him and listened to the sound of his heart, a little quick but mercifully strong.

He stroked the hair off my forehead and tilted my chin up. He wiped my damp cheeks with his thumb and smiled gently. "I'm glad you stayed."

I sat up. "Why? Do you feel worse? Will you be sick again?"

The smile reached his eyes. "I feel fine. Stop worrying."

"I can't help it. You could have died."

"But I didn't." He patted the pillow beside his head. "I'm glad you're staying because I want to lie with you. That's all."

"Oh. Right. But just to sleep, mind. Nothing more. You need to rest."

He laughed softly. "Trust me, I have no strength for anything more than talking."

"There'll be no talking either. Just sleeping."

He sighed. "Very well. Take off your clothes and come to bed."

I removed my shoes and dress but kept on the nightshirt I

wore under it. I climbed into bed beside him and kissed his forehead. It was still warm against my lips, but not hot.

"Who do you think did it?" he asked.

"I said no talking."

"Not even to tell you I love you?"

I smiled against his throat as I snuggled into him. "I love you
too, Dane."

* * *

"It sounds like something the Deerhorns would do," Max said.
"Are you sure it wasn't them?"

"It's highly unlikely," Balthazar said. "They need Dane alive.
For all they know, he's the only one who can give them the gem.
They aren't aware that we all know where it is."

Max crossed his arms as he considered who else could have
tried to poison Dane. He had returned early in the morning from
his shift guarding the Divers' house to discover what had
happened. He'd been as shocked as the rest of us, but reassured
to see Dane sitting up in bed.

Dane looked much healthier. His color had almost returned
and his temperature felt normal too. He still complained of
feeling weak, but only to me and only when I pushed for an
answer. He'd consumed the soup Martha had made for him, but
I wouldn't allow him to have the bread yet. It was too soon and
his stomach needed time to fully recover from the trauma
inflicted on it by the poison.

"It can't be Brant, either," Quentin said from where he sat on
the bed beside Dane, his legs outstretched. "Josie reckons the
Deerhorns have him."

"It must be one of the dukes," Erik said. "To get you out of
the way so they can take the throne."

Balthazar shook his head. "They aren't aware he's *in* the way
yet."

"Someone from Freedland?" Theodore suggested.

Yelena agreed. "They sent an assassin. It's the only
explanation."

"A stranger would have been noticed in the kitchen," I said.

115

"I've met the head cook and he doesn't like anyone in his domain unless they're supposed to be there."

"That means nothing," Yelena said. "Someone bribed a kitchen hand to add the poison to your pie and your pie alone, Dane."

But none of us agreed with her. "None of the staff would accept a bribe to kill him," Quentin told her. "We're like a big family here."

"Families fall out," was all she said before turning her face away.

She looked tired this morning, and not like the ageless beauty I'd first met. The illness on the boat had left her gaunt, and the shock of the poisoning attempt seemed to have added even more years to her sharp features. Her hand shook as she fidgeted with her ring.

Theodore paced the small room, his hands at his back. "It must have been someone who could enter the kitchen and not risk being thrown out."

"Someone who doesn't want me announcing that I am the rightful king," Dane added with a dark look at his mother.

"But no one knows except us," Quentin said.

"I told no one," Yelena said with a sniff.

"You sent documents to the temple of Merdu's Guards in Tilting," Dane reminded her. "Someone knew, and they attacked us in the forest before we reached Merrin Fahl."

I gasped. "You think that attack was an attempt to stop you learning your identity in Freedland?"

"And to stop you claiming your rightful place," his mother added.

"Perhaps," Dane said. "It's also likely that person also attacked us as we tried to escape from Merrin after my release on the scaffold. Do you remember, Josie?"

It all came back to me now, that attack, the one in the forest, and others. "It wasn't just those two incidents. Someone set the Freedland authorities onto us in Noxford outside the inn, then again at Yelena's house when you were arrested. That person must have known where to find you."

It was Yelena's turn to gasp. "They knew where I lived."

"How?" Max asked. "*We* didn't even know where you lived. We didn't know Dane had a mother until then. So how did someone else find out?"

"From me," Balthazar said.

Quentin sat up straight. "You told someone! Why?"

Balthazar lifted a hand off his walking stick, dismissing Quentin's question. "I must have told someone *before* I lost my memory. I found the documents Yelena sent to the master of Merdu's Guards and must have shown them to someone in Tilting before I left to find Dane in Noxford."

My mind raced through the possibilities of who Balthazar had told but dismissed them all. We'd asked his fellow priests what he'd been studying when he disappeared from Tilting, and none knew.

"Someone lied," Max said, his thoughts following the same path as mine.

I lifted my gaze to Dane, but he was looking at Balthazar. Something passed between them, an understanding or acknowledgement. They had both reached the same conclusion.

It took me a little longer, but I reached it too. The realization sickened me. It was the ultimate betrayal. A friendship would be shattered by this and trust broken.

Balthazar could have confided in a number of people before he left Tilting, but not all of them could have sent someone to attack us on the road. Only one had been in Merrin when we were attacked. Only one was here at the palace now and could have entered the kitchen without being ordered out by the cook.

"The high priest of Glancia," I murmured.

"The high priest!" Yelena cried. "Are you sure?"

"Merdu," Max muttered.

Quentin shook his head. "I can't believe it. What an arse!"

"Are you sure?" Theodore asked.

Balthazar and Dane both nodded. "It could only have been him." Balthazar's shoulders sagged, and he lowered his head. "He lied to us when we asked him in Tilting if he knew where I'd gone before losing my memory. I must have done so and confided in him my intention to travel to Freedland and why. We were friends. I trusted him and would have sought his advice. It's the only explanation that fits."

Dane scrubbed a hand down his face. When it came away, he looked even more drawn. He cast a sympathetic glance at Balthazar. "Your memory loss was a blessing for him. It allowed him to cover up his betrayal."

"It bought him time," I added. "Time in which he could kill you, Dane. Or try to."

"But why?" Yelena asked. "What does it matter to him if Dane takes the throne of Glancia from the dukes? Dane is a better option than them."

"I think I know," Balthazar said, rising. "But I want to hear it from him."

I had an inkling too. The more I thought about my encounters with the high priest, the more I couldn't stop thinking about the dinner he'd hosted for us the night before we left Tilting. It was then that he'd heard Dane's name for the first time. Prior to that, he'd simply known him as Captain Hammer.

He'd been going to kill Dane that night after realizing who dined with him. I was sure of that now. He'd asked one of his servants to fetch a phial, telling me it was a tonic for his own health, but it was most likely poison. He'd not followed through with his hastily planned assassination, thank the god and goddess. Perhaps he realized he couldn't get away with it with so many witnesses.

That's why he'd sent men after us to Vytill, then come himself to Merrin Fahl when the attack in the forest failed. He'd been there when Dane was imprisoned for a murder he didn't commit. When we met the high priest in the square where Dane's execution was to take place, he'd claimed to have pleaded Dane's case to the magistrate. But it was more likely he had done the opposite. If it hadn't been for the king's pardon, he would have succeeded in getting rid of Dane without staining his own hands with blood.

After several failed attempts, the high priest had come here in person to stop Dane before he claimed the Glancian throne. He didn't know Dane wasn't going to declare himself. I wasn't sure it made a difference. While Dane lived, he was the rightful king.

"I'm coming with you," I said to Balthazar as he rose to leave. "We must bring guards to arrest him."

"He's the high priest," Yelena said darkly. "One does not simply arrest a high priest."

"Not without evidence," Dane said. "And I'd wager he can't be linked to this." He indicated the pie.

"We can't let him get away with it!" I cried. "At least if he's aware that we know he might stop trying to kill you."

Yelena scoffed. "You're naïve, Josie. We are no threat to the high priest. Our word means nothing against his. He will continue his attempts to eliminate Dane until he succeeds."

"So what do you propose we do? Nothing? That is not an option for me, Yelena."

"Do you think it's an option for me?" She rose and turned to Balthazar. "Gather the dukes in the council chamber. We will address them as soon as Dane is ready."

"Why?" Theodore asked with caution.

"Dane must announce his claim. It's the only way to keep him safe."

A weighty silence filled the bedchamber. Then it was broken by several voices talking over the top of one another.

Mine was not one of them. I glanced at Dane as he argued with his mother, telling her all the reasons he didn't want to be king. But in my heart, I knew she was right. It was the right thing for Glancia and its people, but more importantly, it was the right thing for Dane. By declaring himself, the high priest would be defeated, bringing an end to his attempts to kill Dane. Dane would even have the power to arrest him if he wished.

But Dane becoming king would mean the end for us. The king couldn't marry a commoner, no matter what the law stated or what that king wanted. Glancia needed an alliance with a nation like Vytill. Dane couldn't afford to make an enemy of them. Declaring himself king was the last thing either of us wanted, but if it meant saving his life, I would support it.

"She's right," I said.

Only Dane seemed to have heard me through the cacophony

of voices. He stopped mid-sentence and stared at me. "No, Josie." His deep, commanding tones rose above all others.

The weight of the sudden silence pressed down on me, smothering. Tears pricked the backs of my eyes but I willed them away. I must be strong or Dane would never go through with it. And he had to do this.

"Yes, Dane," I said. "Yelena's right. The only way to keep you safe is to negate the high priest's threats. You becoming king will do that. It will stop the Deerhorns too, and end the war between the dukes. It will solve all our problems. You have to do this, Dane. You *have* to, or the high priest will never stop trying to take your life."

His chest heaved with his deep breath. He looked away, his jaw rigid. But he did not shake his head. He did not refuse.

I turned to Yelena. "Fetch Prince Hugo's letters from the cottage. Max, Erik and Quentin will escort you. Dane, get dressed. Theodore, ask the dukes to meet us in the council chamber. Don't tell them why."

"And us?" Balthazar asked.

"We're going to confront the high priest. I want answers. I also want to make sure he doesn't have an inkling of what we're about to do."

I helped Balthazar to his feet as the guards filed out with Yelena. I did not look at Dane. I couldn't.

"Wait, Josie," he said.

"No, Dane. I won't wait."

"Talk to me."

I shook my head.

"We have to talk about this!"

"There is nothing to say," I said over my shoulder. "This must be done."

I felt his glare boring into my back as I left with Balthazar and Theodore. "Nothing will change between us," he called out.

But we both knew that was a lie.

* * *

THE COOK CONFIRMED that the high priest had indeed been in the kitchen the night before and had asked for a slice of pie. The cook hadn't dared throw him out or deny him the slice.

With that confirmed, we confronted the high priest. We found him in one of the salons, studying a painting of Leon. All the artwork still hung on the walls, even those depicting the false king. The valuable ornaments and gilt furniture were exactly as I'd seen them the last time I'd wandered through these rooms. The servants hadn't touched them. The only difference was the lack of people. We were alone in a chamber that used to be filled with noblemen and women playing cards, gossiping, and preening. There was an eeriness about the empty palace, and a sadness too, like a painted whore ignored by passersby.

"Ah, Bal, Josie," he said upon our entry. "This is a fine portrait, don't you think? He was a good looking young man."

"It's nothing like him," Balthazar said.

The high priest bristled at the brusque tone. His gaze slipped from Balthazar to me and back again. "You both look serious. Has something happened?"

"Dane was poisoned."

The high priest gasped. His jaw dropped. "Merdu, no. That's awful. Truly awful." He took my hand between both of his and gave me a sympathetic frown. "Josie, you poor thing. I want you to know that I will be here if you need me. You are not alone. You have good friends—"

"He didn't die," I said, withdrawing my hand.

The shocked look on the high priest's face was more satisfying than it should have been.

I smiled. "He is up and about as we speak. Fortunately he wasn't hungry last night and ate little of the pie you delivered to his room."

The high priest cocked his head to the side. "Pardon?"

"You heard her," Balthazar said. "You delivered the poisoned slice of pie to Dane's room last night with the expectation he would eat it all. But Dane already ate earlier in the evening and consumed only a small portion. It made him ill, but not terribly." He smiled at the high priest's frozen face. "He has a strong constitution."

The high priest rallied, blinking furiously. "No, no, you're mistaken. I didn't deliver anything to his room."

"You were seen," Balthazar said simply.

The high priest looked to me again. I simply nodded.

"It's all right," Balthazar said, gazing up at Leon's portrait. "There's nothing we can do about it. You are too powerful to bring to justice. No one will believe the word of mere servants over you." He shuffled around to face the high priest. "We just want to know why."

The high priest hesitated, then his throat moved with his swallow. He indicated the painting. "You told me he was a weak man, selfish, greedy and immature. If he'd lived longer, he could have ruined this country and set the entire Fist Peninsula on a path to war."

The high priest had never believed our claims that magic put Leon on the throne and cost the servants their memories. Balthazar seemed disinclined to try to convince him again so I remained silent too.

The high priest wagged a finger at the portrait. "Men like that should not be allowed to rule. They shouldn't have any power at all, let alone the power to affect thousands of lives. Yet they do. They are given power simply because they were born into royalty. It's not right, Bal, and you know it."

I couldn't believe what I was hearing. He'd gone to such lengths simply because he hated royalty? "How does killing Dane change anything?" I cried.

The high priest hesitated.

"We know he's the heir to both the Averlea and Glancian thrones," Balthazar said.

The high priest shifted his stance and nodded slowly. "I see."

"Well then?" I snapped. "Explain yourself."

"Removing him keeps Freedland a republic and gives Glancians the opportunity to install a republic here too."

"Except Glancians aren't interested in becoming a republic. Removing Dane means the dukes are left to fight over the throne. It will lead to war. How does that benefit the people?"

"You can't see the longer view, Josie. You see, neither duke will have enough support to take power completely. That will lead to a weak monarchy and a weak monarchy will bring discontent. Discontent with the monarchy leads to its demise at the hands of its people. Monarchies are dangerous systems. Look what happened in Freedland forty years ago. King Diamedes almost ruined his kingdom through his greed and corruption. But he was brought down by the people, and something new and egalitarian rose from the ashes of the revolution. Freedland is a fine example of what can happen when the monarchy is removed. All nations on the Fist should learn from it."

"You want Dreen and Vytill to become republics too?" I scoffed.

"In time. Glancia is a good place to start, now that it is without a clear king."

"Dane notwithstanding," Balthazar said.

The high priest gave him a grim smile. "Quite."

"He would make an excellent king."

"For a while, perhaps. But power corrupts, Bal. You know that. Or you used to, before you lost your memory. And what of his heir? And his son's heir, his grandson's heir? Dane might make a good king, but good monarchs die and bad ones replace them."

"Bad rulers can be elected too," I said.

"And a different one elected in their place after a brief term." The high priest shrugged. "Which is the lesser of two evils, Josie?"

"How long have you plotted Glancia's path to becoming a republic through murder?" Balthazar asked.

The high priest winced. "I didn't think I would have to resort to murder. As King Alain grew old and frail, no one knew he had an heir. Not even me. Then you showed me those documents from the former princess of Averlea, proving she had married Prince Hugo before his death years ago and borne him a son. You were amazed, shocked, and elated too. You thought putting King Alain's grandson on the Glancian throne would solve the impending problem of the succession, whereas I could see beyond that. Having no clear heir made fertile ground in which a republic could plant its seed and grow. I knew I had to do something before Dane's existence became public knowledge."

"What did you do with those documents?" Balthazar asked.

"I wrote to the authorities in Freedland after you left Tilting and told them what you had in your possession. They burned the documents after they arrested you. Unfortunately you'd already showed them to Dane."

"You knew where to find Yelena and Dane from those documents?" Balthazar asked.

The high priest nodded. "I was able to direct the Freedland authorities straight to you."

"They were imprisoned in a mine," I snapped. "You condemned an old man, your *friend*, to the cruelest of punishments."

"I was assured that he was treated well and didn't work in the mine." The high priest seemed entirely at ease with the role he'd played in events. "I was saddened when I learned of the prisoners' escape and subsequent death after being rounded up. I truly was, Bal. I believed the story the Freedland authorities put out." He indicated the portrait. "Then he showed up."

Balthazar merely grunted.

"He seemed to come from nowhere," the high priest went on. "I would have called him out as a pretender, but he had all the correct documents. More importantly, he had the support from the advisors and dukes. I was devastated. All that effort in suppressing Dane's name and identity, for nothing. Your death too, Bal. All for nothing."

Balthazar leaned on his walking stick. "Leon's lies affected many." He lifted his gaze to me. "Yet he did save us. We all would have perished in that mine, sooner or later, if not for him."

Leon smiled down at us from his portrait in that imperial, smug way of his. He had few good traits, and many bad ones, but Balthazar was right. Leon wishing to become king had saved all of the prisoners from certain death.

"Leon's death was a blessing," the high priest went on, as if Balthazar hadn't spoken. "Once again, having no clear heir meant I could hope for a republic. When I received a letter from the master of Merdu's Guards stating he'd found you here, Bal, I was overjoyed that you'd somehow escaped. I still thought Dane deceased at that point. Your memory loss was fortuitous. You'd forgotten about the documents and Dane's identity, about the prison mine and about my involvement in your arrest. You'd forgotten it all. It was a relief. I could have my friend back with none of the unpleasantness."

"With none of the consequences of your actions," Balthazar countered.

The high priest looked pained. He stepped towards Balthazar, his hand outstretched. Balthazar put up his walking stick, warding him off. The high priest lowered his head. "The night you came to dine at the high temple in Tilting, I hoped to dissuade you from traveling to Freedland. But then I discovered you were with Dane, the heir to two kingdoms..." He shook his head. "It was a severe shock. Not only had I assumed him dead, but I could see all my hard work unraveling before my eyes. I knew you would both learn the truth in Freedland."

"So you tried to stop him going by killing him," I snapped. "And you're still trying."

The high priest stiffened. "For the greater good, Josie."

"You're cruel."

"Me?" He spluttered a disbelieving laugh. "I am trying to *save* Glancia, just as Freedland was saved. Monarchies are cruel systems, Josie, set up so the privileged prosper and the poor are kept poor. Kings and queens should be despised. Monarchies should be brought down and replaced by republics before they turn rotten. Believe me, history has shown that they all become rotten eventually."

"You tried to murder Dane!" I shook my head at him. He sickened me. I could no longer look at him. "Let's go, Bal. We have work to do."

But Balthazar merely gazed at the high priest, a curious frown on his brow. "Sacrificing a small number of souls now to save many in the future. Is that it?"

Relief flooded the high priest's face. "I knew you'd understand eventually. You and I are alike in that regard. We see the bigger picture. We use the lessons of the past in order to stop the future from destroying itself. We are sympathetic but not sentimental."

"I am *not* like you." Balthazar's raised voice echoed around the empty salon. It was strong and stern, without a hint of his frailty.

The high priest stepped back beneath its force. "Bal? Come now, think it through. Use your powers of reason, and you'll see that I'm right."

"Josie's right," Balthazar shot back. "You *are* cruel. But I am not."

He turned and marched out, barely using his walking stick at all. I followed and didn't look back.

"It's over, Bal," the high priest called after us. "He can't gain the throne now. Without the marriage and birth certificates, he has no proof."

"If you thought that, you wouldn't have been trying to kill him up until last night." Balthazar stopped. "We have to be in the council chamber. Care to join us?"

The color drained from the high priest's face. He raced ahead of us and was waiting in the council chamber with the dukes and Deerhorns when Balthazar and I arrived. His face had taken on a deathly pallor.

Theodore looked relieved to see us. "They're annoyed," he whispered.

They looked positively vitriolic, particularly the Deerhorns. As usual, their wrathful glares focused on me. I tried not to let them rattle me. It wasn't easy with Lord Xavier in the same room; his threats from the previous day still rang in my ears.

"Why are you wasting our time?" Lady Deerhorn snapped at me.

"Patience, my lady," Balthazar said.

"Do you have more information about Vytill?" the duke of Buxton asked. "Do you have spies in Phillip's castle?"

The notion intrigued the duke of Gladstow enough that he stopped his restless pacing. Violette joined him at one end of the long polished table and smiled at him. He smiled back, but his gaze wandered around the room. It fell on the high priest, glaring daggers at the doorway.

Dane and Yelena entered, flanked by six guards including Erik, Max and Quentin. Dane didn't bow and Yelena performed no curtsy. Lady Deerhorn's eyes narrowed at the slight, but it was Lord Deerhorn who admonished them.

"You are in the presence of your betters," he snapped. "Have a care, Hammer."

"My name is not Hammer," Dane said. He met the gazes of each duke and Deerhorn and let it linger on the high priest. Despite still looking a little pale and tired, he seemed more formidable than ever. There was no sign of his earlier reservations. He had embraced his destiny.

"Who cares what your bloody name is?" Lord Xavier muttered.

"You should," Yelena shot back. "And you will."

"How dare you speak to my son in that tone," Lord Deerhorn growled. "Who are you? A maid?"

Yelena's spine stiffened even more and her chin thrust out a little further. Despite being shorter than all of us, she had a way of seeming taller. She'd never looked more regal, or more pleased to be asked that question. She'd been waiting for this moment for forty years, and she was going to relish it.

"I was born Princess Yelena of Averlea," she said with haughty conviction.

Murmurs filled the room, and one bark of laughter that came from Lord Xavier. His parents weren't laughing, however. The name was familiar to them.

"After my marriage, I became Princess Yelena Lockhart of Glancia. My husband was Prince Hugo Lockhart of Glancia." She rested a hand on Dane's arm, her lips curved in a victorious smile as she surveyed the shocked faces of the gathering. "And this is our son, Dane, the king of Glancia."

CHAPTER 10

"*T*his is absurd!" the duke of Gladstow blurted out.

Lord Deerhorn barked a laugh. "They're both mad."

Lady Deerhorn snapped her fingers at Max. "Arrest them. It's a crime to make such a claim."

Lord Xavier's eyes gleamed as he licked his lips. "You hitched your wagon to the wrong horse, Miss Cully."

"I said arrest them!" Lady Deerhorn's screech made her daughter flinch. "Sergeant, it's your duty to remove these traitors."

Max didn't move. He didn't even acknowledge that she'd spoken. He stood by Dane's side and waited in silence.

"Captain, what are you doing?" the duke of Buxton asked carefully.

"He is claiming his birthright," Yelena said in a loud voice.

Lord Deerhorn snorted. "She's a crackpot. The entire Averlea royal family died in the revolution forty years ago. Everyone knows that."

"Then why did the Freedland authorities imprison my son on false charges? Why did they try to suppress his true identity? Why did they have him sign this document forcing him to give up all rights to reclaiming the Averlea throne?" She held out her hand and Quentin placed a document onto her palm.

She unfolded it and laid it on the table. The nobles leaned forward as one.

The high priest did not. He didn't even look at the document. "You have no proof of his claim to the *Glancian* throne."

Quentin handed Yelena more folded papers. One by one, she set them down on the table too.

"These are my private letters from Prince Hugo in the lead up to our marriage and before Dane's birth," she said.

The nobles pored over them, quickly scanning the contents and passing the letters around. Lady Deerhorn's face remained impassive, her thoughts difficult to read. Not so her husband and son. The face of the father grew redder with each passing moment, while the younger paled. Lady Violette looked quite ill.

"What about a marriage registration?" the high priest pressed. "A birth document?"

"Lost," Balthazar said calmly. "As you well know, Your Eminence."

The high priest merely shook his head sadly at Balthazar. No one else seemed to have heard his accusation.

The duke of Gladstow snatched up a letter in each hand, scrunching them. "These letters prove nothing!"

"Not by themselves," Dane agreed. "But compare the writing to other letters known to be written by Prince Hugo. You probably have some such letters in your own private belongings, and there will be official documents in the old castle in Tilting."

"I have some letters from him," the duke of Buxton admitted. "I am prepared to compare them. Gladstow?"

The elder of the two dukes flung the letters across the table. They fluttered harmlessly onto the polished surface. "I do not accept this! I want real proof! *Official* documentation."

Yelena tapped her finger on one of the letters. "The proof is in these. Read them. There are details in them that only someone close to the royal family could know."

Lord Deerhorn scoffed.

"Someone here knows I'm telling the truth," Dane said. "He tried to kill me to stop me coming forward."

The high priest shrank back towards the door, his eyes round with uncertainty.

"This man has nothing to fear from me unless he attempts to assassinate me again. If I am to die, he will be the first my men will suspect. Is that clear?"

The high priest gulped.

The lords looked at one another while Lord and Lady Deerhorn exchanged worried glances.

The high priest turned and fled from the room.

Yelena watched him go, a smile of satisfaction on her face. A victory she'd desired for so long was finally within her grasp.

"Your Grace," Dane said to the duke of Buxton. "I value your advice. Perhaps we can meet today to discuss how to proceed."

Buxton's mouth opened and closed without a word passing his lips.

"I know this is a surprise," Dane went on. "But you must see that this is best for Glancia. It means no war of succession. The people can go on as they were."

"Very well," Buxton said. "We shall meet. I'll send for the senior ministers immediately."

"I already have. Some will arrive as early as tomorrow."

The duke of Buxton blew out a breath, but he no longer looked disbelieving. Indeed, he looked quite relieved. "This could be good for Glancia."

"No, it will not!" the duke of Gladstow bellowed. "You only think that because you know you couldn't win."

Buxton rolled his eyes. "You didn't have as much support as you were led to believe. Think about this, Gladstow. He's young and strong, and he comes from royalty on both sides. With a little guidance, he could make a good king."

"You are ridiculous," Lord Deerhorn spat. "You're happy to roll over and let this nobody fuck you because you're too afraid to fight. Well, we're not!"

Gladstow nodded agreement. "He's lying. They both are. They're nobodies."

Yelena's nostrils flared. "We are not."

"Of course you are," Lady Deerhorn said, her tone matching Yelena's. "None of this makes sense. Why has he waited until now? Why has he remained as a mere guard when he could have been king all this time?" She fanned her fingers and pressed the tips to the table surface. Her steely glare settled on Dane. "You saw how Leon imposed himself onto the throne and decided to do the same, but with far less proof."

"That man was an imposter," Yelena snapped. "He took advantage of Dane's memory loss."

"Memory loss?" the duke of Buxton asked.

Lady Deerhorn scoffed. "Another lie."

Dane raised his hands for calm. "I met Leon some time ago in Freedland. I thought I was going to die, that we both were, so told him about myself. I was in no position to do anything about the crown then. The Freedland authorities wanted me dead. Later, I lost my memory and Leon seized the opportunity to make a claim instead. He took my documents for himself. He somehow made copies, changed my name to his, and presented them to the right people as proof. He even employed me as captain of the guards. I was none the wiser to his duplicity."

"How did you discover this if you lost your memory?" the duke of Buxton asked.

"After Leon's death, I went traveling. I suspected I was half-Freedlandian so I headed south. On the way, my memory slowly began to return. By the time I reached Noxford, I remembered my mother. I found her and she confirmed my identity. She'd thought me dead all this time."

If the dukes remembered Leon's dying confession about magic causing the memory loss, they chose not to believe. Dane was right not to mention it. It could undermine his authority and give the Deerhorns and the duke of Gladstow fodder for their theory.

"Remarkable," the duke of Buxton said on a breath. He, at least, seemed to believe.

"Speaking of Leon," Dane went on. "I want to congratulate Lord Deerhorn for capturing his murderer."

"What?" Lord Deerhorn spluttered.

"The guard named Brant. Lord Xavier claims you captured him and are holding him to await trial."

Lord Xavier's eyes widened. "I never said that."

"You told me last night when we met," I said, oh-so sweetly.

Lady Deerhorn turned one of her fiercest glares onto her son. He must have told her I'd promised to hand over the gem, but hadn't mentioned he'd implied they had Brant.

"Leon was an imposter, but Brant should still answer for his murder," Dane went on. "My men will retrieve Brant from you and see that he faces justice. Where is he?"

Lord Deerhorn clamped his mouth shut and turned to his wife.

Her face darkened. "This is outrageous. We're not handing anyone over to you. You are nobody. Nothing! And you cannot tell me what to do."

"Justice must be served," Dane said calmly. "I have an armed guard ready to fetch him if you just tell us where he is. If you don't, there will be consequences."

"For holding a prisoner?" Lord Deerhorn sneered.

"Or for harboring him." Dane shrugged. "I cannot be responsible for what the advisors will think of your actions."

Lord Deerhorn's face grew even redder. "How dare you!"

"He's being held in an abandoned house north of Mull," the duke of Gladstow said.

Lady Deerhorn's nostrils flared and her lips pinched. She looked as though she wanted to order her son-in-law to be silent, or to scold him at the very least. But he still outranked her.

The duke ignored her.

Lord Deerhorn glanced between them. He seemed to be trying to decide who to align himself with; his formidable wife or his powerful son-in-law. With a release of a breath, his shoulders sagged. "The house is a day's ride north, just off the main road near Maiden's Rise."

Dane nodded at Max, and Max left the council chamber.

Lady Deerhorn turned her cold glare onto her husband. "They have the gem," she hissed.

"Magic is just a child's tale," he said without looking at her.

She thumped her fist onto the table then turned to march out.

"One more thing before you go," Dane said.

Erik moved to block her exit, his hand on his sword hilt. Her glare had no effect on him. He simply glared right back.

"The Divers will not be harmed, nor will any of my friends," Dane said. "You don't want to anger me, Lady Deerhorn. I'll have the full power of the law in my grasp within a matter of days. I already have the palace guards on my side. I can arrest you on suspicion of committing any crime. You are not above the law, and you are certainly not above my wrath."

Erik moved aside, and Lady Deerhorn strode off, her heeled boots click-clacking loudly on the tiles. Her daughter and husband followed, then the duke of Gladstow. Lord Xavier's gaze connected with mine before he left too. What I saw in his eyes in that moment chilled me. They were filled with hate.

Dane placed a hand at my lower back. "All right?" he murmured.

I nodded.

"You've made a fierce enemy there," the duke of Buxton told Dane.

"That's old news." Dane indicated the duke should sit. "You must have questions."

The duke of Buxton nodded thoughtfully as he eased onto a chair. "You've answered most, but I would like to hear your plans for Glancia's future. You must have had a long time to think about things and how you'd want your reign to be remembered."

Dane's gaze settled on me. "Not as long as you might think."

* * *

I WROTE a long letter to Meg and sent it with one of the guards riding to Mull. It explained what had happened since we'd left her, and it advised her to remain alert for dangers. The Deer-horns might decide to carry out their threats regardless of Dane's new authority. It was impossible to tell what they'd do next.

With several guards accompanying Max, others at the Divers' house, and some protecting Dane, the garrison was almost empty. I didn't remain long and returned to the cottage with Erik, Theodore, Yelena and another two guards as escort. Dane had insisted we not be left alone for a moment.

Kitty was so relieved to see us, she threw her arms around

each of us, including Yelena. Dane's mother reacted by patting her shoulder then extricating herself.

"Come, Martha," Yelena said, picking up her skirts and heading up the stairs. "We must pack."

"You're leaving?" Kitty asked as Martha raced after her mistress.

"We're moving into the palace."

Kitty turned to me, wide-eyed. "I see I've missed some news."

"You'd better sit down," I told her.

"Prepare to be amazed," Erik declared. "Dane is king!"

Kitty gasped.

"He's not king yet," I said.

Erik frowned. "Why not?"

"Well," I said, taking a seat, "the nobles have to agree that Yelena's letters are not falsified, for starters."

"The duke of Buxton accepted him," Theodore pointed out.

"Yes!" Erik declared. "The others will follow."

Kitty snorted. "Not Gladstow."

"Or the Deerhorns," I added.

Theodore disappeared into the kitchen while Erik and I filled Kitty in on the events of the previous evening and this morning. It was a lot to take in, and not just for her. I was still trying to make sense of it all. It felt quite strange, as if it were happening to other people.

"So Dane will be king and all will be well," Erik finished. "You can come out of hiding, Kitty."

Theodore returned carrying a tray with cake and teacups. "Don't be too hasty. The danger might not be over yet. I think you should wait until the dust settles and Dane has full authority."

I agreed, and Kitty nodded as she accepted a cup from Theodore. "I will wait. I am quite content here, although a little bored." She leaned forward and lowered her voice. "Martha is sweet but she just wants to cook and clean all day. Those are noble pursuits for a maid, of course, but for the companion to a duchess and princess, they make her as dull as dish water."

"And to the future queen of Glancia," Erik said with a wink for me.

"Oh, no," I said, shaking my head.

"Oh yes, Josie. Dane will marry you. He has promised and he does not break his promises."

Theodore beamed over the rim of his cup. "I know it's going to take some getting used to, but you will make a fine queen, Josie. Don't be afraid. We're all here to help turn you from village girl to queen."

Erik plucked at my sleeve. "She will need new clothes. What cloth do they sell in the village?"

Tea sloshed over the sides of Theodore's cup as he knocked it in his excitement. He set it down and beamed at me. "Forget the village shops. Leon wore many fine outfits. You can have the maids unpick them and make dresses out of the fabric. There are some exquisite items in his wardrobe. Cloth of gold and silver, silks of the finest quality... I can't wait to pick out the best pieces for you."

Erik clicked his fingers. "There was a nice cloak he wore once. Wine red with gold vines, leaves and birds stitched all over."

Theodore clapped his hands. "I know the one! There's a matching doublet and breeches too."

Erik lifted his cup in salute. "You will have to be the master of the queen's wardrobe, Theo. Dane will not appreciate your skill as valet. He will not wear red with gold thread. But Josie will."

Theodore blushed as he picked up his cup again. "That's kind of you, Erik, but the job must go to a woman."

"Bah! You are like a woman."

Theodore took a long sip of his tea.

"First, you must think about her wedding dress. Or the coronation dress?" Erik turned to Kitty. "Which will be first?"

Kitty concentrated on her tea as hard as Theodore concentrated on his.

"Kitty?" Erik prompted.

"There will be no wedding," I said.

Erik frowned. "Dane has promised."

"This is a promise he can't keep. Kitty knows it too, don't you, Kitty?"

The men looked at her. After a moment, she set her teacup down with a deep sigh. "You would have made a fine queen, Josie. You're kind, clever, and brave." She blinked rapidly and looked away.

"But that's not enough," I finished for her. "Queens must have diplomacy."

"You will learn the art of politics," Theodore said.

"And most of all," I went on, "they must have connections to other royal houses. That's how alliances are forged, trade is expanded, and wars are averted. Dane will marry Princess Illiriya of Vytill."

Theodore shook his head. "But—"

"No buts, Theo. Kitty understands. The nobles and advisors won't agree to Dane becoming king unless he agrees to marry her."

"No!" Erik all but shouted. "Dane will not accept this."

I set down my teacup and rose. "He already has when he declared himself today."

My chest felt tight, my throat raw. I headed outside for fresh air and sat on the bench seat in the garden. The sun had disappeared behind a blanket of cloud that extended in all directions and looked as though it was here to stay for some time. The stars would not be visible tonight.

Not that it mattered. Dane wouldn't notice them anyway. He was going to be too busy for stargazing from now on.

* * *

THE ARRIVAL of Lady Miranda Claypool the following day lifted my mood a little. She had come with her parents after traveling all night to reach the palace. Her father, the minister for finance, had received a letter the day before from Dane requesting his presence after declaring himself king. He was among the first of the ministers and nobles to rush to the palace, but he wouldn't be the last.

"I'm so tired," Miranda said, as we sat in the parlor adjoining her bedchamber. As a senior advisor, Lord Claypool was assigned one of the better suites that comprised of multiple rooms. We were alone, however. Miranda's father was in a meeting with Dane, and her mother was speaking to other newly arrived ladies.

"I'm so glad you came," I told her.

"And I'm so pleased to be here. I cannot quite fathom the news! It's quite incredible, and I admit that I don't really know why the captain of the guards is now the king."

"It's a long story. The short version is that Dane discovered his past in Freedland and learned that he is the son of a former Freedland princess and Prince Hugo of Glancia."

Miranda squeezed my hands. "You always knew there was something special about him."

I gave her a grim smile. "A little too special."

She drew me into a hug. "Don't worry yet. Wait and see what my father advises. There is still a chance for you two to be together."

Her words might have been hopeful ones, but her tone was not. Like Kitty, she was born into the world of nobles and knew that marriage was a contract between parties. It had nothing to do with love or what either party desired.

"Enough about that," she said, drawing away. "Tell me about your travels." Her smile slipped and her eyes filled with tears. "Tell me how she died."

"Ah. Yes. About that." I stood and took her hand. "Come with me for a ride into the forest."

"The forest? Josie, what is this about? Where are you taking me?"

"To see an old friend."

She gasped. "You *did* find her body. I thought it was strange that it simply disappeared and wasn't found after the floodwaters subsided. But why did you bury her in the forest here and not at her home?"

I refused to answer which drove her a little mad, but she stopped asking me questions by the time we mounted horses in the stables. Quentin and another guard rode with us as an escort, although I doubted the Deerhorns would dare try anything while I was with Miranda. No one had seen them since they'd stormed out of the council chamber the day before, although the maids and footmen said they were still in the palace. Theodore joined us too, since he claimed he had nothing better to do.

When we dismounted at the cottage, Quentin put out a hand to stay me. "We should knock first," he said. "Yelena and Martha have moved into rooms at the palace, but Erik's here. We don't want to walk in on them in the middle of...you know."

"Walk in on who?" Miranda asked.

I handed the reins of my horse to the guard named Jay.

"He should be bloody working," Jay grumbled. "His injury ain't so bad now."

"You can tell him that yourself when he comes out," I said as the door opened.

Erik stood there, entirely naked, scratching his head and yawning. He looked as though he'd just woken up. Miranda gasped and spun around. I didn't bother. I was used to seeing Erik without clothes on after traveling with him for so long. Besides, it gave me a good view of his stitched wound. It was still healing nicely.

"Get out here, you lazy sod," Quentin said.

Erik stepped onto the porch.

"Put some clothes on first!" Theodore cried. "Lady Miranda doesn't want to see *that*."

Erik frowned at Miranda's back. "It is big and frightening at first," he said with a knowing nod. "But you will get used to it, just like the other ladies."

Miranda broke into giggles.

Quentin rolled his eyes. "She's a lady. Be more respectful."

"Kitty is a lady too and she likes to look at my little friend. My little friend has become her—"

Miranda spun around. "Kitty?" She turned huge, unblinking eyes onto me. "Josie?"

I took her hand. "Come inside. There's someone who'll be very pleased to see you, but probably not as pleased as you will be to see her."

Erik stepped aside and Miranda rushed past him. He looked

a little disappointed that she didn't take more notice of his equipage. Miranda was too intent on Kitty to care.

Kitty hadn't yet seen her. She descended the stairs with the self-assured grace of a duchess. The effect was spoiled by her messy hair, her dreamy smile, and Erik's shirt reaching to her knees.

"It *is* you!" Miranda raced to the staircase and threw her arms around Kitty.

Kitty squealed with delight and hugged her back. "Dearest Miranda, you came. Josie, isn't this wonderful? All three of us together again. If only Meg were here." She drew away from Miranda. "Do stop crying, dearest. As you can see, I am not dead."

Miranda pressed her trembling lips together and nodded. She hugged Kitty again and planted a kiss on both her cheeks.

Kitty laughed. "Come and sit down. Josie and I have so much to tell you. Erik, do you mind fetching tea? Oh, *Erik*," she chided. "Did you answer the door to Miranda like that? No wonder she's in shock."

Erik planted his hands on his hips and grinned.

"We're in civilization now, not the depths of Freedland. Go and get dressed."

"You have my shirt," he pointed out.

"Ah. Right. I'll join you and dress too. Quentin, do you mind making tea? Martha left some in the pot. I would ask Josie, but until I know whether she'll be Dane's mistress or not, I can't think of her as a servant."

Quentin puffed out his chest. "I ain't a servant either. I'm the king's best friend."

"Do just make the tea for me." A bat of her eyelashes had Quentin scurrying off to the kitchen to do her bidding. Theodore followed.

While Erik and Kitty dressed upstairs, I sat with Miranda and told her how we faked Kitty's death to keep her safe from the duke of Gladstow.

"It was your idea," I pointed out.

"Yes, but I didn't think it would be so successful," she said. "What luck there happened to be a flooded river!"

Kitty returned as Quentin and Theodore brought in the tea. Her hair still hung down her back and her bodice laces were loose, but she was at least fully clothed. Erik followed her, fastening up his jerkin as he descended the stairs.

"What was the reaction to my death?" Kitty asked as she accepted a cup from Theodore.

"Shock," Miranda said. "Sadness."

Kitty eyed her sideways. "Who was sad?"

"Your parents."

"Only because they no longer had a duchess for a daughter."

"*I* was sad," Miranda said, taking Kitty's hand.

Kitty beamed. "I'm so glad to hear it. What about Gladstow? Did he mourn me at all?"

"He did all the things a grieving husband should. Your burial service was lovely, by the way. You would have liked it."

"Were there lots of mourners?"

"Hundreds."

"What flowers adorned my grave?"

"Daisies."

Kitty wrinkled her nose. "Couldn't he get something prettier?"

"There wasn't much in bloom in early autumn. Not in great quantities."

"But daisies are so common," Kitty whined.

Miranda pressed her lips together to suppress her smile.

"I would have ridden all over Glancia to find exotic flowers for your burial," Erik declared.

Kitty touched his jaw. "You sweet thing. You would mourn me properly too, and not simply do it for show like Gladstow."

Erik gave her a solemn nod.

Miranda watched their exchange with a smile on her lips. "I see you weren't bored on your journey."

"Erik helped me cope with the hardships," Kitty said. "There were many hardships, Miranda. You have no idea the things I had to do. I slept outside with nothing but my cloak for protection. I stayed in disgusting inns that made me wish I was sleeping outside. I hid from bandits and Vytillian guards. I cooked rabbit and peeled potatoes. I didn't wash my hair for days on end. Days! And I wore the same clothes too." She extended her arms forward. "Look at my fingernails, Miranda. I've been trying to clean them ever since we returned, but I fear the dirt may never come out."

Miranda clucked sympathetically. "You poor thing. You've been very brave. Thank goodness you had Erik to distract you from such horrid things."

"Oh yes. He's been a wonderful distraction."

"Thank goodness," I muttered into my teacup.

Miranda shot me a sly grin. "So tell me about the bandits. And why were Vytillian guards after you?"

We spent the rest of the day at the cottage telling Miranda not only about our adventures, but also what we'd learned about magic and the palace servants. We told her everything. She already knew about the magic, but she listened intently as we detailed our other discoveries. By the end, she was quite speechless.

"Say something," Kitty said, eyeing her friend carefully.

Miranda blinked at her. "I don't know what to say. It's all so fantastical."

Kitty placed a hand on Miranda's knee. "You mustn't be afraid of them."

"Of who?"

"The servants. They may be criminals, but some, like Dane, were imprisoned under false pretenses, and others were jailed for weak reasons simply to get them out of the way." She nodded at Theodore.

He seemed surprised to be singled out. "Excuse me," he muttered, rising and collecting the empty cups. "I'd best tidy up. Martha is no longer here, and Kitty shouldn't have to. She's still a duchess."

She smiled sweetly at him. "That's why Theo is my favorite."

Erik pouted. "I thought I was."

I rose to help Theodore in the kitchen. He seemed a little down. His own past must be worrying him, and perhaps he was having second thoughts about staying in Glancia. He must want to learn more about himself.

A knock on the door diverted my course, however. I opened

it to Milo, one of the palace guards. He had not ridden with us to the cottage.

"Captain requests your presence at the palace, Josie," he said. "He asks you to meet him and Lord Claypool in the council chamber."

"Lord Claypool? What does he want with me?"

Milo shrugged.

Miranda traveled back to the palace with me, Theodore, and the guards, while Erik stayed with Kitty. He claimed he was protecting her from discovery, but we all knew the real reason.

A meeting with Lord Claypool in the council chamber seemed very official. There was only one thing the minister of finance would want to discuss with me, and it wasn't a topic I wanted to discuss with him. Even so, a nobleman of Lord Claypool's character wasn't someone to be refused.

He smiled upon my entry into the council chamber and invited me to sit. Dane also smiled, but his was strained. He steered me towards a chair at the head of the table.

"Now will you tell us what this is about?" Dane asked.

Lord Claypool sat but Dane, ever restless, stood at my side, his hand on the back of my chair. When Lord Claypool realized he wasn't going to sit, he clasped his hands on the table and cleared his throat.

"You told me in our meeting just now that you trust me, Dane."

Dane nodded. "You've had Glancia's interests at heart a lot longer than me."

Lord Claypool seemed pleased with his response. "Miss Cully, you might be wondering why I'm referring to him as Dane rather than your majesty or Lockhart or even Hammer."

"Not at all," I said. "Until Yelena's letters can be verified, his identity is unconfirmed. Even then, the nobles must agree that he should be king before he can be given the title,"

He smiled. "I see why my daughter speaks so highly of you. I'm glad you understand my predicament. Now, to the meeting we just had with the other nobles who have arrived today after hearing the news. You should be made aware that many of us support Dane's claim."

I arched my brow.

"I see that surprises you," he said.

"After your preamble just now, I suspected you were going to say the opposite."

"There are some who vehemently oppose him, naturally, but I am not one of them. Dane taking the throne solves many issues the country faces. Those issues are dire. I do not want a war of succession, and I want to see King Phillip taking over Glancia even less." He adjusted his weight in the chair. He was a tall man, strongly built but not heavyset. "The thing is, Dane seems unconvinced."

I glanced up at him.

He touched the back of my neck, his thumb stroking the skin beneath my hairline. "Josie knows I don't want to be king."

"Is that why you asked me here?" I said to Lord Claypool. "To try to convince him it's the best thing for Glancia? Because I have tried. I also think it's the best thing for Glancia. It's the only course of action that will solve everything. Dane knows that, and by declaring himself today, he has agreed to take the throne."

Lord Claypool's gaze lifted from mine to Dane's before falling to Dane's hand, now resting on my shoulder. His eyes closed briefly before reopening. "I don't like to be the one to do this, but...it must be done. It has to be said now, before things get too far." He nodded at Dane's hand. "You two cannot marry."

Dane stiffened. "That is not for you to decide." His icy tone sent a chill down my spine, but Lord Claypool did not even flinch.

"You are both intelligent. You've both been around the palace long enough to know how it is. Noblemen marry noblewomen. Princes and kings marry princesses, or ladies if no suitable princess is available."

"Just because that's the way it has always been, it doesn't mean it must remain that way," Dane growled.

Lord Claypool addressed me. "I see that you understand, Josie, and have already come to terms with it."

My throat was too tight to do anything other than nod.

Dane's hand fell away. He dropped to his haunches, his face

level with mine. His features were hard. "There is no law against us marrying."

"Marrying Josie will not keep Glancia safe from the likes of King Phillip."

"*I* will keep Glancia safe," Dane shot back.

"We cannot fight off the Vytill army. They are weaker without taxes brought in from The Thumb, but they are not yet a poor nation. They are also eyeing our land and harbors. Come, Dane, be reasonable. Be sensible. If you are to be king, you cannot marry for love."

"You did."

Lord Claypool sat back in the chair as if pushed. "I was fortunate that the woman I loved was a noblewoman. But if I were the king, I couldn't have married her. Not when there was a foreign princess available. That is the price kings pay."

Dane shot to his feet and paced to the window. He paused, looking out, before marching back. "I don't accept that price."

Lord Claypool sighed. "Josie? What do you say?"

I drew in a shuddery breath. "Dane must marry Princess Illiriya."

Dane rounded on me. "Josie!"

I turned to face Lord Claypool. I couldn't bear to look at Dane. His face was contorted with disbelief and anger. I gave Lord Claypool a small nod of reassurance.

He seemed to understand. "I'll leave you alone to discuss it further," he said, rising.

"There's nothing to discuss," Dane growled.

"I'm going to suggest in our next meeting tomorrow that we send King Phillip a letter proposing marriage between you and Princess Illiriya."

Dane glared at me, but when I said nothing, he strode off to the window again where he remained.

Lord Claypool's gaze softened as he regarded Dane's rigid back and shoulders. "You'll make a good king, Dane. But if you want to be a great king, you must be selfless. Glancia must always come first." He gave me a flat smile. "Thank you for understanding, Josie. And I'm sorry it has to be this way. I truly am."

He left and closed the door, leaving behind a silence so profound it was suffocating. My breaths became shallow, my skin hot and tight. If I didn't know any better, I would have thought myself ill.

I looked up to see Dane standing with his back to the window, his arms folded, and fury imprinted into every frown line. We needed to talk, but I wasn't sure if I could reason with him when his mood was so dark.

CHAPTER 11

*J*t felt as though we were back to those early days of our relationship when I didn't know how to act around him. Should I hold him or keep my distance? Should I be kind or cold?

In the end, it was Dane who made the decision for me. He strode towards me and clasped my face in his hands. "We don't have to do as they say." His eyes had that haunted, lost look again, like they used to in the early weeks of his memory loss. "We can get married today. Now. Then there's nothing they can do about it."

He grabbed my hand and pulled me towards the door.

I planted my feet to the floor and resisted. "Stop, Dane. Stop making this more difficult than it already is."

He rounded on me. "Difficult? There is nothing difficult about my feelings for you. They're very simple to understand. I love you. I want to marry you." He lifted his shoulders in a shrug. "That's it."

"It's not it. You know how it must be, so stop resisting the inevitable. It'll be easier on us both if we accept—"

"I will *not* accept anything else except marriage to you. I will not accept *anyone* other than you."

His words may have been spoken with a harsh edge, but they were the most wonderful things to my ears. Wonderful yet painful. My heart crumpled. My face too as tears spilled down my cheeks.

Dane drew me into his arms, enveloping me in a fierce embrace. His heart raced, his blood pounded, and I could feel the emotion vibrating through him. He held me for a long moment, stroking my hair, my neck, kissing the top of my head.

I wished it could end there. I wished I didn't have to say more or look into his eyes again and tell him that he must marry someone else, but this was not over. With a shuddery breath, I pushed him away and stepped back.

He stepped forward, and I stepped back again. He searched my face and mustn't have liked what he saw because his frown deepened. "We don't have to do what they say," he repeated.

"We aren't doing it because they say so, Dane. We're doing it because Glancia needs an alliance with Vytill."

He shook his head over and over, his gaze continuing to search mine as if he were looking for the woman who loved him. She was not gone, but she had to hide for now.

"Don't do this to me," he murmured. "To us."

I steadied my breathing and met his gaze with my own. "Do you remember when Leon was king, and the subject of his marriage came up?"

"What of it?"

"You agreed that he should marry one of the princesses, either Illiriya or the Dreen one, when she came of age. You said then that it was something he had to do for the sake of Glancia. Why should he have to marry a princess but not you? How is this situation any different?"

"Because he wasn't already in love with someone," he growled.

I backed up to the table and perched on the edge, my fingers clutching the tabletop. It was so hard to say these things and look him in the eye, to tell him it was for the best when my heart screamed in protest.

"Don't pretend you don't love me," Dane said hotly. "Because I know you do."

I lowered my gaze to the floor, unable to stop my tears again. I didn't even bother trying to deny it.

"I know you think you're doing the best thing for the realm," he went on, gentler. "But how is it the best thing when I can't be a good man without you, let alone a good king?"

My head snapped up. "Of course you can."

"You don't know that," he said.

"And you don't know otherwise."

He grunted. "I somehow doubt that being raised as the heir to two kingdoms by a cold elitist like Yelena made me considerate."

I swiped at my damp eyes to see him better. "Dane, you *are* considerate. You're kind and compassionate. You'll make a great king, with or without your memory. It's in your nature to protect those weaker than you. That has nothing to do with me."

He jerked his head away but not before I saw his eyes moisten. "Don't you dare suggest you'll be my mistress."

"I wasn't going to."

I didn't tell him that I would leave Mull forever. If he was going to reside at the palace with another woman, I didn't want to be anywhere near it.

He strode to the door and pulled it open. "I don't know if I want to be king," he said over his shoulder. "So far, I hate everything about it. But I do know one thing. I don't want to do it without you. I *will* marry you, Josie."

* * *

MEG's sympathetic ear was just the tonic my frayed nerves needed. That and the cup of wine her mother put in front of me.

"I'll give you another when you finish that," she said, patting my shoulder.

"It's going to take more than wine for my heart to heal." I gave her a grim smile. "But thanks anyway. You've been very good to me, Mistress Diver. I'm sorry for all the trouble I've brought to your door."

She sighed. "At least you've brought guards as well. Their protection is a comfort."

"Dane's protection is more of a comfort," Meg added. "Now that he's king, the Deerhorns won't dare touch us."

"I wouldn't count on that," I said. "Besides, he's not king yet."

The news I'd brought from the palace hadn't been news at all to the Divers. Dane's announcement had somehow reached Mull already and spread like fire through the village. The market buzzed with it that morning, and Meg claimed the villagers were enthused about the notion of Dane being their king.

Her opinion was confirmed when Lyle and Mr. Diver returned home from work, an escort of two guards in tow. All four piled into the kitchen, their faces flushed, eyes bright and smiles on their faces.

"It has already begun," Lyle said, peering into the pot warming over the fire.

"What has begun?" I asked.

"A gathering in the village green. Everyone's calling for the captain to be confirmed as king." He punched me lightly on the arm in a rather awkward, not quite brotherly, way. "You'll be queen, Josie."

I sighed.

"Lyle!" Meg snapped. "Don't be so insensitive."

Lyle frowned. "What'd I say wrong?"

His mother handed him a bowl of stew. "Eat this and don't talk."

Mr. Diver clamped a hand on his son's shoulder. "Wise words to live by in a house full of women."

His wife and daughter both rolled their eyes.

Mr. Diver accepted a bowl from his wife along with a kiss. "We'll eat and run," he said. "We don't want to miss the rally in the green."

Mistress Diver frowned at him. "I don't like it. You should stay here."

"It'll be peaceful," Lyle said around a mouthful of stew. "It's just all the villagers showing support for Dane." He shrugged. "It's our way of saying if the nobles don't accept him then we won't be happy. It's likely no one important will listen, but we want to do it anyway."

Despite Mistress Divers' protests, Meg and I returned to the green with the men, including the guards. The gathered crowd was nothing like the mob that had caused the riots in the days before we'd left Mull. While the faces were largely the same, the mood was entirely different. Back then, anger and frustration led them to become violent. Today, a sense of hope bolstered their cheers.

Ingrid Swinson, standing on the edge of the crowd, spotted us and waved us over. "Josie! It's so good to have you back." She gave me a hug.

At the sound of my name, those standing nearby turned around. They smiled and I received more hugs and congratulations. The response was quite different to the one I'd received from Sara mere days ago. Dane's declaration continued to work its magic.

"Isn't this exciting?" Mistress Meekles said. "To think, I've met him."

"Is he as good as he seems, Josie?" Peggy asked.

"He'll make an excellent king," I said. "But it's not yet decided."

"We can still hope." Peggy patted my hand. "Lucky you."

"Um…"

"I remember him from the fire," Peggy's husband said. "Good man. Hard worker."

"And to think he's going to be our new king!" Mrs. Meekles clapped. Those around us joined in and soon the rhythmic beat spread through the crowd.

A chant of "Captain for King" started quietly near the front and built to a steady crescendo when it reached the back. It was interjected with whoops and cheers that would have been heard at the outskirts of the village itself. If Dane were here, he'd be embarrassed.

It was something he would have to get used to. The people of Mull loved him.

The cheers suddenly turned to jeers. I stood on my toes again but couldn't see what was happening. Then several people around me shouted in anger. A woman screamed. The crowd moved as one, knocking into each other, pushing me until I was separated from Meg, Lyle and the guards.

I could just make out Meg's voice calling for me over the crowd's shouts of anger.

"Meg!" I called back as I was jostled further away.

The crowd parted as a horse reared. Its hooves punctured the air, perilously close to cowering villagers. Someone tried to grab the reins, only to pull back when they recognized the rider.

It was Lord Xavier, and he was glaring at me.

Beside him was a man wearing the sheriff's uniform. He sat on the saddle, one hand resting on his sword hilt, his thick brow protruding like a cliff over his eyes.

"Disperse!" the sheriff shouted.

"Why?" someone in the crowd shouted back. "We ain't doing wrong!"

"You are not allowed to gather in large numbers like this! A law was passed after the riots. Disperse!" he shouted again. "Or I will use force."

"This is a peaceful gathering!" someone cried.

Lord Xavier drew his sword and pointed it at the speaker. "I recognize you. You work for my father." He pointed the sword at another man. "And you rent one of our houses."

The man shrank back and the crowd swallowed him up. Some people moved away, muttering and shaking their heads. They were too afraid of the consequences if Lord Xavier recognized them. No one in Mull could afford to go against the Deerhorns. They controlled too much, and with the duke of Gladstow on their side, there was no way to overrule their authority.

Lord Xavier rose up in the saddle. "Hear this! The former captain of the palace guards is a liar! A pretender! A traitor to Glancia!" His face reddened beneath his hat and a bead of sweat dripped down his hairline near his ear. "It is only a matter of time before his claim is disproved and he will have to face justice for the crime he has committed." He sat again and raised his sword. He pointed it at me. A sneer stretched his lips into a thin gash. "Anyone who aligns themselves with the traitor will suffer the same fate as him."

The weight of the crowd's stares pressed down on me, but it was that sneer that opened up a pit of despair in my stomach. I was grateful for Meg's hand wrapping around mine and the guards, Lyle, and several others surrounding me. It was a comfort, yet it worried me too. They would be tainted by being associated with me.

We hurried back to the Divers' house through streets shrouded in dusk's eerie glow. No one said a word until we piled into the kitchen.

"Something must be done about them," Meg exploded. "The Deerhorns should not be allowed to break up a peaceful gathering like that. Where will it end? Can we not have fairs anymore? Is the market considered an unlawful gathering? Did they even tell anyone about this new law?"

"No," her father said darkly. "But they can do what they want."

"They shouldn't be allowed! That's the point."

Lyle scoffed. "Who's going to stop them? You?"

Meg folded her arms and bit her lip.

Mistress Diver glared at Lyle and shooed him out of the kitchen. He rolled his eyes but dutifully left. The guards followed him.

Meg used the extra space to pace the floor, hands on hips. "This is wrong. It's not fair. Without a king, we have no one to turn to, no one we can appeal to."

"Wait for Dane to come to the throne," Mistress Diver said.

"That could take weeks. Months! The Deerhorns can do what they want in the meantime. Besides, Dane's going to be busy with running the kingdom. We need to be able to appeal to someone running the village!"

Her father sat at the table with a heavy sigh. "We can't appeal to the governor. Doing so will put an even bigger target on our heads."

Mistress Diver sat too. She looked as though the stuffing had been knocked out of her.

Her husband placed his hand over hers and gave her a flat smile. "What I want to know is, why did Lord Xavier come at all? The sheriff could have dispersed the crowd without his lordship's presence. If it had turned nasty, he could have been in danger."

"He was preening," Meg spat in disgust. "He wanted to show us how powerful he is. He thinks he can't be touched."

"I wonder if his mother knew he was there," Mistress Diver said.

"She must," I said. "He wouldn't do something as public as that without her approval."

Mr. Diver's words got me thinking, however. The sheriff could have handled the situation, so why *was* Lord Xavier there? Perhaps it was to put terror into the minds of the people, or blacken Dane's name.

Or perhaps he was meant to be seen. But why?

Max.

Max had taken a contingent of guards with him to fetch Brant from the Deerhorns' clutches. Lord Deerhorn might not believe in magic, but his wife certainly did, and she was the dangerous one. She would not sit idly by while her plans were scuttled. Lord Xavier's presence in the village was meant to make us think they weren't going to bother trying to beat Max to get to Brant first. But that didn't mean they hadn't sent a small army in his stead.

"I'd better go," I told Meg and her parents. "It's getting dark." I said my goodbyes and Meg walked me to the door. I wouldn't worry her with my theory. Not yet.

She didn't hear me when I bade her goodnight. She was still distracted by her own anger and frustration. "When this is over, and the Deerhorns have been put in their place by Dane, I hope the governor is forced to step down. He doesn't deserve to be in a position of power. The sheriff too. We just need someone worthy to stand in their place." Her frown deepened and her lips twisted to the side as she thought. "Any ideas who would make a good governor, Josie?"

"There's someone in this village who'd make an excellent governor. She's liked and respected, brave and kind. She cares about people and wants to do the best for the villagers, no matter who they are. She just lacks confidence sometimes, but I think she's getting better." I hugged a stunned Meg then left her to contemplate her future.

* * *

THE LOOK of panic on my face was enough for Dane to request a break in the meeting he was conducting with the ministers and advisors. He ushered me into the small office near the council chamber and cupped my face.

"What is it?" he asked. "What's happened?"

"Nothing. Well, something, perhaps. I don't know. There was a gathering in the village which Lord Xavier and the sheriff dispersed, saying it was illegal."

He searched my face. "Are you all right? Did he hurt you?"

"I'm fine. But it got me thinking. It seemed strange for Lord Xavier to be there. It felt forced, like a show. Then I started wondering why his mother would send him into the village to be seen. I think it was to distract us from what they were really doing."

"Which is?"

"Intercepting Max."

He dragged a hand through his hair. It was already messy, as if he'd spent the afternoon raking his fingers through it repeatedly. Dane hated meetings, and I suspected these ones were rather intense. They were certainly long. It was no wonder he was taking his frustration out on his hair.

"You should send more guards after Max," I urged him.

"He already has several. He'll be fine, Josie."

"But—"

"He'll be fine," he said again. "He's smart and capable. The Deerhorns are on the back foot. Lord Xavier's presence at the gathering today proves it, and I can see in the meeting that Lord Deerhorn is rattled."

"Lady Deerhorn is the one you have to worry about."

He grasped my shoulders again. His gaze held mine. "You're the one who worries me."

I pulled away. "Don't, Dane. My mind is made up."

"As is mine," he said darkly. "Josie—"

"Dane!" called Lord Claypool from the council chamber doorway. "Are you ready?"

Dane lowered his head and sighed. "I'll come to the cottage

when these meetings are finished." He kissed my forehead. "I promise I won't be so..." He waved a hand towards Lord Claypool, watching us with a scowl on his brow like the chaperone of a pretty maid.

"Cantankerous?" I finished for Dane. "Stubborn?"

"Distracted." He went to kiss me again, but I moved away and shook my head.

"He's watching."

He hooked me around the waist and pulled me against his body. "Good." His kiss was as thorough as any he'd given me in private.

* * *

DANE DIDN'T COME that night or the next morning. I awoke after a terrible sleep and yawned through breakfast with Kitty. We were alone in the cottage, with two guards stationed outside. I delivered bread and bacon to them and Kitty followed me out with cups of tea.

"Finish that quickly," she told them. "As soon as I'm dressed, I want you to escort me to the palace."

"What are you planning to do?" I asked, following her inside. "You can't risk being seen."

"It's time to put an end to this. I'm going to show them I'm still alive and—"

"You can't!" When she didn't stop, I caught her by the elbow. "Kitty, no. Not yet. The Deerhorns are already feeling threatened. They're unpredictable right now. If you suddenly show up and declare Violette's marriage to Gladstow unlawful, they'll make trouble for certain. It will push them over the edge."

"But that's the thing, Josie. They have power now because they're connected to my husband through Violette. He's protecting them. But if that connection is severed, their power will diminish." She caught my hands in hers. "Last night, you told me all about the dreadful way the Deerhorns are treating the villagers. They have far too much power now. Gladstow is either too weak to oppose them or doesn't care what they do in his name. I lay awake all last night thinking it through, and I kept coming up with one conclusion. I must rise from the dead. This is all I can do to help you, Meg and the other villagers. It's something good and important. Something *worthy*. I want to do it."

She let me go, and I watched her march up the stairs, her steps determined. There was no doubt she wanted to do it. But I suspected she *needed* to do it, for her own sense of self-worth. While she had enjoyed playing an ordinary woman, she was ready to resume her place as the duchess of Gladstow.

I only hoped the guards could keep her safe.

CHAPTER 12

*T*here was no time to warn Dane of Kitty's plan. She dressed quickly in the gown she'd not worn since the day of her staged death. Between the two of us, we managed to wrangle her hair into a tidy if simple arrangement. She had sold all her jewels but found a pair of suitable gloves to cover her worn fingernails.

The palace was not as busy as it had been at the height of King Leon's reign, but there were enough ladies in the salons to make Kitty's entrance satisfyingly dramatic. Gasps and murmurs passed from chamber to chamber, and by the time we reached the council meeting room, we had quite a following intent on viewing the spectacle.

Erik stood guard on one side of the door with Quentin on the other. Both arched their brows, but only Erik spoke. "Are you sure?" he whispered.

"It's too late to back down now." Kitty lifted her chin and raised her voice. "Announce me."

Erik opened the door. "The duchess of Gladstow." When none of the men looked up from the papers spread out on the table, he cleared his throat, loudly. "The *first* duchess of Gladstow!"

Dane glanced up, followed by several others, including Lord Deerhorn. The duke of Gladstow didn't seem to notice the sudden hush, so intent was he on reading a document. It wasn't until Lord Deerhorn pushed back his chair with a scrape and shot to his feet that the duke finally looked up.

"What is the meaning of this!" Lord Deerhorn demanded. "Gladstow! Explain yourself."

The duke paled. His jowls shook. He stared at his wife with a look of utter incredulity. He didn't speak, and I suspected he was struggling to think clearly, let alone form coherent sentences.

"Magic," someone whispered.

"Witch," someone else said.

Dane stood and offered Kitty his chair. "You are most welcome to join us, Your Grace."

She bestowed one of her best duchess smiles on him. "Thank you for your kindness, Dane, in this and in everything." She sat and faced the group of men, her cheeks a little flushed and her eyes dancing. She was enjoying this. "I must apologize for my intrusion. I know you're all very busy, but I couldn't wait. I awoke this morning after living in a fog, my memory returned. I just knew I had to see my dear husband again. I didn't want him thinking me dead for a moment longer."

The duke of Gladstow continued to stare, but the other lords had been jolted out of their shock. The questions began, with Lord Deerhorn's voice rising above them all.

Kitty put up her hands for calm. "Do sit down, my lord, and I will explain."

She waited until Lord Deerhorn sat again before settling her hands in her lap, the picture of the perfect, demure noblewoman. There was nothing of the silliness about her now, no airy quips or giggles. She looked quite at home in the council chamber full of powerful men.

"I fell into the flooded river on my journey to Tilting. This you know. However, I didn't drown. That day is still something of a blur, and somewhat traumatic to recall."

The lord to her right patted her hand. "Take your time."

She smiled and thanked him. "I was saved by a floating log, but I was washed some way down the river. A local farmer found me the next day on the riverbank. I was weak, half-dead, and I'd lost my memory. I couldn't even tell him my name. He took me to his farm and his wife cared for me, nursing me back to health. Since I didn't know where I came from, I stayed with them."

"Ridiculous story," Lord Deerhorn bit off.

"Why?" Dane asked.

Lord Deerhorn bristled. "The farmer must have heard about the drowned duchess. Surely he knew the woman fished out of the river must be she."

"They live in a very remote spot," Kitty said smoothly, "and courtly gossip isn't important to them. On the few times the farmer went to the village, I suspect it never came up."

"You've been with the farmer and his wife all this time?" Lord Claypool asked.

"Until a few days ago when Miss Cully and Captain Hammer stumbled upon me. Oh, forgive me," she said to Dane. "I forgot, you are not known by that name anymore. Should I refer to you as Majesty?"

"Not yet," Dane said, equally as smooth.

"What do you mean they stumbled upon you?" Lord Deerhorn pressed.

"They were heading back along the same road after their travels, and when they reached the bridge where I was washed away, they decided to have another look. They went further afield than their last search."

"We felt certain someone must have come across her body downriver," Dane said. "Indeed, that's all we hoped for: news of a body. We didn't expect to find the duchess alive and well."

"The duke's men searched downriver," Lord Deerhorn shot back.

"Not far enough, it would seem." Kitty gave her husband a sympathetic look. "I don't blame you, Gladstow. You were in mourning and not thinking clearly. Besides, you weren't to have known that I was rescued and taken to a farm. It was just fortunate that on the day Dane and Miss Cully searched again that the farmer was near the river, otherwise I could still be on the farm."

"How did you get your memory back?" one of the lords asked.

"I'm not really sure. It just came back to me today. Since returning, I have stayed with Miss Cully at a place not far from here, so perhaps it was the familiar surroundings that jogged my memory. Or perhaps I simply needed time. Either way, I asked them not to make my presence known. It didn't feel right without any memory of my past. I wasn't ready. Until this morning, that is, when I awoke with full knowledge of everything. Then I insisted on coming here to see my husband." She smiled at the duke of Gladstow. "I have not had an easy time of it, but these last months must have been truly awful for you."

His throat moved but no sounds came out.

One of the lords coughed. The rest wouldn't meet Kitty's gaze, not even Lord Claypool. The duke of Gladstow finally stopped staring at his wife and pressed his hands down on the table, as if about to announce something. But he said nothing.

The thick silence was broken by Lord Deerhorn swearing. He stormed out of the meeting room.

Kitty's brow wrinkled. "He didn't look very pleased to see me." She gave a small shrug. "Never mind. I was never close to the Deerhorns."

"There's a reason for him being upset by your return, as it happens," said the duke of Buxton. He waited but the duke of Gladstow did not take over. "Would you care to tell her, Gladstow, or should I?"

The duke of Gladstow licked his lips. "I must inform Violette." He did not get up, however.

"I suspect it's too late for that." The duke of Buxton nodded at the door through which Lord Deerhorn had just left. "Very well, since you seem to be having trouble grasping this news, let me explain." He turned to Kitty. "Your Grace, I have something rather shocking to tell you. There is no easy way to say it, so I will just come out with it. Your husband remarried."

Kitty clutched her throat. "Remarried? But I was only gone a short while."

The duke of Gladstow sank into his chair.

Kitty blinked back tears. She would have made an excellent actress. "Who is she?"

"Lady Violette."

Kitty's lips formed an O as she glanced at the door. "Now I see why Lord Deerhorn was so upset. Poor Violette. She'll be devastated."

"It's an unfortunate business for everyone involved," the duke of Buxton said matter-of-factly. "It's a situation that could have been averted if patience and the respectful period of mourning had been employed."

The duke of Gladstow sank even further.

"It's most unfortunate for Violette and her family," Kitty rambled on. "Lord and Lady Deerhorn must have been thrilled when you married their daughter, Gladstow. What a blow this news must be to them, but I'm sure the priests will grant an annulment, and it will be as if nothing happened. There. Problem solved." She put out a hand to her husband. "Shall we retire to the ducal apartments? I would like to change into something else. This gown has seen better days. Do you mind, my lords?"

"Not at all," the duke of Buxton said, rising. "The two of you must spend some time together. These meetings can wait." He smiled, looking very much like a man who had wagered on the underdog and just realized he'd won.

The duke of Gladstow stood and took Kitty's hand, a vacant glaze to his eyes and a slackness to his jaw. He resembled a puppet, or rather a puppet in need of a puppeteer to pull his strings. He didn't seem to know what to do.

A commotion at the door stopped Kitty and the duke in their tracks. Erik moved to block the entrance, sword drawn, barring Lord and Lady Deerhorn.

Unlike her husband and the duke of Gladstow, Lady Deerhorn didn't look confused. She looked furious. "Stand aside!" she demanded. When Erik didn't move, she stiffened. "Get out of the way!"

"It's all right, Guard," Kitty said.

Erik stepped aside, but Lady Deerhorn remained in the outer chamber, her face all thunderous fury, her eyes flashing at Kitty.

Kitty rushed forward and embraced her. "Lady Deerhorn, I am in shock. Poor Violette. I know this is awkward, but let's be friends. We have so much in common, after all. I am Gladstow's wife, and your daughter thought she was, briefly. I don't blame you or her, naturally. If only Gladstow had waited a more suitable length of time after my supposed death, we wouldn't be in this predicament now, would we?"

Lady Deerhorn's nostrils flared.

Kitty kept her sympathetic smile in place. "You must have had grand plans. With a duchess for a daughter, you could have achieved new heights." She leaned forward and whispered conspiratorially. "Not to mention how your star would rise if Gladstow became king after the war. Why, you would have been mother to the queen! Dane's declaration put an end to those dreams, of course, and now my reappearance means dear Violette must go back to being the widow of a count. Never mind. She still has her youth and beauty, and I'm sure everyone will be very understanding and kind to her. Her wellbeing is what matters now, don't you agree?"

If Lady Deerhorn's lips pinched any more they'd disappear into her face entirely. Her chest heaved with her breath, and her fists clenched into balls at her sides. She looked ready to explode.

By contrast, Kitty was all elegant gentility, despite sporting a gown that had traveled to Freedland and back in a satchel and her lack of adorning jewels.

Lord Deerhorn clapped his hands together at his back and glared at the duke of Gladstow, as if he expected him to fix this situation in favor of Violette. But there was nothing Gladstow could do. Not here, in front of witnesses.

Erik used his sword to part Lord and Lady Deerhorn. The reunited couple passed between them, Kitty holding onto her husband's arm and smiling as if she didn't have a care in the world.

"I feel different now," she said in a clear voice as they walked off together. "My time away has matured me and helped me understand more of the world. I was like a child before, but I've changed. Other things must change too, now that I'm back, starting with our staff. I'm going to employ my own servants. You won't mind, will you, Gladstow? You have enough on your plate already, without worrying about such trifles. I'm going to find a new maid, and that dreadful housekeeper will be replaced immediately."

I admired her. She really had come a long way from the weak, spoiled girl who'd been at the mercy of her husband. By announcing her intention to employ her own servants in such a public way, she'd given him no choice but to go along with it. He'd employed them to spy on her and manipulate her. She'd been afraid of them. Kitty might never be able to control the duke, but I suspected she would no longer be controlled by him.

As long as the Deerhorns left her alone.

Dane gave Quentin a nod, and he followed the Gladstows. The lords dispersed; the meeting couldn't continue without both dukes present. Lord and Lady Deerhorn remained behind. He huffed at us, his face a patchwork of red blotches. But it was Lady Deerhorn's calmness that chilled my blood. Her ferocious anger of moments ago had cooled, replaced by familiar steeliness.

"The poor duchess," she said. "She should have stayed at the farm and lived out a quiet existence. Palace life can be so... treacherous for the simple-minded."

Dane came up beside me. "You shouldn't mistake her naivety for stupidity."

Her lips curled in a smile. She turned and walked out, her husband trailing behind.

I let out my held breath. "She looked far too smug for my liking."

"She thinks they're going to get the wishes and undo all of this." Dane took my hand and squeezed. "Max should be back today."

"And if he's not? If their men intercept him on the road?" I pressed my fingers into my eyes. "I wish you'd gone with him, Dane."

"He took a lot of guards with him."

"A lot," Erik echoed. "Come, Josie, I will escort you and Dane to the cottage so you can be together."

"I'll join you later," Dane said. "I promised my mother I'd tell her how the meetings went. I'll be as brief as possible. "

"I'll be in the garrison," I told him. "It's too quiet at the cottage alone."

"You will not be alone," Erik said. "I will be there. We can find something to do together. Now that Kitty is gone, I need a new friend." He winked at me.

Dane scowled. "I think staying at the garrison is an excellent idea." He kissed my forehead and strode off.

Erik chuckled. "It is fun to make him jealous."

We left together and took the hidden passageways to the garrison rather than the route through the salons. The nobles preferred not to see servants unless they were delivering food or wine, and I was as good as a servant to most.

"Kitty was magnificent, wasn't she?" Erik said. "I am very proud of her."

"Are you sure you don't mind that she has gone back to Gladstow?" I asked. "You two have become very close."

"We will always be good friends. But she has her road to follow, and I have mine."

"Where does your road lead?"

"To the maids' quarters."

I laughed. "Thank you for cheering me up, Erik."

"I am glad to be of service."

We walked on, with Erik leading the way. I had never quite learned all the different tunnels through the palace's belly. Erik was quiet for a while and he suddenly stopped.

"I think you should be queen," he said.

I sighed. "Don't."

"But if you will not, then I offer myself to be your lover."

"Oh. Er, that's very kind of you." I set off again, trying to hide my smile from him.

"I will be more fun than Dane," he said, lengthening his strides to catch up. "And I promise to adore you."

"But will you be faithful? I prefer my lovers to give me their full attention."

"That will be difficult," he conceded.

"I can see how you would struggle with it."

"It is not my fault. It is the women. There would be weeping if I have to choose. I am sorry, Josie, but if you insist on there being no others, I will have to decline. Try not to be too sad."

I grinned. "I'll drown my sorrows in ale if the garrison has any."

"There is always ale in the garrison."

There were only two other guards seated at the table, both with their booted feet up, their arms crossed and their eyes closed. I didn't want to disturb them but Erik didn't lower his voice and they both awoke with a start, followed by grumbled complaints.

I ordered them to go to bed in the adjoining sleeping quarters and sat at the table. Erik pulled out a deck of cards and had begun shuffling them when Theodore burst in, using the same internal door we'd used to enter.

"Dane said I'd find you here." He'd clearly heard the news going by his bright eyes. "Go on, give me the details. How did Gladstow look when Kitty walked in?"

"Like he wanted to fall through the floor and disappear," I said.

"I wish I'd been there."

"Where have you been?"

"Going through the king's wardrobe and setting aside anything that could be reused for either you or Yelena."

"Hedging your bets?"

He pouted. "Your relationship is not a joke, Josie. It's most upsetting to think that you won't be queen. I'd rather use those fabrics to make you something, but if you keep refusing to marry him..." He sighed.

I touched his knee. "It'll be all right, Theo."

He threw his hands in the air. "How? You and Dane belong together."

I rested my elbows on the table and buried my face in my hands. I groaned. Sometimes I could pretend that I wasn't affected, that everything would be well, but not always. My friends knew better, anyway. I would never be able to convince them.

Theodore sighed again. "He won't accept your refusal. He has made that clear."

"What's he going to do, kidnap me and force me to say the vows in front of a priest?"

"I wouldn't put it past him."

The door opened again, and Balthazar hobbled in. "I hear the duchess is back."

"And quite in control of the situation," I said. "You'd be proud of her, Bal."

"Why? Because she put herself in danger?" He eased himself onto a chair. "Erik, pour me something from the sideboard."

"The Deerhorns won't dare harm her now," Theodore said, also taking a seat. "If something happens to Kitty, everyone will point the finger at them. Even Gladstow isn't stupid enough to stand by them if Dane became king."

Balthazar conceded the point with a nod. "Let's hope you're right."

"You're forgetting something," I said. "The gem and wishes. Lady Deerhorn was angry at first, but after she calmed down, she had a self-assured look."

"That's her regular look," Balthazar pointed out.

"It was more. They have something planned. It's most likely to do with the gem and wishes. I'm very worried about Max and the other guards. It'll be easy enough to intercept them, kidnap Brant again, take Max or one of the others hostage, and demand we give them the gem." The more I thought about it, the more certain I became. "Lady Deerhorn is not going to let us just take Brant. She'd sell her sons to get her hands on those wishes."

Balthazar glanced towards the door leading outside, as if willing Max to walk in with Brant in tow. The door remained firmly shut.

It opened throughout the day, however, as guards came and went. Dora visited with her son, Remy, and we talked about his lessons and he asked me what Freedland was like. Other servants visited to pass the time or to speak with Balthazar about their work. Some asked when we expected Max back.

Dane did not come. Nor did Max.

The afternoon wore on, and everyone's nerves stretched. The ale didn't calm me; nor did pacing around the garrison or strolling to the stables. In fact, my worry increased when we met with Lady Deerhorn and Lord Xavier there. They lingered by the arched entrance, neither summoning a groom from the stable yard to prepare their horses, nor returning to the palace.

I was glad to have Erik and Quentin accompany me. Even in the open, I didn't want to encounter either Deerhorn alone. Theodore wanted to turn back, but I refused to let them see how much we feared them.

"I want to find out what they're doing here," I said.

"I think I know," Quentin said darkly. "And it ain't to look in on the horses."

Erik rested his hand on his sword hilt. "They are watching for Max's return too."

"Not Max," I said. "Brant's return, yes, but not with Max. They've sent their own men on ahead to intercept our guards. I *knew* this would happen. We should have sent more guards with him."

"He took more than a dozen," Quentin said.

Theodore rested a hand on my lower back. "I'm sure Max will be fine." He didn't sound convinced, however.

We'd been foolish to think Max could retrieve Brant when the Deerhorns knew full well where he'd gone. The proof was in Lady Deerhorn and Lord Xavier watching the road at the point where it disappeared into the forest.

They both turned upon hearing our footsteps on the gravel. Lady Deerhorn promptly turned away again, but not before she tossed out a knowing smile.

"Run back to your lover, Miss Cully," Lord Xavier said. "Oh, wait." His top lip lifted with his sneer. "He can only save you if nothing gets in the way of him becoming king. But something extraordinary would need to happen to prevent him claiming the throne, would it not?"

He waited for my response, but I didn't rise to the bait, and after a moment, he turned around again too.

"You don't have the gem," Quentin spat.

"Not yet," Lord Xavier tossed over his shoulder. "But you'll give it to us when the time comes."

His mother shot him a glare. He cleared his throat and continued to watch the road.

I glanced at Theodore, my brow arched. He merely shrugged. It was Erik who signaled to us, indicating the lurking Deerhorn men just inside the archway to the stable yard on one side of the road and the coach house yard on the other. Unlike their mistress and her son, they were not watching the road. They watched us.

I silently indicated we should leave. If the men they'd sent to intercept Max succeeded in retrieving Brant, then these men could easily overpower Quentin and Erik then kidnap me. The Deerhorns would think nothing of doing it here in the open if they possessed Brant. It would be a desperate act, but they were desperate people with the scent of magic in their nostrils.

Erik suddenly cocked his head to the side and stared along the road. A moment later, I heard it too. The thundering hooves of several horses.

"Is it Max?" Quentin asked, hand shielding his eyes from the afternoon glare.

Lady Deerhorn went very still, but Lord Xavier strode off in the direction of the approaching riders. Erik followed him, but Quentin remained with Theodore and me. Theodore took my hand.

The hooves kicked up mud as the horses galloped towards us. It was impossible to count the number of riders, but there were a good number. At least some wore the crimson livery of palace guards. But not all.

I clutched Theodore's hand tighter.

Quentin squinted at the fast approaching riders, counting out loud. "There are enough, but something's wrong. They're not all our men."

The riders sped past Lord Xavier and Erik. Erik let out a whoop.

It was only then that I began to breathe again. But Erik's elation quickly dampened. He looked back along the road, as if waiting for more riders. None came.

I stopped taking notice. When I spotted Max leading the group, I nearly cried out in relief. Thank Hailia he was safe.

"Where are the other guards?" Quentin asked as Max pulled his horse to a stop near us. "And who are they?" He pointed at the riders following the palace guards. Their hands were tied to their saddle pommels and each horse was tied to the one in front.

"They're our prisoners," Max announced. "They intercepted us as we departed the house where Brant was being kept." He dismounted and handed the reins to a groom. He nodded a greeting at Lady Deerhorn and Lord Xavier. "You wouldn't know who these men are, would you, my lady?"

Lady Deerhorn's jaw hardened. She picked up her skirts and marched off towards the palace, her back ramrod straight.

"My lord?" Max prompted. "Do you know them? It's just that one or two said they worked for you."

Lord Xavier swallowed hard and raced after his mother. Their lurking men followed.

I threw my arms around Max. "It's good to see you. What happened?"

"Where's Brant?" Theodore asked.

"On his way, hopefully."

"Hopefully?"

"I knew the Deerhorns would send men after us, so we left here in two batches. I departed the palace first with a dozen men, and Tom left some time later with another six."

"The first group were a false group," Erik said, nodding in understanding.

"A decoy," Theodore corrected him.

"I stayed with the decoy group," Max went on. "I wasn't sure if the Deerhorns' men realized we left in two batches, but if they did, I wanted them to assume my group would be the one to retrieve Brant, since I was the most senior guard. I hoped they'd follow me and not Tom's contingent. Mine was also the larger of the two groups."

"So they intercepted you on the way?" Quentin asked.

Max shook his head. "Not on the way there, on the way back. My men entered the cottage, told Brant to wait for Tom, then we left again, leaving him behind."

"He just obeyed?"

"He had no choice. He was shackled with only two prison guards for company. They were easily dispatched. Tom's men took the longer route, so they could approach from the north, while we headed off again, going south. Shortly after our departure, the Deerhorn men ambushed us." He watched as the prisoners were led away by palace guards. The jail cells would soon be overflowing.

Erik clapped Max on the back. "We did not doubt you had a plan."

"Never," Theodore said, grinning.

"I was expecting them, so we were prepared for their attack," Max went on. "We overpowered them, although it wasn't easy. They outnumbered us. Rylan's got a cut to his arm, but it's not deep."

They hadn't brought back many prisoners, so the rest must have suffered a worse fate at the scene. The ones being led away sported cuts and bruises but no life-threatening injuries.

"So Brant will be here soon," Erik said with another clap on the shoulder for Max.

"Don't celebrate yet," Max said. "Not until he's here."

"There could have been a second ambush group," Quentin added nervously.

We all looked along the road. It was quiet, the dust having resettled. A weighty silence also settled around us, until Theodore broke it.

"You should clean up while we wait," he said to Max. "You've been traveling for two days."

"I'm not going anywhere." Max eyed the horses, drinking from troughs, through the stable yard archway. "If they're not here soon, I'll head out again."

"The Deerhorns won't acknowledge sending those men," Theodore said.

"Of course they won't," I said, gazing after the prisoners. They stopped as someone approached from the palace. I didn't need to see his face to know it was Dane. His physique was so familiar to me.

A sedan chair carried by two men stopped too, then both sedan chair and Dane continued towards us. It was a fair distance to the stable yard and it seemed to take an age before they reached us.

Just as they did, Erik let out a shout. "More riders!"

We all turned to see them racing towards us at full tilt. The group was much smaller, and they did not wear the crimson palace livery. "It's not Tom," I said, voice trembling.

Max smiled. "Have faith in me, Josie. I told them to wear plain clothing."

I frowned to get a better look at the riders' faces then gasped. I recognized Tom and the men with him. All were palace guards. All except Brant, riding in the middle.

Beside me, Dane drew in a deep breath. His gaze connected with Max's. "Well done, my friend. Your plan worked."

Max nodded back. "Thank you, sir. Er, Your Majesty."

"I'll always be just Dane for you."

Balthazar peered out from the sedan chair. He gave a good natured grunt. "Never doubted you, Max. Right, Josie?"

"Never," I said.

The riders stopped directly in front of us. Tom and the other guards smiled and accepted the congratulatory praise from Dane and Max, while Brant merely scowled from the saddle.

Erik reached up and pulled him down, keeping him on his feet as he stumbled. Then he hugged him. "Welcome home, Brant."

Brant used his shoulder to shove him away. "Get off me, you big oaf. I don't want to be here."

"Then you should have resisted," Tom said. To Dane, he added, "He didn't resist. He already had those bruises when we found him."

"You should have given him more," Quentin piped up. "No one would have cared."

Like the Deerhorn men, Brant's hands were tied, and he also sported a bruised cheek and swollen eye. But where the mercenaries' bruises were only just beginning to turn purple, Brant's were already yellow.

"Take him to the garrison," Dane ordered. "Bal?"

"I'll meet you there with the gem," Balthazar said.

"Take an escort. We don't want anything to happen to you before or after you fetch it."

Balthazar settled back into the sedan chair. "I don't have to fetch it. I'll meet you at the garrison," he said again. "I suggest you use the walk to convince Brant to spend the first wish to get our memories back and the second to save himself."

"Save myself?" Brant echoed, watching as the carriers left with the sedan chair between them, an extra spring in their step. "What do you mean, old man?" he called out. When there was no answer, he turned to Dane. "What does he mean?"

"Maybe you could use the last wish to be smarter," Quentin said smugly.

"Shut your hole, rat."

"Bal means that you are going to die on the scaffold," Quentin went on.

Brant stopped. When Max shoved him, he shoved back. "What is he talking about?"

"Murderers are hanged," Dane said. "Everyone knows you killed Leon."

"You arse," Brant snarled. "I saved you by killing him! I saved everyone!"

"Some of the nobles still think he was the legitimate king, so you've committed regicide in their eyes," Dane went on. "In trials of regicide, the judges are five ministers. The Deerhorns have no influence over them. They can't save you in exchange for a wish."

"I don't care about the fucking Deerhorns." Brant licked his swollen, split lip. "Not after what they did to me."

"You will still have the third wish after you use the second to ask for our memories back. Use it to sway the judges into finding you not guilty."

"When will I face trial?" Brant asked.

"Tomorrow morning. Your hanging will be immediately afterwards."

"*If* I'm found guilty."

"You will be unless you use the third wish to save yourself. No one will try to stop you."

Brant lowered his head, his shoulders slumped forward.

Theodore hooked his arm through mine. "Then all the wishes will be used up," he muttered. "Thank the goddess, everything can return to normal."

"Normal," Brant muttered. "What even is that?"

"We've got news for you," Quentin said. "We learned some things in Freedland about all of us, including you." He spent the rest of the walk telling Brant about the prison mine and our pardons.

Dane remained quiet. The pardons didn't include the men in the palace cells. I wasn't sure if he considered Brant a danger like them and excluded him from the pardon too. If so, Brant could free himself from the scaffold in Glancia with the final wish but be caught in Freedland if he returned there.

By the time we reached the garrison, we'd gathered quite a following. Servants emerged from the service commons and the palace itself, blinking into the sunlight and smiling when they recognized Brant. The noblemen must be inside in meetings, but a few noblewomen crossed the inner forecourt only to pause upon seeing the throng of servants and hurry back inside.

There was no sign of the Deerhorns.

Balthazar's sedan chair stood by the door to the garrison, abandoned. We filed inside and I spotted the two burly carriers flanking Balthazar at the head of the table. Servants packed into the room, bodies pressed against one another. It was hot, but no one seemed to care. A hush blanketed the crowd and the thick air pulsed with anticipation. Max and other guards accepted the praise and thanks of their fellow servants, while Brant endured their jeers. Someone spat on him. He wiped the glob from his face with his shoulder.

Balthazar signaled for Brant to be brought to him. "There were three wishes," he began, with all the showmanship of a narrator introducing a theatrical play. "Leon used one. You have the remaining two. Correct?"

"Get on with it," Brant snarled.

Balthazar sighed and shook his head. "You've been trouble from the outset. It's no surprise to anyone that you ended up in a prison mine. Leon should have asked the sorcerer to leave you behind."

Brant's lips peeled back from his teeth in a snarl. He charged forward and almost got to Balthazar before Dane and Max grabbed him and hauled him back.

"Just give me the fucking gem, old man!" Brant shouted. "Then I can get out of this fucking place and go home!"

Balthazar leaned his walking stick against the table and dipped his hands into the pockets of his robes. "It's in here somewhere."

Brant rolled his eyes.

"Ah." Balthazar removed his hand and opened his fist. The gem throbbed as if alive, its blood-red glow lighting up the faces of those leaning in for a closer look.

Brant's eyes widened, his lips parted with his gasp. His face was scarlet from the gem's light. "I feel it," he murmured. "I feel the magic blooming inside me. It's calling me."

His hands, still tied together in front of him, snatched at the gem like a hungry child presented with food.

Balthazar jerked back his hand, fist closed, just as his other whipped out of his pocket and punched Brant in the stomach.

Brant cried out in surprise and pain. He stumbled forward and would have fallen on Balthazar if Dane and Max hadn't held him upright. "You lied," he spluttered. "Give it to me!"

Balthazar went to punch him again. It was only in that moment that I realized he held a small knife. He wasn't punching Brant, he was stabbing him.

He thrust the blade into Brant over and over again.

CHAPTER 13

*D*ane grabbed Balthazar's wrist and snatched the knife off him. "I can't let you," Dane said.

Max lowered Brant to the floor. Those nearest crowded around until Dane ordered them back.

"Let Josie in!" Max shouted.

"No," Dane said. "She's not doing medical work. I won't let her risk her life to save his. Not even here among friends."

Brant's lips moved, but his whispered words couldn't be overheard above the servants' chatter. He was covered in blood. It gushed out of his many wounds, and his face already showed the signs of a man near death. I bent to him and cradled his head.

Dane crouched beside me. "No, Josie."

"It's too late for medical help. No one can save him now." I looked to Balthazar, his own face ashen. He shook violently. "Only the gem can."

Theodore assisted Balthazar to a chair. "Bal?"

Balthazar shook his head.

"Give him the gem!" My voice sounded harsh, unnatural.

Balthazar shook his head again. "He cannot be trusted with even a single wish. He can combine two into one, like Leon."

"It's murder."

"I have weighed up the options over several weeks, and this

is the only way to secure the remaining wishes." His gaze shifted to the barely conscious Brant. "I'm not sorry for my actions today, but I am sorry it had to be done at all. If you were a better man, someone who could be trusted, it wouldn't have been necessary."

Brant made a gurgling sound in his throat. A weak cough brought up blood and his eyes fluttered closed. He expelled a breath and did not draw another.

"He's gone," I said, laying his head back on the floor. I swiped at my tears, a little surprised that I could shed them for this man. But watching someone in their prime die an unnatural death would always be a difficult thing to witness.

"Bal?" Theodore cried. "Bal, are you all right?"

The crowd gasped. Some fell back, away from Balthazar. He shook uncontrollably, but he was no longer pale. The gem's glow lit up his face. But it was the hand holding the gem that frightened the servants. It was a deep red color, not from the gem's glow, but as if it came from inside him, like a light beneath the skin.

Dane crouched before him and clasped his elbows. "Bal?"

Balthazar simply stared at him, his eyes huge. "I can feel it."

"Put the gem down," Dane said. "You look ill."

Balthazar blinked slowly. "I had to do it. You understand, don't you?"

"Yes."

"Josie?"

I closed my eyes to shut out the image of Brant taking his last breath, silently appealing to me for help. I nodded, even though I was not convinced Balthazar's actions had been right. But it was too late to change anything and he needed the reassurance. He was still here. Brant was not.

"I understand," I said going to him. "You inherited the wishes. But Dane's right. You need to put down the gem."

"Not until I've wished." He drew in a steadying breath and lifted his gaze to Dane's.

A hush fell over the garrison. It was as if they'd all become frozen in time, unmoving, not even seeming to breathe. Some clutched the hands of those next to them. Everyone stared at Balthazar, willing him to say the words.

He opened his palm. The gem gently throbbed, as if willing him too. "I wish for our memories to return."

A bright red light exploded from the gem but petered out as quickly as it had flared. It continued to pulse on his palm like a living thing taking a breath.

The gem may have quietened, but the room burst to life. Gasps and small cries filled the garrison. Some of the servants fell back as if they'd been pushed. They reached for chairs or each other to steady themselves. One or two burst into tears and a small number cheered. Outside, there were shouts of incredulity and joy.

I felt out of place, as if I didn't belong among them. The magic wasn't for me. This moment wasn't mine. It belonged to the servants.

The initial excitement and relief quickly faded, replaced by several people talking at once. Others were noticeably quiet, however, mostly women but some men too. Some even fled from the garrison.

The mixed reactions were not unexpected. Most were learning of their criminal past and remembering the awful things they must have done to earn themselves a prison sentence. I could only hope their time as palace servants would help them see they could be better, that they could be something other than a thief, a thug, or a whore.

But even as I took in the reactions around me, there was one reaction that mattered more. Dane's.

He had been silent since getting his memory back. He'd gone quite still, as if moving would shatter the magic. He stared at the floor. I willed him to look up so I could see his eyes and determine how he felt. Unlike many of the servants, he already knew much of his past and his family, but he did not know himself.

Until now.

"Dane?" I asked softly.

He suddenly looked up, as if hearing his name had woken him from a stupor. His eyes were huge. His face flushed.

"Dane? Are you all right?"

He closed the gap between us and clasped my face in his hands. His kiss was thorough and unrelenting, passionate and skillful. It was the kiss of a man who knew what he was doing, who'd kissed many times before. But it was the kiss of a man who loved and loved deeply.

I raked my hands through his hair and pressed my body against his. He grinned against my mouth then finally pulled away.

"Well?" I asked.

I felt giddy with relief, even though I had told myself over and over that he loved me, and that getting his memory back wouldn't change that. There had always been a doubt. It was only now that I could acknowledge it to myself.

He stroked his thumbs over my cheeks and smiled gently. The haunted look I so often saw in his eyes had vanished, replaced with the spark of life. I couldn't help smiling back. Although my heart was still raw with the knowledge we could not be together when he became king, I couldn't set aside the joy I felt in seeing the real Dane for the first time.

"There are so many things I want to tell you," he said. "Some good, some bad. But for now, there are two things you must know. I attacked Carlos the guard in the prison mine with a hammer because he was cruel." He drew in a breath and released it slowly, as if forcing himself to continue. "Laylana bore the brunt of his cruelty."

Poor Laylana. She would be remembering all of that now. I looked around for her friend, the footman, but he wasn't in the garrison. The number of servants had begun to thin. Those remaining spoke in low voices.

Dane stroked my cheek again and I met his gaze once more. "The other thing I want you to know is that I love you, Josie. There is no one else. I have never felt this way about any other."

I nodded rather stupidly, unable to speak.

"My betrothal to Laylana was just an arrangement between our families. We both went along with it willingly but only because we thought it in our best interests." The corner of his mouth lifted, a shadow of a smile. "I didn't believe in love, so I didn't much care whom I married." He pressed his forehead to mine. "Events have since proven me wrong."

"Oh," I managed to whisper.

His smile widened, and he kissed me again. I sank into his body, hoping this moment would last but knowing it would not. It could not.

Someone cleared their throat and we broke apart. Laylana's footman friend stood there looking stricken. "Something's wrong with Laylana," he said. "Her memory hasn't returned."

"How is that possible?" Dane asked.

We all looked to Balthazar. "The magic didn't tell me it was excluding her," he said. "But I don't know how to control it. I don't think I can control it—or question it." He heaved himself to his feet and pointed the end of his walking stick at the internal door. "I want to see her."

His unsteady pace seemed to get faster the closer we got to Laylana's room. The footman led the way with Dane bringing up the rear. We left the others behind in the garrison, too busy with their own chatter to notice us leave.

The footman knocked and Laylana bade us enter. She smiled and pointed at Dane. "You're going to be the king." She frowned at me then scanned the pictures pinned to the walls around her bed. There were dozens of sketched faces drawn by a skillful hand. I wanted to ask the footman if he'd been an artist before he went to the prison mine, but now was not the time. My heart felt hollow. Laylana clearly hadn't got her memory back.

"Josie," she said triumphantly. "And Balthazar, the master of the palace. According to my notes, you've been traveling and discovered we were betrothed." She pointed at Dane. "But you are in love with Josie, and I am not in love with you."

She smiled and held her hand out to the footman. He took it and sat on the bed beside her. He smiled too, but it was troubled. He silently appealed to Balthazar for answers. Balthazar offered none.

"Now what's this about my memory returning?" Laylana asked.

"I asked her if she could remember everything," the footman told us. "She says she doesn't."

"I know I've lost my memory, as have all the other servants." Laylana glanced from Dane to Balthazar and back again. She frowned. "Are you telling me you've *all* got yours back?"

"No, no." Balthazar shuffled forward and sat on the bed too. "Just some. The magic didn't work as well as we thought. I am sorry that you are not among them, Laylana, but you are not alone. Others share your plight."

"Not quite the same as me." She fingered the fringe of a blanket.

The footman put his arm around her shoulders and kissed her temple. "You're not alone, Laylana. I'm here with you. Always."

She leaned into him and smiled wanly. "I may not know much, but I do know that. Did you get your memory back?"

He nodded.

"And you are not betrothed or...or married?"

He shook his head. "I will be soon, if you'll have me."

She grinned and nodded quickly.

Balthazar, Dane and I left them alone, closing the door behind us. "Why did the magic not work on her?" Dane asked.

Balthazar sighed. "I don't know."

"Perhaps she's too traumatized by what happened to her in the prison," I said. "The mind has been known to work tricks after enduring a harrowing event. My father had a patient who could still feel his arm after it was severed in an accident. He said his phantom arm felt cold in winter, or would itch like mad even though it was no longer there. Perhaps this is Laylana's mind's way of coping with what happened to her in prison."

"Should she see a doctor?" Dane asked.

"She could try, but he won't believe in magic."

"Leave her be," Balthazar said. "Perhaps remembering is not a blessing in her instance."

I took Balthazar's arm. "It was kind of you to let her think she wasn't the only one who didn't get their memory back."

He looked down at my hand on his arm. "Does this mean you've forgiven me for Brant?"

"I understand why you did it."

"But have you forgiven me?"

I hesitated then said, "Yes, Bal. I forgive you." It wasn't a lie, but it wasn't the truth, either. I was still conflicted; shocked, even. The taking of a life went against everything I'd been raised to believe. Yet, if there was no other way, if it was done for the greater good or to prevent something worse from happening… Perhaps, in time, I would see the sense in it. For now, I would hide my troubled thoughts from Balthazar.

At least I would try. He was watching me intently, and I had the distinct impression he could read my mind. "What happens now?" I asked as a means of distraction. "A meeting?"

Balthazar nodded. "We'll gather everyone in the commons."

"After the meeting, we'll have a celebration," Dane said. "I'll notify the cook that we'll need as much food as possible. And ale."

Balthazar stopped and rounded on Dane. "What about the noble guests? Who will serve them?"

"They'll have dinner brought to them as usual. After that, their own private staff will have to suffice. The palace servants are enjoying the night off."

Balthazar grunted and started walking again. "I was expecting an arrogant prince-in-waiting who distanced himself from the rest of us now that you have your memory back. Glad to see I was mistaken."

"You're not. I was like that, before the prison mine. But a lot has happened since then. I changed."

"Your mother won't like it."

Dane's smile didn't waver. "Not in the least."

As much as I wanted to speak to Dane privately, I knew it would have to wait. Besides, I wanted to celebrate with the servants too.

My mood dropped dramatically when we returned to the garrison and I spotted Brant's body wrapped in a blanket. I suspected Theodore had seen to it. He was one of the few left in the garrison, along with Quentin and Erik. Most of the other servants had dispersed.

"Max has gone to the village to see Meg," Quentin said in answer to Dane's question.

Dane indicated the body. "Help me get him out of here. We'll take him to the prison cells and bury him tomorrow."

"I remember him in the mine," Quentin said, watching on as Erik and Dane carried Brant out between them. "He was a bit of an arse, and I didn't like him, but he wasn't all bad. He took a beating for me, once."

"As did Dane," Theodore said. "More than once. Erik too, and Max, and a few others. All of them are palace guards now. They protected some of us from the prison guards who thought cruelty was a sport."

Quentin sat and dragged his hand through his unruly hair. For the usually jovial lad, he'd suddenly become quite serious. "I remember it all now. The beatings, the starvation, thirst and fear, the hard work, day and night."

"It was unrelenting," Theodore bit off. "Leon was right when he said he saved us. If not for his wish, we would all be dead by now, even the strongest."

It was a sobering thought, knowing the lives of so many had been saved by a greedy, selfish man. I made a silent promise to remember him more fondly in future.

Balthazar poured ale at the sideboard and handed a cup to Quentin. "The sorcerer turned our protectors into palace guards and made Dane the captain. That is not a coincidence. That was based on who they were, on their nature. Dane was a natural leader. He led by example. Everyone looked to him for how to act, what to say, or for protection."

"Brant respected him," Theodore went on. "Dane was the only one Brant respected."

"That's because Dane beat him up and put him in his place," Quentin said with a half-smile. "Brant was a turd when he first arrived in the mine. He wanted to be the toughest, the one we all feared. But he didn't count on Dane. After that confrontation, he always did as Dane asked, or Hammer, as we knew him then."

Theodore accepted a second cup from Balthazar. "You were good with numbers and being organized, Bal. That's why you were made master of the palace. I was fastidious and good with fabric and clothing, so I was made valet."

"Were you a draper?" Quentin asked.

"A tailor to the royal family of Dreen."

Quentin looked impressed. "That's a highly skilled profession. You must have been well regarded to work for royalty."

Theodore grunted. "Not enough to save me from being thrown into a Freedland prison mine for loving the wrong person."

"How can you be arrested for that?"

"My lover was the justice minister's son."

Quentin's cheeks pinked. "Merdu, Theo. Why'd you risk your life for that?"

Balthazar smacked Quentin's leg with his walking stick and scowled at him. Quentin shrugged and mouthed, "What?"

But Theodore didn't seem as upset by the question as I expected him to be. He simply sighed into his cup. "I did it because I was in love, and I thought he was in love with me and would protect me if we were found out. Apparently he wasn't as in love with me as I thought. His father gave him an ultimatum. Either quietly stand by while I was arrested and removed from the country, or lose his allowance. He chose his allowance."

"Turd," Quentin said. "You're better off without him. Right, Josie?"

I rubbed Theodore's shoulder. "You're better off staying here," I said. "Don't go back to Dreen. Besides, Dane will need you when he becomes king. If it was left to him, he'd only wear black." I frowned. "Or perhaps that'll change, now that he remembers clothing can be worn in other colors."

Quentin chuckled. "You're going to need a maid too, Josie."

"Don't, Quentin. Dane's marrying Illiriya, and that's final." I put up my hand when he protested, but it was the return of Dane and Erik that stopped him.

"Tell us about you," Theodore said to Quentin. "Why were you arrested? You never told us when we were all in the prison mine together."

"Aye, who did you annoy?" Erik asked.

"My father," Quentin said.

"What did he do to you?" Dane asked.

"It's not what he did to me, it's what I did to him. I hit him over the head with an iron rod. He didn't die, if that's what you're thinking. He survived. But I wanted to kill him in that moment."

I pulled up a chair and sat beside him. I touched his knee. "What happened?"

"He's a blacksmith in Logios in Dreen. He wanted me to be something more than him, so when I showed early promise with learning, he pushed me to join the college of engineers. But I hated it. I didn't study so I failed and was thrown out. My father got real angry and started hitting me. He just kept punching and kicking me, calling me a disappointment, over and over. Ever since my mother died, he drank most nights, and when he was drunk, he turned violent. That day, he hit me until I fell. I landed near the furnace, grabbed an iron bar he'd been about to work on, and smashed it into his head."

"Someone must have seen it happen," Dane said. "They must have reported you to the authorities."

Quentin lowered his head. "My father reported me. I was arrested, and because it was my own father, the magistrate said it was a heinous crime and sentenced me to the prison mine."

Balthazar clasped Quentin's shoulder. "You are welcome to make the palace your home now. I'll see that there's always work here for you."

Quentin merely shrugged a shoulder. "Maybe."

"Or you can go to medical college if you want," I said. "We'll find a way, even with your criminal record."

"I'll see to it," Dane said, ruffling Quentin's hair. "You don't have to return to your father's house."

Quentin gave him a sheepish look. "My father was real sorry when I was sentenced to a prison mine in Freedland. He thought I'd just end up in a regular prison for a short while. I think he regretted reporting me."

"He has more to regret than that," Balthazar said. "I may not have children, but I like to think I'd make a better father than yours."

Erik thumped Balthazar on the back so hard that Balthazar almost lost his balance. Erik caught him and steadied him, his grin still in place.

"But why did the sorcerer make Quentin a guard?" Erik squeezed Quentin's arm. "He is puny."

"To protect him?" Balthazar said with a shrug. "You, Dane, Max and the others took care of him, just as they took care of Leon in the mine. Perhaps the sorcerer thought it best to keep him close to you."

Erik punched Quentin lightly and winked at him when Quentin frowned back. "Lucky you. Being a guard is the best. Better than a footman."

"What about you, Erik?" I asked the Marginer. "Were you arrested for horse theft?"

"Aye," he said. "In Freedland."

"But why did you leave the Margin in the first place?"

"I slept with the wrong woman. She was the wife of my clan's chief." He sighed theatrically. "She was beautiful but far above me. I was one of her personal guard, but she ignored me. Until one day, she stopped ignoring me and slept with me." He grinned. "My smile and charm won her affection."

"But her husband found out," Theodore said. He must have heard the story when they were prisoners together in the mine.

"Aye, the chief wanted to kill me. In the Margin, when a man's wife strays, the husband and the lover must decide who wins her by hand to hand combat." He raised his fists and settled into a fighting stance. "But he knew I would win. I was young and handsome."

"Being handsome doesn't count in a fight," Quentin said, smirking.

"I was strong and good with my fists. He could not beat me. So he sent an assassin to kill me in my sleep. But I awoke and fought the assassin off then escaped. It was the only way to keep my freedom. If I stayed, I either win the fight or he sends another assassin and I die."

Quentin frowned. "Isn't winning the fight a good thing?"

"No! Because then I would have to marry his wife. She was beautiful and lovely, but I did not wish to marry her." Erik wrinkled his nose. "Marriage is for men like you and Dane." He winked at Dane. "Men who can only love one woman. I have to love many."

Quentin rolled his eyes. "You don't *have* to."

Erik blinked up at the ceiling, as if giving this serious thought. Then with a shrug of his shoulders, he dismissed the notion. "You are wrong. I have to. It is who I am."

Dane poured himself an ale but had barely taken a sip before announcing he should leave to see that celebrations were being prepared. "We'll wait for Max to return before we have our meeting in the commons." He pecked my cheek before I even knew what he was doing and turned to Balthazar. "I almost forgot in the excitement. The gem. I should keep it safe for you until we decide what to use the third wish on."

Balthazar jangled his pocket. "It's here. It's safe."

"We will protect him," Erik said. "Me and Quentin, and Max when he gets back."

"We'll all go to the commons," Theodore said, rising. "The Deerhorns won't trouble us there."

Dane was about to leave when Balthazar beckoned him back. "You should know that we were right about the high priest. I did tell him what I'd discovered about you in the temple's archives. I wanted his opinion. He suggested we burn your parents' marriage document and your birth registration. He wanted Freedland to remain a republic. With that evidence in existence, he could foresee the Averlea royalists winning once they got enough support."

Dane nodded, as if it were just another piece of the complex puzzle of his life. He didn't seem to care overmuch. I suspected he'd long since come to terms with how events had played out—and the high priest's role in them.

"Dane's mere existence threatened to end the republic," I added. "Or so the high priest thought. He hoped the prison mine would do what he couldn't."

"What about Glancia?" Dane asked. "Did he care what happened here?"

"He wanted to kill two birds with one stone," Balthazar said. "Your death would mean neither the Averlea nor the Glancian throne would have an heir. Freedland would remain a republic and the Glancian dukes would battle it out but hopefully have no clear winner, sowing the seeds to becoming a republic."

"No doubt he would have helped those seeds grow by speaking seditious words into the right ears," Dane added.

"I couldn't believe it when he suggested sending assassins to murder you. I couldn't condone that, not until I'd determined for myself what your plans were. I left Tilting that night and raced south. I warned you immediately upon my arrival in Noxford, but it was too late. The high priest's message reached the authorities before you could go into hiding."

"Thank you, Bal. I'm glad our accusations weren't way off."

"I'm prepared to tell the dukes and other nobles what he did," Balthazar said. "If it's what you want."

"The high priest will refute your claim. He'll say you're lying."

"And I will say I'm not. I think with Yelena's letters from Prince Hugo, it will be enough."

Dane gave a single nod. "Let's not worry about it. We have something to celebrate, and I intend to do just that." He glanced at me then strode out of the garrison.

We followed behind at a distance. I was quite happy to maintain a slower pace. I wanted to find out more about their pasts.

"Do you remember Leon in the prison mine?" I asked.

"He whined all the time," Quentin said. "Such a little turd."

"He was a fool," Balthazar added. "But he'd been orphaned from a young age and brought up by a troop of actors in Vytill. Acting was his whole life. He knew nothing else. I think he spent so long pretending to be someone he wasn't, he could no longer maintain the façade in the mine when the situation became desperate. That's when his true nature came out."

"He wasn't too bright," Theodore said on a sigh. "He mocked King Phillip when he was in Merrin."

Quentin snorted. "I might have failed at engineering, but he failed common sense."

"Is that a subject they teach at college?" Erik asked.

Theodore laughed softly. "No, but it should be."

We continued the walk towards the two forecourts, the palace's northern wing on our right. It was some distance and it seemed even further thanks to Balthazar's plodding pace. We rounded the first of the pavilions flanking the forecourts to see some of the servants milling around the fountain, talking. Dane stood on the porch steps with the two dukes and Kitty, her hand wrapped tightly around her husband's arm.

Dane said something to the dukes then continued on his way towards the commons, situated behind the far pavilion. The dukes gave brief bows to his retreating figure.

Kitty spotted us and excused herself. The duke of Buxton gave a short bow as she departed. Kitty's husband, the duke of Gladstow, merely scowled. Both retreated back into the palace.

Kitty took my hands in both of hers, a grin splitting her face. "Dare I hope these celebrations are because you all got your memories back?"

"It is true," Erik said, smiling.

"I am so thrilled for you all!" She glanced behind her towards the palace entrance. "I would embrace each of you but I'd better not. Gladstow is probably watching."

"How is it with him?" I asked.

"Fine. I got rid of all the servants we brought here and I am using palace staff for now." She flapped her hand in the air. "Piffle. They're gone. Like magic, it was." She giggled.

"Be careful with him. He's no fool, and he likes being in control."

"Don't worry about me. I'm determined not to let it get as bad as it used to be. If I have learned anything on our journey it's that I must take control and responsibility. If I wanted to eat, I had to cook. If I wanted clean hair, I had to wash it. If I want trustworthy servants, I must hire them myself. Good staff won't make everything better between Gladstow and me, but at least I'll no longer feel like an unwelcome visitor in my own home."

"It's a start," I assured her. "A good start. But you know you can always come here if you need to get away from him again."

She arched her brow, a sly smile on her lips. "Does that mean you'll still be at the palace after Dane becomes king?"

I sighed. "Of all people, you know he can't marry me."

"I wasn't suggesting marriage, but as his lover—"

"No! Dane would never do that to his wife."

"Nor to you, Josie," Theodore added. "Kitty, it's up to Josie and Dane to determine what happens next."

"Not true," Balthazar said, walking on. "Not true at all."

Kitty held me back and reassured me once again that being the king's mistress could be a position of power and influence. I cut her off. I didn't want to hear it. We parted, she returning to the palace and me heading to the commons with the others.

The commons courtyard was filled with servants in conversation. Not all looked happy, but there was an overall sense of positivity and hope. Dane was nowhere in sight, but I spotted him a little later, in deep conversation with some men dressed in gardening clothes. More and more servants turned up until the courtyard brimmed with excited faces. They spilled into the large dining room adjoining the courtyard and outside the commons building. There must be no one manning the gondolas on the lake, or the menagerie, orangery or laundry. All the inside staff, footmen and maids, were present too. Only the kitchen staff were missing. The delicious smells wafting to us from the enormous basement kitchens confirmed they were still working.

I could not approach Dane, surrounded as he was by servants. Balthazar was popular too, shaking hands with the staff who wanted to thank him for wishing back their memories. He answered their questions about the magic and the sorcerer, albeit vaguely.

"They all think the sorcerer is a person walking amongst us," he told me later. "But it is not a physical entity, just an intuition, a feeling, something that resides within the wish holder, compelling him to use the wishes." He tapped his chest. "It's like an ache, a longing. It must have been difficult for Brant holding the wishes but denied the gem."

"You sound sympathetic."

He eyed me sideways. "I didn't want to kill him, Josie."

I nodded.

He settled both hands on the head of his walking stick. "You don't forgive me."

"I didn't say that."

"You don't have to."

"Josie!" shouted a familiar voice.

I looked up to see Meg heading towards me through the

crowd. Max was behind her, but he was waylaid by a footman who wanted to speak to him and clap him on the back.

She hugged me, grinning, and then hugged Balthazar. "I hear you played a significant role in this, Bal."

"Perhaps a little too significant."

Her smile turned sympathetic. "You must feel awful. You don't look terribly well."

"It's the third wish, calling him," I said. "Bal, why don't you sit down?"

"This is a little overwhelming," he said, turning away. "But first, we should start the meeting, now that Max is back. Have you seen Dane?"

I stood on my toes and looked over the sea of heads. As if he sensed me, he looked up. I waved him over.

He joined us, telling those he passed that it was time for a meeting. It turned out to be a brief session, with Dane announcing that everyone was free to leave the palace or stay as a member of staff, but Balthazar would appreciate notification of everyone's intentions as soon as possible.

"So Balthazar is staying?" someone asked.

"I am," Balthazar said. "This feels like home to me now."

"And you, sir?" one of the guards asked Dane. "Are you going to be king?"

"My situation is not yet settled," Dane said. "What happens for me next depends on the decisions of others. I'll let you know as soon as I know."

"But you'll be staying here or in Mull regardless, because of Josie."

"Yes." He then reminded them they had pardons from the Freedland authorities and could safely return there if they chose. His final words were about the prisoners in the palace cells.

"Those men are the only ones who deserve to remain locked away. The crimes they committed here, after losing their memories, mean they won't ever be released. They can't be trusted in society. You are not like them. You may have been sent to the same prison mine, but after you lost your memories, you didn't commit another crime. That's all I need to know about you. I don't care what you did before, it's what has happened since that matters. That's why I trust all of you to remain here as staff. Consider the loss of our memories as a line. What you did on one side of that line is irrelevant. Only what you've done on this side is important. Take advantage of the second chance the sorcerer gave you. Don't cross back over that line. Stay on this side and you will not regret it."

Applause, cheers and whistles erupted. Everyone wanted to shake his hand or thank him, and to wish him good luck. He was edged away from us by the tide. With Meg chatting to Theodore and Quentin, I took the opportunity to talk to Max.

"Well?" I asked. "Have you asked her to marry you?"

"Not yet. I'm working up the courage."

"Just ask her, Max. There's nothing standing in your way now." When he wouldn't meet my gaze, I added, "Is there?"

"Her parents don't know about my past. They won't want her with a fellow like me."

"You mean a kind-hearted, loyal and trustworthy fellow? No, Max, that's not the sort of man they want for her at all."

He gave me a lopsided smile. "Fine. I'll ask her tomorrow and we'll speak with them together. There is some good news. Balthazar should hear this. Bal!"

Balthazar joined us, his wrinkles angled into a frown. "It's madness in here and will only grow worse when they start drinking."

"They have a lot to celebrate," Max said. "As I do. I wanted you to know, I remember it wasn't me who started the fire in the goldsmith's shop in Noxford. I'm innocent of that crime, at least."

"Congratulations," Balthazar said wryly. "But we suspected as much."

We'd suspected the person who'd killed the goldsmith and his wife had started the fire to cover up the murders, but it had troubled Max ever since learning he'd been arrested and sent to the prison mine for arson.

"There's more," he went on. "When we were inside the prison, I learned who did start it. He bragged about getting away with murder, only to be arrested for something else later." His gaze connected with Balthazar's. "It was Brant."

Balthazar leaned heavily on his walking stick. He nodded, his gaze unfocused. "I see."

"I thought you might like to know."

"Why? Because it justifies me killing him?"

Max shrugged.

Balthazar shook his head. "It's still not enough."

"Enough for what?"

"For Josie to forgive me." Balthazar walked off through the crowd.

I let him go, not sure if he wanted me to follow or if he preferred to be alone.

Thankfully I was soon distracted by the appearance of Miranda and Kitty, dressed in maids' uniforms. They looked so odd that I burst out laughing.

"It was Miranda's idea," Kitty said cheerfully.

"You were the one who wanted to join in the celebrations," Miranda chided with a smile.

Kitty grinned. "I feel as though I should. These are my friends, after all. Without them, I wouldn't be alive today." She threw her arms around me. "Isn't it wonderful, Josie? I'm so happy for all of them."

Erik came up behind her and wrapped his arm around her waist. He planted a kiss on the back of her neck. "I like the uniform on you. You should come to me like this."

She swatted his shoulder. "I won't be coming to you again, Erik dearest. Don't look so upset, you know it must be this way."

"Aye, but I miss you."

"Look at all the lovely maids here. Surely a man like you will be too busy to miss just one."

"But you are special. You are my duchess."

She kissed her fingertips then touched his cheek. "And you are my dear Marginer. I shall cherish the moments we spent together."

I looked away so as not to intrude and spotted Yelena making her way to Dane. She interrupted his conversation. She spoke to him and he said something back, shaking his head. He turned away, but she grabbed his arm, forcing him to look at her again.

Whatever she said next had him frowning and shaking his head again. Then they both looked in my direction.

CHAPTER 14

*D*ane wove his way through the crowd to me, took my hand, and led me outside. His mother followed.

"Don't walk off on me," she snapped.

"I'm not walking off; I'm going somewhere we can talk. It's too loud here." He led us behind the commons where still more servants could be found. We had to walk almost to the end of the southern wing of the palace overlooking the orangery before we could be alone.

"Slow down," Yelena growled.

Dane finally stopped but didn't turn around. He looked over the orangery and formal lawn, with its paths and statues, towards the small lake where we used to meet sometimes if we wanted to be alone. The water looked calm in the early evening twilight. Dane's eyes, when he faced us, were anything but calm.

"If not because of her then why?" Yelena asked, picking up the conversation they must have started inside.

"My mother expected me to return to Freedland and reclaim my birthright now that my memory has returned," Dane told me. "I explained that I won't and that my decision has nothing to do with you, and that's the truth."

"Then if not Josie, why?" Yelena asked again.

Dane's fingers tightened around my hand. "My reasons

remain unchanged. I have no interest in the Freedland throne. They're better off as a republic—"

"Nonsense. They're better off with a strong, capable leader such as yourself." She clasped his other hand between both of hers. "You belong on that throne, Dane. Averlea is your home."

He snatched his hand away. "Not anymore. My decision is final."

She flinched as if he'd snapped his fingers close to her face. "I don't understand. You have your memory back now. Why are you still like this? Why do you not think as you used to?"

Dane scrubbed a hand over his jaw, hesitating.

"What was he like before?" I asked Yelena.

"Sensible," she said snippily, annoyed at my interruption. "He understood his obligations and embraced them. He welcomed his duty and looked forward to the day he could claim the Averlea crown for himself."

"I've changed," he growled.

"Because of *her*."

"Because of what happened to me since my arrest last year. The prison mine changed me, and then the loss of my memory and working here changed me more. I used to do what I was told. I was dutiful, to a fault."

"Duty is not a fault."

"It is when that duty is the worst outcome, not just for the people of Freedland but for me too."

She scoffed. "How is becoming king bad for you?"

"There was not enough support. Our coup would have failed, and I would have been executed. Is that not a good enough reason?"

"There *was* enough support."

He shook his head. "Ever since regaining my memory, I've been going over the numbers. It wouldn't have worked. We didn't have enough money or mercenaries. I can see that now, but I couldn't see it then. I believed what I was told. I didn't question it; I didn't dig deeper."

"You weren't stupid, Dane."

"But I was naïve. I believed I should reclaim the throne because it was the right thing to do, the natural order, that a son in my position must do his duty, whatever the consequence. I never thought about what was right." He tapped his chest. "I also never thought about what I truly wanted."

She made a scoffing sound again, but it settled into a brief, dry cough.

"Yelena, are you all right?" I asked, touching her elbow.

She shook me off. "Are you saying you never wanted the throne?"

"That's what I'm saying," Dane said. "Back then, I lacked the courage to voice my opinion and go against what you and people like the Rotherhydes wanted."

"You are the bravest person I know. You certainly never lacked courage."

"In that I did."

She stared at him, her features hard, not a hint of a tear in her eyes. But there was no denying her age now. She looked tired, drawn, like a woman well past her prime. I wondered if her own ambitions had finally exhausted her or if disappointment at Dane's decision aged her prematurely.

He adjusted his grip on my hand. "I matured in the mine and here, as captain of the guards. I became the man you always claimed me to be."

"You *were* that man already."

"I wasn't. I know that now. From this moment on, I make my own decisions, and they are based on what I want, not what you want for me. And my decision is final. I won't be returning to Freedland. Glancia is my home."

Her gaze slid to me, ice-cold. She picked up her skirts and went to march off, only to stop. "Then the Glancian throne will have to do. You ought to know I have just come from speaking to the two dukes. I urged them to write to King Phillip with an offer for his daughter's hand. They agreed that she is the only acceptable bride for you. For Glancia. *Both* dukes agreed, Dane. There's no getting out of it now."

He stiffened. His fingers tightened so much that I had to touch them with my other hand. He relaxed a little as he watched his mother walk off towards the palace, but his features remained firm.

"Come with me," he said, turning to the orangery.

I resisted, planting my feet onto the ground. "No, Dane. We should go back to the commons."

He heaved in a deep breath as if stopping himself from throwing me over his shoulder and hauling me off. "Very well. I'll say what I want to say here."

He dipped his head to meet my gaze. His eyes still simmered with anger, but each throb of his pulse brought back a little more of his humanity.

"I was an arse," he said.

I couldn't help the bubble of laughter escaping, and that dispersed the last vestiges of his anger. He smirked.

"It's true," he said. "I was an arse to everyone in Noxford, before my arrest. Laylana only agreed to marry me because her brother promised her a very good allowance. To be honest, she was somewhat greedy and narcissistic."

"So you weren't very nice. Is there a point to this story?"

"I just wanted you to know that I was arrogant and self-centered. Leon was a good actor in that regard. He mimicked me well."

"But that was the old Dane," I said. "The Dane from before the prison mine."

He nodded. "I meant it when I told Yelena I never wanted to be king, even then. Not really. I would have taken the throne if it was presented to me, but I certainly didn't want to work for it."

"You pretended to want it to appease her."

He nodded again. "But I meant it when I say I've changed. I grew up. I'm not that person anymore, thank the goddess." He smiled gently and stroked the underside of my jaw with his knuckles.

I moved away and headed off in the direction of the commons. He fell into step alongside me. "You called her Yelena just now," I said.

"I only call her Mother to her face. Martha brought me up. She's more like a mother to me. I should go and see her. I feel bad that I haven't treated her as she deserves."

"Like a mother."

"Like *my* mother," he murmured.

Someone waved at us from the commons. "Is that Quentin?" I asked. "What's he holding?"

"Two cups, probably containing ale. He wants us to join him."

"You go see Martha. I'll tell him you're on your way."

Dane caught me around the waist and trapped me against his body. His gaze softened. "I'll let you go, for now, but this conversation is not over. Not until you believe me when I say I *am* going to marry you."

"You heard what Yelena said. It's impossible. I know it, Dane, and I've accepted it."

"I don't believe you."

"But—"

He put up a finger to silence me. "I won't hear anything more about it unless you want to tell me the date you've set for our wedding." He let me go and walked off, his steps purposeful.

"You're still an arse!" I called out.

He flashed me a grin over his shoulder. "But you love me anyway."

"Definitely still arrogant and self-centered," I muttered as I walked off to join Quentin.

* * *

MEG and I returned to the cottage sometime during the night, taking a contingent of guards as protection. Max was among them but Dane was not. I'd left him deep in conversation with Balthazar and Theodore. The guards had continued their celebrations at the cottage but ran out of ale some time before dawn.

I fell asleep in a chair downstairs with Quentin lying on the floor beside me and Erik sprawled in one of the other chairs, snoring softly. The stairs creaked and I cracked open an eye. I smiled.

"Good morning, Max," I said, my voice gravelly.

He froze with his boots in one hand and his doublet in the other.

"Are you hungry? I'm about to cook some breakfast."

"Um."

"Will you ask Meg if she wants breakfast?"

He went back up the stairs. A moment later, Meg came down.

"You've terrified him," she said with a smile. "He thinks you're going to chastise him for taking my virtue."

"I will chastise him, but only to tell him he shouldn't have taken so long. I've known for some time that he's in love with you."

She hooked her arm through mine, stepped over Quentin, and steered me into the kitchen. "I suspected, but I don't have much experience with men. I wasn't sure how deep his feelings ran. Not until he came for me yesterday, directly after getting his memory back." Her smile widened. "He said he wanted me to be the first person he told about himself. About his true self."

I hugged her arm. "He's worried what your family will think of his criminal past."

"They won't like it, but I don't care. Being with him is my decision and they need to accept that. I refuse to be smothered anymore."

I picked up a pan and went in search of eggs in the larder. "I'm glad to hear it. You're quite formidable when you want to be. I don't envy anyone standing in your way now." I scooped up the basketful of eggs and returned to the kitchen.

Meg fanned the glowing coals in the fireplace with a cloth. "Is that your way of encouraging me to put my hand up for a council position again?"

"I was still referring to marrying Max, but very well. It can be about that too."

She smirked. "Very coy, Josie. Is that how you plan to win Dane over?"

"I'm not trying to win him over, I'm trying to get rid of him." I studied the basket of eggs and sighed. "He says he's still going to marry me. I thought once he got his memory back he'd see how impossible it is, that he'd just *know* he had to make a strategic marriage. But he's still refusing to entertain the thought of marrying Princess Illiriya, even though everyone else talks of it as a foregone conclusion. Including me."

She took the pan from me and placed it over the low flames. "I still can't believe he's the heir to two kingdoms. I also still struggle to believe the extraordinary events that led him and the others here."

"It is extraordinary," I agreed. "And tragic too, for the lives that were shattered in that prison mine." I thought of Laylana and many others who'd endured so much there. Some might wish they'd never got their memories back.

"What about the last wish?" Meg asked. "What do you think Balthazar will use it for?"

I gasped as a thought occurred to me. "I hope Dane doesn't try to convince Balthazar to wish for me to marry him."

"Why not?"

"Because it should be used on something important."

"Marrying you is important."

"I mean something for the wellbeing of everyone."

"I wish you'd think about yourself, for once, Josie. Anyway, I'm sure Balthazar will use it wisely."

"Even so, I'm going to the palace after breakfast."

I was summoned to the palace before I'd finished my eggs, however. I headed off with the bleary-eyed guard, along with an equally bleary-eyed Quentin and Erik. If the Deerhorns knew where to find me, they'd be wise to ambush us now. The guards were not at their sharpest.

"Did Dane say why he wanted to see me?" I asked the guard who'd delivered the message as we rode back to the palace.

"He said he needs to announce something important, and he wanted you there."

The image of Dane and Balthazar in conversation last night came to mind. They'd looked in earnest. Whatever they'd discussed had been serious.

My modest escort led me through the palace's service corridors to the vast complex of formal and informal rooms that made up the king's apartments. The antechamber to the council meeting room held little furniture. Attendants were not expected to sit. The only seating was the throne covered in crimson velvet. Leon's personal insignia of two entwined Ls embroidered into the cushioned seat in gold thread now looked like the boast of an inadequate man.

None of the nobles noticed my entrance until Dane, standing

beside the throne, acknowledged me with a nod. Even then it was only the Deerhorns who followed his gaze.

"What's she doing here?" Lord Deerhorn demanded. "She has no right."

Dane silenced the quiet chatter with a raised hand then lowered it. "Erik, please bring in a chair for Balthazar and anyone else who requires one."

Murmurs rippled around the chamber as the noblemen and women considered this strange request.

"But this is not a room for sitting in," one of the lords protested. "Only you should sit." He indicated the throne.

Dane looked surprised by the seemingly offhanded comment. It was more than a simple statement of fact. It proved that this lord accepted Dane's status as king. Going by the many nods around the room, others did too.

"Yes, try it out," the duke of Buxton urged.

Dane shook his head.

"Go on. It's yours."

"Not yet," Dane said.

"But it will be. We've decided, haven't we, Gladstow?"

The duke of Gladstow nodded. The murmurs increased in volume, but not in protest—in agreement. No one spoke against Dane's claim. Not a single person. I could no longer see the Deerhorns, however. They must be seething.

"I'll stand," Dane said, as Erik carried a chair to the front and situated it beside the throne.

Balthazar sank onto it with a grateful sigh. Then he stamped the end of his walking stick into the tiled floor. The room hushed once more.

"Before Dane Lockhart speaks, you should know that someone in this room tried to stop me bringing him here," he said. "It was almost two years ago when I first discovered the marriage and birth documents his mother sent to the master of Merdu's Guards. As the temple archivist, I stumbled upon them during a routine reorganization. Uncertain as to what it all meant, I spoke with my good friend and superior, the high priest of Glancia."

All heads swiveled towards the high priest, standing utterly still by the window. He stared straight ahead, hands clasped at his back, not quite looking at anyone.

"But he denied seeing those documents," the duke of Gladstow said.

"He lied."

Whispers became gasps. Someone protested that he couldn't accuse the high priest of dishonesty.

Balthazar merely shrugged. "He lied and then he had me accosted in Freedland, where the documents were confiscated. They've most likely been destroyed." He adjusted his grip on the head of his walking stick and fixed his glare on the high priest.

The high priest's gaze suddenly sharpened into focus. "This is an outrageous lie! And I considered you a friend."

"My point is," Balthazar went on. "I have seen the documents you all asked for as proof of Dane's claim. That proof has been destroyed, and now there is only my word over the high priest's."

The high priest scoffed. "Why should they believe you? *I* am the high priest of Glancia! I am the conscience of the kingdom!"

"I know you did what you thought was best for the kingdom," Dane went on. "I have no wish to see you punished for your crimes."

Balthazar wagged a finger at Dane. "You saw the documents too, when I presented them to you in Noxford."

Dane nodded. "The high priest alerted the Freedland authorities to their existence," he said. "It's why I was arrested and thrown into prison when I had committed no crime."

More gasps of shock sucked the air from the room.

"How awful for you," one of the ladies declared.

"Our own king imprisoned!"

"He was only the heir at that point," Balthazar said. "King Alain was still alive."

"Nevertheless, strong words should be issued to the high minister of Freedland," Lord Claypool said. "Perhaps trade sanctions until a formal apology is received."

Dane watched on with a confused frown as the voices grew louder with the nobles speaking over one another. It was left to the duke of Gladstow to quiet the room.

"The documents are now irrelevant anyway," he said to Dane. "No one doubts your claim. The letters from Prince Hugo to your mother, the former Princess Yelena of Averlea, have been accepted as evidence."

Dane arched his brows at the duke of Gladstow. I understood his surprise. The duke's unquestioning agreement was unfathomable. There could only be one reason for it—Kitty. She must have somehow convinced him.

"We *all* accept her evidence," the duke of Buxton assured Dane.

Not a single noble disagreed. I tried to see the Deerhorns' reactions, but they were out of my line of sight.

"Good," Balthazar declared. "Then Dane's authority is accepted."

"It is," the duke of Buxton said. "We can have the formal documentation drawn up today for signing. After that, the rest is mere pomp for the people."

Dane settled his hand on the throne's back, steadying himself, perhaps, from the shock of how easy it had all been. He'd expected a fight, not just from the duke of Gladstow and the Deerhorns but from others too. But not a single dissenting voice could be heard. I suspected the Deerhorns didn't dare when the tide was clearly in Dane's favor.

I blew out a held breath and met his gaze. I nodded. He nodded back, but did not look as satisfied as I thought he would.

"We'll adjourn to the council chamber now, shall we, Your Majesty?" the duke of Buxton asked.

Dane shook his head. "I haven't yet begun."

"Pardon?"

"The reason I brought you all here this morning is not about evidence of my claim."

"Is it about your queen?"

Some heads turned to me. Their frosty regard left me in no doubt what they thought of me marrying their new king.

"No," Dane said. "This is about Glancia's future. A future without a king or queen. A future as a republic rather than a monarchy."

CHAPTER 15

*T*he silence stretched and deepened. Nobles glanced at one another, frowning. Then the outbursts erupted.

"Why?" asked one.

"What's wrong with a monarchy?" asked another.

"This is Glancia, not some barbaric backwater."

The voices became louder, the questions more rapid. Dane looked to Balthazar and Balthazar merely lifted his shoulder, as if telling Dane he'd expected this response.

Dane let the nobles continue until the noise level became deafening. Then he whistled for silence. The room instantly quietened, although the chatter didn't stop altogether.

"I don't understand," said one noblewoman near me. "Are we now at war with ourselves?"

"What will happen to us?" her friend said with gravity. "To the nobility?"

"Let me explain," Dane said. "Ever since learning I am heir to the Glancian throne, I have been considering the situation. I had a lot of time to think in prison, and since, and I came to realize that Freedland has a good political system in place."

"It's corrupt!" the duke of Gladstow declared. "Taxes are too high."

"And the nobles were all stripped of their property and titles," Lord Deerhorn shouted over the other voices. "Is that what you want here? Are we to be turned out of our own homes?"

Dane called for calm again, but it took longer before he could be heard over the dissent. "I said the Freedland system was good. It's certainly not perfect. But we can learn from their mistakes. To address your immediate concerns, I am not proposing any nobles be stripped of anything. You can keep your property and titles, and any rights that were fairly and legally come by will remain."

That produced a few sighs of relief.

"As for corruption, Freedland experiences some, it's true, but so do we. Governors and officials are often appointed based on personal ties, or even bribery, rather than merit."

Uncomfortable murmurs and shuffling of feet ensued.

"What I propose is for the people to vote for a high minister to oversee the governing of Glancia," Dane said.

"What? All of the people?" asked a lady in a shrill voice.

"If they wish."

Somebody snorted. "That'll be an administrative nightmare."

"It'll provide employment," Dane shot back. "A republic means Glancia will not be reliant on a single person of nobody's choosing to govern—and govern well—for decades. If the king is a tyrant, the kingdom suffers. A republic will ensure that never happens."

"But you'll make a good king," the duke of Buxton protested.

"Perhaps," Dane said. "But I have a temper. I have no taste for diplomacy and little patience to learn it. I'm stubborn and arrogant, so I've been told."

I pressed my lips together to suppress my smile. Dane didn't look my way, but I knew that was directed squarely at me.

"I will hate every moment of being king, and that's not what Glancia deserves. Further," he said, raising his voice over the protests, "What if my firstborn son lacks the qualities a king needs? Or his firstborn son? What if my heirs are more like Leon? Or worse, like my grandfather, King Diamedes of Averlea?"

A hush fell over the gathering.

"We are in a unique position here," Dane went on confidently. "We have this opportunity to change the course of history, to shape a better future for Glancia."

"But we have a king, and you seem nothing like Diamedes," the duke of Gladstow said. "Why change things now? Why not worry about overthrowing a bad king when the time comes?"

"If a republic is created now, with the approval of the ruler, it will be done in a bloodless, peaceful manner. I'll manage the transition for two years. At the end of those two years, we'll hold an election and the people can vote for the candidate they deem best to become high minister."

"Who will choose the candidates?" Lord Claypool asked.

"Anyone can be a candidate. They will have to register and then—"

"Do you mean my stable hand can be a candidate?" Lord Deerhorn sneered. "Ridiculous. Is that the sort of person you want running the country?"

"Your stable hand might know what's best for the people," Dane said.

Lord Xavier snorted. "Ridiculous," he muttered in echo of his father.

"Can women be elected?" asked Lady Claypool.

"Yes," Dane said.

That produced another round of surprised mutters. I smiled. This was going to take some getting used to, for all of us.

"The details still need to be worked out, but that's why I suggest a two-year transition," Dane said. "We can look to Freedland for advice and use the parts of their system that work and discard those that do not. We will put in place a better system, and make Glancia a beacon for fairness, the envy of every nation on the Fist Peninsula."

"You would deny your heirs the opportunity to rule?" the duke of Gladstow asked, incredulous.

"My heirs can stand for election as high minister, just like anyone else. If the people think they'll make a good leader, then they'll rule until the people no longer think that and vote them out."

"You're doing this so you can marry whomever you want, aren't you?" Lord Claypool asked, not unsympathetically. "You know King Phillip won't want his daughter married to a man who will be leader for only two years with no guarantee beyond that."

Dane's smile was hard. "You seemed not to have heard me the other times I told you, so I will say it again. I will marry Miss Cully whether I am king or not."

Lady Claypool glared at her husband and said something under her breath to him.

"It's irrelevant now anyway," he muttered. "If this proposal goes ahead, he won't be king."

Satisfied, Dane surveyed the room again. He let his gaze settle on the Deerhorns. "Let this be a warning. Corruption will be exposed and punished. Not just corruption in the process of choosing a high minister, but past corruption in the assigning of governors, sheriffs and other local officials. Perpetrators will be dealt with according to the law."

The crowd parted and Lady Deerhorn marched through it, her skirts billowing behind her as she strode from the chamber. Her husband and son followed in her wake. Either they didn't see me, or they deliberately avoided looking my way.

I released another breath. It was over. They held no more power. The gem and final wish were in our possession, the duke of Gladstow was no longer married to Violette, and Dane was now in charge. In a matter of days, they'd lost everything they'd clawed back after rioters destroyed their castle. It was an immeasurable relief. I couldn't help smiling.

I caught Dane looking at me. He smiled back, even though the nobles were not yet won over. Some seemed to be, but most were worried about losing their own power or having a commoner in charge of the country. Dane had some way to go before convincing them.

Balthazar pushed to his feet. "Is this what you want, Dane?" he asked.

Dane nodded. "It is. A republic is the best system for Glancia. For her people. It seems the high priest worked against me for nothing."

The high priest collapsed against the wall, as if he needed the support to hold him up.

The room heaved a collective sigh. Some nobles began to leave. Others stayed to talk. The duke of Buxton shook Dane's hand and assured him he would see that everyone was brought around to the notion of a republic.

Then, in a complete surprise, the duke of Gladstow also shook Dane's hand. I couldn't hear what they were saying, but it looked favorable. If both dukes agreed to Dane's proposal of a republic then surely the rest of the nobles would follow.

"What a sensation!" Kitty said as she joined me. "I didn't know he was going to declare Glancia a republic, did you?"

"No."

She clicked her tongue. "Tell him he must share his ideas with you before going ahead with them next time. It's what couples do."

"Gladstow doesn't share his ideas with you."

"*Loving* couples." She leaned closer. "Anyway, Gladstow did tell me he wants to get on Dane's good side. He thinks I'm one of Dane's closest friends now, through you, so considers himself fortunate that we are still married. He'll ask me to use that relationship with Dane to some advantage or other, of course."

So it was true. His ready agreement to Dane's proposal was indeed thanks to Kitty. She had swayed him, indirectly and unwittingly. "We'll be sure to let him continue to believe you have influence with Dane," I told her. "It will keep you protected."

"Most assuredly. Before his eagerness to please me wanes, I'm going to ask him to buy me a cottage near here so I can visit you whenever I like. I'll get him to put ownership in my name."

"Cottage?"

"Very well, a mansion. Just a small one, no more than six or eight bedchambers. With any luck, the Deerhorns will need to sell off an asset or two to pay fines for their corruption."

I laughed, feeling giddy with relief and happiness. Not only was Dane getting what he wanted, and he would not have to be king, but with both dukes on his side, gaining the support of the other nobles should be smooth.

And we could be together.

"The look on Lady Deerhorn's face when she stormed out of

here was priceless," Kitty said, grinning. "I shall never forget it. She was furious—but anxious, too."

"A dangerous combination in a Deerhorn." I looked to Balthazar, now getting up from the chair. Four guards surrounded him. It might not be enough. The Deerhorns would be more determined than ever to get their hands on the final wish, and the only way they could get it would be to kill Balthazar.

"Oh dear," Kitty said.

I followed her gaze to see Yelena striding into the room. Going by the thunderous look on her face, Dane had not informed her of his intentions for Glancia, and she had just learned it from someone else.

She stood in the middle of the room, both feet planted on the entwined LL emblem tiled in gold on the floor. She wore a simple but elegant cream and blue gown of lustrous silk that must have been hastily made from the clothes in Leon's wardrobe. With her hair neatly arranged, and jeweled rings on her fingers, she looked every bit the princess.

Her color worried me, however. If it weren't for the two pink spots on her cheeks, her face would have been too pale.

She waited for Dane as he finished speaking to a group of noblemen and Balthazar, her lips pinched. The men finally bowed to Dane and left. As they passed through the doorway, a movement in the shadows caught my eye. Martha stood there, waiting meekly for her mistress.

"How dare you," Yelena snapped at Dane when the noblemen were gone.

Balthazar signaled for me to leave with him, but Dane asked me to stay. He dismissed my guards, however, and asked them to wait outside.

Once the door was closed, Dane invited his mother to sit. He indicated the throne. "You might as well sit there. It's as good a place as any."

"Don't be glib," she spat. "*You* should be sitting on it. You and only you."

"So you've heard about the republic. I'm sorry you had to find out—"

"Why didn't you consult me before making the announcement?" she asked.

"Because it doesn't affect you."

"Doesn't affect me! Of course it does. You are my son!"

"I'm the one losing the throne, not you."

"I learned of it through gossip as the ladies left here. Do you know how that feels, Dane? To learn of something so significant from strangers?"

"Yes."

She flinched then began to cough. She recovered quickly, but I suspected that was only because she fought it.

"I'll fetch water," Dane said, striding past her.

"Get back here. I haven't finished." She squared up to him. He was much taller than her, but even ill, she was a formidable force.

Dane settled his gaze on her. It held no anger, but there was no sympathy either, and certainly no love. "I'm sorry you had to find out that way, Mother. But I didn't inform you because I didn't want this lecture before I spoke with the nobles. I needed a clear head. I planned to speak to you immediately afterwards, but it seems gossip is faster than me."

She drew in a deep breath. "Did you do this because of Josie?"

Dane indicated me, standing behind her. "She's right there, Mother. And no, I did not. I did it because it's the best thing for Glancia."

She closed her eyes, and I worried she'd faint. Dane caught her elbow, but she shook him off with a violent jerk. She pierced him with a sharp glare, all signs of illness gone. "Everything I have striven for—everything *we* have striven for—gone." She clicked her fingers. "Like that. In an instant of selfish folly."

Dane huffed out a humorless laugh. "And here I thought it was the least selfish thing to do."

"Don't treat this as a joke!"

"I'm not. I'm sorry you feel aggrieved—"

"Aggrieved! I feel betrayed, Dane. Betrayed by my own son." She thrust out her chin. "You should at least have consulted me before making the announcement. You don't want to make hasty decisions about something so important."

Dane sighed. "Do we have to go through this again? Ever since I renounced my claim to the Freedland crown—"

"Averlea," she ground out through a clenched jaw. "It's *Averlea!*"

"Ever since I renounced my claim, and learned that I was king of Glancia, I have been thinking about this. It's not a recent idea. I've thought long and hard. I've consulted wiser heads than my own."

"The master of the palace?" she sneered. "If it weren't for him, we wouldn't be in this situation." She suddenly turned on me, eyes bright amid her pale face. "Or her. You may argue that you didn't renounce the throne so you can marry her, but I will never believe it." She picked up her skirts and marched out of the room.

Dane followed, but he let her go once he reached Martha. He caught Martha's elbow and asked her to stay a moment. She smiled sweetly up at him, brows raised in expectation.

He suddenly bent and hugged her. "Thank you, Martha," he said quietly.

When he pulled away, she had tears in her eyes. Her smile softened and she patted his cheek. Then she raced after Yelena.

Dane watched her go, his chest rising and falling with his deep sigh.

I touched his arm and he turned to me, a lopsided smile in place. "All right?" I asked.

"I am, but I'm not sure if Yelena will ever forgive me."

"Then that's her burden."

He circled his arms around me and kissed my forehead. "Finally we can be alone," he murmured.

I warded him off with a hand to his chest, earning me a frown. "I'm worried about Balthazar. The Deerhorns will remain a threat until the third wish is used. We should decide what to do with it, sooner rather than later."

"Agreed, but that's a discussion that requires all of us present. We'll meet tomorrow morning. Don't worry, Josie, I've given Erik orders to double Balthazar's escort and for the Deerhorns to be watched at all times."

It was a relief to hear, but I wouldn't relax until that third wish was used and the Deerhorns informed.

Dane rubbed my arms. "I know you worry about him. You care for him like a father, and he thinks of you as a daughter." He gave a wry twist of his lips. "Yelena could learn much about parenting from him."

"She hasn't had an easy life," I said. "She was passed from family to family from the age of ten after witnessing her parents' murder. It's difficult to give love when you've never been the recipient of it yourself."

"She could have been the recipient. When I was a boy, I craved her love. She gave me her attention only when I did well at my studies or training, but she never once praised me. If it weren't for Martha, I would have been starved of love."

I touched his face to force him to look at me. "Thank goodness for Martha. You seem to have quite a good grasp of it."

He settled his hands on my hips and dipped his head. "More recent friends have helped too. The most important of whom is standing before me, looking at me with adoring eyes."

"Adoring?" I mocked. "You're mistaking that look for admonishment."

He pulled back. "Admonishment?"

"I wished you'd talked to me about your plan to form a republic before you announced it to the nobles." I winced. "Sorry. I sound like Yelena."

"I admit I should have told you. I should have told both of you. I didn't discuss it with Yelena beforehand because I was a coward and wanted to delay a confrontation with her."

"And in my case?"

"I wanted to surprise you."

I laughed. "It was certainly a surprise. But a good one."

He tugged me closer and circled me in his arms before kissing me deeply.

When we finally broke apart, he said, "We have a lot to discuss, but let's start with the most important. What is the minimum length of time before a couple can wed after making an official application? In Freedland, it's three weeks."

"Glancia too."

"Then we'll go to one of the temples."

"When?"

He smiled. "If not today then tomorrow."

"Very well," I said. "There's more important things to discuss, anyway. Such as what to do with the third wish."

"Agreed." He tugged me towards the throne.

"And we should decide where we're going to live."

"Here for two years," he said.

"And after that? What are your plans?"

"We'll talk about that later." A sly smile curved his lips as he kept tugging me towards the throne.

"We should also discuss your plans for Glancia, at least in broad terms," I said.

"Politics is so dull."

I chuckled. "You're the leader of this nation, for good or ill. You have to discuss politics at some point."

"True, but not now." He scooped me up into his arms. "Now, I'm going to ravish you."

I gasped. "Dane! There are no locks on these doors!"

"You want to do it here?" He looked around. "On the throne?"

"Isn't that where you meant?"

He carried me out of the antechamber, through the council chamber, the formal sitting room, a games room, the private dining room, a small chamber of indeterminate function, a small library, private office, and finally the king's bedchamber. We did not stop there, however. He carried me through to the adjoining bedchamber, assigned to the captain of the guards.

"This door has a lock on it," he said, pushing the bolt across. "And the bed is more comfortable than the throne."

I smiled against his mouth. "It's also far away from the rest of the palace. Not many will think to look for you here."

He smiled too. "Politics and administration can wait. I have more important things to do."

* * *

OUR TIME together was over all too briefly. Dane needed to attend meetings while I went in search of Meg. I found her at the forest cottage, about to return to Mull. She was in a bit of a lather.

"Josie, thank goodness you're here. Tell Max that my parents will not be angry about last night."

"Wellll…"

She gave me an arched look. "I sent word that I was staying here with you. They will assume Max was in the garrison where he should be."

"That's all right then." I turned to Max. "What they don't know won't make them cross."

He considered this a moment. "But we should be honest with them."

"No!" both Meg and I cried.

Meg took his hands in hers and kissed him lightly. "I adore my family, but they're overbearing sometimes. They don't need to know we spent last night together. But we should tell them about our plans for the future."

"You're getting married?" I asked.

She nodded, smiling. "Just as soon as we can. You and Dane?"

"The same." I hugged her then Max too. "It looks like we'll all live at the palace together for a while. You'll be made captain of the guards, Max."

He shrugged. "Maybe."

"Definitely. There's no one better qualified. You proved that by outwitting the Deerhorns when you fetched Brant."

"Speaking of the Deerhorns," he said. "Are you returning to the palace? I'll escort Meg to Mull, but you need to be properly guarded. Until the third wish is used, you're still in danger."

"My escort is outside. They'll accompany us all to Mull. I can't wait to see your parents when you tell them, Meg. They'll be so pleased."

* * *

WE TRAVELED at a rapid clip along the village road, staying alert. There was no sign of the Deerhorns, but they would do well to remain at the palace. They could not kidnap me when I was with so many guards. It wasn't just Max and my escort that protected us, but a number of staff accompanying the duke of Buxton and the minister for justice joined us. The duke and minister rode in an official palace carriage. One of the doors gleamed with fresh black paint where Leon's personal insignia had been covered. The door on the other side still sported the Lockhart family crest of key and prancing deer. I wondered if that would soon be painted over too. What would replace it?

I asked one of their men why they were going to the village, but he didn't know.

We parted ways at the edge of the village, and we headed to the Divers' house. I remained outside to allow Meg and Max to speak with her parents alone.

The door opposite opened and Bessie Tailor emerged from Doctor Ashmole's cottage. She felt her way with one hand against the wall. Her near-blind eyes sought out the sun, but she wouldn't be able to see more than a general lightness. Nobody accompanied her.

I went to help her navigate the steps, my escort of guards in tow. "Bessie, it's me, Josie Cully. Can I help you?"

"Josie!" She squinted in my direction. "Is that really you?"

"It is," I said, taking her arm. "Step down now."

"I thought you were at the palace, measuring up the queen's chambers." She laughed at her own joke, revealing a lot fewer teeth than the last time I'd seen her.

"What happened to your teeth?" I asked.

"They were old, like me, so Doctor Ashmole said I should have them removed before they cause me trouble."

"So they weren't causing you trouble yet?"

"They were fine."

"He shouldn't have done that. It's not necessary—"

"My, my," came a brittle voice behind me.

"Ugh," Bessie muttered. "The viper speaks, unfortunately."

"Giving out medical advice again, Miss Cully? Didn't you learn from the last time?"

I glanced over my shoulder to see Mistress Ashmole looking down her nose at me, her arms crossed. "Just having a chat with an old friend," I said.

I assisted Bessie down the next step and she assured me she could get home alone from there. "Although one of your nice young men could offer to help, if you can spare one."

"Are you sure you can't see?" I teased.

"I can see their shape," she said.

"How did you know they're not women?"

"They smell like men."

I laughed and signaled to one of the guards to take her to her home in the next street. "She'll let you know which one it is when you reach it."

I watched them go and was about to return to Meg's house when Mistress Ashmole spoke. "I've been the midwife ever since your departure."

"I hope you found the task to your liking."

She sniffed. "It's menial work. You may take back the role."

I arched my brows as she disappeared inside. I was still recovering from the conversation when she handed me my midwifery pack. "All the instruments are in there. You won't find any missing."

"I suspect nothing less from you, Mistress Ashmole." I went to walk off, but she spoke again.

"It's impossible for you to have made a living as a midwife. Perhaps with the apothecary shop, you could have survived if you lived frugally, but there isn't enough midwifery work. You *must* have been doctoring to support yourself."

Perhaps I was bolstered by recent events, with Dane becoming king then interim leader of Glancia, and with the Deerhorns being outwitted, but I couldn't let her comment slide. "I didn't simply give up the apothecary business. You took my premises, my ingredients, everything I had in storage. How was I supposed to continue?"

She humphed. "They tell me you're clever, resourceful. Clearly you are not."

She was the sort of person for whom inflicting an injury wasn't enough. She liked to dig her thumb into the wound too. I loathed her with every fiber of my being. Before I could think of a retort, however, she disappeared inside and slammed the door.

"Bloody awful woman," one of the guards said.

I returned to Meg's house and spent some time with her family until Mistress Diver suggested we visit some of the shops for wedding things.

"Have you thought about your gown, Josie?" she asked.

"Not yet," I said as we walked into the village with a small army of guards behind us, including Max.

"We'll see what the draper has in stock."

"Probably not much," Meg grumbled. "He doesn't use Deerhorn merchants for his supplies, which means his own deliveries will most likely have been delayed or blocked altogether."

We inspected the bolts of cloth in stock anyway and listened to the draper's complaints about his struggling business. Then we spent a leisurely afternoon moving from shop to shop, mostly greeting friends rather than actual shopping. News had already reached the village about the republic, and they had many questions, some of which we could answer, many we could not. I wasn't familiar enough with the concept and what it meant for the ordinary person to explain it.

"Little will change for most of us," I assured one shopkeeper.

She looked somewhat disappointed until Meg chimed in. "Things will certainly change for the better around here, though. Dane is going to end corruption. The Deerhorns will have to unblock supplies or be arrested for hindering trade."

She was bombarded with more questions, many of which she could answer. She knew a surprising amount about commerce and the law. Certainly more than me.

"That's because you had your head buried in medical texts growing up," she told me when I asked her about it. "Whereas I grew up with Lyle and my father coming home at the end of the day and discussing current events, politics, economics."

"Meg," Mistress Diver whispered. "Don't talk about such things in front of the sergeant. It's unattractive in a woman."

"Max knows what I'm like."

Her mother looked uncertain.

"Meg's interest in village affairs is one of the many reasons why I love her," Max assured Mistress Diver.

It was just the right thing to say to assuage her and she smiled, albeit unconvincingly. "Still, a wife shouldn't let such interests get in the way of her home duties. Isn't that right, Josie?"

"Uh..."

"You won't allow your medical interests to get in the way of Dane's work as leader, will you?"

"Actually, I'm going to be the village midwife again. Mistress Ashmole is no longer interested."

"Oh."

"I'm also considering petitioning the colleges in Logios to allow women. As the wife of Glancia's leader, I might have some sway. At the very least they'll have to grant me an audience or risk offending not only Dane, but all of Glancia too."

Meg hooked her arm through mine. "Good for you, Josie." Her mother looked as though she was about to protest, but Meg indicated the building ahead. "The duke and minister are leaving the governor's office. I wonder what they wanted with him."

"Let's find out."

"You're going to address a duke?" Mistress Diver cried.

"Stay here if you like," Meg told her.

She and I hurried towards them before they departed. They didn't get into their carriage straight away, however, but seemed to be issuing orders to the governor's men guarding the entrance. By the shocked look on the guards' faces, the orders were extraordinary.

They saluted the duke who then trotted down the steps to join the waiting justice minister. Behind him, the door opened suddenly, forcing the two guards to jump out of the way. The governor emerged. He stomped down the steps like a petulant child denied a treat and headed off, away from the duke's carriage.

"I wonder why the guards aren't escorting him," Mistress Diver said, frowning. "They always do, nowadays. He's worried about retaliation, ever since the riot."

"Your Grace," I called out to the duke. "May I ask what's happening?"

He paused, one hand on the open carriage door. "Of course you may. It is your village, after all." He indicated the minister for justice. "We were sent here to investigate reports of corruption in the appointment of the sheriff and governor. Upon being confronted with several accusations that he committed fraud and corruption on the Deerhorns' behalf, the governor stepped down, effective immediately. We didn't even have to present evidence."

Meg and I exchanged glances.

"So...he's gone?" Max asked.

The duke nodded. "The sheriff will most likely fall on his sword too. We've already spoken to him with the same accusations, and he said he will consider his position. I doubt he will continue in the role after he hears of the governor's resignation."

"I don't understand," Mistress Diver said. "Who is in charge of the village if we have no governor?"

"His assistant will step into the role temporarily, until a replacement is chosen by the councilors. If the sheriff also decides to leave, his men will have to make do until the new governor appoints a new sheriff."

"Do the Deerhorns know?" I asked.

"Dane went to see them as we were leaving the palace. As lord in these parts, Deerhorn had to be informed." The duke gave us a smug smile. "I don't think they'll be very pleased to hear that all deals made with this governor will be deemed null and void."

"Will they have to give back the land they bought for next to nothing after the Row burned down?" Meg asked.

"They will."

"Extraordinary," Mistress Diver said on a breath.

"I wish I was there to see Lady Deerhorn's face," Meg said.

"So do I," said the duke. "So do I."

We waited until the crier emerged from the council building and announced the resignation of the governor. He then went on his way to walk around the village, calling out the news. He gathered quite a following of stunned listeners before he'd got very far.

We headed back to the Divers' house, meeting Lyle and Mr. Diver along the way. They'd heard the news and were as shocked as us but had more to say on the subject.

Meg was very quiet, however, not joining in on their excited conversation. Since she was remaining behind in Mull, we said our goodbyes outside the Divers' cottage. I wanted to reach the palace cottage before it grew dark.

"Is something wrong?" I asked Meg after her family retreated inside.

"Nothing. I'm just thinking."

"About becoming the next governor of Mull?"

She looked around to see if anyone had overheard, but her family had all gone. Max, however, gave her a nod of encouragement. "An inexperienced nobody can't simply step into the role of governor," she told us both. "The councilors will never choose an uneducated woman."

"Perhaps not for governor, but I think they would consider you for a position on the council now that one has become vacant."

"Especially if the people of Mull let it be known they want you," Max added.

Meg sighed. "My parents wouldn't allow it."

I took her hands in mine. "You're a grown woman, Meg. Your decisions are your own to make. Besides, you'll no longer be living with them soon. You'll be with Max, and if he thinks it's a good idea then how can you refuse?"

Her smile began slowly and spread, lighting up her entire face. "I think I will apply."

I drew her into a hug. "This village needs you."

"It's not just that," she said, pulling away. "I want to prove that women can be councilors—or even queens—and do a good job of it without being ruthless like Lady Deerhorn."

"Perhaps you will run for the high minister's role in two years' time."

"I don't know about that, but perhaps other women will see that it's possible."

"Meg Diver, councilor of Mull. It has a nice ring to it."

"Meg Bullitt, councilor of Mull, sounds better," Max said.

* * *

THE GARDEN STAFF were lighting the torches along the drive when I arrived back with my escort. The forecourts, pavilions and the palace itself were already well lit, welcoming us. I wanted to see Dane before I retired to the cottage, but after waiting in the garrison for some time, I gave up and went in search of Balthazar instead.

His heavily guarded office signaled his presence inside. "You're still here?" I asked.

He looked up from the paperwork with a weary smile. "There's much to be done. The servants are starting to indicate whether they're staying or going, more and more nobles are arriving, and some staff have not been performing their duties to optimum levels in recent weeks."

"You're working too hard. All of that can wait until tomorrow. Come to the garrison with me."

"Or I can finish this." He indicated his papers.

I sighed. "You should relax and enjoy life."

"Why? Because I'm old? The day I stop working is the day I die."

A distant shout set my nerves on edge. I joined the guards at the door as they drew their swords. Another shout echoed along the tunnel as the flickering light of a torch signaled someone's approach.

The guards raised their swords.

"Rylan! Zeke!" Quentin rushed out of the darkness, torchlight picking out the worry in his eyes. "We need help. The prisoners have escaped."

"From the palace cells?" one of the guards asked.

"Of course from the bloody cells," Quentin snapped.

"How?" Zeke asked.

"Don't know. We can investigate later, but we've got to round them up before they hurt someone. The Deerhorns's mercenaries will probably leave the vicinity and not cause trouble, but the other three are evil. They can't be trusted to roam the grounds or village at night. Come on, we need help!"

Rylan glanced into the office. "We have to protect Balthazar and Josie."

"Go," Balthazar said, rising. "Josie and I will join the staff in the commons. We'll be safe there."

"Zeke, take two men with you," Rylan said as Quentin ran off again. "The rest of us will escort Josie and Bal to the commons then help you look for the prisoners."

Zeke and another two guards raced after Quentin. We followed as quickly as Balthazar's gait would allow, with three guards in front of us and three behind. I held onto Balthazar's arm to steady him so he could walk faster. The sooner we reached the commons, the sooner our escort could leave us and join the hunt.

"How did they get out?" I muttered. "There's always a guard posted there."

"The question isn't how," Balthazar said. "The question is, why? Why did someone release them? Because they did not escape on their own. They had outside help."

Hailia and Merdu, he was right. "The Deerhorns must have done it," I said.

Flickering torchlight up ahead signaled the approach of another party. "This way," came a man's voice. "It's through here."

Brisk footsteps tapped on the flagstones and a shadow appeared on the wall of an adjoining corridor.

"Halt!" Zeke said. "Identify yourself!"

A chuckle echoed off the walls. The footsteps didn't break stride and a figure emerged from the other corridor. Torchlight lit up the tangled gray hair and dirty features of Kai, one of the escapees.

"Arrest him!" Zeke ordered the two guards alongside him.

"Wait!" I said. But it was too late. The two guards lowered their swords to grab the unarmed Kai, grinning at them like a madman.

Just as they accosted him, two swordsmen dressed in black with cloths covering their lower faces emerged from the darkness and struck down the guards. Kai removed a knife from his belt and raised it. He ran at Zeke. Zeke struck him, felling him before he'd got too far, but the action meant he was not in the right position to fend off the attack from the swordsmen.

A sword ran him through and he fell before the three guards who'd been behind us could reach him.

The remaining guards engaged the two attackers, but when another two came out of the dark corridor, they were outnumbered.

I grabbed Balthazar's arm while reaching into my pocket for my knife with my other hand. "Back to your office."

He didn't move. "We can't outrun them."

I followed his gaze to see one of our guards fall. The remaining two could not hold off for much longer. "We have to try!"

Even before the words had left my mouth, another figure rushed out of the darkness. Lord Xavier! His twisted grin split his face as he came at me, knife raised. The blade shone in the torchlight, momentarily blinding me, but not before I saw the look in his eyes. I would never forget it. It was one of triumph, ecstasy, and pure evil. I'd seen evil before, but I'd never seen such thrill at the taste of it. He knew he had us. We were trapped.

I pushed Balthazar, urging him to leave me. I must block Lord Xavier from getting to him. Balthazar and the last wish had to be protected at all costs. If Lord Xavier killed him, he would inherit the sorcerer's magic.

But Balthazar wouldn't budge. He was shouting. We were all shouting, even Lord Xavier, as his blade descended.

I went to dodge it, but Lord Xavier kicked out. His booted foot smashed into my thigh. I slammed into the wall, hitting my shoulder hard against the unforgiving stones.

I didn't fall, however, and quickly recovered. My thigh and shoulder burned with pain, but that didn't matter. None of it mattered. Lord Xavier was raising his knife above a cowering Balthazar's head. Balthazar tried to strike him with the walking stick, but Lord Xavier batted it away.

"Wish for him to leave us alone!" I shouted at Balthazar.

A movement near the entrance to the other corridor caught my attention. All our guards lay dead and Lady Deerhorn was stepping over their bodies. Her smile was as slick as her son's. The last wish was within their grasp and they knew it.

"Do it!" she screeched.

Lord Xavier stabbed Balthazar in the stomach.

Balthazar clutched at the protruding knife as he slipped to the floor, his lips moving but no sound coming out. He fell into a crumpled heap and his eyes fluttered closed. His hand fell away from the knife handle as blood soaked his clothing.

My scream filled the corridor.

But through it, I could hear Lord Xavier's joyous cry. "I can feel it! I can feel the magic, Mother. The wish is mine!"

CHAPTER 16

"*D*o it!" Lady Deerhorn cried. "Do it now! Get the gem and make the wish!"

Lord Xavier could not be allowed to get his hands on the gem. He could not speak the words. I lunged at him, my knife raised to strike.

He shoved me in the chest. I struck the wall again, the back of my head smacking into the stones. Dizziness swamped me.

Lord Xavier fell to his knees and rifled through Balthazar's pocket. He pulled out his hand, the gem enclosed in his fist. I lurched towards him. The room spun. My legs buckled. I fell to my hands and knees as black spots danced before my eyes.

"I wish for my family to be the most powerful on the Fist Peninsula, now and forever." The words rushed from Lord Xavier's mouth as clear as day.

He laughed, tipping his head back, and let out a whoop. His mother clasped his face in her hands. I had never seen her smile a proper, happy smile. It was like her son's, all twisted cruel joy.

"We've done it," she said. "We have done it!"

Grief, anger and desperation propelled me towards them. I lunged but Lord Xavier caught my wrist and overpowered me. My knife clattered onto the flagstones. He pinned me to the wall, his fingers clasping my face like a vice and digging into my jaw.

"You will regret fighting me, my pet," he spat. "But I regret nothing because now your punishment will be all the sweeter."

He let me go only to press himself against me, keeping me trapped against the wall. His breath reeked, his body's stench enveloped me. I wanted to throw up. I tried twisting my face away to avoid his kiss.

His vile wet mouth descended.

A cough saved me from the revolting fate. It came from Balthazar.

He was alive!

Lord Xavier let me go and spun around to see Balthazar staring up at him from the floor. He clutched the knife protruding from his stomach and his beard twitched with his attempted smile.

"What is this?" Lady Deerhorn spat at her son. "You said you felt the magic! You don't possess it if he's not dead."

Lord Xavier opened his fist to reveal the stone in his palm. It was just an ordinary stone, not the gem. "Where is it?" he growled.

"Gone," Balthazar whispered.

"Don't talk," I urged him. "Save your strength."

I took a step towards him, but Lady Deerhorn blocked my path. She pressed the point of my surgical knife to my throat. "Give us the gem," she said through gritted teeth. "Or Miss Cully dies."

"I can't give you the gem if I wanted to," Balthazar gasped out. "I don't know where it is."

"Who does know? Who did you give it to?"

He swallowed. "The sorcerer."

"What?" she exploded.

"Only the sorcerer knows where it is."

It suddenly dawned on me what he was saying. "You've used the third wish," I said.

He blinked up at me. "Why do you think the lords all agreed to Dane's republic so easily? Even Lord Deerhorn."

"You wished for *that*?" Lady Deerhorn screeched.

He fought for a breath. "I wished for them to agree to whatever Dane wanted. If that was a republic or him as king…"

That meant he'd used the third wish yesterday. He'd known all this time and not told us. "Why didn't you say?" I asked.

"To draw them out. Dane will arrest them now for treason, murder…"

He winced in pain. I tried to go to him, but Lady Deerhorn shoved her arm into my chest, pinning me against the wall as her son had done. I couldn't fight him off, but I could fight her.

I struck out and punched her in the stomach. The pressure on my chest lightened and I was able to sweep her arm aside, pushing the blade away from my throat. I struck a quick blow into her wrist and another at her throat.

She let go of the knife and fell to her knees, coughing and grasping her throat. I picked up the knife and used it to ward off Lord Xavier and their swordsmen.

"Get back, or I will cut you."

He bared his teeth and lunged at me. With a flick of my wrist, the blade sliced his cheek. He hissed and clutched at his face. "You bitch! Get her!" he ordered the mercenaries.

I backed away from the approaching swordsmen. "Someone will have heard the commotion and sent guards," I warned them. "You won't have much time to escape. It's over for the Deerhorns, but you can still get out of here alive if you go now."

They needed no more urging and sprinted off down one of the corridors.

"Get back here!" Lady Deerhorn shouted. "Your work is not finished!"

They continued on.

I fell to my knees near Balthazar. "I'm going to remove the knife, but the moment it comes out, I must put pressure on the wound. This will hurt."

"It's all right, Josie," he rasped. "I'm old. You know I cannot survive this."

I wrapped my hands around the handle, but his suddenly widening eyes had me turning around, expecting to see Lord Xavier or Lady Deerhorn coming at me again.

But it was Dane and Theodore, followed by Erik and Quentin. I had not heard their footsteps. The look on Dane's face was one of deep anxiety.

"Josie?" His voice sounded strangled.

"Help me." I turned back to Balthazar. "We need to stop the bleeding."

He knelt beside me and wrapped his hand around the blade handle. I pressed down against the sides of the wound and nodded.

I tried to block out Balthazar's groan of agony as Dane removed the blade. To my utter relief, it appeared as though the knife hadn't been thrust to the hilt. The extra layers of clothing Balthazar wore due to the colder weather had stopped it entering all the way.

"Tear off some of my underskirt," I instructed Dane. "Long lengths to bandage him."

He did as told while I continued to press down. I didn't want to release the pressure until I knew the bleeding was slowing so there was nothing to do but wait and keep Balthazar comfortable.

Theodore came into view as he knelt on Balthazar's other side. Balthazar closed his eyes and rested his head on Theodore's lap.

"Bal?" Theodore whispered, tears streaming down his cheeks.

"He's still breathing," I said. "Dane, help me bandage him."

"Who wielded the knife?" Dane asked as we carefully bandaged the wound.

I glanced behind me to see the Deerhorns standing very still, swords pointed at their throats. Quentin and Erik looked as though they'd be glad to ram them through. Dane only had to say the word.

"Lord Xavier, but I'm sure it was under his mother's instruction," I said.

"Execute him," he said to his men.

"No!" I cried, as Balthazar's eyes flew open.

Erik and Quentin obeyed me, but those sword points had drawn blood from the soft flesh. Lord Xavier was shaking, his breathing rapid. Lady Deerhorn's chin lifted in defiance, but her eyes filled with worry.

"Josie, if he dies…" Dane said gently.

"The third wish has been used," I told him. "There are no more to inherit. The gem has already vanished." I nodded at the stone now lying on the floor, forgotten. "Bal used that to trick them."

Dane blew out a deep breath as he studied the ceiling. "Thank the god and goddess."

"It's over," I said.

He looked to Balthazar, so pale and frail in Theodore's arms. He rested a hand on my arm. "Will you be all right while I escort them with Erik and Quentin? I'll send men back to help with Bal."

I nodded and attempted a smile. I wanted to reassure him that Balthazar would be all right, but I couldn't.

"Take them to the prison cells," Dane ordered his men.

"The cells!" Lord Xavier cried. "You can't do that! The cells are for commoners."

Dane nodded at Erik who grabbed Lord Xavier's arm and marched him along the corridor.

Quentin took hold of Lady Deerhorn, but she shook him off. "You will regret this," she snarled at me. "When I tell them you've been doctoring, there'll be no escaping severe punishment for a repeat offence. Let us go and I will keep quiet."

"Not doctoring," Dane said. "Merely doing what anyone would do and try to stop the bleeding." He gave me a slight shake of his head, warning me to not help Balthazar or give medical advice while they watched on.

But I would not be intimidated by her anymore. She had no more power over me and I wanted her to see that, to know it deep in her bones. I stood and approached her. Quentin shifted his stance, nervous about me getting within her reach.

"Don't be afraid, Quentin," I said. "She isn't armed and she has no capacity to hurt me."

"You vulgar little whore!" she spat.

I smiled. "And you are a greedy, cold, hateful woman who got the moronic, revolting son she deserved. From now on, you'll get everything else you deserve too. Oh, and you might like to know that thanks to my medical knowledge, Balthazar will recover. Your son couldn't even thrust a blade all the way into an unarmed old man."

Up ahead, Lord Xavier tried to wrench free of Erik. The Marginer punched him in the stomach. Lord Xavier bent over, coughing.

"Stay quiet or I will cut your other cheek," Erik said.

"I will tell everyone that you used your doctoring," Lady Deerhorn said in a guttural growl.

I shrugged. "Who will care? The governor has resigned, the sheriff is on notice, and you heard Balthazar. The lords and ministers will do what Dane wants."

Dane's brows drew together, but he didn't ask for more information.

"No one will take your side anymore," I went on. "I'll be surprised if your husband keeps the estate after this. The other noblemen might wish to see him stripped of all privileges. Nor would I expect him to visit you in prison. It's quite disgusting down there. Don't worry. I'll see that you and Xavier don't starve. I'll ask the cook to prepare something special, just for the two of you. I hope you like offal."

"You bitch! Whore! Witch!" The echoes of her screams continued to drift back to us long after Erik and Quentin marched them away.

I drew in a deep breath and blew it out slowly, then I knelt alongside Balthazar again. I took his wrist and felt his pulse. It was weak, the beats slow. The bandage was already soaked with blood. I pressed my lips together to suppress my crying, but tears escaped anyway. I didn't want to look at Theodore. He would most likely be worse.

"Don't cry," Balthazar whispered.

"Shhh, save your breath," I said, wiping my eyes with the back of my hand.

"After I tell you that I'm proud of you, my girl. So proud." His eyelids drifted closed again.

* * *

BALTHAZAR SLEPT in his bed in a Mother's Milk induced slumber, the covers hiding his heavily bandaged middle. I'd cleaned the cut and inspected it. The blade had missed all vital organs, thankfully, but he'd lost a lot of blood. Theodore helped me stitch the wound. He'd insisted on locking the door, claiming he didn't want anyone disturbing Balthazar. I think he was more worried about one of the dukes or nobles walking in and seeing me performing a task that only a doctor should do.

Neither Theodore nor I would leave Balthazar's side until Dane returned. He brought Max and Meg with him. One of the guards had ridden to Mull to bring them back in case the worst happened. They would both want to be here if it did.

They gazed at Balthazar, lying motionless in bed, then pinned stricken looks upon me.

"He's alive," I whispered. "But very weak."

Dane signaled for me and the others to join him. Theodore shook his head and remained in the bedchamber. Outside in the service corridor, Dane leaned back against the wall. He looked exhausted.

"Have the remaining escapees been recaptured?" I asked.

"They're back in the cells." He indicated the bedchamber door. "What are his chances?"

"It's too soon to tell."

"What happened?" Meg asked. "The guard knew so little, only that the Deerhorns stabbed him to get the wish."

"They have to be executed," Max said darkly.

"They might be yet, if Balthazar doesn't live," Dane said. "I've spoken to the justice minister. He says attempted murder doesn't hold the death penalty, but it will see them sent to a prison mine in Freedland."

Meg gave a humorless huff. "How ironic."

"They killed the guards," Dane said heavily. "The justice minister says he can push for charges of murder or even treason. Killing the king's guards is considered an act of violence against the king and therefore treason. But since I am not king, he's not sure how to proceed."

"I meant we have to execute them now, before..." Max

nodded at the door. "In case the worst happens and they inherit the third wish."

"The third wish is gone," I said. "Bal used it yesterday to wish for the nobles and advisors to agree to whatever Dane wanted."

Meg and Max stared at me, mouths ajar. I laughed, partly with sheer relief that the threat the Deerhorns posed was finally over, and partly because they looked so odd.

"What do you mean, whatever I want?" Dane asked carefully.

"I don't know the exact wording he used for the wish, but it seems he did it so there'd be no opposition to you becoming either the king or interim leader of the republic."

"He should not have wished for anything so broad."

"You can tell him that when he wakes, but I think he knew what he was doing. Bal doesn't do things without careful thought first. Besides, he knew he could trust you."

Dane grunted and crossed his arms. "Why didn't he tell us yesterday?"

"He wanted to draw the Deerhorns out so they would do precisely what they did to him today and be caught in the act. He knew we would try to avoid a violent confrontation by telling the Deerhorns the third wish was used. That would render them harmless, but not see them arrested. He wanted them gone from our lives for good."

He'd done it for me. It was his way of protecting me, now and in the future, long after Balthazar himself was gone.

Dane lowered his arms to his sides and stared at me, mouth open, just as Meg and Max had done.

"He's mad," Max said with a shake of his head. "He could have been killed."

Meg took his hand. "I don't think death worried Bal as much as having the Deerhorns free did. He saw it as the only way to remove them without their deaths being on anyone's conscience."

"He's still alive, and I will do everything I can to make sure he stays alive," I said.

"Will you call Doctor Ashmole?" Max asked.

I bit the inside of my cheek. "I should..."

"Why?" Meg asked. "You're as good as he is. Better, perhaps. I've seen you tend to knife wounds many times before. Doctor Ashmole can do nothing more."

"But it's the protocol. I wouldn't want to give him ammunition to use against me. If he or Mistress Ashmole complain to the sheriff, he will have to arrest me, and Dane shouldn't interfere. The republic is too new to test his position. I know the wish dictates that the lords and advisors have to agree with his desires, but this a matter for the sheriff, and he's not under the spell."

Meg gave me a sly smile. "Don't worry about the sheriff."

I frowned. "Why not?"

Meg simply continued to give me that maddening smile.

Max put his arm around her shoulders and kissed her cheek. "My wife-to-be spoke to the sheriff this morning, before we heard about this incident. She reminded him that the governor has been forced to resign and the Deerhorns' influence has been severely curtailed, thanks to the duchess of Gladstow's reappearance and Dane becoming leader. She convinced him that the Deerhorns are no longer in favor and are in danger of having their power diminished even further."

"How prophetic that turned out to be," I said.

"I don't think you need to worry about the sheriff," Max said with a hint of pride in his voice. "He won't support the losing side."

Meg smiled up at him and accepted his light kiss. "Do you think it'll be all right if we sit with Bal for a while?" she asked me. "Perhaps Theodore can have a rest."

"You could ask him, but he hasn't left Bal's side yet. I'm sure he'd like some company, though."

I remained outside with Dane as Meg and Max disappeared into the room. Once the door closed, Dane gathered me in his arms and kissed me thoroughly. It was just the tonic I needed after the emotional day.

We broke apart when someone behind me cleared their

throat. Five servants stood there, all of them leaders of their respective departments. I recognized the bad-tempered cook, and Wes the head keeper of the menagerie. Behind them stood Lewis the head gardener, as well as the grand equerry, the grand huntsman, and the grand forester.

"Miss Cully." Wes cleared his throat again. "Is he... Will he...?"

"It's too soon to tell," I said. "He's resting peacefully now."

"Can we see him?"

I hesitated. "He needs to rest. I'll send someone to fetch you when he wakes."

They nodded, glanced at Dane, and shuffled off.

Dane and I slipped inside. We sat with Balthazar until the Mothers' Milk wore off and he awoke. He tried to sit up, but Theodore gently forbade him.

"You should lie as still as possible," I told him. "Doctor's orders."

"Ashmole's?" he rasped.

"Mine."

Theodore helped him sip from a cup and plumped up the pillows, earning a glare from the patient.

"Stop fussing," Balthazar grumbled.

Max grinned. "You're feeling better already."

"I feel like I've been stabbed in the stomach. It hurts."

"Now you sound like Quentin." Max clasped Balthazar's shoulder and his smile softened. "We're glad to hear your complaints, my friend."

Balthazar returned the smile. "I'm glad to be voicing them."

"You did a stupid thing," Meg admonished him. "You could have informed someone of your plan."

"You wouldn't have let me go through with it."

There was no denying the truth of that, so nobody tried.

"Next time, make sure you're armed," Dane said. "And don't drag Josie into it."

"She wasn't supposed to be there. And I wasn't expecting them to draw some of my guards away by releasing the prisoners."

"It was a neat way to distract us." I leaned forward and kissed his forehead. "You did a fine thing today."

"Debatable," Dane said, arms crossed.

"You would have done the same thing," I shot back.

He scowled but conceded the point with a nod. "So am I all powerful now?" he asked Balthazar, voice dripping with sarcasm.

"If having the nobles agree to your proposals is power, then yes," Balthazar said. "Use it wisely. Josie, you must control him."

"I can control myself," Dane said. "I won't ask them to agree to anything at all. I'll merely make suggestions. Every proposal must be debated and voted upon fairly."

"And if the Deerhorns are freed?"

A muscle in Dane's jaw pulsed. "Except that. I'll demand justice for their crimes."

Balthazar reached out a hand and Dane took it. "I trust you."

"Just get better soon, and you can keep me in check yourself. You have three weeks. That's when Josie and I are marrying."

"Us too," Meg piped up.

"I'll be there, even if I have to be carried on a litter," Balthazar said.

Theodore made his excuses and opened the door, only to pause. "Uh," he said, turning to us. "There are some people out here who wish to speak to you, Bal. Can they come in, Josie?"

"Two at a time," I said, rising. "And they can stop only briefly." I stood at the head of the bed to keep an eye on proceedings and monitor Balthazar's condition.

Dane, Meg and Max made their excuses and joined Theodore as he opened the door wider. Dozens of servants filled the corridor.

Theodore clapped his hands for attention. "Form a line, please. You two, in you go. Just say a few words then leave."

I touched Balthazar's shoulder. "It seems you have a few friends among the servants."

He grunted good-naturedly. "Perhaps. Or perhaps they want to make sure I'll live so they'll get paid on time."

* * *

I SLEPT on a roll-out bed in Balthazar's room that night. He rested peacefully, and the following morning, his pulse felt steady. He still looked deathly pale, and had difficulty lifting so much as a finger, but he ate everything I set before him.

I left him in Theodore's capable hands mid-morning to report on his condition to Dane. I was waylaid several times by servants inquiring after Balthazar, but eventually found Dane in one of the salons in the king's apartments. He was surrounded by noblemen and women, but they didn't appear to be having a meeting. Rather, the discussions going on around him seemed informal, an air of cheeriness about them.

He saw me and broke away from the duke of Buxton. "How is he?"

"Better than I expected," I said.

"And you?"

I smiled. "Also better than I expected. I feel as though a huge weight has been lifted from my shoulders."

He clasped my hand in his. "As do I. Everyone knows about the Deerhorns. We're waiting for Lord Deerhorn to join us. He was informed last night of events and was summoned to the palace this morning. The dukes want to question him about his involvement in the attack."

"And you?"

"I want to throw him in jail with his wife, but they told me he can't be arrested if she acted alone." He squeezed my hand. "As much as I want to, I won't use the power granted to me from the wish to convince the nobles otherwise."

"That's very restrained of you."

He grunted. "I think if I can restrain myself with this, I can restrain myself with anything."

"You're very strong," I teased.

"You have no idea."

All the conversations suddenly ceased as everyone turned to the door. Lord Deerhorn stood there, searching the faces, two guards flanking him. His gaze finally fell on Dane. He stiffened, lifted his chin, and bowed deeply. When he straightened, he approached. The guards moved with him, hands on sword hilts.

"My Lord Lockhart," he began. "I want to apologize for my

wife and son. I am deeply offended by their actions yesterday, but I want to assure you I had no idea what they planned. If I did, I would have stopped them from doing something so utterly foolish."

"Foolish?" the duke of Buxton asked.

"Despicable," Lord Deerhorn spluttered. "Detestable. Nasty and vile." His face grew redder as he spat out each word. "It's my deepest regret that I didn't know what they were up to."

"How could you not?" one of the nobles asked. "You're the head of the family."

Lord Deerhorn swallowed heavily. "I admit that I should have controlled my wife. I am sorry that I could not. She has never been a dutiful, agreeable wife. She has always been willful and, sadly, my eldest son grew up in her image. I should have taken him in hand earlier and steered him away from his mother's viciousness." He finished with another swallow and carefully watched Dane's reaction.

Dane stood with his hands at his back, looking every bit the king addressing an errant subject. I doubted he knew they all saw him as the king rather than an interim leader of the republic. If he did, he might try to appear less regal.

"I don't expect you to control your wife," Dane said. "She's capable of making up her own mind, as is Lord Xavier. Both know right from wrong, yet they willfully chose to commit grave crimes for their own gain."

Lord Deerhorn nodded quickly, making his jowls shake violently. "Yes, yes, they did. I don't understand why they attacked the master of the palace. Perhaps they were mad. I've long suspected something was wrong with my son." He tapped his temple. "And my wife encouraged his...excesses."

"What I do expect is for you to follow the law and have common human decency," Dane went on.

"Of course, of course. And I would humbly suggest that I always abide by the law."

Dane arched his brows. "I could list a number of incidents where you have either directly or indirectly harmed the villagers of Mull."

"Sir, those incidents were all my wife's doing! She forced my hand! She was greedy, corrupt. You must believe me! My second son, Greville, and I are both innocent." The rise of his voice made him sound small, weak, and afraid.

"I have no doubt that you were complicit in at least some of your wife's endeavors, but without proof, I can't accuse you officially. Consider yourself on notice, however. Don't test me. Don't do anything to draw my ire or I will see that Lord Greville inherits not a single brick or blade of grass on the Deerhorn estate. Is that clear?"

Lord Deerhorn bowed deeply again. "Yes, my lord. Thank you for your generosity and understanding."

He rose and looked around at the stern faces of his peers. None would side with him now. Even the duke of Gladstow turned up his nose at his former father-in-law.

"You're still a nobleman of Glancia and have every right to attend meetings," Dane said. "We're about to have one now, to discuss the future of the republic. You're welcome to stay and discuss the proposals."

Lord Deerhorn suddenly grasped Dane's hand and kissed the back of it.

Dane snatched his hand away. "Don't do that. I'm not king." He signaled for the noblemen to make their way to the council meeting room so they could begin.

Once they were gone and we were alone, he turned to me. "Should we trust him?" he asked.

"We have no choice," I said. "But I do think he'll try to stay on your good side, if only for Lord Greville's sake."

He kissed the top of my head. "I'd better join them. Meet me later?"

"I'll be in Bal's room."

"Be dressed for a ride into the village."

"Why?"

"To go to the temple and officially give notice of our pending nuptials."

"Don't cut the meeting short if it's going well. We can go to the temple another day."

"The republic can wait. Our wedding is more important."

"Try telling the nobles that."

He tilted his head to the side and eyed the door through which they'd gone. "Challenge accepted." He kissed my forehead again then headed off in the direction of the council meeting room.

CHAPTER 17

*O*ur wedding was not a quiet or small affair. We decided to conduct it in the palace gardens after Theodore warned us that all the servants wanted to attend, and Meg said many villagers planned to as well. I'd worried that the noblemen and women wouldn't like having their accommodations overrun by commoners, but Dane convinced me otherwise.

"The garden is large enough for everyone," he said in the days leading up to the ceremony. We stood on the steps overlooking the formal hedges and paths that stretched to Lake Grand, sparkling in the distance. It was the perfect spot for our wedding. I couldn't imagine it being anywhere else. The palace was such an integral part of the fabric of our relationship. "Besides, the palace doesn't belong to them," Dane added.

"Who does it belong to now?" I asked.

"The republic of Glancia. It'll be used by advisors, ministers and their staff. Foreign delegations will stay here, and high-ranking nobles during meetings. There'll be public theatricals and musical evenings, fairs and other events that all Glancians can attend. The forests will be reopened for controlled hunting and foraging, and the menagerie and orangery will be used for the study of zoology and botany." He touched his fingers to mine. "One of the pavilions will be dedicated to the study of medicine, surgery and midwifery. Anyone with a serious interest in any of those endeavors will be welcome to attend, not just those trained in the Logios surgeon's college."

"Women?"

"It would be strange not to allow women when one is over-seeing it."

I frowned.

"Will you do it, Josie?"

"Me?" I blurted out. I laughed but he didn't join in. "Is that wise, Dane? Some doctors will be upset that an uneducated female is in charge."

"You're not uneducated. Besides, if anyone complains, they can leave. I suspect Doctor Ashmole will stay away."

"Even if he wanted to, he'd be too busy with his new practice in Tilting," I said.

On the evening Meg had been chosen as the newest village councilor, mere days before our wedding, Doctor Ashmole announced his intention to leave Mull just as soon as a new doctor arrived. No one asked him to stay. Meg said she would put forward a proposal at the first council meeting to have my fine overturned so that the cottage could be returned to me, but I declined the offer.

"Give it to a family in need when the Ashmoles move to Tilt-ing," I said. "My home is with Dane, and for the next two years his home is the palace."

"Poor you," Meg had teased.

I wasn't inclined to consider the palace a good place to live, however. Only our private apartments were truly private. Everywhere else was open to nobles and officials. I would concede that our rooms were very comfortable, and the space was many times larger than my old cottage. It would also be nice not to have to do domestic chores, the bane of my exis-tence. I could concentrate on teaching Mistress Swinson the science of midwifery so that she could take over from me, as well as see to the conversion of the pavilion into a medical school.

But all of that would come after the wedding.

The day dawned overcast but I saw little of the morning. I was too busy being dressed, coiffed, and primped by various maids in the apartments that had been reserved for the queen that never was.

"Do a twirl," Miranda said, making little circles with her finger.

I did as asked and received sighs of appreciation.

"You look beautiful," Meg said. She came in to hug me, but was warned away by Kitty.

"Don't ruin her hair!" Kitty cried.

"That dress is perfect," Meg went on. "Theodore, you have excellent taste."

Theodore bowed. He had re-entered the dressing room after I'd put on the gown and fussed over it until it was just right. His critical eye spotted a loose gold thread on the train which he mended with deft fingers, but otherwise, it was indeed perfect.

The cool season meant a light, summery gown wouldn't be suitable, so we'd chosen the highest quality silk in frost-white from the draper. Theodore spent an entire week sewing it into a figure-hugging shape with long sleeves. A second over-sleeve kept my upper arms warm then fell away from the elbow. Theodore had spent the next two weeks overseeing three village dressmakers as they embroidered an elaborate gold vine pattern interspersed with seed pearls on the sleeves, the high collar and the train. He'd sewn on the horizontal gold military-style braids across the bodice himself and presented me with a wide gold belt in delicate filigree that morning to finish off the outfit.

"I found it in Leon's wardrobe," he admitted. "I hope you don't mind."

"Not at all. If it weren't for him finding that gem and wishing to be a rich king, we wouldn't be here today." I studied myself in the looking glass and spared a thought for the selfish, immature Leon who'd asked for more than he could handle. Then I dismissed him. Today was for happier thoughts.

"I adore weddings," Kitty exclaimed, clasping her hands together as she studied me. "I can't wait for yours, Meg."

"I'm so glad I delayed it a week," Meg said as she inspected her hair in the looking glass. Not once had she self-consciously touched the birthmark nor tried to cover it up with powder.

"It is rather a lot of work for you on top of the councilor's duties," Kitty said sympathetically.

"Not for that reason. Since all of my guests are here, they're going to need a week to recover."

I laughed. Like Meg, I expected it to be rather a long day and night. The palace kitchen had been preparing for weeks. I'd instructed the cook not to make anything elaborate, as there were a lot of mouths to feed. There'd been a great deal of running about for the rest of the staff this last week, too. Servants seemed to not have time to stop and talk to me. None would tell me what Balthazar had planned.

He'd been directing proceedings from his bed, despite my protests. He claimed he'd left the preparations up to Theodore, but considering Theodore spent most of his waking hours working on my wedding gown and the dresses of my attendants, I suspected Balthazar was lying to appease me.

A band struck up a merry tune in the distance and Kitty clapped her hands. "That's the signal. It's time!"

Meg peered out the window and gasped. I went to look too, but was ordered to stop by Theodore and my three attendants.

"It must be a surprise or Balthazar will murder us," Miranda said. "Well," she added as she admired my gown. "Are you ready to dazzle Dane?"

Meg snickered. "He was dazzled a long time ago."

It was quite a way from the queen's chambers down to the gardens, particularly at the slow pace Theodore forced us to walk. When the doors leading outside opened, I gasped at the sight in front of me. The grand terrace leading out to the gardens was filled with villagers and servants. They cheered upon seeing me, and I was clapped and congratulated as I traversed through the crowd.

Garlands of leaves and flowers marked out the path's edges and white perfumed petals covered the paving stones. The flowers were not in season, yet the head gardener had managed to keep them alive in his orangery glasshouse. Balthazar must have used every last one. Exotic lemon, orange and oleander trees in pots had also been positioned at intervals along the path and down the steps leading to the main fountain. The sun came out at that moment and rainbows formed in the fountain spray.

"That's an auspicious sign," Kitty whispered.

"Poppycock," Miranda whispered back. "It's a trick of the light. But I will admit it's quite beautiful."

We rounded the fountain and headed towards Dane and his groomsmen. Theodore strode ahead of us so he could stand beside Balthazar, seated in a chair to Dane's left. On Dane's right stood Erik, Quentin, and Max, all looking handsome in their crimson guards' uniforms.

Dane stood tall between them. I considered myself slightly biased, but he was the most handsome of the men, in his captain's uniform. Nobody had told him he couldn't wear it now that he was no longer the captain of the guards, and I was glad of it. He looked very fine, and the gold braiding at the shoulder matched that on my gown's bodice. I took in the details of his uniform, of the flowered arch he stood beneath, and the local Mullian priest waiting patiently to the side.

But it was Dane's face I wanted to commit to memory. I never wanted to forget this day, or the way he looked at me. He seemed slightly bemused, somewhat over-awed, but most assuredly loving.

Then he smiled, and it was dazzling.

* * *

THE WEDDING DAY turned into the wedding night with music, dancing, and feasting. The air turned cold, but Balthazar had organized fire pits to be brought out to keep everyone warm. When I stood on the palace terrace and looked back towards Lake Grand, the gardens were ablaze with light.

"You did a wonderful job, Bal," I said, taking his hand. "But I hope you didn't over-exert yourself."

"I haven't lifted more than my finger," he said.

"You lifted your finger to point at me on many occasion," Quentin grumbled. "He had me running all over the palace issuing directions."

"Not just you," Erik said. He put his arm around my waist. "Can I kiss the bride? Is that custom here?"

"Only on the cheek," Dane said.

Erik pouted. "Pity. In the Margin, men can kiss her on the mouth."

"You're making that up," Max said.

"How do you know?"

"Because I know you well enough to know when you're lying."

Erik grinned and looked around. "I must go. I see maids over there who need me."

"They're ladies, not maids," Theodore called after him.

He waved off Theodore's concern and kept walking.

"Should we be worried about him?" Meg asked.

"He never persists where he's not wanted," I said, watching the four noblewomen smile as he joined them. By the looks of things, he would be welcomed in precisely the way he liked.

"You should retire, Bal," Theodore said with a worried frown.

"I will." Balthazar looked towards Lake Grand. "Soon."

Yelena joined us, with Martha stopping a few steps away. Dane beckoned her over and put his arm around her shoulders. "Are you enjoying yourself?"

"Oh, yes," the maid said, smiling. "It's wonderful. The music is perfect, the dancing and food...it's all so wonderful."

"Make sure you try the confectionary. The cooks have worked hard all week."

"I will. Thank you, Dane, and congratulations to you both."

Dane addressed Yelena. "Are you warm enough, Mother?"

She adjusted the fur-lined cloak around her shoulders. It was too big for her, and I suspected it had been taken from Leon's wardrobe along with the jewels adorning her neck. Theodore frowned as he studied her up and down with a calculating eye.

Yelena took Dane's hand between her gloved ones. "I wanted to wait until the ceremony was over to tell you both that I'm leaving."

"Leaving?" Dane echoed.

"I'm returning to Freedland. Martha will come with me."

Dane frowned at Martha. "Why?"

Martha lowered her head.

"Because it's our home," Yelena said. "We don't belong here with these people." She waved a hand that encompassed me and the crowd beyond.

"Does this have something to do with my decision to turn Glancia into a republic?"

"No-o." Her hesitation was telling. "I will admit that I feel deeply hurt by some of your decisions, but that's not why I want to go. I want to be home for... I just want to go home."

She meant she wanted to die there. I had warned Dane mere days ago that I suspected Yelena was dying. He hadn't said anything at the time and not brought it up since.

I eyed him carefully, but his only reaction was to hug her. When they parted, they were both dry-eyed.

"I'm sure she will seek you out tomorrow," Yelena went on, "but I ought to tell you that Laylana is returning with us, and her new beau, too. I don't envy her informing her brother that she intends to marry a footman, but that's her decision, and I've learned I have no sway in how others live their lives."

Dane stiffened. "I'm sorry if my decisions hurt you. That was not my intention."

She nodded. With an adjustment of the cloak, she headed inside.

Martha went to follow her, but Dane caught her elbow. He waited until Yelena had disappeared from sight before he enveloped Martha in a hug that was longer and warmer than the one he'd given his mother. When they parted, both had tears in their eyes.

"Take care of her for me," he said.

She gave him a wobbly smile and a nod.

"And take care of yourself too," he added. "I hope to see you back here one day."

"You will always be welcome," I told her.

She hugged him again then hugged me. "I couldn't have wished for anyone better for him," she said. "You won't let him get away with anything."

I laughed. "I'll do my best to keep him out of trouble."

She hurried off to catch up to her mistress, just as Erik rejoined us along with Quentin, Meg and Max.

"Ready?" Balthazar said.

"For what?" Dane and I both asked.

"You'll see, Mistress Lockhart," Quentin said with a grin.

"It's Lady Lockhart," Max chided.

Quentin saluted. "Right. I forgot. Lord and Lady Lockhart." He pulled a face. "It sounds weird."

"I know," Dane muttered.

I hooked my arm through his. "We'll get used to it together."

"I like the sound of that." He kissed me lightly then tapped Balthazar on the shoulder. "When's this surprise of yours happening? I have important business to attend to in our chambers."

"Patience never was your strong suit," Balthazar said. "It's about to begin. Watch the lake."

They all looked at the lake, but Dane studied me. "I happen to think I've been very patient this evening."

The loud explosion cracked through the night air. Screams erupted from the crowd, but they quickly turned to squeals of delight as fireworks crackled. Tiny stars of light lit up the darkness above the lake. Another firework went off, followed by another and another, dispatched from barges on the water.

"Oh look, Dane," I said on a breath. "They form a love heart."

He stood behind me and circled me in his arms. He lightly nipped my ear. "Seems appropriate."

"Magical," I murmured as more fireworks brightened the sky to sounds of awe from the onlookers.

"It ain't magic," Quentin said. "It's just a little explosive powder, a fuse—"

Max smacked his arm.

Quentin rubbed it but was distracted by another firework, this one climbing higher in the sky than the others before exploding into a thousand golden stars. As the stars rained into the lake, a flaming arrow shot from the shoreline arced through air. It struck something in the dark in the middle of the lake. The flames quickly spread to reveal the entwined letters of J and D. The initials appeared to be floating on the lake surface, with no barge in sight. The guests gasped in delight.

"I take it back," Quentin murmured. "That *is* magical." He turned to Balthazar, his eyes wide. "Are you the sorcerer?"

Balthazar chuckled. "If I were, I'd have given myself a stronger body a long time ago."

Quentin watched the fireworks fade away. "But if you are, can you make me taller?"

Erik clapped him on the shoulder. "You are a very handsome young man. All you need is confidence. Like me." He tapped his chest. "Come, I will show you how to get any woman you desire." He dragged Quentin off by the elbow.

"Erik, I already have a woman."

"Aye, but I will show you how to get another, and another. Why stop at just one?"

Max drew Meg to his side. "I can think of an excellent reason," he told her.

She grinned and threw her arms around him.

Dane tugged me away from them, towards the palace doors. "Thanks for the surprise, Bal," he called back. "But my patience has worn out."

Balthazar dismissed us with a wave then signaled for Theodore to help him inside.

Dane and I got as far as the entrance foyer where he scooped me up. "Come with me, Lady Lockhart. I've got my own surprise to show you."

I gave him an arched look as we headed up the stairs. "I've seen it, Dane. It's hardly a surprise."

He grinned. "It's not that."

"Then what is it?"

"Patience, my lady."

He carried me all the way to the king's apartments, which we'd decided to make our home for the next two years. He opened door after door without setting me down until we reached the door to a room that I'd never been in.

Indeed, I didn't even know the panel in the wall was a door until he opened it. The room on the other side was hardly big enough to be called such. It was more of a nook with a window overlooking the celebrations in the formal gardens below. A cushioned window seat looked inviting, but wasn't the most wonderful thing about the room. That honor went to the books nestled into shelves set into all the walls.

I gasped as Dane set me down, and went to inspect the spines. "These are medical texts," I said.

"Your father's books," he said. "I retrieved them from your cottage. Doctor Ashmole didn't mind, but his wife scowled at me the entire time. Although I've never seen her not scowling, so perhaps it's the way her face settles."

"There must be hundreds! Far more than my father ever owned."

"I spoke to the high priest before he returned to Tilting and asked him to send back anything he could find that looked remotely medical from the high temple's library. He owed us that." He gazed around the room. "It seems he felt guilty."

"Very." I circled my arms around Dane's neck. "Thank you, Husband. This is already my favorite room."

He beamed. "Good. Now let me take you to my favorite room." He scooped me up again and carried me to the bedchamber.

THE END

Want more from the world of *After the Rift*? Read the standalone spin-off THE WARRIOR PRIEST. Starring Rhys, who appeared in *The Temple of Forgotten Secrets* (*After The Rift* book 4), THE WARRIOR PRIEST is a one-off novel available from September 2025.

Read on for a description.

EXCERPT: THE WARRIOR PRIEST

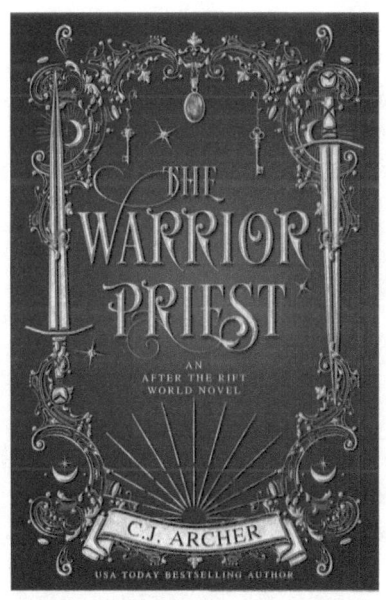

About This Book

A warrior priest sworn to an oath of celibacy, and a spy fleeing from her past. A magical mystery, a forbidden temptation and a destiny they cannot escape.

Jacqueline (Jac) has survived on the streets ever since

escaping from the clutches of her ruthless uncle, the city's powerful governor. He craves more than political influence and believes a legendary talisman in Jac's possession can give it to him.

To survive, Jac has honed her skills as a thief, catching the eye of Rhys Mayhew, a brother in an order of warrior priests. Rhys enlists her as a spy, and their partnership soon deepens into more. But Rhys's faith demands strict adherence to oaths of denial, and when he is unexpectedly elevated to the position of master of his order, he faces an impossible choice: his duty or his growing attraction to Jac.

As her uncle's net tightens, Jac seizes a chance to become an assassin's apprentice, leaving the city for months of grueling training. When she returns, much has changed—except the forbidden nature of her bond with Rhys.

When her uncle learns of her return, Jac's life is in grave danger, forcing her and Rhys to unite. Together they unravel the secrets of the talisman and confront dangers both old and new. But the greatest danger of all is to Rhys's loyalty, as resisting Jac becomes more difficult with every passing day.

Chapter 1

I first met Rhys Mayhew when he plucked me out of the path of a runaway horse with one hand, a half-eaten apple wedged between his teeth. He told me later that he could only spare one hand because he didn't want to put down the tankard of ale he held in the other. He didn't spill a drop during the rescue, nor when he shoved me behind his three companions standing side by side near the entrance to the inn. The first and only drop fell when my pursuers arrived. I watched through the gap between two burly men sporting the symbol of the warrior priests' order on their belted, knee-length brown tunics as Rhys pointed the tankard in a southerly direction.

He removed the apple from his mouth. "He went that way."

"Thank you, Brother," one of the constables said as he ran off.

The fatter constable stood with hands on hips, his chest heaving as he sucked air into his lungs.

Rhys handed him the tankard. "You look like you need this more than me."

The constable gulped down the contents with the same enthusiasm he'd shown for pursuing me. He gave the tankard back and swiped a gloved hand across his mouth. "Merdu bless you, Brother." The constable set off.

Once he and his colleague were out of sight, I turned to run.

Rhys grasped me by the back of my doublet again. The leather was so thin, the seams so old, that it began to rip.

"Let me go, oaf!"

Rhys released me to the sounds of his priest brothers chuckling. He gave me what remained of the apple. "Walk with me. I have a business proposition for you that will put an end to your need to steal. It'll even put a roof over your head." He gave his friends a look and they wordlessly entered the tavern.

I fell into step alongside my savior, although I suspected he shortened his strides so I didn't have to trot. His offer intrigued me. More than that, I knew what it could mean—a way out. When a warrior priest made you an offer to end your starvation, you took it. Famous for their discipline, sacrifice and rigid adherence to their oaths, including celibacy, I felt safe assuming he didn't want me for my body.

I greedily ate the apple, hardly swallowing one bite before taking the next.

"Slow down," he said. "You'll give yourself a stomachache."

I didn't slow down. I finished it, core and all.

We turned the corner and I realized we were in the inn's courtyard. A groom led a horse into one of the stables while its rider strode to the rear door of the inn, a worn leather satchel under one arm. Another groom swept the cobblestones, while a third sat on a bale of hay, watching a boy struggle to roll a barrel across the uneven ground. No one paid us much attention. Our conversation wouldn't be overheard.

"What do you want me to do?" I asked.

"A little spying here and there."

"Why?"

"Because you rarely make a mistake like the one you made today."

He was right. Today had been different. I'd seen my mother's uncle for the first time in almost a year. While I was confident I'd done enough to change my appearance since then, seeing him again had brought back ugly memories. Panicked, I'd fumbled then dropped the carrot I'd stolen from the costermonger's cart. He'd noticed and shouted "Thief!", drawing the attention of constables who'd happened to be passing by.

I studied the priest. He was classically handsome with his tanned skin, short brown hair and clear blue eyes, but it wasn't merely his face that would have the women of Tilting lamenting he'd chosen a life of celibacy. Tall, even for a Glancian man, and broad across the shoulders, I would have guessed he'd be capable of wielding a sword even if I hadn't seen his order's badge on his tunic.

Yet it wasn't his good looks or impressive physique that made my heart flutter. There was something else, something I couldn't quite define. The spark in his eye and tilt of his lips made it seem as though he went through life in the best of humor, as if nothing troubled him and never would. For someone like me, whose life had shrunk to living in dank sewers and stealing scraps to survive, Rhys was magnetic.

I learned later that he was only twenty-four when we met. That age never quite felt right. It seemed too old for the mischievous, youthful air that clung to him, and too young for the responsibilities that would one day burden him. But I didn't think about that until much later.

"You've been watching me," I said, a challenge in my voice.

"You're quick and nimble. I've seen you steal a bag of nuts at the market without the stallholder noticing, or some ells from a man's pocket, also unnoticed. You have light fingers, and being small helps you slip away easily, or simply to blend in. Despite your poor attempt at a disguise, people usually take you for exactly what you want them to see—a boy."

I resisted the urge to touch my cropped hair and instead settled my feet further apart, as I'd seen lads on the cusp of manhood do. "I am a boy."

"You must think I'm an idiot to fall for the girl-disguised-as-boy trick."

I gave in without a fight. For some reason, I wanted him to know. "In my defense, people usually are idiots."

"'In my defense?'" he mimicked. I'd never quite been able to lose my upper-class accent, and with him I'd barely even tried to hide it. "The child speaks like she just stepped out of her tutor's schoolroom."

"I'm not a child. I'm seventeen."

He scoffed. "Nice try. You're thirteen, fourteen at most. Tell me, why is an educated girl living on the streets as a boy?"

"None of your business." It was a pathetic response, but it was all I could think of at the time. He'd unbalanced me with his assessment. He was right—I was educated, a girl, and living on the streets disguising myself as a boy. He only got my age wrong. I was seventeen. Perhaps if he'd studied my figure more closely, he'd have noticed, but he kept his gaze firmly fixed on my face.

"What's your name?"

"Jac."

"Short for Jacqueline?" When I didn't answer, he said, "My name's Rhys Mayhew. I'm a brother in the Order of Merdu's Guards." He tapped the badge depicting a sword crossing a blazing sun stitched into the tunic at his chest.

"I noticed."

He removed a small pouch from his pocket, tossed it in the air and caught it. The clinking of ells had me salivating. The apple had been my only food that day. "An advance payment." He dropped it onto my outstretched palm. "There'll be more if you meet me back here tonight when the temple bell strikes eleven."

I stared at the pouch. "How do you know I won't run off with your money and not come back?"

"You won't."

"But how do you know?"

He smiled, revealing a dimple in each cheek, and signaled to the ostler to bring his horse.

Weeks later, Rhys admitted that he hadn't known, he'd simply gambled on me being desperate enough. Once again, he was right. Even though my thieving kept me from starving, I was tired of always looking over my shoulder, tired of living in squalor, and sleeping with one eye open and my back to the wall. His offer was the best thing to happen to me since I ran away from my great-uncle's home. I had no choice but to accept, if I were to survive.

Before the ostler could bring out Rhys's horse, the two constables walked past the entrance to the yard and just happened to look through the archway directly at us.

"There he is!" shouted one, pointing at me. "Brother, you've caught the thief! Thank you. Now hand him over."

Rhys regarded the advancing constables as if he didn't have a care in the world. In truth, he didn't. It was me who'd be thrown into prison if I were caught, not him. All he had to do was reassure the men that he had indeed caught me and was about to take me to the sheriff's office. He could claim I escaped on the way. The lie would keep his reputation pristine and me free.

Instead, he spoke to me under his breath. "I feel like having a little fun. Do you, Jac?"

The constables strolled toward us, swords still in their scabbards. They weren't worried about me attacking them, and they were entirely unprepared for Rhys working against them. "If your idea of fun is saving me, then yes. Do you have a plan?"

"Of course." He clapped me on the back, grasping a fistful of my jerkin as he did so, and marched me toward the constables.

My stomach plunged. He was apprehending me, after all.

Although I didn't say a word, he must have felt me tense beneath his grip. "Have faith, Jac." The laconic drawl defined the carefree twenty-four-year-old Rhys Mayhew. His words, however, would one day haunt me.

Faith would tear us apart.

"Slip past them while I distract them," he went on.

"That's your plan?"

"You underestimate how distracting I can be."

"Ha! Nobody underestimates that."

His grip loosened. "Good sirs! The lad is a slippery fish, but no one outwits a brother of Merdu's Guards." He angled us between the constables and the exit, then released me. "Here you go."

I ran.

Behind me, I heard the constables shouting at me to stop, then at each other to go after me, then at Rhys for blocking the way. "You're obstructing us on purpose!"

I didn't hear Rhys's response, or perhaps he didn't give one. The next moment, as I sprinted down the street, he drew up alongside me. "Turn left," he directed. "Get lost in the market."

The market was always busy, and it was easier to disappear as long as you darted around carts, stalls and people without knocking anything over. Easier, that is, if you were small and nimble. Rhys was surprisingly fleet for a large man, but he wasn't in the least unobtrusive. Everyone noticed him.

I risked a glance behind us. "They're still following."

"Surprising. I thought they'd run out of steam by now."

He leapt over a wooden crate while I darted around it, only to have a wheelbarrow full of cabbages thrust at me. I wasn't sure if the cabbage seller did it on purpose or if it was an accident, but it slowed me down as I lost my balance.

Rhys grasped me around my waist before I fell, and tucked me into his side, lifting my feet off the ground. Not only was it an ungainly position, he would have felt all of my feminine curves, what little curves my undernourished figure had.

"Put me down! I'm not a sack of potatoes."

He glanced around and finally released me. "Down that lane," he ordered. "We need to get out of the market. Coming here was a bad idea."

"I could have told you that if I'd known your plan," I tossed over my shoulder as I ran.

"It would have been a good plan, if you'd avoided that wheelbarrow."

"How was I supposed to avoid it when it was shoved directly at me? I don't have legs like a giant leaping spider," I said pointedly.

"I've been compared to a few creatures before, not always favorably, but never a spider." How could he sound so calm? My heart thundered in my chest, not only from fear but also exertion. I was used to sneaking, not running for my life.

I dared another glance back at the pursuing constables, only to trip over the uneven cobblestones.

Rhys once again grabbed my jerkin, causing the beleaguered seams at my shoulders to finally rip apart. "You're good at thieving, not so good at escaping."

"I don't usually need to escape," I spat out between labored breaths. "Today is not a good day."

"Cheer up. It's about to get better."

"Why?" I followed Rhys's gaze.

He looked directly ahead where a brick wall loomed. The lane came to an end. The only exit was behind us, where the constables were still in pursuit.

"How is that better?"

He flashed a grin. "Change of plan."

"What plan?"

He stopped and linked his fingers together, forming a cradle. "Up you go."

I looked up. The building was the only single-level one in the entire lane. With Rhys's help, I could escape across the roof. But could he climb up without any assistance? There was nothing for him to stand on to give him a boost.

"Now, Jac." It was the tersest he'd sounded throughout the entire escapade.

I glanced along the lane. The constables had slowed, but there was no way to get past them out of the lane. "What about you?"

"Don't worry about me. I've been in stickier situations than this and got out of them."

"With Merdu's warriors at your back," I said as I placed my foot into his hands. I grasped the roof tiles and hauled myself up. Rhys made it easier, pushing me as high as he could.

Despite a niggling doubt, I wasn't too concerned about him. Constables wouldn't arrest a warrior priest.

Below me, the constables drew their swords and faced off against Rhys. They were alone in the lane. There were no witnesses. They could attack him with no one finding out what they'd done. Rhys had to rely on his own skill with the sword, and two against one weren't favorable odds.

But he didn't even draw his sword. He simply ran at the wall below and leapt. Using the wall as leverage, he stretched up to grasp the overhanging roof. Swinging his legs, he managed to get half of his body onto the roof. But one of the tiles broke under the weight. He slipped.

"Rhys!" I grabbed his shoulders. The pendant around my neck emerged from beneath my shirt as I leaned forward.

I doubted I played much of a part in saving him, but somehow he managed to keep both arms on the roof while his body dangled down. Seeing an opportunity, the two constables leapt at his legs.

At that moment, Rhys swung them up again. This time, the tiles held, and he pulled himself onto the roof. He lay on the sloping tiles and grinned at me. "Don't look so terrified, Jac. I won't let anything happen to you."

I tucked the pendant back under my shirt. "Merdu and Hailia, you're mad! Why didn't you just give yourself up? Or will you be thrown out of the order if your master hears of this?"

He sat up. "Never. I'm his favorite." He stood and peered over the edge of the roof, just as two hands suddenly gripped the tiles from below. "Isn't that interesting."

I scrambled to my feet. "What is?"

"They're still going. I'd have put money on them giving up by now. Come on. We'd better get a head start. You're going to need it since you don't have legs like a giant spider." He indicated I should go up the roof ahead of him, much as a gentleman signals to a lady to enter a room first.

To the tune of grunts coming from the two constables as they tried to get onto the roof, I used all fours to balance as I scrambled up the tiles. "If you get me killed, I'm coming back from the afterlife to haunt you."

"Our religion doesn't believe in ghosts."

"Then it's lucky I don't believe in religion."

The ensuing silence felt heavy after the lighthearted moments we'd shared during our escape, but I needed to concentrate on my balance as I navigated the roofline, so gave it no further thought.

I came to a stop as the building butted up against a taller one.

We'd need to repeat our climb if we were to continue that way. The only other way out was down the sloping roof on the other side then dropping into what appeared to be a courtyard surrounded by buildings. In other words, we would be easy to trap down there.

I turned to face Rhys. "I don't fancy going up again."

"Afraid of heights?"

"No. I'm tired of being chased."

He glanced over his shoulder. "Do you have a plan?"

One of the constables was on the roof, although he looked unsteady on the steeply sloping tiles. He was calling down to his colleague, instructing him on the best way to get up.

"Unlike you, yes."

I was glad to see the humor return to Rhys's eyes. I wasn't sure why it bothered me that he'd been offended by my heathenism. All I knew was that I preferred his mischievousness.

"I have some skill with a knife," I said. "I presume you have some skill with a sword. If we work together, we might have a chance."

He chuckled. At the time, I had no idea why. Later, I would witness Rhys's skill for myself. Even with his eyes closed and a hand tied behind his back, two bumbling constables would offer no opposition. If I'd known that then, I would have found his actions even more baffling. Why didn't he just fight them then and there?

Perhaps he didn't want to harm them. Or perhaps he was simply enjoying himself.

"I have a better plan," he said.

"It's about time," I scoffed. "What do you propose?"

He looked down at the courtyard.

"But we'll be trapped!" I said.

"I told you, Jac. Have a little faith."

"Fine," I ground out. "Do I go first or do you?"

I'd not even finished speaking before he was on his way down the sloping roof. He hung onto the edge and swung himself down to the ground, landing deftly on his feet. He held his arms up to me. "Jump. I'll catch you."

I stared at him, open-mouthed.

Behind me, the constable stood on the ridge of the roof. "Got you," he snarled.

I jumped.

Rhys caught me effortlessly. He didn't set me down immediately, however. With his hands at my waist, I was pinned against his body. The cloth of his tunic and the shirt underneath hid nothing, not the ridges of muscles across his chest, rising and falling with breaths that had suddenly become ragged for the first time. Could he feel the contours of my body through the layers of my disguise? Was that why his gaze suddenly heated as it locked onto mine?

Eye to eye, chest to chest, I could easily kiss him. I wanted to kiss him. It was as if a madness had come over me, taking control. I'd never felt this brazen, this much desire and need. Rhys consumed my thoughts, even to the exclusion of my own safety, and I hadn't even known him an hour.

I reached up my hands to bury them in his hair, when he suddenly lowered me to the ground.

That's when I heard a door behind me crash back on its hinges. I suddenly turned to see the second constable barreling out of the house and into the courtyard. He drew his sword. "You should be ashamed of yourself, Brother."

Rhys put his hands in the air. "Let the lad go. He's just a hungry child."

"I thought you had a plan," I hissed.

"Who says it's not going how I wanted it to?" he hissed back.

"You wanted this to end in our surrender?"

"Not ours. Just mine."

"I'm not letting you do that for me."

"All will be well. Nothing will happen to me, Jac. You can still escape through the sewers. I'm standing on the grate. When I step off, open it quickly. Climb down the ladder then continue left. Always go left. Eventually, you'll come out at the river."

"I know the way. You're not coming with me?"

"I'll stay up here and keep him busy. Don't worry, I won't let him follow you."

I glanced up to where the constable on the roof was carefully navigating his way down the slope, arms out for balance, his attention focused on each slow, cautious step.

Rhys stepped off the grate. I bent down and wrapped my fingers around the bars.

"Stop!" The constable in the courtyard advanced.

Rhys moved to block him, his hands still in the air. "I said, let the lad go."

The constable, however, thrust his sword point at Rhys. "Move aside, Brother."

Rhys glanced at me. "What's taking you so long?"

"It's stuck," I said.

"Pull harder."

"Easy for you to say."

He grunted, conceding that he must have miscalculated. He swore under his breath, and the fingers of his right hand twitched, as if he wished he held his sword. For the first time since the pursuit began, he seemed rattled.

The constable ordered Rhys to step aside. Rhys hesitated before complying. The constable drew in a relieved breath then came for me.

I pulled out the iron grate and swung it at him. It hit his arm, and he lowered the sword with a grunt of pain.

I sprang up and ran past him, grabbing Rhys's hand as I did so. "Your plan needed a slight modification."

To the shouts of both constables, we raced across the courtyard. Just as we were about to enter the building, the constable on the roof cried out. I glanced back to see the constable on the ground look up at the same moment his colleague rolled off the roof. He dropped his sword in order to catch the man.

Both tumbled to the cobblestones in a tangle of limbs and curses.

Rhys and I ran on, out through the building and back down the lane. We reentered the market briefly before turning down another street then another. More twists and turns later, I was quite out of breath.

Finally, Rhys stopped when we reached the river. It was then that I noticed we still held hands. As if he'd just realized, too, he released me. I bent over double in an attempt to catch my breath.

After several moments, I straightened. Rhys's eyes were bright, his lips curved with his smile. He wasn't in the least out of breath. "I told you I had a plan," he said.

"That was not part of your plan."

"Wasn't it?"

I narrowed my gaze at him, no longer sure if it had been or not.

He started to laugh, and I couldn't help laughing along with him. Perhaps it was the danger and excitement we'd just shared, or perhaps it was because he made me feel safe, but in that moment, something exploded inside me. It was heady and all-consuming, and it awoke every part of me in such a way that I was utterly and completely absorbed by the feelings coursing through me.

Rhys made me feel wonderful, alive, special.

If I made him feel that way, he didn't show it. As his laughter faded, he simply pointed upstream. "You can find your way home by following this until you reach the crooked house, then go right, then left at the high fence."

"Oh," I managed to say. "Right. I mean left. Right." Hailia, stop me.

Still smiling, Rhys sauntered off, one hand resting on his sword hilt. "Don't forget: tonight at the eleventh hour."

I watched him walk away with an overwhelming sense that my life would be different from then on. A believer would say that Merdu, the god of change, had me in his sights. I was no longer sure if I believed in the power of the god and goddess. Like Rhys's, their plans seemed poorly considered.

All I knew was that meeting Rhys would be just the beginning.

Chapter 2

Three years later, I peered out of the window in a room where Rhys used to take his lovers. According to Mistress Blundle, the old woman who rented rooms on the ground floor, Rhys had a string of them before he became a priest. I discovered he hadn't stopped when he became one of Merdu's warriors, however. He simply became more discreet.

Not discreet enough, though, and I told him so after I overheard two women discussing him in the street as he passed by. He'd assured me that liaison had ended and he never took women to our secret meeting room anymore. From the way he avoided my gaze, I wondered if he still had lovers but just took them elsewhere. I decided I didn't want to know, so I didn't try to follow him and find out.

There was very little I couldn't find out. That was why Rhys hired me. I found things out for him, and sometimes for myself. Sometimes I found things out about Rhys, like Mistress Blundle's offhanded mention of women. Her comment intrigued me enough to investigate the ownership of the secret room. A little nocturnal excursion to the Glancian property office revealed the entire building had been owned by Rhys's father until his death when Rhys was aged just thirteen. I knew Rhys had been raised by the order after he became an orphan, then taken his priestly vows once he reached eighteen, the legal age of majority. According to the records, the building's ownership had been formally transferred to the order at that point, no doubt along with any other belongings Rhys possessed. The second-floor room had been left vacant, however, and Rhys continued to have access. I wondered how many brothers in his order knew.

After the first time he employed me to undertake a little spying, we changed our meeting place to that room, and we've met there on and off for three years. If he wanted to speak to me, he lit a candle and placed it on the windowsill, and I did the same if I had something to report. The central location of the building meant it wasn't out of our way to walk past and look up.

What began as sporadic meetings whenever he had a job for me became more frequent. Then they became daily. Sometimes we discussed a task he needed me to do, but usually we just talked or watched the stars in silence from the balcony. He was my friend—my only friend—while I was just one of many to him.

I watched him stride across the street, his cloak billowing

behind him like a sail. Even in the poor light cast by the flickering torches, I could make out Rhys's brown hair, a little darker than the blond of most Glancians, and his impressive physique. Once he was out of my sight, I counted slowly from one so I was ready for him to enter when I reached nine. As usual, he'd taken the steps two at a time. For someone who possessed patience in abundance, he had a distinct dislike for the slowness of stairs.

He removed his cloak and tossed it over the back of the armchair, one of the few pieces of furniture in the room, then placed his gloves on top. "Rain is in the air. You should stay here tonight, Jac, instead of going home."

"A little rain doesn't bother me."

It was an old argument that he repeated every time bad weather struck Tilting. Rhys paid me enough so that I no longer had to live on the streets, but even if I didn't have a roof over my head, I would refuse his offer. If I stayed in the same place where he and I met to exchange information, Mistress Blundle and the other neighbors would grow suspicious. Rhys may have owned the house once, but he didn't anymore. The master of his order might put a tenant in if he found out Rhys met a woman here, even if she was just his information gatherer, not his lover. That's if they realized I was a woman. I still passed myself off as a boy.

Rhys was nothing if not persistent. "But it's cold tonight."

"Stop whining, you big baby. Put on an extra hair shirt before bed if you're cold."

He crossed his arms over his chest. "Only zealots wear hair shirts, and I don't get cold. My muscles keep me warm." He flexed his arms, to prove the point. "You're skin and bone, Jac. Still. That reminds me…" He dug into the pocket of his tunic and produced a slice of honey cake wrapped in a cloth. "It was the cook's special treat after dinner for the celebrations." He handed me the cake.

It was rare for the priests to be given treats. All of the orders, whether dedicated to the god or goddess, had rules that required their priests and priestesses deprive themselves of worldly goods. I would argue that delicious food wasn't a worldly good, it was a necessity, but my argument would fall on deaf ears. If Rhys's friend Andreas was to be believed, Merdu's Guards dined on gray sludgy gruel twice a day. Then again, Andreas was prone to exaggeration.

I accepted the cake. "Thank you."

"Don't thank me, thank Rufus."

"He knows I like honey cake?"

"I stole it from his plate when he wasn't looking. You don't expect me to give up my own honey cake, do you?" He ruffled my hair.

Ruffled! He still saw me as a child. Sometimes I think he also still saw me as a boy. If my mother was alive, I'd be dancing at balls and playing the pianoforte, wearing pretty dresses with my long blonde hair elegantly arranged. Yet here I was, sitting on a windowsill, eating honey cake brought to me by the man I loved, who treated me like a fourteen-year-old boy.

I ate the honey cake as the first drops of rain splattered on the windowpanes, and tried very hard not to dwell on something I couldn't change.

Rhys built a small fire in the fireplace then warmed his hands by it. "You were at the parade ground this morning. Did you enjoy our display?"

"I did. There's nothing more exciting than watching over-sized men with oversized opinions of themselves pretend to fight each other with wooden swords."

He shot me a wry smirk over his shoulder. "Blame the master for the swords. I wanted to use real ones for authenticity, but he thought drawing blood while the king, governor and high priest all watched on was a bad idea. Can't think why. What do they expect from the protectors of the faith?"

"You had all the ladies swooning."

"Andreas had them swooning."

I rolled my eyes. I wasn't sure if Rhys was truly unaware of the effect he had on women, or whether he was just being modest. "How did you see me? Half the city was there, and I had my hood drawn low."

"I didn't." He sat in the armchair, stretched out his long legs, and smiled slyly. "You just confirmed it. You're a good spy, Jac, but don't get caught. Your captor will have the truth out of you before you're aware you're being interrogated."

"This is hardly an interrogation, and I had no need to keep my presence at the parade ground a secret from you."

His smile faded. "Just don't get caught when you're spying."

"I'm too good to be caught."

"You're forgetting how we met."

"I've gotten better at escaping since then." A lot better, thanks to Rhys teaching me how to balance and use my small size to my advantage. "Besides, I was distracted that day."

He arched his brows, waiting for me to tell him what I'd seen that I'd found so distracting. When I didn't respond, he added, "Promise me you'll be careful, Jac. Don't get complacent."

"I promise. What's brought this on?" It was nicer than I thought it would be to have someone worry about me, particularly when that person was Rhys. Perhaps he'd always worried about me, just never expressed it.

He crossed his legs at the ankles and stared into the flames. The light flickered across his face, highlighting the strong angles of his jaw and cheeks and giving his eyes a moodiness that wasn't natural on him.

I got up and stood between him and the fire. "Rhys? Do you have a new job for me?"

"You're good, Jac, but I think I'll ask someone else." He shrugged without meeting my gaze.

"For Hailia's sake, just tell me about the job. If I feel it's beyond me, I'll reject it, but don't pretend there's someone else you can ask because there isn't. I'm your best spy."

After a moment, he lifted his gaze to mine. "And you accuse me of having an oversized opinion of myself."

Despite my irritation, I couldn't help my smile. "What's the job?"

"I want you to look for a document in the governor's office."

I went very still.

Rhys missed nothing. "What is it?"

I shrugged, dismissive. "What's the document?"

He narrowed his gaze. "A declaration giving Tilting's governor the power to make decisions without the agreement of his council."

"That can't be allowed! He'll change laws to his advantage,

assign contracts to businesses linked to his own interests... It's dangerous to give a man like him so much power."

Rhys's gaze narrowed further. "That's why we need to know if it's just a rumor or not. If the document exists, I want you to find it. I don't need to see it. I just need to know what it says. The governor can't be given more power. He already pays the magistrate and sheriff to do his bidding. This will be disastrous for the city."

"The king won't allow it."

"King Alain has other things on his mind. Things that involve his kingdom, not its capital city."

"Such as?"

"Such as the fact he's dying and has no heir. If he dies soon, which is looking likely, there'll be a power vacuum. Filling it will keep the nobles busy fighting amongst themselves and possibly fighting off the king of Vytill."

He was right, although I'd never given it much thought. The ruler of our neighboring kingdom was a distant cousin of King Alain's. Glancia would be swallowed up by Vytill unless we went to war with them and chose a new king from one of Glancia's dukes instead. The problem was, which duke? If they both wanted the crown, it could result in a civil war between their factions.

I knew nothing about the dukes, but I did know that Glancia couldn't afford to go to war, either with its richer neighbor, or with itself.

"I'll go tonight," I assured him.

He put up a hand. "Slow down, Jac. There's a lot of security at the governor's office. It requires preparation to learn the guards' movements—"

"The cleaners arrive as dawn breaks, just before the guards change shifts. The guards will be at their sleepiest and won't notice an extra cleaner, and if they do, they'll simply see a youth blackened by chimney soot."

He rose without taking his gaze off me. He never studied me with such intensity. It was unnerving. Yet it warmed my insides, too. "How do you know when they change shifts? Or when the cleaners arrive? I've never asked you to break into the gover-nor's office before, so this should all be new."

I shrugged.

"And why the hesitation when I mentioned the governor?"

"I didn't hesitate."

"You did. You also showed an uncommon interest in the exis-tence of such a document. You've never shown an interest in knowing the implications of any job I've tasked you with before."

"That's because they've always been petty or dull or both." It was mostly true. I never took an interest because the jobs didn't directly affect me. The machinations of noblemen and rich merchants mattered nothing to my day-to-day existence.

This was different.

I might as well not have spoken. "Why, Jac? Why the interest this time?"

I crossed my arms, but when I realized that made me seem defensive, I lowered them to my sides. "You're mistaken. I'm not interested."

"Merdu, Jac, are we not friends?"

I flinched at the vehemence in his tone. "We are."

"Then why don't you trust me? I trust you."

"It's easy to trust me because you know I owe you. I'd be in prison if it weren't for you, or dead."

It was his turn to flinch. "I had no idea I was just the source of your next meal. But then, I have no idea about anything when it comes to you. You tell me nothing, no matter how many times I ask."

"You haven't asked in a long time."

"Because you wouldn't tell me anything!" He stormed off toward the door, snatching up his cloak and gloves, only to stop before opening it. He lowered his head, and his shoulders slumped. "I thought we were friends, Jac," he said again, without turning to face me.

"We are. We are, Rhys." I surged toward him, only to stop myself before I pressed my palm to his back. "I do trust you. I was annoyed just now because sometimes I hate that you can read me so easily."

He half turned and watched me through his thick dark lashes.

I could trust him. I knew that in my bones. It was time to tell him. "You're right. There is something about this particular task that affects me, more than any other you've assigned."

He faced me fully. He didn't speak. He hardly seemed to be breathing. His intensity, so unlike his usually carefree self, was unnerving.

It was why I blurted out my confession in a rush. "The governor is my uncle."

Rhys slumped back against the door. He stared at me. "You're the governor's niece!"

"Great niece," I said. "He's my mother's uncle."

His brow furrowed. "I remember when you were abducted. The entire city was looking for you, including me and all of the other brothers. Merdu and Hailia...you weren't abducted, were you? Otherwise you'd reveal yourself and return home. You ran away. You didn't want to be found."

"I hid in the sewers while the city searched for me. None of the other homeless vagrants and orphans realized I was a girl after I cut my hair and changed my clothes." I fingered the short strands at the nape of my neck. Sometimes, even now, my reflection startled me when I caught a glimpse of it. I looked nothing like that long-haired innocent sixteen-year-old who'd believed her uncle had her best interests at heart. "If they had, they would have turned me in for the reward."

"The search was called off when your burned body was found after a fire in a warehouse at the docks. The sheriff claimed the investigation revealed the building was used by child abductors who hid them there until they had an opportunity to transport the children out of the city by riverboat. Everyone assumed you'd been one of their victims."

"That fire was a stroke of luck for me, although sadly not for the real victim."

"Or the so-called child abductors. The governor was so upset he tortured them when they were caught."

"They were indeed child abductors, according to some of the

children in the sewers. If there's one good thing to come out of this, it was their capture."

"The governor was brutal, so I heard."

"Not because he was upset over losing me. He wanted something of mine. He must have tortured them to find out why it hadn't been on the body, and what they'd done with it." I removed the blue-green cabochon pendant on the end of the silver chain I kept around my neck.

Rhys barely even looked at it. He couldn't stop staring at me. "Is it a family heirloom?"

I nodded. "It's been handed down through the female line over many generations, so my mother said. It's the one thing that was truly mine, and the only thing I had of hers. Yet my uncle wanted it."

"You ran away from a comfortable home because he wanted your necklace?" He shifted his feet and finally his gaze slid away. "Or was there another reason?" He suddenly and violently shook his head. "No, you don't have to answer that. You don't have to tell me anything if you don't want to."

"It's not what you're thinking. He never touched me. To the outside world, it looked as though he took me in because he was my only relative. But in truth, he only gave me a home to get his hands on this." I held the pendant higher, wanting Rhys to take a closer look, to marvel at the stone that I'd marveled at for many years. "All my parents' worldly goods, including me, were given to my nearest male relative, Uncle Roderic. My mother had gifted me this stone on my sixteenth birthday, shortly before she died. She called it a talisman, and claimed it held power put there by the sorcerer himself. That power could be drawn upon by the one who possessed it. Family legend says it must be passed down the female line. My mother didn't know how to extract the power or even what it does—the details were lost long ago—but she made me promise to always keep it on my person. It was that power my uncle wanted for himself. Within minutes of me moving into his house, he asked to see it. When I refused to hand it over, he spent the next few weeks alternately trying to trick me into giving it to him or attempting to take it from me. When he realized I wouldn't give it up and couldn't be tricked, he ripped it right off me. Then he locked me up."

"Clearly you stole it back."

"My first theft. My mother may have given me this pendant, but my father gave me a few skills that he thought might prove useful one day."

I smiled, remembering those lessons. My father had died when I was ten. It was just my mother and me for another six years, until she caught a fever. It had happened so suddenly she'd never been able to make alternative arrangements for my upbringing. Either that, or she hadn't known how cruel her uncle could be and thought he'd make a fine guardian. He'd hidden his true nature from us. From everyone. He still did.

Rhys continued to stare at me, not the stone. Nor did he seem to have taken in what I'd said about the pendant's power. He probably thought it was nothing more than an old family tale, passed down from mother to daughter with a wink as they bonded over something that all wished was true but couldn't possibly be. After all, women held no power in Glancia. Indeed, none of the kingdoms on the Fist Peninsula recognized women as having legal rights when they had a male relative to control them. I wasn't sure about Freedland, that republic full of rebels at the very southern end of the peninsula, but I doubted it was different. My uncle's desperation to get his hands on the pendant was the first clue the story about its power might be true. Since then, I'd wondered how it would work, if it were. If it held power, I had no idea how to unleash it.

With access to the old archives at his order's library, Rhys might be in a position to find out. Even if he couldn't, I didn't regret telling him. I did trust him, and I wanted him to know that.

I held the pendant higher and finally he took notice. He picked it up by its chain. "It's pretty."

"Hold it to the light and you'll see a star in the center."

He angled it toward the fireplace. "So there is. It's as if it shines from within." He went to pass it back to me but stopped. He held it near my face. "The stone is the same color as your eyes."

I was thankful for the poor light when a blush infused my cheeks. I took the pendant and lowered my head as I put it back on. "My mother had the same color eyes, as did her mother and hers, and so on, according to family lore. I liked to think that an admirer of one of my ancestors found the stone while out walking one day and noticed it matched his beloved's eyes, so he had it polished and gave it to her as a gift."

"It's a nice story, and more realistic than the one about a sorcerer putting power into it for some unknown reason then giving it to your ancestor, also for some unknown reason."

His response was hardly surprising. I didn't really believe it myself. "You don't think it could even be remotely true? Not a shred?"

"No, Jac, I don't. I believe in Merdu, Hailia and the minor gods and goddesses. To admit the existence of a sorcerer is blasphemous. Not that I would admit it, because I don't believe sorcery exists."

I tucked the gemstone back under my shirt. It was warm against my skin from Rhys's touch. "The Zemayans believe in a sorcerer."

"Some do. Most don't. They tell their children stories about the sorcerer to scare them into behaving. Nowadays, most believe in the gods and goddesses that we do here on the Fist, led by Merdu and Hailia." A gust of wind rattled the windowpanes, catching his attention. "I should go. I've changed my mind about breaking into the governor's office. I don't want you to do it. It's not worth the risk. All will be officially revealed sooner or later anyway."

That may be true, but it would help Rhys to know in advance. Or, rather, his order's master. I presumed that's who ultimately employed me, since Rhys had no money of his own to pay me. Merdu's Guards might not be responsible for catching criminals who broke the law—that was the job of the sheriff and his constables—but they could be called upon to quell unrest that threatened the city's peace, since Glancia's high priest lived here in Tilting. It made sense to be aware of potential conflicts before they arose.

Rhys made to leave only to stop again. "I'm sorry you had no one after your mother died, not even the man who was supposed to protect you. I can't imagine what it felt like being all alone."

"You were younger than me when your father died, and you had no other family."

"I had the order. Master Tomaj was my father's good friend and took me in without question. The brothers became like real brothers to me. We're a family. Thanks to them, I've never felt alone."

I wondered if that was why he'd joined their ranks when he turned eighteen, because he wanted to stay close to the men who'd become his family. But that wasn't a question I felt comfortable asking, even if he was my best friend.

He rested his hand on the door handle. "I'm glad I found you, Jac. Now you have brothers, too." He slipped out and closed the door softly.

My vision blurred as tears welled. He was right. His friends had become my friends over the last three years, and I was extremely grateful for them. But mostly the tears welled because an ache had settled into my chest. I didn't want Rhys to feel like he was my brother. I wanted him in an entirely different way. One that his religious order forbade.

*You can read a longer excerpt on CJ's website

Available from 2nd September 2025:
THE WARRIOR PRIEST
An *After The Rift* World Novel

ALSO BY C.J. ARCHER

SERIES WITH 2 OR MORE BOOKS

The Glass Library

Cleopatra Fox Mysteries

After The Rift

Glass and Steele

The Ministry of Curiosities Series

The Emily Chambers Spirit Medium Trilogy

The 1st Freak House Trilogy

The 2nd Freak House Trilogy

The 3rd Freak House Trilogy

The Assassins Guild Series

Lord Hawkesbury's Players Series

Witch Born

SINGLE TITLES

The Warrior Priest

Courting His Countess

Surrender

Redemption

The Mercenary's Price

ABOUT THE AUTHOR

C.J. Archer has loved history and books for as long as she can remember and feels fortunate that she found a way to combine the two. She spent her early childhood in the dramatic beauty of outback Queensland, Australia, but now lives in suburban Melbourne with her husband, two children and a mischievous black & white cat named Coco.

Subscribe to C.J.'s newsletter through her website to be notified when she releases a new book, as well as get access to exclusive content and subscriber-only giveaways. Her website also contains up to date details on all her books: http://cjarcher.com She loves to hear from readers. You can contact her through email cj@cjarcher.com or follow her on social media to get the latest updates on her books:

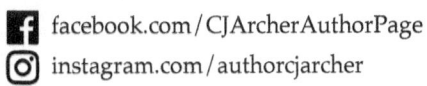

facebook.com/CJArcherAuthorPage

instagram.com/authorcjarcher